Here's the letter breakfast table:

Dear Tris Healy,

Please keep reading this letter no matter how confused or alarmed you become. It will be worth it.

You're probably wondering who I am and how this letter ended up in a time capsule. My name is Susan Granger, and I truly wrote this letter fifty years ago—before your birth parents even met. How then could I know your name and address? You told me in a dream—the same dream you will have soon.

Here's the gist. If you haven't been opened to your past-life memories yet, brace yourself. Reincarnation is real. I am who you were in your last lifetime. When I was twenty-eight, I received a letter like this one from my former self.

I know. I know. I didn't believe it either. I researched the letter's origin, I hunted for alternate explanations, and I even doubted my sanity. But the letter began a process that led me to accept the truth. This will happen to you, too.

We're not like everyone else. At some point, we always wake up to who we really are—that life is continuous, and we are a soul, not a person. There is comfort in this. But in our case, there is also a sobering responsibility associated with this awareness.

We're on a multi-generational mission, and we've been carrying it out for millennia. This mission will come to fruition in your lifetime.

Praise for Verlin Darrow

My mystery—Blood and Wisdom—was a finalist (runner up) for best mystery of 2018, the New Generation Indie Book Awards (the largest nonprofit book contest in the world).

Comments by another author about my fantasy thriller:

"COATTAIL KARMA isn't just a book. True, it's an exciting, fine piece of writing with plot twists galore, peopled with characters that behave like villains and metaphysical superheroes. And it's certainly fun to read. But it's so much more than that. In other words, Verlin Darrow's outrageous fantasy masquerades as something that readers can easily grasp and be wildly entertained by, but along the way he also shares wisdom and his own quirky take on the meaning of life in mind-blowing fashion. Who can write such stuff and get away with it? Verlin Darrow can...and did."

Prodigy Quest

by

Verlin Darrow

Prodigy Quest

Cover Art by *The Wild Rose Press, Inc.*

The Wild Rose Press, Inc.
PO Box 708
Adams Basin, NY 14410-0708
Visit us at www.thewildrosepress.com

Publishing History
First Edition, 2021
Trade Paperback ISBN 978-1-5092-3690-9
Digital ISBN 978-1-5092-3691-6

Published in the United States of America

Dedication

To plagiarize myself:

This book is dedicated to everyone who's learning to thrive in free fall,
or beleaguered by thoughts like science fiction stories written by drunk monkeys,
or trying to stuff awareness back into the benign Pandora's box it arrived in,
or trying to arm wrestle life into submission,
or struggling to give yourself permission to be where you're at,
or trying to waltz with a badger,
or unfolding yourself and trying to return to the simple, blank sheet of paper that you once were before you became the complex, completed origami who is reading this dedication.
In other words, I dedicate this book to all of us walking around in these outlandish human disguises.

Acknowledgments

I greatly appreciate all the help, support, and love that I've received from my wife, Lusijah. Like my gracious beta readers—Nancy Whiteside and Anne Jacobs—she provided candid and detailed feedback about this book. The bulk of the excellent (and necessary) editing fell to Eilidh MacKenzie, my colleague at Wild Rose Press. This is our third novel together, and I get better and better at minimizing my customary writing flaws, thanks to her expert suggestions. I also want to thank my biggest fan, Rev. Donald Fox, for his decades of appreciation.

Chapter 1

After I made an appointment with Marc Dalcour, I told my parents I needed to be at his office in two hours. I'd been lucky. It was either that or wait five weeks for another opening in his schedule.

"Isn't therapy a bit pricey, honey?" my mother responded. "I know what that doctor said, but…"

"…it isn't in our budget, son," my father added. "It'll need to come out of your savings account. And I'm not convinced any ten-year-old needs a headshrinker."

They'd read that properly parenting a gifted child required solidarity, so now they finished each other's sentences. And I'd thought they couldn't get any more annoying.

"No problem. Our insurance covers it," I told them.

"There's no co-pay?"

"No. I just need a ride there. His office is down near the lake."

"All right," my father grumbled. "I'll drive you and wait around for an hour while you chat with a stranger instead of one of us. He'll probably have some interesting magazines in his waiting room, or maybe I'll just stare at the goddamn wall."

"Great!" I strode away. I'd learned early on to ignore this sort of passive-aggressive nonsense.

On the drive there, a man pulled up next to us in

the left turn lane at the stoplight by the Vons grocery store just south of downtown Ojai. I could feel him staring at me, something I'd grown accustomed to since appearing on *Who's the Genius?* It's funny how one can sense scrutiny without visual confirmation. In this case, goosebumps prickled on my arms for no discernible reason. I studied the driver to ascertain why my body had responded this way.

About sixty years old, with long, straggly black hair cascading from under a blue baseball cap, he sported a bushy beard and wore oversized sunglasses. After a moment, it became clear he was wearing a wig and a fake beard—not even convincing ones. Why?

As my father pulled away from the light, the man tucked his elderly silver pickup truck into the lane behind us.

"I think we're being followed by a man wearing a disguise," I told my father.

"You need to keep that imagination of yours in check, Tris. We've talked about this."

"He really is wearing a wig and a fake beard."

"That's not our business. He's probably on the way to a costume party."

"He changed lanes to get behind us," I reported, turning my head to keep an eye on the truck.

"People change lanes all the time for all sorts of reasons. This is the kind of thing that makes you have mental health problems—like this panic thing yesterday. You need to calm down and enjoy the ride. Look at all the nice trees."

The truck was a fair distance behind us now, and I spied another figure in the passenger seat who hadn't been visible before. I couldn't make out any details.

Had this person ducked down and hidden as the driver surveyed me? Once again, why?

"They could try to kidnap me," I told my father.

"Just stop it, Tris. I don't want to hear another word."

When we pulled into the asphalt parking lot of Dr. Dalcour's office, the truck continued past us—with only one occupant visible.

We arrived quite early, which wasn't surprising since my dad was almost always early to everything in an effort to never be late. Next to where I emerged from our car, roots from an adjacent sycamore had buckled the elderly concrete, and I almost tripped. I glared at the soaring tree, spying several battered doll's heads hanging from one of its lower branches. Were I prone to fanciful thoughts such as omens, I might have been concerned. As it was, I simply returned my gaze to the uneven pavement of the two-story brick building's parking lot. A near fall was enough embarrassment for one day. Two would be intolerable.

A few minutes later, we sat in a generically decorated, shared waiting room—three other therapists occupied the suite—and at first we were the only occupants. I caught a whiff of lilac—a legacy from whoever had recently preceded us, or perhaps a practitioner's trick to establish a desired ambience. Add a bed and we could've been in a midlevel chain motel room. The amateurish artwork on the cream walls— watercolor prints of mountains, lakes, and a rainbow arcing across an unnaturally blue sky—were hard to bear. Why stop there? Why not dogs playing poker?

After a few minutes, an obese woman waddled in and sat as far from us as she could. I reasoned that this constituted normal behavior under the circumstances, given the stigma that still existed around mental health.

The woman's posture struck me as incongruent with her body type. In my experience, strikingly upright posture tends to be correlated with a fit figure, perhaps from a yoga practice or a career as a dancer. This patient displayed legs like sausages below the inappropriately high hemline of her billowing emerald green dress. Fat hung from her upper arms like whatever simile creatively describes fat arms. Honestly, I can't think of one.

The woman's face wasn't all that round—another anomaly for a severely overweight person in my brief life experience. Framed by frizzy brown hair, her features reminded me of my aunt Patricia. Close-set blue eyes sat above the patient's snub nose, which, in turn, perched above substantial, glossy lips. Her receding chin sank back into her substantial neck.

She tapped her feet, picked at her nails, and shifted several times in her overburdened chair. In a film, her actions might be deemed overly dramatic, even hammy. Here, her behavior struck me as within the (abnormal) bell curve.

I continued to peek at her out of the corner of my eye and tried to diagnose her to pass the time. I settled on generalized anxiety disorder, a common ailment, albeit less prevalent than depression. The woman seemed full of energy, ineffective at managing it, and quite worried about her upcoming session with one of the therapists.

Dr. Dalcour emerged from his office to meet me right on time, which I appreciated. He shook my dad's hand and insisted on seeing me by myself—another source of kudos. He told us that first sessions were an hour and a half. Then he had my dad sign some sort of consent form, which I would've liked to examine.

The other patient suddenly stood, rushed over, and inserted herself before I could form any in-depth impression of Dalcour. Numerous metal bracelets jangled as she moved, as if someone like that needed to announce her approach. "I need a minute of your time," she gasped, out of breath from her journey across the room. "Doctor, it's life or death!"

Now, she'd definitely be panned for overacting in a movie review. But who knows how crazy people behave when they're panicky and desperate, as she so clearly was?

He paused and then turned to me. "Do you mind, Tris? If you do, I'll summon a colleague."

"It's okay. Go ahead." I liked his deep, resonant voice.

"I promise I won't be more than five minutes."

I nodded.

In four minutes—I timed him—he was back, with no sign of the aggrieved woman. He noticed my puzzled expression. "I have another door to the parking lot in my office."

"Ah."

He'd buzzed down his thinning blond hair in a drastic manner, which I preferred to whatever attempt he might've made to obscure his version of early onset baldness. His oblong face was top-heavy with a high, broad forehead. Where his face tapered to a square, but narrow jaw, something between a dimple and a vertical crevasse divided his two-day stubble. Leathery skin spoke to an adolescence misspent in the sun. My guess was the beach and not outdoor labor. I couldn't picture someone with Dalcour's alert chestnut eyes picking oranges in an Ojai orchard. Sparse eyebrows arched over a bony brow that hovered above a slightly crooked nose, perhaps from a sports injury. With his height, I could see him playing competitive basketball.

Even in his blue chambray work shirt and new jeans, Dalcour could play a character in a Shakespeare tragedy—maybe Hamlet's uncle. He'd be around the right age—forty or so. When I tried to remember this character's name, a memory of Meriwether Lewis attending a performance of *King Lear* popped up. The actors had spouted Shakespeare's lines with deep southern accents, which rendered their performances unconvincing.

I pulled my attention back into the moment as I entered Dalcour's office. It was an effort.

"Sit wherever you like," he told me, gesturing in a manner that encompassed the entire room, which held only three possible seats.

Two lightly curtained windows spread diffuse sunlight throughout the room, which softened the edges of everything, as if objects weren't as separate as they usually appeared.

A floor-to-ceiling oak bookcase dominated the far wall, and one shelf of the bookcase sported a variety of colorful wood animal carvings that I recognized as Oaxacan. The remaining shelves were crammed with books, mostly professional trade paperbacks, including a bright yellow one titled *Jousting With Adolescent Clients: A Handbook For Intrepid Therapists*.

Two armchairs faced each other, five feet apart in front of a drawerless cherry desk. On closer examination, this elegant piece was clearly a table pressed into service to support Dalcour's computer and an array of manila files, pens, and bright yellow cough-drop packages. Had he recently shopped for the latter and then failed to tuck away his purchases in one of the stacked, gray metal filing cabinets in a corner of his room? Was he ill? The drops were sugar-free. Was he diabetic? Would that affect our work together?

I selected the black leather armchair that seemed to be Dalcour's usual roost. A legal pad and a coffee mug sat on a small round table beside it. On the floor beyond it, a healthy-looking houseplant climbed a wooden stake in a teal ceramic pot. Its dark green, oversized leaves had vertical, off-white streaks, which resembled spilled house paint.

Dalcour didn't so much as raise an eyebrow at my seating choice. He scooped up the items on the table and settled in across from me in a distinctly less expensive chair. Then he asked why I was there.

"Don't you know who I am?"

"Well, I know your name, Tris. Until you tell me more, that's it."

I sighed. "So now we're going to waste time on this. Great." I crossed my arms and glared at him.

He smiled back. "Yes, we are. Tell me about yourself."

"I'm a boy genius. I'm famous for being one." I don't know why I began the session in such a huff. It hadn't been my intent. Perhaps my behavior was a defense mechanism; my subconscious may have perceived Dalcour to be a threat to the status quo of my psyche.

"How's that going?" he asked.

"That's it? That's your idea of transpersonal therapy? 'How's it going?' "

"That's how we start, or at least how *I* start. Let me ask my question a different way. Is your intelligence a factor in whatever concern has brought you into my office? Is that why you're mentioning it?"

I considered that. "I'm not sure." I admired Dalcour's careful word selection—intelligence instead of genius and concern instead of problem. He wasn't endorsing anything in particular by the way he framed things. I might be a genius, or I might not be. I might have serious problems, or perhaps I didn't. So many people immediately displayed their assumptions.

I imagined Dalcour's vigilance was necessary with touchy clients. Then it occurred to me that he might consider me one, based on my response to his initial question. Were we jousting?

"Tell me what it's like to be a genius," he said. He was going for it—pushing all his chips in the pot— accepting my words at face value before he knew them to be so. A good tactic, I thought, despite his initial hesitation, which, paradoxically, I also admired. So far, so good.

"In my case, it's not easy," I told him. "I was adopted, and my parents are not only stupid, they're also greedy, exploitive, and emotionally immature."

"Do you consider yourself to be emotionally mature?"

"No, clearly I'm not." Why had he picked that out of my list of adjectives? "But I'm ten years old, I'm not raising a child, and at least I *know* I'm immature."

He nodded. I liked his nod. It was minimal and crisp. "Do you know your birth parents?"

"No. The ones I have won't even tell me if *they* know them."

"How about we circle back to my original question?" He picked up his mug and sipped whatever was in it. He hadn't needed so much as a glance at the mug on the table beside him to retrieve it. "What concern brings you in?" he asked. "Or is it someone else's concern—someone who finds your behavior inappropriate?"

"As you'll discover if you pass this audition, my behavior is almost always inappropriate by ordinary standards. But I don't care." I paused and scratched the side of my nose. It didn't itch. That was just something I did sometimes. "I think I need to ask you a few things before I answer you."

"All right."

"Do you think we are more than just the person we seem to be?"

"Yes, I know we are." Dalcour scratched his nose, too. This was called matching—a way to connect with someone and put them at ease. In the brief interval between calling Dalcour and commencing our session, I'd studied therapeutic interventions online.

"Do you have personal experience with any sort of transcendental state?" I asked next. If this man only understood metaphysics from an academic standpoint, I wasn't going to divulge my story.

"Yes." He smiled, encouraging me to continue. Strategic smiling could be useful to a therapist, too, I'd read.

"So you're informed by this when you talk with someone in here?" I asked.

"Yes." He accompanied this with another crisp

nod.

"I've endured extremely inexpert sessions with other psychologists who treated me like a lab rat. My parents lent me out to researchers."

"I will not treat you like a lab rat." His tone was emphatic. I expected him to nod again as he spoke. He didn't.

"What would you do if someone told you they remembered a past life?" I asked, leaning forward. This was the key question, after all.

"I would listen."

"And after that?"

"I would say whatever I felt was the most helpful to say when that moment arrives. If I pay attention closely enough, I'll know what that is."

I liked these answers. "And you maintain confidentiality—even when your client is only ten years old?"

"If you don't want me to, I won't tell your parents anything substantive."

Dalcour was easy to talk to, and so far he hadn't uttered anything stupid. I took a deep breath. "Yesterday, suddenly, I was flooded with the memories of Meriwether Lewis, who I intuitively understood to be a past life of mine."

"This is the Lewis of Lewis and Clark?"

He didn't seem to be taken aback at all. I could've told him I had a hangnail or my foot itched. I guess he was inured to wild stories since he probably worked with thought-disordered people. At least I wasn't declaring I was Jesus.

"Yes," I replied. "Lewis was Thomas Jefferson's personal secretary, too."

"I didn't know that."

"I'm probably the world's greatest authority on him now. Do you want to know how he was toilet trained?"

Dalcour smiled. "Absolutely not. Tell me more. How did you weather the experience?"

"It was overwhelming. I passed out." For a moment, I was back onstage at *Who's The Genius?* at the TV studio in Van Nuys. I must've demonstrated my distress to Dalcour.

"Are you all right?"

"Sure."

"Where were you at the time?" he asked. All his attention was on me in that moment—absolutely all of it. I was disconcerted since no one else I'd ever met had ever managed this—or even seemed to want to.

"The first time, down in L.A. in a television studio winning a quiz show."

"Ah, you're the one from *Who's The Genius?*" He leaned back, taking in the implications of this. For the first time, his eyes were off me, veering up and to the left.

That gave me a chance to breath more freely. "Yes. The one and only. They took me to a hospital, where even more intense memories sent me back into unconsciousness."

"Another historical figure this time?" His focus was back on me. I liked it, however intense it might be.

"No, more Lewis."

"Tell me about these memories," he instructed, "and don't leave out the feelings this time."

"It's hard to describe." I did my best, and Dalcour seemed to understand, as much as anyone could. I left out the feelings again. I had just met this man, after all.

"That's remarkable," he pronounced when I'd finished. "Do you think you're crazy?"

"I know I'm not."

"It's certainly unlikely. There aren't many psychotic ten-year-olds running around, and they're nothing like you. Plus, your story is so similar to mine that if you're delusional, so am I."

My eyebrows raised involuntarily, and my mouth dropped open. "Really?" My head cocked to the side on its own, too. "You've remembered a past life, too?"

"Yes."

This was an ideal scenario. I had chosen this man wisely. "What did you do afterward?"

"After my memories showed up?" Dalcour asked.

"Yes."

"I've just lived my life since then—worked, eaten, loved—the human condition. No matter how extraordinary or wonderful peak experiences may be, they don't transform us into something beyond our nature—not while we're still in these bodies."

My head uncocked. I'd been viewing Dalcour's face on a diagonal. In that position, his nose was like a forward slash on a keyboard, giving me a choice of which half to look at.

"You know," I said, "when I take a moment, all this sounds ridiculous, especially when someone uses nonscientific language as you just did. I wish I could simply renounce what happened."

"You could try, but trust me, it doesn't work out in the long run. Awareness is like a benign Pandora's box."

I considered this. "I get it. Once I know, I know.

Do you think all awareness is benign?"

"In the long run, yes."

After that, Dalcour wanted to hear what he called my life story. I concisely filled him in on what I considered the germane background he needed, focusing on the features of my life that set me apart from other ten-year-olds. When I'd finished navigating this, a thought occurred to me. I asked Dalcour if he'd paid attention to the aspects of my life I hadn't chosen to share.

"Not quite as much, but yes, I can glean quite bit about clients' orientations and priorities from what they leave out. Sometimes a client will only discuss her relationships or work history. Another might only talk about his childhood up to a certain age." He gazed at me for a while. "You'd make a good therapist," he said. "You notice things. Your narrative reflects that."

"Thank you. Just because I'd be good at it doesn't mean I want to do it. I don't know how you stand it. I don't care about other people's problems all that much, and if I did, I'm sure I'd get sick of hearing about them in short order. You've got to understand; I'm really, really good at all kinds of things, so that alone isn't a particularly meaningful criterion for choosing a profession."

"I understand."

"What else can you tell about me?" I asked.

"You mean from your life story, the omissions in your life story, or my general impressions so far?"

Clearly, I'd meant my life story, but now I was curious about his overall impressions. Dalcour was far from clueless, so he had probably introduced this more global option for some therapeutic purpose. Also, I was interested in how he'd tell me. Would he be brutally frank, overly diplomatic, or something in between? Perhaps I could find out something useful about *him.*

"The latter," I told him.

"All right. I'll skip all the obvious. Why waste time telling you you're smart and developmentally advanced?" He paused. "Are you sure you're ready for this? I'm thinking you want the unvarnished version. Not everyone does—not so soon, at least."

I nodded. "Please be candid."

"Okay. You're overly self-confident given your inexperience, and you rely on your intellect at the expense of developing other parts of yourself. This is to be expected in your circumstances. You have an affinity for precise language and expect this in others, but you're constantly disappointed. Expanding that phenomenon, you have trouble accepting who other people are, as well as what they do. You no longer expect people to live up to your standards, but it's been hard to let go of yearning for this. You also project unenforceable rules onto them. If you could be in control of other people—no, the whole world—you think it would be a far better place. All of this breeds cynicism and arrogance, which don't serve you well, and you know it. But the main thing is that you're scared—not just about these memories you've had. You fight knowing the baseline of fear that rules you. You want to be other than who you are—someone who matches your ten-year-old's ideals. So you view yourself with a bias and block your awareness of whatever defies that." He paused and gazed at me mildly, perhaps trying to soften the effect of his words. "How am I doing so far?"

"Fair to middling," I managed to croak. At that moment, I was, in fact, terrified, not that I wanted to let Dalcour know that. My gut clenched, my heart raced, and my chest tightened to the point where I had to struggle to breathe. When I glanced at Dalcour, I could see he noticed all this.

The man's words proved he possessed X-ray vision—well, the psychological version of it. How could he know so much—perhaps more than I did—when I'd only been in the room with him for an hour? I'd been markedly censorial about what I'd shared, too. I felt naked—no, worse than that—transparent.

"You're scared right now, aren't you?" Dalcour asked.

"Maybe."

"I'm sorry. I thought it was necessary to show off to gain your respect and motivate you to return. I sense that people have to prove themselves to you, especially intellectually, or you don't have time for them."

"That's true, but you were doing all right in that department before your synopsis of my character." The words were a refuge from the feelings. If I focused on choosing just the right words, my attention remained on a safe topic.

"If I'd realized that, I would've toned it down," Dalcour said, shifting in his chair. "I apologize. But let's stop talking for a moment. I want you to sit and tune into the body sensations that have arisen with your fear. Can you do that?"

I nodded and gave it a try. Apparently feeling body sensations was not my forte. I could only tune in to the tension and shakiness for a few seconds before my mind intruded. I remembered previous iterations of strong fear, I wondered how I looked while I was supposed to be focusing on sensations, and I pondered how often Dalcour and I should meet. I even planned what I would do if a major earthquake rocked his office.

After a few tortuous minutes of this, I'd had enough. I reported my experience, and Dalcour suggested I periodically "sit with my body." "I want to see you again tomorrow at the same time," he added.

"I thought you were all booked up."

Dalcour leaned back, making me aware that he had been leaning forward ever since my fear had arisen. "You need what you need. I'll work it out."

****

I pondered my first session with Dalcour while I ate dinner and pretended to listen to my mother prattle about a neighbor's son who had won a pie-eating contest. Really? This was the new gold standard for family dinner conversation? Gluttony for cash prizes?

Dalcour had made me feel something. That wasn't easy—not with me. It wasn't that I completely disavowed my emotions—my responses to Lewis's memories demonstrated the fallacy of that notion. I just protected myself from anyone manipulating me into emotionality.

Dalcour had snuck in the back door with his exposition about who I was, enticing me to become invested in what he said. Then he'd been smart to focus on my body and not on the emotion itself—something I wouldn't have agreed to try. At least, not in a first session.

And he was right about all of it. I *was* fear-based. Much of my braggadocio and belittling behavior was in the service of keeping myself convinced I was truly a genius. If I demonstrated others' inferiority, it proved my superiority. Only I knew how much of my supposed intelligence was actually a byproduct of a near-photographic memory.

I *did* block awareness of this insecurity, too—as best I could, anyway. And I *was* arrogant. And all the rest that Dalcour had delineated. I couldn't imagine his peers approving his behavior—so much, so soon—and with a kid (technically)—but it suited me. It induced me to come back, and it provoked a new level of self-examination.

When we'd exhausted the topic of pie eating, my parents wanted to hear about my session.

"What part of confidential don't you understand?" I tried.

"Oh Tris, at least tell us if you talked about us," my mother said, her mouth half full of orange Jell-O. "Did you blame all your problems on your father and me? And are you panicky like the doctor said? What diagnosis did this man give you?"

"We focused on me, and no, I don't have panic disorder. That's all I'm saying. Therapy only works if it stays private."

"Okay, fair enough," my father said. "But just tell me this. Is this psychologist a Christian? He looks Jewish. That's all I'm saying."

All I could do was roll my eyes. I understood he was ignorant and doomed to think such things. I just wished he'd suppress their expression.

Chapter 2

I will never forget the moment the alien memories
flooded me. How could I? Even what led up to them is
etched in my mind.

I perched my ten-year-old butt on a wooden stool
between two other quiz-show contestants on a gaudy
soundstage. I served as the main attraction on *Who's
The Genius?*, having achieved a level of fame
commensurate with whoever was currently hurling a
football the most accurately. After three triumphant
weeks, I'd been invited to Super Genius Week. The
media was already calling me the smartest boy in the
world, which might be true, but regurgitating facts on
TV was certainly an inadequate measure of that.

Bright lights glared at us on the expansive,
carpeted stage in the oversized Quonset hut that
crouched on the perimeter of the studio grounds. It
always smelled like stale cigarette smoke in there,
despite signage denying nicotine addicts their fix.

I sweated profusely in my black polyester slacks
and the tight yellow tee shirt my parents made me wear,
which sported a heart-shaped photo of them across my
concave chest. My legs always wanted to shake when I
was on camera, and they ached when I didn't let them.
My heart thumped against my ribcage, and my eyes
smarted.

When we were about a third of the way through the

show, the studio audience applauding, gasping, or sighing as the monitors directed them to, Marv Merlin announced a commercial break. I climbed down, stretched my legs, and observed the spectacle of our patently insincere host.

A voluptuous Latina in a tiny red dress trotted over to touch up his makeup, and Marv tried to fondle her while she danced around him, dabbing at his unnaturally orange face. Eventually, Marv successfully brushed nonexistent lint from Tammy's behind, a more serious encroachment than the previous day's effort, which entailed stroking her hair. I liked Tammy. She'd calmed me down on multiple occasions while I waited backstage for shows to start. She didn't deserve this type of harassment, and I'd told her so just that morning. There were steps she could take.

"Are you kidding?" she'd responded. "This could be my big break. What if they decide to have someone bring Marv the question cards or something. I'll be right here, won't I? There's always a lot of grabbing in show biz. You wouldn't understand."

Once we resumed our seats, Marv restarted the taping by booming out "This is a two parter, contestants, so listen carefully before you answer. Who was Thomas Jefferson's first term vice-president? And please name where he was born and where he died."

I rang in, using the button on the oval plastic device I clutched in my clammy hand. "First of all, Marv, that would be a three-part question, unless you honestly believe that consolidating birth and death locations is a viable method of organizing your material. Also, there's no such word as 'parter.' To answer your question, it was Aaron Burr, and he was born in Newark, New Jersey, and is buried 36.86 miles to the southwest in Princeton."

"Correct!" He worked to maintain a smile. After several weeks of this, I'm sure he would've preferred to gut me like a fish. For my part, I missed no opportunity to make Marv look foolish. Besides mistreating Tammy, he purported to have been a child prodigy himself, sporting an IQ of 160. What a load of crap.

In hindsight, since he was merely reading cards he'd been handed, and my behavior was, of course, extremely boorish, I'm sure I was the one whom viewers vilified.

I drank in the obligatory applause, and a lout shouted, "Go git 'em, Sonny Boy!"

Marv continued. "Here's your follow-up question, Tris. Who was Jefferson's personal secretary, and why was he famous?"

"Meriwether Lewis. He was the Lewis of Lewis and Clark."

Suddenly, I stood in an old-fashioned parlor, with lit oil sconces on the brocaded burgundy walls. I smelled wood smoke, although there was no fireplace in sight. Several colorful, silk Persian rugs adorned the hardwood floor, clashing with the heavy red drapes covering a picture window on the wall to my left.

Two men sat on an overstuffed brown settee before me, gazing at each other with enmity. I recognized the one on the left—President Jefferson.

"That will be all, Meriwether," he said, without breaking his gaze from the fierce-looking man next to him. "Mr. Burr and I have personal business to attend to."

"Very well," I replied in a low adult voice.

What the heck! What just happened? What the heck was going on?

It wasn't a vision, a hallucination, or a dream. I *remembered* it, like any other memory. More and more of these scenarios cascaded through me—building to an overwhelming blur of images and voices. I saw face after face, vistas of mountain ranges, interiors of libraries, and a row of shabby outhouses. I heard cannons, a marching band, and the dulcet tones of my mother telling me to buck up on my first day at school. One after the other, the memories flooded me, faster than I could assimilate them.

Marv said something which I didn't hear. Someone else spoke. Then my legs gave way, and I fell to the floor. I heard myself muttering something about what was happening to me, and then I passed out.

Chapter 3

They cancelled the rest of the taping after I wobbled back into consciousness, unable to speak a complete sentence. As an infant, my first words had been a complete sentence, replete with a pause for a comma.

In an emergency room, lying on a hard, cold gurney while a female doctor in a white lab coat loitered at a nurse's station, the torrent of alien memories slowed, and I began to sort them. Meriwether Lewis had been dispatched to the westward expedition by Jefferson. Some of the memories of those years could only be described as harrowing. Others were totally boring. Still others shocked me. He had led an extraordinary life.

I don't how I knew these were *my* memories, nor did I have any way to make sense of them. In an effort to convert the experience into something more palatable, I considered the possibilities that I was hallucinating, delusional, or just letting my imagination run wild in some convincing new fashion.

But I knew what I knew. The knowing emerged from some essence within me—a realm I never knew existed. *I* had lived this life.

While I lay waiting on my back, bright fluorescent lights glaring at me, I pulled my phone from my pocket and researched the phenomenon of past-life memories.

Others reported flashbacks such as mine. Some of these people were branded crazy, and clearly they were. Others subsequently found validation in the New Age community. No one else described the onset of past-life memories as so sudden or detailed as mine.

Unbidden, I was thrust into remembering how Meriwether/Me had been murdered at the age of thirty-five. Historians pronounced his/our death a suicide, and I did ponder ending my life many times due to my sexual orientation, but I was killed by a jealous lover at an inn in Tennessee.

A flood of feelings surged through me. As Meriwether, I feared for my life, felt love for my assailant, and was even concerned for his fate once I was gone. Would he be hanged, racked with guilt if he weren't caught, or pleased he'd exacted his revenge? Could he ever love again? He hadn't been an evil man, just a lost soul driven mad by circumstances. These sentiments arose from deep-seated compassion, a quality with which, as Tris, I wasn't at all familiar.

Then a new set of his memories drifted into my consciousness—a gentle parade this time, allowing me to ponder or savor each as I pleased. Most were mundane by ordinary standards, anchored by some emotion associated with the circumstances. For example, when Lewis spied a girl at a tavern who resembled his sister at that age, a tender love flowed through him. The moment lasted seconds for both of us, but for me it once again represented a profound, novel experience.

Similarly, remembering when the Lewis and Clark expedition fought with a hostile indigenous tribe in Oregon, Meriwether's bravery and resolve were almost too alien to understand. Why didn't the expedition just turn around and go home?

All told, I cycled through a dozen intriguing scenarios. Clearly, Lewis lived in a far rawer era, one in which death was more casually risked.

Then I was back in the emergency room. Apparently, I'd passed out again, which prompted the doctor to finally treat me. One of this thirtyish woman's eyes listed to the side, as though she were simultaneously examining me while she studied a nurse's name tag beside her. This did not inspire confidence.

She hovered, pestering me with questions about what I'd just said as I'd regained consciousness in the emergency room. Apparently, it was something intriguing, perhaps along the same lines as my utterances on *Who's The Genius*? Simply repeating that I didn't remember failed to dissuade her from pestering me. When she finally proffered questions on germane topics—my symptoms, medical history, and the like, I cooperated with a sigh of relief.

My parents rushed into the room a few minutes later, crowding me from both sides, a physical metaphor for their psychological oppression.

"My poor baby," my mother crooned. "You just get better. Don't worry about anything. The show runner said they'd wait for you to come back."

"Marge, don't bother our lad with all that," my dad admonished. "The important thing is that his mind hasn't been damaged. Has it, son? The world needs that wonderful mind of yours."

"I'm fine," I told them.

My mother smelled like fresh bread—apparently

she'd been baking—and my father smelled like cigar smoke. He didn't smoke. Both men he worked with did, and he'd come straight from a job site.

"What was that you said on the air, son—just before you passed out?" my father asked. His tone was as solicitous as he could manage—about fifty percent of what anyone else would say.

"I don't know. What did you hear?"

"Something about a special book. I couldn't make sense out of it."

The doctor spoke up. "I doubt his words meant anything. He said much the same thing here when he wasn't fully conscious. He doesn't even remember he did."

"So you're saying his brain's not right?" my mother exclaimed, her voice rising in pitch. Each successive word spurred her to a higher level of concern.

The doctor tilted her palm up as though she were a crossing guard dealing with a reckless child. "Not at all. He'll probably be fine." An accompanying frown either belied her words or expressed her disdain for my parents. I rooted for the latter.

"Probably?" Now my mom was really scared.

I understood. From my parents' perspective, if our family wasn't receiving the benefit of my intelligence, I was just an arrogant problem child and the family was a lot poorer. I'd have hated to raise me in either case.

"You're upsetting my wife," my father growled, glaring at the doctor for all he was worth. "I'd like you to apologize."

Thankfully, my doctor was having none of this. "Your son needs to rest," she told him, "so I need you two to wait outside. We'll be running some tests, and we'll let you know the results as soon as we get them."

Begrudgingly, they filed out. My dad turned to aim scowls at both the doctor and me as he reached the door. What did *I* do? Fall down? Pass out? How was that *my* fault?

"Thanks," I told the doctor when the duo had departed. "I don't see why I'd talk about a book, though. Are you sure about that?"

"You really do need to rest, and we really do need to run tests," she replied. "Never mind about anything else." First she'd quizzed me mercilessly about what I'd said, and now she wouldn't even address the topic.

"I know what happened. This wasn't a seizure or anything else medical."

She leaned over me, orienting her face with mine. Did they teach this in Bedside Manner 101 in medical school? Her misaligned eye stared at my shoulder. Her unnaturally smooth, chocolate-brown skin gleamed in the harsh lighting. "I don't believe in self-diagnosis. Our opinions are too biased, and very few of my patients have attended medical school."

"It's not what you think," I told her in my best I-know-what-I'm-talking-about voice. "Trust me. I'm the smartest boy in the world." That didn't seem to register.

"Be that as it may, a sudden loss of consciousness is always a medical issue. What if you'd been standing on asphalt when you passed out? You could've sustained a traumatic brain injury. Do you want the IQ of a four-year-old for the rest of your life?" She gazed at me expectantly, awaiting a concessionary answer to what had sounded to me like a rhetorical question.

"My four-year-old self could probably negotiate

26

life better than most adults," I told her, "but that's not the point. This is a boundary issue. Whose body is this? Do you own it?"

"Technically—legally—your parents do," she responded, backing away now and folding her arms across her ample chest. "I empathize with you, having met them. But they call the shots, so here I am. For better or worse, you're stuck with me. Do you want to do this gracefully or kicking and screaming?"

I considered that. "Go ahead, I guess."

While I waited again, I discovered I could solicit memories of particular times in Lewis's life. This yielded me an exhausting march in the Whiskey Rebellion, an unpleasant bowel movement, and a dull lecture expounding on the importance of regular crop rotation.

As I suspected, the tests failed to indicate any physical problem. My doctor decided I'd suffered a severe panic attack. I suspect this was her default diagnosis when all else failed. Heaven forbid a doctor should admit she was stumped. I was released to my parent's care, with an admonition to drink more water and find a "particularly expert" therapist.

"It's not easy being different," the doctor told my father when my parents and I turned to leave the crowded, noisy waiting room where she'd delivered her news. The doctor was surprisingly short, I finally noticed. I guess looking up at her from a gurney and an examination table distorted my perspective. For that matter, her nostrils were substantially smaller than I'd thought. Like the entire ER, she exuded an unpleasant chemical smell. "I'm sure Tris experiences more stress than most children," she continued, her good eye trained on my father's face. "This can lead to anxiety."

"Well, I'm sure you know a lot about being different, don't you?" my father barked, either referring to her misaligned eye or her ethnicity. He did this type of thing when he didn't like someone.

"Shut up, Dad," I snapped. "Just shut up for once."

Chapter 4

At dinner, while a hard rain pounded onto the roof, I put in my earbuds and listened to Haydn. Watching my folks gobble their food, I was struck by how Germanic their features were. I could easily see them in a World War Two film, perhaps as Nazi farmers chasing a Roma family through their cornfield, pitchforks in hand.

My mother's face was broad and flat. Her deep-set, muddy brown eyes reflected a lack of awareness. Large ears dangled beside her rouged cheeks. As usual, she wore clip-on earrings. On this occasion, they resembled miniature nautilus shells, with a tiny, bright pink bow glued onto each. She often augmented her accessories and clothing. Her friends encouraged her by paying her lavish compliments whenever she trotted out a new iteration of her over-the-top aesthetic.

My father wasn't strikingly "Aryan" in terms of the fabricated Nazi ideal. His skin tone was too dark, for one thing. Nonetheless, his fierce countenance commanded authority from those who didn't see through his bravado to the insecurity that lay underneath. To me, this was evident in a shiftiness in his watery eyes and the uncertainty expressed in the corners of his toothy mouth.

Every bit of him was burly, from his oversized neck all the way down to his tree trunk calves. And curly black hair sprouted everywhere. I suspect he'd been allotted a disproportionate amount of testosterone in his roll of the genetic dice.

For the millionth time, I was glad I'd been adopted.

As soon as I'd finished a delicious plateful of lasagna and vanilla pudding—my mother was an accomplished cook—I removed my earbuds and pushed back from the table.

"Where are you going?" my father demanded. "We don't leave the table until we're excused in this house, young man. Your mother is still eating. And we need to talk about what you said to me at the hospital. It's not okay to tell me to shut up. You know that, Tris. I don't care if you were sick. That doesn't excuse disrespectful behavior."

Usually, I'd apologize after this type of incident to keep the peace. What did it matter what my father thought? This time I didn't feel like it. I turned to Mom from where I stood behind my chair. "Do you mind if I leave before you finish?"

She shook her head and started to answer. "No, I..."

"That's not the point," my father interrupted, controlling his tone and volume with some effort.

Now my mother nodded her head reflexively. To head off conflict, she suddenly minded my leaving. She and I had each developed a strategy to sidestep my dad's wrath. If she agreed with Dad in the first place, she wouldn't have to apologize after his fireworks like I did.

I raised my voice for emphasis. I knew my father found this objectionable as well. "What are you going to do? Send me to my room? That's where I'm heading, anyway."

"That's it!" he roared. "Go to your room!"

I knew I could get him to say that. If either of my parents didn't give me permission to go to my room, all I had to do was goad my dad into demanding it.

My room didn't reflect my personality. When money had rolled in from my early intellectual efforts, my mother's first spending spree entailed hiring an interior decorator and following this clueless woman's recommendations to the letter. The decorator's idea of a stylish and appropriate bedroom for a five-year-old child prodigy included cowboy wallpaper and a bed shaped like a racing car. Thankfully, I'd established an office in a corner of the room, replete with an L-shaped metal desk, two filing cabinets, and the latest upgraded laptop.

If adult men required a man cave, this was my equivalent, albeit devoid of a billiard table, a wet bar, or a giant television. Men were like adolescents in wrinkly bodies, weren't they? What precluded them from embarking on a life path that included a learning curve? It was all clueless straightaways with men, wasn't it? Perhaps my perspective was skewed by years of close observation of my father's modus operandi.

As I lounged in my cushy desk chair, I began shaking. I couldn't control it. I stumbled to my stupid bed, curled up on my side, and sobbed. Eventually I fell asleep and dreamt I was Thomas Jefferson's dog. In the dream, I kept biting Meriwether Lewis, who presented his leg as though he enjoyed being bitten. He tasted like asparagus, for what that's worth.

Upon awakening early in the morning, I pondered recent events as I lay in bed. *It could have been worse.*

The memories represented an augmentation, not a diminishment of who I'd been before they arrived. Sure, it was proving hard to incorporate them, but that was no wonder, given the sheer quantity of them.

In the light of day, the metaphysical implications of the past-life memories were quite challenging. I was—had been—an atheist. I'd believed all religions promoted comforting, superstitious delusions that had served mankind poorly through centuries of religious conflict and repression. None of its varied theses could be proved, rendering them useless. This stance had embodied a purely mechanical, causal view of life. Yes, aspects of quantum physics defied Newtonian and possibly Einsteinian principles, but these were still disputed theories, easy to discount.

Now everything seemed to be more mysterious and far-reaching than I'd thought. This scared me, which I experienced in that moment as an alarming array of physical sensations, including sweaty palms, increased heart rate, and a preternatural alertness—no, vigilance.

When I believed surface reality was all there was, when I closed my mind to the unknown…Well, that all sounded extremely short-sighted now.

An alarming thought popped up. What if I remembered more lives? How many were there? Could I hold them all? If I hit my limit, what then?

I stumbled to my laptop and discovered most traditions were loath to pick the number of incarnations a typical soul underwent. I did find one reasonably legitimate source who asserted that 850,000 lives were usually required to "complete the cycle"—whatever that was. So according to this well-respected guru, at any given point, a soul might be living its first or its

850,000th life. Clues as to which it was rested on the nature of the circumstances and issues a person faced. Compulsively beheading people was an early reincarnation sort of thing, while mediating international peace talks bespoke reincarnation maturity.

Obviously, even I wasn't equipped to hold thousands of previous life memories. The very idea scared me all the way to tears.

Ten minutes later, still crying like a helpless infant, I realized some of my tears were driven by unacknowledged grief—the loss of my cherished operating system. A part of me knew I couldn't cling to my mechanistic world view in the face of recent events. I'd entered frontier territory, albeit of a different ilk than Lewis's journey westward.

The question was, what should I do about it? How could I explore what I'd discovered? I decided to brainstorm a list of possibilities.
- Find out more about Lewis.
- Try hypnosis.
- Consult an expert, if there were any.
- Do nothing and see what happens.
- See a therapist, based on the ER doctor's recommendation.
- Try a mind-expanding drug.
- Continue researching past life material, theories about the soul, metaphysics, etc.
- Seek out a local New Age community.
- Meditate, chant, or establish some other spiritual practice.
- Run away from home—to Iceland?

I reviewed my list. As always, running away from

home had made the cut, although the Iceland destination was new. The second to last entry spoke to my desperation. Meditate? Really? Me? I considered each of the other items.

I didn't perceive any value to researching Lewis's life since I already knew all about him.

I ruled out hypnosis since I didn't wish to surrender my will to anyone. I probably wasn't hypnotizable, anyway.

Doing nothing simply wasn't in my DNA.

I'd probably be too nauseated by a gaggle of New Agers, even if they shared helpful concepts.

I was too scared of drugs to try a mind-altering substance, and I suspected I needed psychic glue more than solvent at the moment.

I would continue my research, of course, but that felt insufficient.

This left consulting an expert or seeing a therapist. I placed the latter at the glue end of a glue-solvent spectrum, which was a plus. An expert could educate me about reincarnation, while a therapist could help me maintain my psyche amid the stress of adapting to the new me. Then I had a flash of inspiration. That was why I employed brainstorming; it loosened something creative in me.

Suppose I combined my remaining two options by finding a therapist who knew a lot about reincarnation, or was a Buddhist or a Hindu himself? Perhaps there were entire schools of therapy based on these traditions. After all, clinicians in India and Tibet were unlikely to achieve satisfactory results utilizing interventions based on Freudian sex themes.

I returned to the internet, and sure enough,

Wikipedia described Transpersonal Psychology as "a sub-field or school of psychology that integrates the spiritual and transcendent aspects of the human experience with the framework of modern psychology. It is also possible to define it as a 'spiritual psychology.' The transpersonal is defined as 'experiences in which the sense of identity or self extends beyond (trans) the individual or personal to encompass wider aspects of humankind, life, psyche, or cosmos.' It has also been defined as 'development beyond conventional, personal, or individual levels.' "

Perfect. Now to find a practitioner who wasn't a moron.

Chapter 5

My family rented a two-bedroom condo carved out of an avocado grove outside Ojai, California. Ironically, this was the same patch of land my father had grown up on before *his* father lost the orchard to foreclosure. This scenario highlighted the chasm between established agricultural families in Ojai and the valley's newcomers. The former tend to be conservative and resentful (from being displaced from their farms and orchards). The latter embrace upscale southern California culture, and many of them demonstrate scorn for their poorer, less-educated forerunners.

These days, Ojai is small, quaint, artistic, and unusually spiritually oriented. I don't mean religious. Twelve miles inland from coastal Ventura, my hometown sits in a pretty east-west valley an hour and a half north of Los Angeles. Wealthy city dwellers stream in for weekend excursions, shopping at upscale art galleries, herbal remedy shops, and our venerable locally owned department store. Ojai also has a disproportionate number of expensive boarding schools, specialty restaurants, and retreat centers.

The morning after my first session with Marc Dalcour, the weirdness continued. I generally prefer not to use the word "weird." It's been co-opted by the media and pop culture to represent an undifferentiated grouping of whatever unusual phenomenon someone is too lazy to describe accurately. Its inelegance offends me. But what other word captures the flavor of the two letters addressed to me I found at my place at the breakfast table?

The first letter:

Dear Sir,

The enclosed envelope was found in a fifty-year-old time capsule that we recently opened at the county courthouse in San Marcos, Texas. Perhaps a relative of the addressee is still living at this residence. We don't feel we have the right to open the envelope, nor do we have the resources to research this matter further.

Yours,

Velma Patton, County Clerk

The second letter:

Dear Tris Healy,

Please keep reading this letter no matter how confused or alarmed you become. It will be worth it.

You're probably wondering who I am and how this letter ended up in a time capsule. My name is Susan Granger, and I truly wrote this letter fifty years ago—before your birth parents even met. How then could I know your name and address? You told me in a dream—the same dream you will have soon.

Here's the gist. If you haven't been opened to your past-life memories yet, brace yourself. Reincarnation is real. I am who you were in your last lifetime. When I was twenty-eight, I received a letter like this one from my former self.

I know. I know. I didn't believe it either. I researched the letter's origin, I hunted for alternate explanations, and I even doubted my sanity. But the letter began a process that led me to accept the truth.

This will happen to you, too.

We're not like everyone else. At some point, we always wake up to who we really are—that life is continuous, and we are a soul, not a person. There is comfort in this. But in our case, there is also a sobering responsibility associated with this awareness.

We're on a multi-generational mission, and we've been carrying it out for millennia. This mission will come to fruition in your lifetime.

How are you doing? Take a break if you need to. Walk around the block. Eat a cookie. I gather you're only a boy, which puzzles me. I can only trust that powers greater than I know what they're doing. Perhaps your parents will help you.

Ready for more?

Here's the mission. We've been writing a book since writing began, refining and adding to it through the centuries. It currently contains all the distilled wisdom that humans are capable of grasping. There is no more to add. It's finished.

Your job is to get it published. We're counting on you to find a way, whatever the current state of publishing might be.

Now, prior to this task, you will need to retrieve the one and only copy of the book from its hiding place.

Tonight you will have a dream that will confirm my words and guide you. Trust it. From now on, your dreams will be reliable sources of information. When your mind is quiet, the universe will speak to you— when you're awake as well, if you can still your mind enough.

Of course, you'll still check on the legitimacy of the time capsule and all the rest (I've left you confirmations if you research this hard enough). Who wouldn't? But when all is said and done, you will go look for the book.

Bring the book to a safe place.

DO NOT READ IT!

Not yet. It will be sealed. Leave it sealed. You are not ready (no offense).

We love you. All of us who were you love you.

Susan

So there it was. Meriwether's memories had loosened my proverbial lid, and now it was about to be twisted all the way off. Two days ago, I would've dismissed the letters as a silly prank. Now I couldn't.

Of course, as soon as I finished my french toast, I ran to my laptop and researched for all I was worth. For one thing, it let me postpone feeling my emotions, which might be overwhelming. I was not at all happy these had become such a prominent element of my experience.

I maneuvered through several Texas newspaper archives, eventually discovering an article and several letters about the San Marcos time capsule, as well as Susan Granger's obituary.

She'd been the head librarian in town—which sat in the middle of the state, a half hour south of Austin. A respected member of the community, she'd spearheaded the time capsule project by writing letters to the editor, which included the following phrases: "I'm keen to pass on vital information to a relative of sorts who's bound to read it in fifty years." And "I believe strongly that what we place in our capsule could help humanity become wiser. I know this will strike your newspaper's readers as an exaggeration, but it will mean a lot to one important young person."

Chills ran up my spine as I read. When I reached the last sentence, I couldn't breathe. I staggered to my bed and collapsed onto it, bruising my knee against one of the racing car's taillights that adorned the foot of the frame.

So now who I was in a past life—my last one, apparently—was sending me on a mission to change the world. I began exploring this by examining whether it could still be a hoax. I was a celebrity, after all. Maybe a crazed fan had rigged up something to trick me. I didn't believe this line of thinking, but once again, it helped me suppress my emotional response.

I checked the newspaper website to see if it was a real site. It was. I called the woman at the San Marcos courthouse who had forwarded the time capsule letter. She was legitimate, and she'd sent it.

I decided to bring the letters to my therapy session. I was only ten, after all. How could I sort this out on my own?

"Hello, Tris. Come on in. What's that in your hand?" Dalcour had buzzed his hair down further, creating the illusion that his high forehead was even higher than it was. Once again, I was struck by his square, narrow jawline.

"Letters. Read the top one first." I sat in the client chair this time and handed them over.

He did, taking his time. He wore a cobalt blue polo shirt and khaki slacks. He'd shaved since our first session, and his thinnish lips looked a bit dry and cracked.

When he was done reading, he looked up sharply. The sudden movement seemed out of character. "Who do you know who might want to mess with you?" he asked.

"No one. I think the letters are real."

"Why's that?"

I told him about my research.

He frowned. "Despite that, surely there's a more rational explanation than what the letter writer proposes."

"Coupled with my memories, I'm not so sure."

"When a magician seems to do an impossible trick, do you assume it's real magic? And when you find out how a trick works, isn't it always something mundane?"

"Sure. Point taken. But what if I have a big dream tonight like the letter says? What then?"

"We'll cross that bridge if we come to it. I may be a transpersonal therapist, but I'm also a skeptic when it's called for."

"I understand."

Dalcour paused and thought for moment, characterized by a slightly dreamy look in his brown eyes. "Did you know people are suggestible about what they dream?" he finally asked.

"You mean I might dream something about the letter simply because Susan Granger said I would?"

He nodded.

"I believe that phenomenon is associated with weak minds."

"Perhaps." He just gazed at me for a while as the clock ticked, counting off how many seconds of our session he was wasting.

"Tell me what to do," I said, perhaps for the first time in my short life.

"That's not my role. Let's explore that question

together."

"All right."

"What are you feeling right now?" He leaned forward. When he fished for feelings, Dalcour liked to close the gap between us.

"What's that got to do with anything?" I didn't appreciate being bossed around, especially when I was directed to do something unpalatable.

"Our feelings serve as wake-up calls and clues about what's going on. It's a resource, Tris."

"Maybe for some people."

"Just try it. Tune in for a moment. Consider it an experiment if you wish."

"Fine."

I tried to step away from my mind and just notice if there were any feelings lurking behind the scenes. This proved impossible. "I feel confused," I tried. That wasn't fear or anger or something along those lines, but it was better than nothing.

"And what's it like to feel confused?"

"What do you mean?"

"Do you like it?"

"Of course not."

"Are there any bodily sensations associated with it?"

"My head hurts a little."

"Great!"

"You're glad I have a headache?"

"I'm glad you were able to notice it."

I didn't know what to say to that. "Look, I've got to figure out what to do. Should I go look for this book? Do more research? Do nothing for a while and let all this sink in?"

"Those all seem like viable options."

I snorted. "That's no help."

He maintained a half smile. "Sorry."

Facing a dead end with this, I focused on something else I'd been wondering. "At this point, what do you think the likelihood is that I'm wrong about all of this—that I'm just crazy." I knew I wasn't, but I wanted to see where I stood with him. "In percentage form, please."

Dalcour shook his head slowly. "I don't think it would be helpful for me to answer that."

"You're asking me to be honest and forthcoming, right? Well, I'm asking the same of you."

He studied my face and then nodded just as slowly as he'd shook it. "All right. It's been my experience that when I've encountered situations like this in the past, ninety percent of them have had a pathological explanation. But it seems likely that you fall into the ten percent range, Tris."

I took a moment to consider Dalcour's perspective and thought of something else. "Have you entertained the idea that someone's playing a trick on *you*? Maybe I'm an actor some colleague of yours hired to confound you."

"I've ruled that out."

"How?"

"I think we're getting pretty far afield from your main concern. What do you think of the third option you mentioned?"

I appreciated that he assumed I'd remember the order of what I'd listed earlier, which, of course, I did. "I like the wait and see strategy, at least until or if I have that dream the letter mentioned. The dream could substantiate things for me if it entailed a correspondence to the real world."

"What do you mean?"

"Well, suppose it told me to go look under a rock in a park to find a clue, and I did and it was there?"

"That would be compelling evidence, and I'd love to explore that more, but our time's up. Are you comfortable coming to see me daily now?"

"Sure."

"Same time?"

"Okay."

Chapter 6

I almost had a friend. Burt. He was twelve, another genius recruited by a particularly annoying team of psychology researchers in Pasadena. As part of a twelve-week study, we'd fraternized outside the lab and reported on our experiences. Don't ask me why. My father liked to say that "egghead scientists" have their heads up a certain bodily orifice, which my father was always happy to name. I won't. But some psychologists did seem to be woefully out of touch with what normal people cared about. To be fair, others were remarkable, compassionate individuals.

Anyway, it had been fun to argue with Burt over whose parents were more clueless, or which of the researchers most aptly fitted my father's description.

I decided to call him. He'd called me a few weeks back, and I hadn't bothered to return his call.

"Burt, it's Tris Healy."

"Oh hey, can you hold on a minute?"

"Sure."

I could hear accordion music, Burt yelling at someone to turn it off, and then a loud bang, as though someone had dropped a brick onto a resonant surface.

"I'm back. How are they hanging, bro?" Burt affected a loutish manner, perhaps to fit in with ordinary kids, or perhaps just to amuse himself.

"Actually, I'm in the midst of a personal crisis."

"Whoa. What's up?"

I hadn't decided on how candid I would be, which was unlike me. In that moment, it felt appropriate to share most of what had happened. I left out the Dalcour part since my medical history was no one else's business. I also synopsized the letter from Susan Granger in a more abbreviated fashion than it probably deserved.

Burt listened quietly and paused before replying. "As a scientist, I'm open to all possibilities, however unlikely, so I want you to know I'm not dismissing your story, Tris. But I also think you should know that mental illness may be the root of your problem."

"I'm aware of that, of course."

"Have you talked to a professional?"

I decided to trust him a bit further. The risks outweighed the benefits. "Yes. He's skeptical, but helpful, so far."

"Good for you. Stay grounded."

"What does that even mean? Isn't that a New Age concept?"

"My therapist uses it all the time, and he's decidedly Presbyterian."

"You see someone?"

"Sure," he told me. "But let's get back to your crisis. Are you waiting to see if you dream about this book you're supposed to find?"

"Yes. Do you think I will?"

"Beats me."

"What would you do in my situation?"

"Duck and cover, bro. Duck and cover."

"Isn't that a wartime term? Something that's derived from soldiers in World War One trenches?"

"I don't know. You're such a literalist, Tris. Lighten up."

"I'm done," I said, and I hung up. So much for reaching out to a supportive friend. All he'd offered were cryptic idioms.

I attempted to distract myself that evening, but my focus was uncharacteristically poor. I perused a series of textbooks covering widely variable academic fields. None held my attention. Eventually, I resorted to viewing several TED talks about the global economy, a passive activity which usually didn't suit me.

As I lay in my absurd bed at ten o'clock, anticipation and a minor dose of fear kept me from falling asleep for quite some time. Here's what I dreamt later that night:

I strolled down a dirt road, dust in my nostrils, surrounded by odd-looking trees. I was taller than in real life and when I held a leg out to take a look at it, it was bare and quite tan. I wore a black dress and tan work boots. This didn't upset me, as it didn't seem important in the dream.

Each tree was shaped like a menorah, with nine trunks soaring up from a common, roundish base. It was warm and sunny in the dream, but the trees were leafless as though it were the dead of winter. At the top of each tree trunk, a small wrought iron platform supported an identical short-haired tan puppy. They all stood in unison and began barking simultaneously. The cacophony was almost unbearably loud.

Suddenly they stopped, and for some reason, that let me know I was in Texas. A boy called to me, and my attention was pulled to the road up ahead.

"Susan!" the boy shouted—in my voice.

It was me. I wore a navy blazer and red tie—an outfit my mother had recently picked out for a publicity photo. Once again, my dreamer self—Susan Granger—wasn't particularly alarmed by any of this.

"Who are you?" I asked in a woman's southern drawl.

"I'm you in your next lifetime. Here's what I'm here to tell you. Hide the book so the clues in this and subsequent dreams will lead me to find it fifty years from now."

"The wisdom book? How do you know about that?"

"Never mind," the boy—me—told me. Well, me as Susan Granger in the dream. "I have something else important to tell you," he continued. "My name is Tris Healy, and here's my mailing address. Write both of those down as soon as you wake up. You'll need them later."

"Why?"

"You'll figure it out. We trust you." He told me his address.

Then the puppies started howling, and the boy disappeared.

My dreamer self—Susan Granger—stood there, trying to make sense out of what had just happened. Before I could, my body slowly began to fade—becoming less distinct at first, and then transparent, and then disappearing entirely. Instead of being alarmed by this, I relaxed more and more as the process continued. Finally, I was left on the road without a body to inhabit, which felt sublime—peaceful and clear. I was ethereal—a specter—with no worries or cares.

Then the dream ended. I woke up, wrote it down,

and tried to remain in an elevated state. The bliss lingered briefly, but ironically, exerting an effort to hang onto it dissipated the lovely mood.

After telling Dalcour the dream in our session later that rainy day, he asked if I found the dream inconclusive, which struck me as odd.

"From your question, I assume you do."

"I don't know what to think, and I'm not sure it matters. What matters is what it means to you. I should've asked an open-ended question instead of leading the witness. That's a legit objection in a court of law."

"Yes. And please don't use pseudo words like legit."

He nodded. Today he wore the least formal clothes so far—worn gray corduroy pants and a plain black T-shirt. A compact blue knapsack sat on his desk next to his computer, and a pair of white running shoes were haphazardly strewn in a corner by the vast bookcase. Otherwise, the office was much the same.

"I guess I don't know what to think," I continued. "On the one hand, it was so radically different from any other dream I've had that it's easy to think it originated externally. On the other hand, the so-called clues in the dream weren't particularly helpful. Should I look for a synagogue or a dog breeder to find the wisdom book? Maybe the menorah trees represent Hanukah. But how does that direct me?"

"Why don't we look at some of the other features of the dream? What associations do you have with Texas?"

"It's where Susan Granger lived. I don't think I mentioned that before."

"No, you didn't. Do you think your book is hidden there?"

"So you believe there could be a book?"

"Let's work with it as a metaphor for now. I don't think we need to get hung up on that question."

I glared at him. "It matters to *me*."

"Wouldn't sharing my opinion deflect us from exploring more relevant material? Tris, I'm not going to let you lead us away from *you*." He'd been frowning, which apparently he belatedly noticed since now he switched to an incongruous smile. "What did you feel when you woke up?" he asked.

"I felt great. I guess it was a carryover from the end of the dream—when I was disembodied and peaceful."

"What do you make of that?"

"It could've been a glimpse into some deeper reality—maybe what it's like when we don't have bodies." This popped out of me without forethought.

He frowned and leaned back so far in his chair I thought he might tip over. Then he paused before tilting forward and speaking in a faster, crisper voice. "I get flashes of intuition, Tris, and I've learned to trust them. I think you're right about that." Apparently he sought my permission to continue because it wasn't until I nodded that he kept talking. "What did you feel when I just shared my intuition?"

Here we were again. I was sick of questions like this, but since Dalcour had been so forthcoming, I threw him a proverbial bone. "Interested."

"Strictly speaking, that's not a feeling, Tris. It's a cognitive state. I'm fishing for a core emotion like sadness, fear, anger, or joy."

"I guess I was…uh, happy." I just said this to head

off more discussion on the topic. What mattered to me was the meaning of the dream. I studied his face, looking for clues about how to get us back on track. I hadn't noticed before, but he was a good-looking guy, all things considered. He could've leaned against a sports car in a print advertisement. The combination of his alert eyes and the default setting of his mouth—a half smile—inspired trust. If he implied it was a good car, then it probably was.

"Why the constant emphasis on feelings?" I finally asked. I sensed that Dalcour wouldn't be willing to completely change subjects yet. "I know you stated they were clues about reality, but that doesn't seem to justify your dogged focus on them."

"We need to get you out of your head. It doesn't serve you to experience life from that vantage point so much of the time."

"I disagree."

"Let's table our conversation about the meaning of the dream until tomorrow. I'd like to think it over." He waved his hand in the air as he said this. I didn't perceive any correlation with his words. "But before we stop today, I want to make sure you're okay."

"What do you mean? That's a very vague term."

"Open-ended, I'd say. Here's why I ask. Some people have difficulty managing radically new information. It creates stress—puts us in a mental vise—and we all have an Achille's heel—a weak area—whether it's depression, anxiety, medical problems, substance abuse, or whatever. I'm checking in with you to see if any of these have gone *sproing*. Has the vise action of stress triggered your inner spring?"

"I don't have any weak areas," I told him. "You're mixing metaphors, and I don't think 'sproing' is a real word."

"Yes, that was my point, Tris." His mouth twisted sideways. "I was testing you to see if you'd notice I used a made-up word."

"Are you mocking me?" I was more curious than offended.

"Yes, I guess I am. Sorry. Let's explore your stress level another time when I don't feel so frustrated. You may not realize it, Tris, but you can be challenging to work with. You have your own ideas about what we should talk about—you don't like yielding to my expertise. And you frequently rebut what I say without really taking it in and considering it."

"Aren't you supposed to put your feelings to the side in order focus solely on me? Isn't that what my insurance company is paying for?" I was dodging his feedback. I hadn't solicited any criticism, had I?

He frowned now, furrowed his sparse eyebrows, and raised his voice. "Why don't I prorate your fee this session so you don't have to pay for the one-eightieth of the time I acted unprofessionally."

I calculated the exact percentage. "That's inaccurate," I told Dalcour. "It's more in the neighborhood of one-six hundredth. And I hardly think that's worth refunding."

He winced this time and told me in a measured voice that our session was over.

On the ride home with my dad, I considered Dalcour's behavior—at least until we got into a fender bender near our condo with a Mercedes driven by an older man in an expensive suit. While exchanging insurance information by the side of the road, my father's loud epithets prompted the other driver to jump back into his car and take off.

I was disappointed by Dalcour's display of poor emotional regulation. I knew from my reading he was never supposed to say anything about his own feelings, let alone mock a patient. I consoled myself with the notion that he'd allowed himself to be authentic—telling me what was going on with him—albeit in an inappropriate way. He'd probably broken his rules because he cared. I forgave him.

Because of the dream, I spent the afternoon researching Judaism, which had never particularly interested me. Like Catholicism, it was obviously obsolete, serving the needs of a long-gone demographic with its pointless rituals and ridiculously simple concepts. To my mind, it also represented an arrogant version of an us-versus-them dynamic. The chosen people. Really? Chosen for what? To be reviled for their snotty attitude? When I realized these thoughts were in the same ballpark as my father's overt anti-Semitism, I vowed to upgrade my perspective.

Eventually I started coupling words and phrases in Google search, which had borne good results in the past, however esoteric the subject. When I juxtaposed "synagogue" and "puppy"—I wonder if I was the first person to ever do so—I found something beyond intriguing.

A congregation in Austin, Texas—a short journey up the interstate from Susan's hometown of San Marcos—was hosting what they called an "adoption festival" for dogs and cats. A pdf of a poster revealed more details.

The event was in three days, and the logo of the synagogue was a menorah. The photograph of the dog on the poster was the puppy in my dream.

Chapter 7

I was sure now the letter was true—all of it—despite never having experienced any Meriwether Lewis memories about the wisdom book. He was, after all, another karmic ancestor and had probably played a role in its development.

Despite my newfound certainty, in my next session with Dalcour, following my synopsis of recent events, I acceded to his request to brainstorm other possibilities.

"I'll get us started," he said. "Suppose you'd become clairvoyant and could dream future events and past lives. There are people who make a living purporting to do such things."

"I suppose we can't rule that out, but that's not my experience."

"You wouldn't be the first person to go through something untoward and then construct meaning out of it that veered away from consensus reality."

"You're back to saying I might be delusional, which is quite insulting now that you know me—and I thought we'd ruled that out—but I guess it's your job to brainstorm along those lines. I'll go ahead and respond civilly since I understand I annoyed you last session with my behavior, and I'd like to avoid doing that today."

I paused, and Dalcour nodded his appreciation of this admission. "I apologize for *my* behavior last session," he told me. "Thanks for bringing it up. It's not an excuse, but I had a really hard day yesterday. Shortly before you came, I tried to hospitalize one of my clients, but she ran off when the police showed up to escort her."

"That does sound challenging," I agreed, as empathetically as I could. "But back to me. Let me remind you I'm a genius with a well-chronicled grip on reality. Since your profession trains you to diagnose everyone, have you considered this bias may be driving your point of view?"

"First of all, geniuses are more, not less, likely to suffer from mental health problems." He sneezed suddenly, and I pulled back from the minor violence of this. "Sorry. It's just allergies."

I sniffed the air, detecting faint paint fumes.

Dalcour continued. "You're right that ten would be a very early age for a full-blown mental disorder to show up—I think I said that earlier—but obviously you're out of synch developmentally with your birth cohort. Anyway, I'm not insisting you have a delusional disorder. I'm brainstorming."

"You only brainstormed one item," I pointed out.

"So far, sure. But okay, forget about that one. I'm not trying to rile you up, Tris. Here's my point. How can anyone be sure about the meaning of strikingly novel life material after only a few days? Why not hold a working hypothesis lightly in your hand? I'm reminded of something a wrestling coach told me once. 'Sometimes you need to let go to get a better hold.' "

"I want to go to Austin to the pet-adoption festival," I blurted out.

"Yes, but you're ten. What do your parents think of

the idea?"

"I don't know. I haven't mentioned it, and I hope not to. They wouldn't understand."

"So how can you go?" He took a sip from his mug. Glazed with a dark green sheen, this one featured tiny white coffee mugs dancing on even tinier legs around its circumference.

"I could pretend to be older," I said.

"They check IDs before you go through security, don't they?"

"I could pretend I was with a family."

"How?" Dalcour cocked his head.

"I don't know. Maybe I could pay a family to escort me." I heard the uncharacteristic improvisational nature of my responses. I was grasping at straws; it was as though my brain had become unmoored, floating in the air above me.

Dalcour shook his head, a bit faster than usual. "That seems very unlikely. Why don't you reconsider the idea of discussing your plan with your parents?"

I pondered the matter for a bit and came up with a new idea. "You could take me."

"No, I couldn't."

"I'd pay you."

"It's out of the question. And it's time to stop. Will I see you tomorrow?"

"Yes. I don't need to leave for Austin until tomorrow evening at the earliest."

Dalcour stood and started walking to the exterior door. "I think you're going to have to let that go unless you can talk your parents into taking you."

"Just think it over. We can talk about it again tomorrow, okay?"

He nodded his head. "Sure." He didn't mean it.

Later that day, I researched flights, ground transportation, and AirBnBs in Austin. The latter were a scarce commodity that weekend because of an audiologists' convention. How many audiologists were there? I managed to make a reservation for three nights in a stone cottage behind an unimpressive home in West Austin. The owner was obviously eccentric. His online description of the amenities he offered must've eliminated a lot of potential guests. Perhaps he did that on purpose to troll for people he liked. The room came with its own "antique dartboard, dolphin-themed punchbowl, and a complete set of minor key harmonicas."

Now I just had to find a way to get there. I used my father's credit card number, which I'd long since memorized, to book a flight. Once I managed to get to Austin, I'd use Uber, and the driver probably wouldn't request proof of age to ride across town. In case it was a problem, I researched diseases and birth defects that made young adults look like children, and I chose one to tell anyone who questioned me.

An unaccompanied kid my age would be allowed on a flight if a parent handed him off and presented a letter in which the other parent gave permission. Then there had to be a family member or someone I recognized at the other end. Since the airline employee who'd shepherd me through the Austin airport to this phantom loved one was unlikely to use a leash or handcuffs, I could probably elude him or her. I ran fast for my age. Perhaps my birth father had been a champion sprinter in high school.

So I forged all the required documentation and

studied theater techniques in order to convince or bribe some stranger at the airport to pretend to be my parent and hand me off. That was the one variable I couldn't control. I thought about hiring someone I knew to drive me there and play the part, but I couldn't think of anyone who wouldn't snitch to my parents.

By the time I retired to bed, I'd decided that a reasonably presentable homeless man was my best bet. I'd take buses to get to the airport, and then I'd tell my hand-selected bum I was running away from an abusive father who beat me, and he was a policeman so I couldn't contact the authorities. If I spoke in my natural genius voice, he'd probably assume I was quite a bit older than I was.

My mother didn't trust banks since "they were always getting robbed in the movies," so she kept a stash of bills inside a roll of toilet paper she hid under a pile of sweaters in her closet. All the sweaters were bright red, which tells you something about her sense of style.

I took five hundred dollars and left the rest. Then I packed a knapsack and tried to fall asleep. Tomorrow would be a big day, and the following one—the dog adoption day—even bigger.

Chapter 8

The next morning, Dalcour wasn't himself. His hair was mussy. I love that word—mussy. My grandmother used to say it at every opportunity. His shirt was wrinkled, too. And he worried the air with his hands as we sat across from each other.

"What's up?" I asked.

"I had two significant dreams."

He was working hard to maintain a professional tone of voice. I liked him the most at that moment. "Tell me about them," I said. "Then I'll interpret them and charge *you* at the end of our session."

"They definitely relate to our work, Tris. I was elderly, and my wife and I sat in wooden rocking chairs on a covered front porch. There was a small table between us with two tall glasses of iced tea on it. It was very hot. For a while we just watched the street as several 1950s cars drove by. Then my wife told me about a time capsule she wanted the town to bury on the courthouse lawn. I told her that sounded fun. Then I woke up and wrote it down. When I fell asleep again, I dreamt you and I were in Austin, sitting in a small living room with limestone walls and a few odd objects on a shelf across the room from us."

"Was there an antique dartboard?"

"Yes! Did you dream that, too?"

"No, I made a reservation for that room last night.

There were a bunch of harmonicas too, right?"

"Yes!" Dalcour grinned excitedly. "This is remarkable!"

"So who's delusional now?"

"You're taking this in stride, aren't you?"

"I've had several days to get used to it. It's new to you. Well, it's newly *real* to you. We've got a mission to complete. We need to find that book." Calmness permeated my body, and strong resoluteness surged in my mind. My posture stiffened, and I felt invincible. This was the first time I'd ever experienced this phenomenon. I liked it very much.

"Let me think this over," Dalcour told me. He closed his eyes and leaned back in his chair. I watched him think, which was quite boring since his facial expression never changed for the five minutes his mind was elsewhere. Surely he'd had time to consider the matter between waking up and meeting me. Periodically I glanced around the office, noticing things I'd been too self-absorbed to see before.

A koa ukulele hung from a wall-mounted clamp in the corner behind me, above a compact stereo system on a shelf that, in turn, sat above cereal-box-sized walnut speakers. The house plant beside Dalcour tilted to the right at the same angle as one of his legs, and an engraving on a small gray rock in the soil proclaimed *Don't Believe Everything You Think*.

Finally he blinked his eyes open, nodded several times, and spoke again. "I think you're right. We need to go to Austin." He frowned for a moment before reforming his mouth into a wry smile. "And I need to fill you in about some of my history so my decision will make sense to you. I'm not choosing to offer help outside of this office lightly. I've never done it before, and I don't intend to do it again." He paused again, this time exhaling loudly before continuing. "As a child, I shared your difficulty connecting to my family. I wasn't adopted, but I was different. I told you early on that I remembered a past life too, but I didn't tell you it happened to me when I was fourteen. Not only didn't I get any support around this, I was told I was going to hell for blasphemy. When I tried to take an interstate bus to where I believed I'd lived before, my parents had state troopers haul me off it in handcuffs and keep me in jail overnight to teach me a lesson. I won't tell you what happened to me in there."

"I'm sorry."

Dalcour waved away my concern, although his face was grim. "My point is, now that I know everything you've told me is real, someone needs to step up and make sure *you* get a chance to follow *your* path. That someone is me. Here I am."

"Thank you." Tears formed in the corner of my eyes, which confused me. Did I feel sorry for what he'd endured? Was it simply his kindness that was tear-inducing?

"Stay with the feeling," Dalcour suggested. "Don't go up into your head and try to figure it out."

A salty tear dripped down my cheek into my mouth; I was simply sad. It didn't matter why. The feeling subsided a few moments later, and a thought occurred to me. "Given your history, you might get something out of going to Texas too, right?"

"I hadn't thought of that, but yes. It'll probably be healing for me to be along for the ride—the ride I wish I could've made on my own all those years ago."

"Do you think my parents will be okay with us going? If we sneak off, they might call the police."

"I'll clear it with them—tell them we're off to a retreat or a training."

"I can create a phony pamphlet if it proves necessary." I told him about the flight I'd booked. "There was a seat on the plane next to mine as of yesterday."

"I'll nab it when we're done. Where's the BnB? Near the synagogue?"

I rattled off the address. "That's not close, but it was the best I could do."

"How are you feeling about all this?" he asked.

"Excited." I hadn't realized this until I said it, which was interesting. Some part of me knew more about my emotions than my conscious mind did. My hands vibrated, and my head nodded several times in rhythm with some inner tune I couldn't quite hear. Then a flash of fear surged through my chest. My emotions were running wild. I reported this to Dalcour.

"The attempt to control our feelings—or life in general, actually—fuels a lot of anxiety," he said. "And it's scary and sometimes depressing when we learn we can't."

"What do you mean?"

"You're kidding yourself if you think you're in charge of your life, Tris. No one is." He clasped his hands together as though to comfort himself in the face of what he was saying.

"Then what's going on instead? Are you talking about predetermination or an old-school God in the sky running the show? I expect better of you, Dalcour."

"Call me Marc. No, I mean there are too many

unknowable and unmanageable variables in addition to our minds and willpower. We could both perish in a natural disaster in the next few minutes. I could meet the love of my life waiting on line to board our plane. Think about all your current circumstances. Which of them did you personally engineer—or even imagine?"

"You've got a point. But if we don't live our lives as though we're in charge, what then? Knowing the truth of what you say doesn't suggest an alternate way to proceed, does it?"

"It does. We need to learn how to accept our lack of the empowerment we yearn for and make the best of our lot on a daily basis. This means letting go of expectations that we can control emotions, outcomes, and all kinds of other things."

"That's nutty."

"More so than what's happened over the last few days?"

"Another good point. Of course it isn't. Clearly, I need to update my thinking. My previous perspective is ill-equipped to make sense out of all this."

"Just keep an open mind. We'll find out what we need to know simply by paying attention as we move forward."

"How do you know that will work?"

"It always does."

"Not to be contrary, but I sincerely doubt that."

Dalcour—Marc—was true to his word. By dinner time, he'd obtained written permission from my mother and father for our trip. What sort of parents entrust their young son to a virtual stranger on an out-of-state trip? Suppose Marc were a molester or a human trafficker? Despite my burning desire to go to Austin, I couldn't help thinking my mother and father were abandoning their responsibility to keep me safe. As usual. Many of the research scientists I'd been leased out to had been solely interested in advancing their careers.

The next morning, Marc picked me up in a hybrid SUV, and we headed to the LA airport—a two-hour trip. The interior of his vehicle had not been cleaned in quite some time. Several CDs were loosely stacked in the console as well, endangering their integrity. Marc's musical taste was even more alarming—Christmas carols in June? Two CDs of Finnish folk music?

The sun glared off the rear window of the car ahead of us, so I pulled down the SUV's hefty visor. Limited to the side window, I watched the overly familiar parade of homes and businesses en route to Ventura. After ten minutes or so, I began noticing novel details.

The incongruously Tudor house set back from the highway on a sweeping curve needed a new roof. A huge mailbox shaped like a dirigible peeked out from under a tangle of vines in front of a green and white manufactured home. And a young goat stared wistfully at the meadow across the road from where he was tethered next to a strip mall. I felt sorry for him.

"Tris," Marc began as we merged onto the highway connecting Ojai to the coast, "I think we need to set some ground rules for our quest."

"Quest? You think this is a quest?"

"Sure—like in a fantasy book or an epic poem. We're setting out to find a wisdom book against all odds—or at least contrary to logic. And we're obviously ill-equipped for the task, aren't we?"

I put my feet up on the dash—something I'd only

been able to do since I grew a bit recently. In my stocking feet, the nubby texture of the plastic dash almost tickled. "I don't think so. On paper, we're an impressive team. I'm the brains of the outfit, and you're savvy about people. We'll go to this adoption fair and find some big clue, or maybe the book itself. I'm sure of it."

"Even if we do find it, the next step will be daunting. We're supposed to get the book out into the world, right? That may prove to be the hardest part."

"Why's that? Who wouldn't want to publish legitimate wisdom?"

"The relevant question is who would? I wrote a self-help book—well, a self-help manuscript. Not a single literary agent would even read it."

"Why would you want an agent? Don't they just take a percentage of your royalties for things you can do yourself?"

"No major publisher will even look at a manuscript unless it's been submitted by an agent. And they earn their commission and then some for all the things they do."

"This book is bound to be better than yours. No offense. I'm curious about it, though. What was yours called?"

"*Congruence Therapy: Aligning Ourselves With Life*."

"Ah, I see where you're going with that. It sounds helpful to me."

"Thanks. Here's an even bigger catch-22 in non-fiction. You pretty much have to be a celebrity or have another platform of some sort that guarantees sales ahead of time."

"What do you mean by platform?"

"A built-in readership. You could be renowned in your field or successful with a previous book, for example."

"You're a psychologist. That's not enough?" I asked.

"Hardly. Then there's the business of the book's content. One person's wisdom is another person's boring drivel."

"That's a little extreme, don't you think?" I was surprised Marc was being so negative. Perhaps he role-modeled positivity in our sessions but couldn't sustain it out in the world. It was almost as if he'd sat around making a list of all the reasons our quest was doomed before we even began.

"I suppose you're right," Marc admitted. I turned to watch him. Marc's profile wasn't as handsome as his frontal view. It highlighted his bony brow, and his chin was a bit protuberant. "I still have feelings about my unsuccessful manuscript," he continued. "Maybe a fairer statement would be that we can't count on a given editor appreciating our book's wisdom as wisdom. All in all, it's a crazy-making industry—and I know crazy."

"Nothing ever gets done if one enters into a project with a defeatist attitude," I parroted, having read this some time ago.

"From the mouths of babes. You're right. Let's assume we have the tools and the backing of the universe to get the job done. That gives us the best chance to succeed."

"Don't call me a babe. I don't like that."

"I'm sorry."

"So you mentioned ground rules," I reminded him.

"Are you assuming a parental role? I hardly think that's necessary." I scratched the side of my nose for no reason again. The habit was becoming less frequent, but still surfaced periodically.

"I owe that to your folks. But don't worry. I won't infantilize you or enforce any restrictions for anything less than good cause. Your limited experience makes you vulnerable in some situations." He paused to avoid a truck that careened from the slow lane into ours. We'd entered Highway 101 a few minutes before, and people drove much more aggressively on their way to Los Angeles. "I propose you let me be in charge of anything I feel a need to manage on behalf of us both."

"That's a bit of a blank check, isn't it? Suppose I disagree?"

"Then you'd yield to my judgment. Those are my terms."

I wished I could see his whole face to read how determined he was, but he kept his eyes on the busy road. "So this is a take it or leave it deal? Can't we discuss the matter as peers?"

"We aren't peers in many respects, Tris. Mental acuity only goes so far. Frankly, you think more of yourself than the evidence supports. As you say, I know people. That will probably matter more than who is purported to be more intelligent."

"Purported?"

"You know your story. You don't know mine. I could be a genius too, for all you know. So how can you compare?"

He certainly hadn't seemed like one so far. Quite intelligent, yes. Perhaps he'd learned how to hide a truly superior mind to fit in better, a choice I'd always eschewed. By the time we arrived at the airport parking lot, I'd decided Marc was making a point about assumptions, not claiming a particular intellectual status.

Getting through security and boarding the plane turned out to be relatively simple once my parents' letter granted us some sort of special pass. Also, the pretty gate attendant recognized me from TV.

"What an honor!" she gushed. "The smartest boy in the world right here. Tris Healy!"

"It's nice to meet you." I shook her hand, which was surprisingly strong.

"Can I ask you a question?"

"Sure."

"What's the square root of 13,304?"

I thought for a long moment. Numbers aren't my strength. "115.342966842"

"Is that right? I'm going to write that down on your ticket stub. Will you sign it?"

"Sure."

Marc watched all this with mild amazement in his eyes. Clearly he had no idea how much of a celebrity I was. I'd actually forgotten myself.

When we'd found our seats behind a bulkhead and settled in, he spoke excitedly. "You *have* a platform. A big one, apparently. What if the smartest boy in the world wrote a book? Would you want to read it?"

"Of course, but I don't know how to write, and I wouldn't want to take credit for someone else's work—not even my past lives'."

"Since it *is* your lineage who wrote it—your *soul*, your most *essential* self—it *is* you that wrote it."

"That sounds like sophistry, Marc, no matter how

you emphasize certain words. You know what I mean."

"Well, we'll see."

Later, as the half-empty plane taxied and took off, I considered what it would be like to lend my name to the book and be known as both the smartest *and* the wisest boy on the planet. My ego was flattered by the notion at the same time the rest of me recoiled. Things were bad enough the way they were. I didn't need to live under an even more powerful microscope.

Chapter 9

By my reckoning, quite a few hours passed before anything noteworthy happened, unless you counted how hot it was on the pavement outside the Austin airport.

We finally arrived at our AirBnB in our diminutive Korean rental car. It had been hard to find, despite our GPS, nestled as it was in the hills just west of Austin proper. A flat-roofed limestone cottage behind a plywood geodesic dome, a makeshift plaque at the foot of its long driveway proclaimed that a noted folk singer had written all his "major milestone songs" in it, begging the question of who he was. As we drove up beside the cottage, a tall sixtyish man sporting a long gray braid emerged from the back door of the main house, smiling and waving.

"Welcome, brothers," he drawled as we emerged from our car.

"Thanks," Marc replied.

"Call me Chet."

"Hi, Chet. I'm Marc. This is Tris."

Chet's well-worn face was friendly, but something in his deep-set eyes hinted at complexity. He was more than he seemed—more than just friendly. I'd met other old hippies in Ojai, and for the most part, what you saw was about all there was. I attributed this to drug usage, which I'd read created a type of suspended animation around personal development. Perhaps Chet had uncharacteristically eschewed drugs as a youth.

Clearly he was Caucasian, but his nose and lips could've been transplanted from an African American man. The former was quite wide at the bridge and then flared out even more around his substantial nostrils. Chet's lips were almost girlishly plump. I would've thought this out-of-place duo of features—both racially and by gender in terms of his lips—would render any man ugly. Somehow, in combination with his squarish face and substantial height, Chet passed for reasonable-looking. I theorized that his oversized features were farther away from my gaze than normal because he was so tall, which made them appear smaller. Then I immediately discarded this theory. I needed to stop concocting wacky theories and just pay attention, as Marc suggested.

"Can I help you with your luggage?" Chet offered. "Show you your digs? I know all the best Tex-Mex and barbecue places in town, if that's your thing."

"Thanks," Marc responded. "We're good for now."

"It would be more appropriate if you speak for yourself," I told him. "I'd like to know who the folk singer from the sign is, and which Mexican restaurant is your favorite, Chet. For that matter, do you know anything about a pet adoption that a synagogue in town is sponsoring?"

"I'm him. I'm the folk singer. I lived in the cottage before I built the dome. The Mexican restaurant depends on whether you like authentic—greasy and cooked with lard, which I dig—or Americanized, which most of my guests prefer. And no, I don't know anything about pet adoptions. I had a dog once, but she was struck by lightning, believe it or not. After that…"

"Would we know your whole name if you told it to us?"

"Sure. Chet's my middle name." His reasonable tone failed to express the annoyance in his eyes. I'd interrupted him during his dead dog story. I guess I would've been annoyed too.

"I want to try an authentic place," Marc enthused, jumping in to lighten the mood.

"El Frontera on Fifth Street."

"Thanks," Marc and I said in unison.

"Can we bring anything back for you when we go?" Marc asked Chet.

"That's kind of you. I'll think it over. One thing you could do is write in the notebook I keep just inside the front door of your place. I ask everyone to write one sentence—what's the most profound thing they know?"

Marc looked at me and raised his eyebrows. "A book of wisdom, huh? We'd be happy to."

"So y'all are in town to get yourself a pup? Where are you from?"

I answered. "We're from Southern California. And all I said was 'pet adoption.' We might be getting a cat or even a lizard, for all you know." I wasn't sure why I'd adopted this tone.

"Oh, sorry." He looked down into the hard-packed dirt between his home and the cottage behind it as though the next thing he should say was written there. "Y'all just look like dog people, I guess." He looked up, seemingly pleased with his response.

"We're actually doing some research about an ancestor," I told him. Off the cuff, that was the best I could come up about our quest without resorting to outright deceit. I hadn't thought how to describe our mission.

In the minuscule bedroom of the AirBnB, twin beds huddled against opposite walls in the minuscule bedroom of the AirBnB, separated by a rickety rattan table. The kitchen was almost spacious, with avocado-colored appliances and a huge microwave that looked as though it belonged in an army mess hall—at least the movie version of a mess hall, which was all I knew. The modest living room completed the triumvirate of rooms. Heavy, dark furniture crowded its borders, and a faded brown, oval braided rug sat squarely in its center. An altar-like table rested against the wall next to the front door. The aforementioned harmonicas and such sat next to Chet's guest book. Hanging on the wall just above the table was a small print of an oil painting—a portrait of Meriwether Lewis.

Marc either didn't notice the portrait, or, more likely, had no idea what Lewis looked like. Personally, I remembered sitting for that painting, which had been excruciatingly boring. I decided not to say anything to Marc. I didn't want Chet involved in our business.

After dropping our carry-ons on our respective beds, we sat in sagging beige armchairs across the living room from one another.

"The room in my dream was a lot like this one," Marc told me. "Not identical, but uncannily similar. Mine had an old-fashioned TV in the corner and a bowl full of bananas on that table over there. And there wasn't a coatrack or that poster of Janis Joplin."

"I like the poster. Do you think Chet knew her? She was from Texas, and he said he was a famous musician."

"I don't know. Maybe."

"So what'll we do now?" I asked after a moment of silence. "Scout the site? Find people associated with the adoption event?"

"Let's just have fun tonight. Maybe go hear some music if there's any that doesn't start too late. Austin is the live music capital of the world, after all."

"The whole world? That's American centrism, isn't it?"

"I think you mean centric, not centrism. Centrism is a political term."

"Yes, of course." My face must've reflected my irritation.

"I guess I don't really need to correct your vocabulary."

"No, you don't."

Dalcour seemed to be a top-notch therapist, but his in-the-world self was fraught with typical human foibles. In this instance, I think he couldn't resist catching me out; perhaps he was intimidated by my intelligence.

"So how do we find out where to go for music?" Marc asked. He knew the answer. He was throwing me a bone as penance.

"Chet, of course."

We headed to the back door of the main house after we'd cleaned up and unpacked. Constructed of unpainted, slightly warped plywood, it responded to Marc's repeated knocking with a hollow, dead sound.

"I'd be happy to show you around," our host told us after he finally answered the door wearing nothing but a lime green towel around his waist. This wasn't precisely what Marc had asked a moment before. "I haven't made the scene in ages," Chet added.

My eye was drawn to two circular scars that adorned his bony ribcage.

"That would be great," Marc responded before I could say no. I was surprised by what Marc said next, which struck me as quite rude. "Bullet holes?" he joked, gesturing toward Chet's scars.

Chet paused before replying. He looked uncomfortable. "Cigarette burns."

"Whoa. An abusive father?"

I cut in. "Marc, you're getting a little personal, don't you think? This isn't a therapy session."

"No, it's all right." Chet's pained facial expression spoke otherwise. "A crazed fan kidnapped and tortured me. And why are you calling him Marc? He's not your father, is he? Should I be worried about you two?"

"I'm so sorry about what you've been through." Marc reached into the back pocket of his jeans. "Here's a letter Tris's parents signed so no one would need to worry about us. I'm Tris's psychotherapist. I'd be happy to show you some ID."

Chet didn't take the proffered paper, but instead studied my face. "I knew there was something different about you. You don't talk like other kids. So you're crazy, huh?"

"Hardly. I'm gifted beyond your ability to understand."

He nodded. "Grandiose personality disorder?" he asked Marc. "Mild psychosis? Well, no worries. It's nothing a synagogue with adoption animals can't cure. Ha ha ha."

I didn't appreciate this so-called jest, and I was about to tell him so when Marc changed the subject back to Chet's scars.

"Your crazed fan story is like something I read in a novel once."

Once again, his comment seemed out of character. Why didn't he care about the pain or fear such an assault would've triggered? He was so attentive to emotions in our sessions. I'd constructed an all-too-specific picture of how Marc would behave socially. What seemed out of character might be squarely *in* character—a character I hadn't had a chance to meet yet. Another possibility was that there was something about Chet that made Marc want to know more about him. What would that be?

"Actually, there are two books about it," Chet reported. "But I won't let them do a movie. Being famous was a previous incarnation, really."

I exchanged a meaning-laden look with Marc. So far, we had Chet's wisdom book, Lewis's portrait, and now a mention of reincarnation. The scale was tipping toward something meaningful.

"Who *are* you?" Marc asked.

Chet smiled ruefully. "If a fan tortured you, would you continue to be a public figure? Would you use your original name? Maybe you'd even change your face with hours and hours of painful surgery."

"I understand."

We all just stood there for a long moment.

"I'll see who's in town," Chet finally told us. "If there's nobody special, there are plenty of great local bands. What kind of music do y'all like?"

Marc and I looked at one another, and then we both shrugged. "All kinds, I guess," he said.

"No Christmas carols," I chimed in. Chet stared at

me. Marc smiled.

"Well, that makes it easy. Anything but carols. Maybe we ought to go for something you aren't likely to hear back home."

"That sounds good."

"Are you headed to La Frontera for dinner?"

"Yes," I replied.

"We could all go, and then head off to hear music after—if you don't mind the company, I mean."

"Sure, that would be great," Marc replied in high-handed fashion. Why do older people think they know best simply because of a chronological advantage?

Back in the cottage, I complained to Marc that he'd once again made an unwanted unilateral decision. "Your need to be in charge is understandable in some respects," I told him. "But in relatively trivial matters, don't you think empowering me would be a good idea?" I was proud of utilizing the vocabulary of the psychology world to make my point.

"I'm sorry. You're right. It's a habit left over from a previous context."

We wrote in the wisdom book by the front door before assembling in Chet's driveway. I was curious to see what Marc considered his most insightful sentence.

His nearly indecipherable handwriting yielded "It's all Love."

"Do you mean that literally?" I asked.

"Yes." He wouldn't say more.

I wrote "There is more to life than meets the eye." I thought it nicely refuted Chet's jocular assertion that I was grandiose. After all, I implied there was a mystical realm, but I didn't claim to know anything about it.

I flipped back to earlier pages. There were only

four. Perhaps this was the second volume of the guest book or Chet had only recently set up his BnB. Some typical entries: *Live it or live with it. The meaning of life is pizza. Remember the golden rule.* And my favorite: *Satan loves hypocrites.*

Whoever had decorated La Frontera obviously didn't care how other Mexican restaurants approached this aspect of their business. The owners had inherited a space that had obviously been an Italian restaurant and hadn't bothered to redecorate. An amateurish mural of the Bay of Naples sprawled on the wall behind round tables with red and white checkered tablecloths. After the three of us wandered to a corner table without an invitation to do so, I saw that the table coverings were plastic and sported encrusted salsa and other less defined stains. I stifled my repugnance, at least verbally.

Chet stared at an attractive redheaded woman sitting by herself across the room and almost fell seating himself. "That's one of my exes. She dumped me when I had my breakdown."

"Wow, that's cold," Marc responded.

The older man shrugged. "She's not a bad person. Everyone has their limits."

Our middle-aged server lugged giant laminated menus to the table. A brightly colored Mexican blouse tented over her ample bosom, and a thick, black braid snaked over her shoulder, reaching down past the front of her blouse to well below her waist. I could only hope that she'd toss this health hazard back where it belonged before she carried our food to us.

"Howdy, gents." Her Mexican accent co-mingled with a Texas twang. "Don't pay attention to anything on the menu that's got chicken in it. We're out of chicken cuz some chicken-eating college students cleaned us out."

"No worries," Chet said. "We're carne asada guys. Right, fellas?"

"Sure," Marc said. I glared at him, and he amended his answer. "Well, I can only speak for myself. Tris might want any number of things."

Chet's former partner approached our table after the server departed. At first it was hard to look past the fiftyish woman's hair. Some redheads' locks were truly red, some auburn, and some, like this woman's, were bright orange. She'd piled her hair on top of her head like the swirls on a soft ice cream cone, and what looked like a shiny black chopstick pierced this mass at the back. Both ends of it peeked out from behind her ears.

Her facial features were pleasing to my eye—regular and harmonious. I especially liked her large eyes, although I wondered if their Kelly green color had been enhanced by colored contact lenses. Her carefully applied makeup over very fair skin and flowing black dress suggested vanity, or at least a flair for the dramatic. If I could've edited this woman's face, I would only have thickened her thin lips a bit—maybe given her Chet's. Hers hinted at a propensity for sharp rebukes. Perhaps Chet had earned them when he'd been married to her.

Our host scrambled to his feet, and they hugged in a markedly tentative manner, her hands barely touching his back. When they'd separated and shared wary looks across the obvious psychological chasm between them, Chet turned to us.

"Marc, Tris, this is Suzanne Granger."

I inhaled involuntarily and drew back from the table. Was the whole trip going to be littered with crazy coincidences? "Any relation to Susan Granger?"

"My grandmother. How would you know about her? She was just a librarian down in San Marcos."

"Can you sit with us?" Marc said. "I'm sensing we need to explain some things to you and Chet."

Confusion crawled across Suzanne's face, starting at the bottom, where her lips pursed tightly. By the time it got up to her forehead, indecision took hold. But she sat down at the vacant seat across from me, anyway. "I hope this isn't some lame attempt to get us back together," she said to Chet as he lowered himself back into his seat. "I'm sure your friends think it's a good idea, but you and I know it isn't, don't we?"

"It's nothing like that," Marc said. "I'm about to tell you something fantastic—very hard to believe. You are both associated with it, for better or worse."

"Hold it," I said. "This is another example of you making decisions for both of us. I'm not sure these coincidences indicate anything definitive. And my personal narrative is mine to share."

"So what do you want to do?"

"Look," Suzanne said. "I don't know who you people are, and I have flan to finish."

"This is the smartest boy in the world," Marc said. "Tris Healy. And I'm his therapist and spiritual advisor."

"You're the boy from the quiz show?"

I nodded.

"What body of water lies between Borneo and Sumatra?"

"The Java Sea."

"Who invented the slide trombone?"

"That's a trick question because no one knows. It was probably an anonymous Flemish instrument maker who supplied the Burgundy court. This was sometime in the latter half of the fifteenth century. And your idea that the ability to regurgitate trivial facts represents intelligence is absurd."

"Okay. That sounds like you. You know you come across as an arrogant ass on that TV show?"

"Hardly. I'm a refreshing change from the robots I compete against," I informed her.

"In other words, you shoot your mouth off about how great you are all the time."

Marc spoke up. "I mentioned who Tris was simply to convince you to bear with me—to listen to the life-changing story I'm about to tell you." I glared at him. "We need to do this, Tris."

"They'll just think we're crazy."

"Not if they're really a part of this," he replied. "And if they aren't, what does it matter if two random people think we're delusional?"

I mulled that over. "Your logic is impeccable."

"Who talks like that?" Suzanne leaned forward and frowned. "You're just trying to make other people feel inferior."

"First of all, if the shoe fits…And secondly, I'm speaking in precise language because that's what best communicates what I wish to communicate."

"Did you learn English from eighteenth-century literature?" Her tone was scornful. She grabbed a handful of our tortilla chips, which she had no right to do.

"Partially, as a matter of fact," I told her. "Do you have enmity for that as well? Does Defoe rankle you? Is Swift an arrogant miscreant for satirizing English society?"

"That's what I mean. You're showing off. You're thinking I don't know the authors of that era, and you're rubbing my nose in it. It's not kind."

"First of all, I reiterate my shoe-fitting aphorism. You probably don't. And who says I should be kind? A lot of harm has been done by people who haven't been forthcoming in the name of kindness." Suzanne was lucky I held back some of the more caustic remarks that occurred to me.

She calmed down a bit. "You're partially right about the authors. I know Jonathan Swift but not the other one. And I don't remember anything Swift wrote besides *Gulliver's Travels*, but so what? Who cares? And when it comes to kindness, it has to be wielded with wisdom, taking into account all the causes and circumstances of a given situation."

"I think we're getting sidetracked here," Marc said.

"Of course we are," I agreed. "But she started it— in a most unkind fashion, I might point out." I gave myself permission to continue. "Another thing I'd like to mention is that you, Suzanne, seem to be spouting the Buddhist party line—the whole tired causes and circumstances thing. I'm guessing that you're about two years into studying…let's see…Tibetan Buddhism."

She sat back suddenly and stared at me. "How could you know that?"

I smiled and remained silent. I'd had enough of her. She was abrasive, critical-minded, and downright rude—a very bad Buddhist, in essence. I could've pointed that out and supplied supporting evidence, but why bother? She wasn't worth it.

Instead, I glanced at Chet, who was grinning, obviously enjoying our interchange. Marc, on the other hand, seemed to be engrossed in studying our facial expressions, as if we'd revealed significant aspects of ourselves. Perhaps we had.

I strongly preferred to be done with Chet and Suzanne, especially Suzanne. Since I believed they would dismiss Marc's information out of hand, I no longer feared the outcome.

"Go ahead, Marc. Tell them whatever you want."

"Here goes. Put on your proverbial seat belts," he told the two Texans.

Chet pantomimed just that, and Suzanne waved her left hand dismissively. She wore three large rings on it, each of them featuring turquoise stones.

"Tris and I have begun remembering our previous lives, and he was your grandmother—Susan Granger. That's for starters."

"That's ridiculous," Suzanne said heatedly, apparently angry that he was trying to make a fool out of her.

"Ask me something only she could know," I said. "Perhaps some memory of a confidential conversation." I didn't know if I could summon Susan's memories the way I could Lewis's—I'd yet to try. But failing to convince these people would constitute a satisfactory outcome, anyway.

"All right. Fine. What unusual thing happened to me when I was with my grandmother when I was nine?" She smirked.

I cleared my mind as best I could, and a memory

bubbled up to the surface. "Somebody put a pig on a merry-go-round with you, and it bit you. Seven stitches on your shoulder. I was there, babysitting my granddaughter—you. I felt terrible about what happened."

Her jaw dropped—literally. She looked like she could stuff an orange in her mouth instead of the tortilla chip that rested on her tongue.

"Let's see the scar, shall we?" Marc said. "There's your proof."

Suzanne pulled herself farther back from the table as though he might grab her and shove her dress off her shoulder. "That's all right," she said hurriedly. "It's there."

"Later," I continued, "you made friends with the pig and bought it a birthday present. That same day, you ate too much ice cream and vomited on your dad's shoes."

Suzanne stared at me and nodded.

Chet spoke up. "I remember being an usher in a 1920s movie house—just snatches of my last life—random memories, really. But I know reincarnation is real."

"You forget I know you're crazy, Chet," Suzanne said. "Anyway, Tris could've found out about the pig some other way."

"When you were about to go on your first date," I told her, "as Susan Granger, I took you aside and told you to kick the boy in his 'sensitive area'—those were the words I used—if he tried to kiss you. Afterward, when the date went poorly, I consoled you by slipping you a candy bar you weren't supposed to have." I turned to Chet and Marc. "My daughter Beth was

85

obsessed with weight, so she kept Suzanne on a short leash when it came to desserts." I looked at Suzanne. "I'm so sorry you went through that. I talked to her numerous times, but she wouldn't budge."

"Oh my God! It's true! You sound just like Grandma." She started to get up from the table. Part of her just wanted to get away from me. Then she settled back down, adjusting a lock of hair that had dropped over one of her eyes.

Marc spoke up. "Let's order. That's enough for now." He gestured to our server, and she lumbered over. My research on Mexican food indicated that cheese enchiladas were the least likely menu item to harbor dangerous bacteria, so I ordered two. The others boldly endangered their health by choosing various high-risk items. How our species has stayed alive through the millennia is a mystery to me.

While we waited for our food, after an initial period of stunned silence, I continued narrating our tale. "That's not the hardest part to digest. I was also Meriwether Lewis. And—"

"He was my great-great-grandfather!" Chet proclaimed. "Or something like that. I mean genetically, not karmically."

"Of course," I said, intending to be facetious. There was no "of course" about these remarkable coincidences. "We're all connected in weird ways, aren't we? And it keeps getting weirder. If I didn't know better, I'd think we were all making this up, or working from a science fiction film script."

I glanced across the table to see how these statements had been received. I didn't want Chet or Suzanne to think I was calling them liars.

Marc spoke up before I could properly evaluate their reactions. "And I dreamt I was Susan Granger's husband. Do you want to test me, too, Suzanne? I think I know things I couldn't know. I can tell you exactly what your grandmother looked like in the dream, and what we drank out on our porch in the evening."

"No, that's all right." She'd only ordered a frozen margarita, which arrived at that point. She took a huge gulp and grabbed a few more tortilla chips. "I guess it makes sense that Tris is a psychic. All that brainpower…"

"I'm not," I told her. "Let me continue. There are verifiable aspects of this that I want to tell you. That will help."

She nodded, stuffing her mouth with salsa-slathered chips now. It was disgusting. How many of these would she engorge herself with?

"Your grandmother—me—left a letter for the current me in a time capsule that was recently opened, and—"

"I got a letter from it last week! It didn't make sense to me at the time, but now I guess it does. What did yours say?"

I quoted it verbatim, emphasizing the part about my needing to find and publish the wisdom book. Then I recited all the relevant URLs that provided proof of the capsule's legitimacy. Suzanne stared at me. Chet turned to his phone and had me repeat the website address of the San Marcos newspaper archive.

Our food arrived, and I dug in. The enchilada sauce was tangy and quite unlike any Mexican food I'd sampled back home. It smelled as good as it tasted.

"So what did you dream about the night you got

your letter?" Suzanne asked. Her bright eyes gleamed in the reflection of her glass.

"It's all true!" Chet reported, looking up from his oversized phone. "This is exciting!"

I told them about my dream and the synagogue's poster I'd seen online, including the identical dog in both. Marc chimed in about his dream, and then we simply ate while Chet and Suzanne attempted to make sense out of it all.

Suzanne's face reflected her inner conflict—rather melodramatically, in fact. Once again, it seemed to me as if she might be involved in theater. Chet, on the other hand, seemed to be accepting things a bit too blithely. Perhaps the "breakdown" he'd referred to had loosened his grasp on ordinary reality.

After a while, Marc attempted small talk—how great the food was, his impressions of Austin so far, and the like. Everyone ignored him. I found it odd that he continued nonetheless.

Following this, Suzanne stated several times how shook up she was, but her expression and body language no longer reflected that. If I were her, I might be teary or pale or shut down emotionally—as displayed by frozen facial features. How had she recovered so quickly from such shockingly eerie revelations?

"So what does all this add up to?" Chet asked after we'd finished eating.

Marc spoke. "Tomorrow, we'll go to the pet adoption event and stay alert for clues."

"You mean all of us?" Suzanne asked. "I'd like to help, but I have a life—a job."

"What do you do?" I asked.

She grinned, and for a moment she looked like someone else—someone I could like. "As it happens, I'm a literary agent."

Marc laughed. "That's perfect! Of course you are."

"I thought they were all in New York," I said. I couldn't envision her in that role. Agents had to be personable to cozy up to editors and coddle their stable of writers. Suzanne was *not* a coddler.

"Not anymore," she told me. "It's done with emails and phone calls these days unless you've come out of a publishing house and know editors to wine and dine."

"Would we know any of your authors?" Marc asked.

She rattled off a string of nonentities. Even I hadn't heard of any of them.

"So would it be fair to say that you're not particularly successful?" I raised an eyebrow for effect, which I'd once spent an afternoon perfecting.

"I'm just getting started, and it's a hard business to get up and running, especially these days. Look, Tris, obviously we got off on the wrong foot. I'm sorry I was so rude. I've had a hard day."

"I suppose I could be a little more humble on TV," I told her, grasping onto the only reciprocal concession I could muster. I certainly wasn't going to apologize for anything I'd said earlier that evening.

Marc spoke. "What's going to happen with that? Weren't you in the middle of taping when you passed out? Don't they want you back?"

"Geez, I forgot all about it. That's not like me. Supposedly, I'm recovering from my collapse on the set."

"Why don't you call your parents?" Marc

suggested. "I told them you'd check in every day, anyway. Find out what the story is."

"Okay."

"Before you do," Suzanne said, "I can tell you what's been happening on the show the last few days. They showed the one where you said something about the book and then you passed out, and then they did a retrospective of your best answers from prior shows to fill out the half hour. Actually, it was moving—the first time I gave a crap about you. Since then, they suspended Super Week until you're well enough to come back."

"Thanks. I guess my parents haven't given the all clear to the producer. They probably want Marc to straighten me out so I don't jeopardize my cash-cow status."

"That's harsh," Chet said. "I'm sure your parents want the best for you, Tris."

"You don't know them."

I rose and strode to just outside the restaurant, which was in a sketchy neighborhood with all sorts of unsavory characters stumbling past. While I positioned myself, making sure I maintained eye contact with Marc through the glass door, two men wearing women's clothes strode by and a foul-smelling homeless woman rambled past me with a reluctant, scraggly cat tied to her worn belt with twine.

The day had finally cooled down. Now it mimicked what I was accustomed to back in Ojai, albeit with more moisture in the evening air.

"Hi, it's me," I told my father.

"Where are you? What's happening? Are you eating right? Are there a lot of Mexicans there? I know we've got our share of them, but I've heard the Texas ones are worse."

"You know I don't appreciate that kind of talk. I'm not going to keep checking in with you if you're going to keep that up."

"Sorry, son. I just worry about you when you're away."

"Then why did you send me away all the time when I was little?"

"It was for your own good, Tris. We didn't know what to do with you. We wanted you to have a better life than we could make for you on our own. Plus, all the research about your brain has gotta help with the whole science thing, right?"

I sighed. "Sure. Anyway, I'm fine. We just had a nice dinner and tomorrow…" I just realized that I didn't know the specific fiction Marc had concocted. "Well, that should be fun, too."

"Fun? I hope you're taking this trip seriously, Tris. It could lead to big things for all of us."

"You don't know the half of it."

"What does that mean? Are you holding back on me?"

"It's just an expression. I apologize. What's happening with the show?"

"No problem there. They're happy to wait for you and their big ratings, plus we're in discussion with another network about having you host a new show with other smart kids as contestants. They'd compete against you for prizes like bikes and trips to amusement parks."

I didn't need to address this idea for now. Chances are, nothing would come of it once the TV people realized how painful it was to deal with my parents. That happened a lot.

I told my father I needed to go, and we hung up. My mother would be upset I hadn't talked to her and would probably call me right back, so I shut off my phone on the way back into the restaurant. By now, it was seven thirty.

"I've got to go," Suzanne reported when I returned to the table. "I've got a busy work day tomorrow. But let's swap phone numbers and stay in touch."

"Tomorrow's Saturday," Marc said. "Are you sure you have to work?"

"All right. You caught me. I just need to step away from this and get my head on straight."

"Sure, that's fine. But let's be honest with one another." He paused and made a point of looking her in the eye. "We're all in this together."

"That's a good anthem for life in general, isn't it?" Chet said. "I wrote a song about that once."

I noted this clue about his identity. Sooner or later, I'd ferret out his secret past, if he didn't tell me first.

So we exchanged numbers, Suzanne took off, and the three of us looked at one another blankly for a moment. Then our server toddled over and placed her meaty hand on her hip.

"You're hogging the table. We don't make any money if people just sit there after they're done."

I was ready to point out that no one was waiting for a table, and we had a perfect right to stay where we were unless the restaurant had posted clearly defined policies concerning occupancy. Marc rendered all this moot by immediately apologizing and standing up.

Outside the restaurant, walking to the car, I asked

Chet when the music he'd selected started.

"Well, they say nine thirty, but I know these guys and it'll probably be more like ten. Is that okay?" He'd had two beers, and I could smell them on his breath.

"One thing I share with other ten-year-olds is a need for a good night's sleep, so no, it won't work for me. Marc, you could go. I don't mind."

"I can't leave you alone."

"Why not? What's going to happen?"

"It's safe at my place," Chet added.

"If we put aside physical safety," Marc responded, "I believe that leaving you alone at ten would qualify as child neglect in the eyes of the law."

"Aw, nobody cares about that stuff in Texas," Chet said. "My folks locked me in the backyard with our dogs starting when I was seven."

"And how did that work out for you?" Marc asked.

"Okay, yeah. It wasn't great. But what I'm saying is that nobody ends up behind bars for something like that around here."

"Nonetheless," Marc said, and that was that.

Chapter 10

Back in our room, while I read about Texas history and geography, Marc spoke on the phone with the colleague who was covering for him while he was out of town. He squirreled himself away in the bathroom and ran the exhaust fan to maintain confidentiality.

That night, I dreamt I sat cross-legged in a makeshift treehouse across the street from our condo in Ojai. It was about fifty degrees, and I shivered in shorts and a T-shirt. Two enormous men came to my parents' door, and I could hear their interchange with my mother as though I were a few feet away. They said they were government agents and they needed to speak to me, but I knew they weren't. Then it started to rain, and I woke up.

Once I'd shared my dream, Marc asked me what I thought it meant, but before I could answer, his phone rang—a cheery chirping.

"Hello?" he answered. Someone spoke. "I'm going to put you on speaker so Tris can hear." He placed the phone on the rickety rattan table between our twin beds. It looked as though that was about as much weight as it could bear.

"Good morning, Tris and Marc. This is Suzanne Granger."

"Good morning."

"Someone broke into my house and stole my time

capsule letter while I slept last night." Her voice was shaky.

Marc replied, "Are you okay? Do you feel safe now?"

"I called my brother, and he came over with his dogs, so yes. But I'm concerned there may be dangerous people out there working against us—trying to get the book for themselves."

"That's a bit of a leap," Marc said. "I don't see why you'd think that."

"You don't know what was in the letter. My grandmother told me I'd meet some out-of-state people soon whom I could trust—that's y'all, I'm thinking. Then it went on to say I should watch out for evil religious people who might harm me."

"Like a cult?" Marc asked.

"I don't know. She just said I should watch my back because of these people." Suzanne's tone expressed annoyance, as though Marc's perfectly sensible question represented an unhealthy curiosity.

"Why would the letter—or the book, for that matter—incite anyone to criminal behavior or violence?" I asked. "And what sort of cult is both interested in wisdom and also embodies evil?"

"More to the point," Marc said, "how could anyone know about your letter in the first place?"

"I'm just telling you what the letter said and what happened. You two don't have to argue with me. My grandmother also sent me a clue about finding your book in the letter. At least I think that's what it was. Now someone else has it, too."

"What was it?" Marc asked.

"And why didn't you tell us about it last night?" I

added, peeved at the haphazard way she was doling out information.

"That doesn't matter, Tris," she said. "My nana's letter said 'get the dog who looks like a horse.' So now someone else might show up at the synagogue and get that dog instead."

"If such a person exists, how would they know about the adoption event?" Marc asked. "We only know to go there from a dream."

"If you were in Austin, and you were told to go get a dog, where would you go?" Suzanne asked.

"Good point," Marc conceded. "This event at the synagogue seems to be well publicized. Did your letter mention any particular role you were supposed to play?"

"It said I should get the book published once other people found it." She stated this like a grade school student reciting what her teacher had told her to memorize.

"I have a question you didn't answer before," I told her. "And I think it does matter, no matter what you say. How did anyone know about your letter in the first place? Did you tell people about it? The San Marcos newspaper didn't mention any letters in their article about opening the time capsule."

Suzanne seemed flustered, which I would not have thought I could sense on the phone. I could hear her breathe more rapidly. "I talked to my sister and a few friends. Why not? I still think that wondering about that is a luxury we can't afford right now. And I'm tired of all these questions. We need to make a plan."

Last night, she couldn't wait to get away from us. Now she was directing us to make a plan, probably to distract us from her admission that she had revealed the letter to others. This sort of subterfuge didn't bode well. Was Suzanne a manipulative person on top of all the rest?

"Do you think you were followed last night to the restaurant?" Marc asked. "If you were, then they know about us."

While she said no and explained why, I thought over this new development. Then I spoke up when she finally paused.

"Here's my theory. Someone, or possibly a group of people, might have known that messages from Susan Granger in the time capsule were important. And maybe they were able to obtain the addresses on your grandmother's envelopes from someone at the courthouse in San Marcos. You were easy to get to since you're right here in Austin, bearing the same name. Now that they have the information about what the dog looks like, they might think they need to combine that with what was in our envelope."

"That makes sense," she conceded. "I'm not saying it's true, but it makes sense."

"This is all speculation," Marc protested. "Let's not get paranoid. All we know is that someone robbed Suzanne. Did they take other things?" he asked.

"Yes."

"There you go. It was probably a kid or a drug addict grabbing whatever he could to pawn or sell."

"A letter?" I said. "You'd have to ingest a lot of drugs not to be able to tell the difference between something sellable and a sheet of paper. Plus I dreamt last night that people came to my parents' house to find me. It wouldn't surprise me if that were true, and that would support my hypothesis. In fact, let me call my parents. Stay on the line, Suzanne. I'll put it on speaker for everyone."

I called and rested both Marc's and my phone on my chest. I wasn't taking any chances with that rickety bedside table.

My mother answered after quite a few rings. "Oh, Tris. I'm so glad you called. There are people here to see you from…Where did you say you were from again? Oh, that's right, the public health department. Apparently, some letter that was sent to you may have some special germs on it. I've looked everywhere, but I can't find it. They had me wear a big gas mask I had to take off to answer the phone. I'm just glad your father wasn't here to see how silly I looked in it. And now my hair is a mess."

I could hear a gruff male voice in the background. "Let us talk to him, ma'am."

I hung up.

"Was that wise, Tris?" Suzanne asked. "Maybe we could've found out something useful."

"I panicked." I was embarrassed to admit that, but direct contact with crazed cult members or criminals was a far cry from merely talking about them.

"It's okay, Tris," Marc said. "We did find out some important things."

"Like what?"

"There are at least three of them—one to rob Suzanne and at least two to shakedown your parents. That's assuming all these people are connected. So this isn't a kid or an addict. And obviously this isn't the way public health officials act. We can presume they know we're in Austin now, whether we were followed from the restaurant or not. Your mother had no reason to hold back that information. Does she know where we're staying?"

"No. I made the reservation online, and I have my laptop with me. I suppose a first class hacker could get into the AirBnB database."

Suzanne spoke. "We don't know anything about them. They could have infiltrated some secret government agency that has access to satellite imagery or something. Maybe they're Chinese spies or terrorists. I don't think we should take any chances. I'm taking my brother's dogs and heading to my cousin's place in Elgin. I suggest you do the same. And make sure you're not followed."

"Are you representing any thriller writers?" Marc asked.

"Well, yes."

"I thought so. Perhaps these kinds of things are on your mind these days, and after all, your sense of security was just breached. Why would spies be chasing esoteric knowledge?"

"Plus you said before it was a cult," I pointed out.

"I did not. *You* said that, Tris." Her shallow breathing was quite audible. "Fine. Do whatever you want." She read off her cousin's address and abruptly hung up.

"I just don't like her," I told Marc as we continued lying in our beds. It felt odd to wake up in the same room as a non-family member. Not alarming, just odd.

"I don't blame you," Marc said. "And to tell you the truth, I'm not that comfortable with Chet, either."

"Why?"

"I'm not sure. There's just something off about

him. What's your take on him, Tris?"

"Well, he said he'd had a breakdown. And on top of that, he's an eccentric old hippie and a former celebrity, isn't he? I think that explains a lot." I stretched, which triggered a long yawn. "Basically, I'm not crazy about Chet, either. Unfortunately, we're not the ones picking our team here, are we? At least he's colorful."

"That he is. I guess it's more than politics that makes strange bedfellows."

After our morning ablutions, we knocked on Chet's back door. If we hadn't been saving the world, we would've anyway, since the price of the room included breakfast. The day was sunny again, and my weather app had told me the high temperature would be ninety-two.

"Come in, come in. I've got eggs any way you like 'em."

He wore a T-shirt with a stylized graphic of a busty female Aztec warrior—there hadn't been any, of course—and cut-off jean shorts. He was barefoot.

The inside of the dome house was disturbingly free of right angles. I was disoriented for a few moments as we paraded through the living room to a kitchen alcove.

Surprisingly, chrome and leather mid-century furniture dominated the interior landscape. A smoked glass coffee table in the living area typified the outdated style. Three slim, shiny legs created a tripod that supported an asymmetrical shape not found in nature or any interior design magazines since the mid-sixties. A self-consciously modern pair of raked chairs looked to be impossible to climb out of, assuming someone was brave enough to fall into them in the first place.

He noticed my gaze. "Believe me, I didn't pick out any of this ugly crap."

On the walls, blown-up photographs of black and white New York street scenes alternated with colorful acrylic abstracts. These seemed even more out of character. Why would a Texan wish to be surrounded by these images? I realized I held a narrow, stereotyped view of the state's residents. Why *wouldn't* they like this type of art? As my mother liked to say, "There's no accounting for taste, said the lady as she painted her cow purple with yellow polka dots."

While Chet cooked scrambled eggs and toasted dark, German bread, Marc filled him in on our conversation with Suzanne. We sat around a normal, scarred pine table about ten feet from an upscale stovetop.

"I think we're up against a very twisted spiritual organization—extremists," Chet pronounced as he served us. "If you think about it from the perspective of who wants wisdom real bad…"

"You might be right," Marc said. "I've thought about it, and I can't think of anything more plausible. People in cults can certainly be dangerous. It's my experience that fringe religions attract troubled people."

"Absolutely," Chet agreed. "I was in a Hindu cult for a while, and most people there were like me—they'd signed up because they couldn't make it on their own. In other words, we were all screwed up. Then after we were in the ashram, we thought we had all the answers about everything from our guru. Thinking you know crap people can't know makes you feel like you're above regular human stuff. Morality and all that don't matter much anymore."

"Who was the guru?" I asked.

"Sri Bhaktiji."

"I read one of his books," I told him. "Pretty standard stuff, I'd say. But I still don't understand why people oriented around wisdom would be aggressive and break the law. Aren't these behaviors antithetical to a religious organization's stated values?"

Marc spoke up. "Like any group of humans subject to the human condition, there are issues of power, ego, greed, and every other human failing. Surely you've read about historical cults with creepy leaders who brainwash their followers and take all their money. In this case, perhaps a guru wants to take credit for the book to become more famous and recruit followers. The thing is, as Chet said, a lot of extremists feel they're above the law. Anyway, let's focus on how to handle the situation. We're not going to get anywhere trying to nail down who these people are, let alone what their motives might be."

"Here's what I think," I said. "They'll be on the lookout for me. I'm the recipient of the letter, and they'll know what I look like, but they may not know much about Marc, and they certainly don't know Chet." I looked down, lost in thought for a moment. "They also know there's a significant horse-like dog out there somewhere. Maybe they suspect that without the information in my letter, knowing about the dog won't be that helpful. So maybe they'll keep coming after me. I don't know. And what kind of dog looks like a horse, anyway?"

"A Great Dane?" Chet tried. "Or one with a long face?" He opened his mouth all the way and raised his eyebrows in a comical attempt to create a stretched version of his visage. His oversized nose and mouth maintained a sense of width despite his efforts.

"Anyway," Marc said, "I suggest that Chet and I pose as a gay couple who fall in love with whichever dog feels right at the synagogue. That leaves you safely out of the picture, Tris. We could say we live on a ranch or someplace else great for a dog, Chet."

"Here's another idea," I said. "A better one, I think. Suppose we doctor up a dog of our own—maybe use markers that make him look horse-like—and then we bring him with us as a red herring. If I have him on a leash at the event, they might grab him instead of the real one. Like you said, they'll be able to recognize me, which could trick them about the dog. After they run off, we'll adopt the right dog and see where that leads us. Maybe Fido will have a map hidden in his collar or something."

"I have some feedback," Chet told us, shaking his head. "First of all, no one would believe I'm gay. I'm too manly. And frankly, if I were, I'd never be with someone like you, Marc. No offense. Then as far as the other dog idea goes, can we really do that to a poor critter—put him in the hands of evil-doers? That doesn't feel right. And maybe they'll want to kidnap Tris, too—to get the information in his letter. Even if he doesn't have it on him, they know he'll be able to tell them every word in it from watching the way he wins on that dumb-ass TV show."

"You've seen the show?"

"Sure. Who hasn't? You're famous, bro. The future Einstein. Just don't go making nasty bombs like him."

"That wasn't Einstein."

"Whatever."

"We're off track again," Marc said. "We need to discuss the options we came up with. They're just precautions, of course. I still think it's unlikely anyone wishes us harm." He ran his hand through his stiff, short hair. For a moment, I wished I could do that to see how it felt.

"I wasn't finished with mine," Chet protested.

"Okay, go ahead."

"I say we go to the synagogue with guns—in case these other people show up. We don't know if they will, but if they do, a gun's the best deterrent."

"You have guns?" I asked. "I thought you were a hippie."

"Even hippies have guns in Texas. I'll take the Glock, and if you're not experienced with shooting, Marc, you can have the little Smith and Wesson. We probably won't use them, anyway. The idea is to have them in our hands to scare off anybody who shows up."

"Isn't brandishing a weapon a felony here?" I asked. "It is back home."

"I dunno. Does that matter?"

"I guess not. But what about me? I could hold a gun, too."

"Sure. I've got a little bitty one for you. We'll leave it unloaded, though."

"No way," Marc said. "No guns. Where there are guns, the threat of violence goes up, not down."

"Where'd you get that?" Chet asked.

"It's a valid statistic."

Chet laughed. "A statistic, huh? You California people slay me."

"We need to refocus," I said. Then I suggested we take a vote on our three options. We each voted for our own idea.

"How are we going to settle this?" I asked.

Marc responded. "I'm invoking executive privilege and picking the safest choice—Chet and I go look for the dog while Tris stays out of sight. We don't have to be a gay couple to do that. And the two of us have a better chance of dealing with anything untoward than I would by myself."

"Okay, whatever you want." Chet nodded furiously. "I'm along for the ride."

I nodded my assent as well. It certainly was the option least likely to lead to disaster, if not success. Secretly, I hoped Chet would bring a gun anyway. What if the interlopers had weapons? Wouldn't we want to be able to shoot back?

The brick synagogue sat in an older area of south Austin, on the far side of Interstate 35, which clearly served as a de facto demarcation of upscale (white) neighborhoods versus poorer ethnic ones (Mexican-American and African-American.) Gentrification had made inroads nearby, but a flat-roofed taqueria still squatted next to the temple, and next door to that stood a seedy laundromat. Perhaps a classier synagogue served another demographic elsewhere in Austin.

A banner with sky-blue letters on a field of white proclaimed the pet adoption event over simple wooden doors, which were swung all the way open. As we cruised by, I peeked at this scene from where I crouched in the back seat of Chet's first generation Prius. Islands of weeds and prickly pear cacti marred an otherwise immaculate, perfectly rectangular lawn. A band of raised flowerbeds hugged the base of the structure, displaying an array of red and purple flowers.

Chet parked at the end of the block, and Marc called me on his phone from the front seat, placed it in his shirt pocket, and put it on speaker. I'd be able to hear what was said in the synagogue, and with mine muted, no one would know I was eavesdropping from the car.

Since Chet had opted out of the role of a gay impersonator, he would be the dog adopter, and Marc would be a friend who'd help him pick one out. Ironically, our host wore a salmon-colored ribbed tank top and light-yellow cargo shorts, which befitted an effeminate gay man. Marc's green polo shirt and khaki shorts, by contrast, projected the "manliness" that Chet claimed to embody.

"Welcome, gentlemen. Shalom," a cheery woman said over my phone a couple of minutes later. "Don't worry about what's happening in the temple—it's Shabbat, after all. Are you dog or cat people?"

"Dogs."

"The dogs are out back—obviously, we have to keep them separate—so just go down that hall to the left. You're among the first to arrive, so the pickings are good."

"Thank you," Marc said.

As Marc and Chet exited the building, Marc described the area behind it for my benefit. "Why look, Chet. It's a patio made of limestone slabs, and behind it there's a grassy area with a temporary cyclone fence enclosure."

"I can see that. I'm not blind, for Christ's sake." I could picture Marc raising an eyebrow or winking. "Oh, I get it. Yeah, there must be two dozen dogs in there. Why don't we go closer and take a look?"

"Sounds good. Try not to bump into the fourteen other people grouped around the low fence, most of whom look like families with young children."

"Okay."

I could only hope that no one else could hear this stilted interchange. On the other hand, I appreciated the opportunity to envision the environs.

I could hear other people now, although I couldn't make out words. I lay flat on the back seat of the car with my phone glued to my ear. The day's heat was escalating already, threatening to drive me out to find shade.

"Hey, what about that one?" Marc asked. "The one with the brown spot on its back. That looks like a saddle, doesn't it?"

"It looks more like a mutant peanut to me."

"Do you see a more promising candidate?"

"There's that big guy in the corner," Chet said. "I think he's been staring at me."

"It does look like he's fixated on you. I wonder why. Maybe we could get face time with both dogs and see what happens."

"That sounds like a plan," Chet agreed. "Excuse me, Missy. Could we meet a couple of dogs?"

A tentative young voice replied, "Of course. That's why we're here. Who do you like?"

"The one over there with the peanut on his back," Chet told her.

"That's Chuckie. I think his spot looks like someone spilled a hot fudge sundae on him. He's great. You'll love him. I do."

"You know all the dogs?" Marc asked.

"Most of them. They're from the shelter I volunteer

at."

"Can we get dibs on the Great Dane-looking guy sitting in the corner, too?" Chet asked. "I mean, we want to meet Chuckie, but we wouldn't want someone else to grab the big one before we get a chance to check him out, too."

"Understood. No worries there. Ferdinand's an odd duck. I'm sure he was abused before we got him. If anyone besides me approaches him, he turns around and lies down."

"Gotcha. Let me ask you this," Marc said. "Which dog do you think looks the most like a horse?"

"What an odd question. Are you going to race him? We can't allow that."

"No, no. It's just that...uh...we had an eccentric relative whose last wish was that we get a dog who looked like a horse."

I liked this answer. Marc had found a way to not exactly lie, but not to sound like a nut, either.

"You're kidding," the young woman said.

"I'm not."

"Well, let me think." I visualized her surveying all the animals and making up her mind. Her chosen image of a sundae on Chuckie's back made me picture her as overweight, and her timid voice made me think she was screwing up her courage to deal with the weirdos beside her. "I guess Mildred—the little white one over there."

"Why's that?" Chet asked. "When I look at her, all I see is a ball of fur."

I felt sorry for a furry dog in the Texas heat. I'd already sweated through my clothes in the car. My back stuck to the beige vinyl back seat of Chet's car.

"That's the thing. When she came in—and she's

been with us for a while—she'd been shaved, and you could see how much her frame and legs look like a miniature racehorse."

"You're not just saying that to get us to take an unpopular dog?" Marc asked.

"Well, there might be a little bit of that mixed in. I really love Mildred—she's my favorite. But honestly, she does look a little like a horse. I'll hold her fur down, and you can see for yourself. And mostly, she's been unadoptable because of medical problems, but those have been dealt with."

"What medical problems?" Marc asked.

"Mildred has a mild form of epilepsy. She doesn't convulse, she spaces out. It's called an absence seizure. When she comes back, she's a little scrambled for a while. This leads to some behavioral problems sometimes. You can't count on her paying attention like a regular dog. She's totally sweet, though. It makes up for the rest, and she's on an implanted med, so she only spaces out every now and then, or when she's stressed."

"Okay," Chet said. "I'm sold. Can we meet her?"

"Sure. Let me get her out. Y'all can commune over by the gazebo. You see where we fenced in that area over there? Find some shade, and I'll see you there in a jiff."

"Yes. That would be great. We'll meet you there."

A few moments later, Chet spoke sotto voce. "Marc, do you see those guys who just came out of the building? I don't like their looks."

"Me neither."

I wanted to shout, *What* do they look like?"

"If those are dog lovers," Chet added, "I'm Janis Joplin. Maybe we should take a different dog to throw them off and then come back for the right one later."

"He or she could be gone by then. And we don't really know who those guys are. Lowlifes adopt dogs, too. Their being here doesn't make them *our* lowlifes."

I heard my partners walking on a gravel path and then taking a step or two onto a wooden deck.

"Hey, maybe they'll think that's a saddle on Chuckie like you do," Chet said. "If I squint real hard, I can almost see it. They might take him on their own even though he's the wrong dog because that's really a weird peanut on his back."

None of this chatter was doing me much good. I toyed with the idea of speaking sotto voce myself—asking Marc to activate his phone's video function so I could suss out whoever had arrived for myself. But I didn't know if anyone else was in hearing distance. A minute passed in which I only heard breathing.

Gravel crunching preceded the young woman's arrival. "Here you go," she said. "Mildred, meet…"

"Chet and Marc. Hi, Mildred."

"Let me show you what she looks like under her fur."

"I see it," Chet said after a few moments. "Even her face is kinda like a donkey or something."

"Well, that's not very flattering, is it, Mildred?" the young woman said. "By the way, I'm Maria."

Marc spoke up. "It looks like those two men are interested in Chuckie."

"It does, doesn't it?"

"I wish we could be sure that Mildred was the right dog for us. Can you tell us more about her?"

I could hear Chet muttering things to the dog while Marc and Maria spoke.

"Sure. Someone found her on the street in San Marcos behind the public library. And…"

"We'll take her," Marc said. "This is the one for us."

I smiled and pounded my fist into my thigh. It was all I could do to keep silent.

While Chet and Marc filled out paperwork and satisfied Maria's boss that Chet would be a responsible dog owner who lived in an animal-safe environment, I fended off an older man on the sidewalk beside me who'd peered into Chet's car and was concerned about me. I had to hurriedly turn down the volume on my phone to do so, which meant I missed what happened next behind the synagogue.

"Honestly, my dad just stepped away for moment."

"I reckon it's been a long moment, son." He leaned in the open window, his elbows resting above my head. I was still lying flat, just to be on the safe side.

His breath smelled of alcohol, despite the time of day. And he looked like a walrus, with his bushy, gray mustache and droopy cheeks. His rheumy eyes and thinning, greasy hair further disqualified him as a parental consultant.

"Be that as it may," I said, "this isn't any of your business."

"The welfare of children is everyone's business— or it ought to be, anyway. And why are you lying down like that? You should sit up to talk to an adult. Unless you've got special needs?" He raised his bushy black eyebrows, which drew my attention to his rheumy, pale blue eyes.

"My need is for you to leave me alone. What do I have to do to get you to go away?"

He frowned, which made the corners of his bushy mustache turn down along with his mouth. Now he resembled a sad walrus, if walruses could be sad. "In all conscience, I can't do that. As a retired deputy sheriff, I know what can happen to a child left alone on the street."

"I'm a grown midget," I said.

"Don't lie to me. I know you're not." He was affronted, as though no one had ever lied to him before.

"My dad told me not to talk to strangers," I tried.

"Good for him," the man said, leaning in farther. "That's my point. Suppose I was a pervert."

"Maybe you are. I think I'll call the police." I reached for my phone as I glared at him.

He held up his worn hands in surrender. "Okay, okay. I give up. I just hope I don't read about you in the newspaper tomorrow."

"Me too."

In my haste to keep my determined well-wisher from hearing my phone, I'd actually hung up. I tried to call Marc back, but he didn't answer. I lay there another ten minutes, sweating and wondering when the others would return, hoping no more good Samaritans stopped by. Then a gunshot rang out.

Chapter 11

From a half a block away, a gunshot is still remarkably loud—at least this one was. I peered over the windowsill and saw several pedestrians flatten themselves on the sidewalk in front of the synagogue. They probably thought some deranged anti-Semite had embarked on a murderous spree.

A minute later, I spied Chat and Marc sprinting toward me. Chet sported an oversized pistol in his hand, while Marc held a bundle of white fur—Mildred, I presumed. Just before they got to the car, a burly man in overalls emerged from the building behind them and fired a handgun into the air. Sitting up now, I jumped in my seat, adrenaline surging through me.

"Stop!" he shouted. "Stop in the name of the law!"

Chet and Marc piled in the car, and if it hadn't been an elderly Prius, we would've screamed away from the curb, leaving rubber in our wake. As it was, we could only hope our head start would keep us safe.

My heart pounded the hardest it ever had, and energy shot down my limbs. It was hard to sit still, so I didn't. I swiveled to watch the gunman sprint away from us toward a black van. Then I rocked back and forth, wishing there was something I could do to influence how the next few minutes would turn out.

"That was a police officer?" I asked after we turned the first corner.

"Hell, no," Chet said. "That's just what he wants us to believe. How's Mildred doing?"

Marc replied, "Not great. I think her epilepsy kicked in."

I turned around to face the front seat, where Marc cradled her gently in his arms as Chet built up a head of steam. Hot air rushed through the open windows, along with the tang of barbecue.

"Hell, she's better off if she doesn't have to be here for a car chase," our driver replied. He veered onto a side street, almost going up on two wheels. We passed a sad-looking cemetery with no visible grass or landscaping, a strip mall with a gaudily decorated massage parlor and a chain convenience store, and then turned again down a long alley between a row of board and batten homes.

I watched through the rear window again and didn't see anyone following us, which made it easier to calm down, even as adrenaline continued to flood my system. "At least we're likely to be getting better gas mileage than our pursuer," I pointed out.

Chet laughed out loud. "You've got balls, Tris. You're all right. You don't see anyone chasing us, do you? I don't."

"No, I don't either."

Marc turned and glanced at me. "Humor in the midst of crisis, Tris. Good for you."

We never saw whomever we'd escaped from. On the way back to Chet's house, Mildred regained awareness, and Marc passed her back to me. Then he filled me in on what had happened back at the synagogue while I stroked her incredibly soft, white fur. I liked her right away, and I think she liked me too. My parents kept me away from animals. They said animals had diseases.

Marc told me the guy in overalls and a younger man in a Mormon-looking black suit had attempted to "confiscate" Mildred, asserting she was a "witness to a major crime." Maria was ready to hand her over until Marc asked for ID and the younger man snarled, "Screw you," and pulled a revolver out of his waistband.

"Chet shot him in the leg," Marc reported.

"Really?"

"Really," Chet told me. "It was me or him."

"I doubt that," Marc said. "He just wanted to scare us into giving up the dog."

"He'll know better next time he tries to scare someone, won't he?"

"So now we're wanted by the real police?" I asked.

"I guess so," Chet said. "It's not as bad as it sounds, though."

"How's that?" Marc asked.

"I dunno. It just felt like it was time for someone to say something positive."

"Well, we did get Mildred," I said. "I mean, that was our goal, right?" I needed to counterbalance the sense of doom that was pervading me. Guns? Wanted by the police? I hadn't signed up for all this.

"You're sticking up for this madman?" Marc asked. "You weren't there, Tris. It's one thing to hear a gunshot. I was there. It's damned traumatic."

"It'll all seem worth it in the end, don't you think?" I was trying to convince myself, and I almost did.

"It *was* worth it right there with those dogs," Chet pronounced. "I'd shoot that bastard again in a heartbeat."

"How's Mildred doing back there?" Marc asked, exasperation in his voice.

"Okay, I guess." I stroked her furry back. "I don't know much about dogs beyond what I've read."

"Don't worry. We'll take care of her," he assured me.

"I'm not worried. Well, not about that."

"I hear you."

Suzanne called just before we got to Chet's. Marc put her on speaker.

"Hi, boys. Did you get the dog?"

"Yes."

"No problems?"

"Well, I don't think we could say that," Chet admitted.

"Chet shot a guy in the leg," Marc told her.

"Oh, no! Not again!"

"Again?" Marc and I said in unison.

"Well, it was only one other time," Chet told us.

"What happened?" Suzanne asked. When Chet told her, she said she might've done the same thing.

"Is this a Texas deal?" Marc asked.

"Absolutely," she said. "We don't let people push us around down here. But I'm getting a little tired of people belittling Texas—making out like there's something wrong with us for being the way we are. I get enough of that from snooty editors and New York literary agents."

"Sorry," Marc said.

"She's always been a little touchy," Chet said.

"Yeah," Suzanne said. "Especially when you say things like that, so just shut the hell up, Chet."

"So are you in?" I asked. "You haven't been clear about that. Can we can count on you to help get the wisdom book published?"

"Yes, I'm in. I told you before. Feel free to let me know how I can help about anything, but keep Chet away from me as much as possible."

"Aw, don't be that way, darlin'."

"Bite me." She hung up.

I let Mildred loose when we got to Chet's. It felt safe up his long driveway, and if I were her, I'd want to explore, which she did, sniffing noisily and squatting to pee on several nondescript spots—a tree root, a flat rock shaped like Sudan, and an overgrown concrete sundial. I guess they weren't nondescript to an olfactory-oriented species.

After this, she came running back to me and jumped up on my leg several times until I figured out she wanted me to pick her up. I did so, and she stretched her little head up to lick me in the face, which of course I didn't allow. A snout that had just been snuffling in the dirt was not going to be communing with my face any time soon—if ever. Canine diseases aside, there was no reason to introduce alien bacteria into my system.

We hadn't stopped to buy any dog food, water bowl, or other pet owner paraphernalia. Chet rustled up facsimiles of these from somewhere in his dome home, employing a plastic Flintstones cereal bowl for a water bowl, from which Mildred lapped greedily.

We all met in our rental studio's living room. Chet said it would be cooler in there. The limestone walls did help some. Marc and I sat on the couch, and Chet faced us in a chair, his legs casually crossed. Mildred sprawled on my lap, where she fell asleep almost immediately.

Chet removed one of his white running shoes and rubbed the ball of his foot through his brown sock. "So what now?" he asked.

"Perhaps your role in our adventure has come to an end." Marc crossed his legs too and leaned back. So sometimes he used therapy techniques like matching out in the world. That seemed like cheating somehow—gaining an unfair advantage.

"Oh, I don't think so. You still need me. I know the area. And I know how to be a successful fugitive."

"That doesn't fill me with confidence."

"It was back when I was a radical, and then again after my breakdown—years ago."

"What about when you shot someone before?" I asked.

"Yeah, then too. But the guy had it coming. Trust me."

"Well, that's the thing, Chet," Marc told him, "I don't think we *can* trust you. I made it clear I wouldn't allow guns to be a part of our quest. Then what did you do? If we can't trust you about something like that, how am I going to keep Tris safe?"

"I just did what I needed to do if you wanted to get the dog. You should be thanking me."

"Did it occur to you I might've been able to protect us and disarm that man without using a gun?"

"What do you mean? Are you some sort of kung fu whiz?"

"More or less. If you had let me take care of things, we wouldn't be in trouble with the police and no one would be lying in a hospital bed."

"I doubt that."

Marc moved about as fast as anyone I'd ever seen, leaping to his feet and snapping a kick that stopped inches short of Chet's wide nose. Then he held that position, balanced on one leg.

"Holy crap!" Chet exclaimed.

"Ditto," I chimed in. "That's amazing, Marc. How'd you learn that?"

"I started training as part of rehab after a car accident when I was fourteen. In graduate school, I taught at a small dojo. And it's kenpo, not kung fu."

"Do you use it a lot?" Chet wanted to know.

"Actually, very little. The last time I needed it was probably ten years ago."

"Remind me not to make you mad," Chet said.

"It's too late." Marc smiled wryly, lowered his leg, and sat down.

I let out my breath, which I hadn't realized I was holding. Marc's balancing act alone was enough to take my breath away.

After a few moments of silence, I spoke up. "I'd like to revisit the 'what now' idea, whether Chet is involved or not." I squirmed under Mildred's furry little body. She generated an alarming amount of heat for such a small creature.

"Sure," Marc said. "What are your thoughts?"

"I think we have to wait for another dream to tell us what to do next."

"Perhaps, but remember that Mildred was found in San Marcos, by the library where Susan Granger worked." He was a bit out of breath. "What if we drive down there and follow Mildred while she roams around? Maybe she'll lead us to something. What have we got to lose?"

"We still have most of the day free," I agreed, "and I'd like to see what it's like there, anyway."

"It wouldn't hurt for us to get out of town right now," Chet added. "I changed my face like I said before, but some people around here know this one."

Marc frowned. "You're the shooter, and you've got a record. I don't think it makes sense for you to be out and about, even down the interstate a half hour or so. But no one's looking for a son and his dad playing tourist. For that matter, people might recognize Tris and want an autograph or something. Who would suspect that the smartest boy in the world was involved in a shooting?"

"The bad guys know what Mildred looks like," I pointed out.

"We could get her to wear a disguise," Chet said. "Are there wigs or hair dye for dogs? What about one of those doofy vests?"

Marc frowned again, but Chet's inane remark gave me an idea. "Let's shave off her fur. It's hot enough that she'd probably appreciate it, anyway, and she'll look totally different. Remember when Maria showed you her figure under there? That made her look like a miniature horse, right?"

"Yes. Great idea," Chet said, nodding vigorously. "I've got a hair buzzer."

Mildred didn't think it was a great idea. She had another one of her seizures shortly after Chet started running his electric clipper down her back. On the plus side, this made her compliant—well, zombie-like, really. On the negative side, she came out of her episode ten minutes later in a very confused state. I don't think she knew where she was or who we were. I had to entice her into my arms again. Now she was almost slippery without her fur.

"I certainly wouldn't recognize her," Marc said. "How about we have some lunch and then Tris and I hit the road. We'll come back and give you a full report, Chet."

"All right. If that's the way you want to play it."

I checked the national news on my phone, and Marc called the therapist who was covering for him while Chet prepared a lunch in his dome home. I found the coolest spot on Chet's property, under the eave at the back of our cottage. From there, I could see through a raggedy hedge to a neighbor's well-groomed lawn. Ten minutes later, spongy white bread and bland egg salad awaited us at an aged red picnic table under a spreading pecan tree. Mildred liked hers.

"Maybe we should find out what dogs eat," I suggested.

"We'll stop by a pet store on the way back," Marc assured me.

The trip down to Austin's junior cousin—San Marcos—was mildly interesting. Mildred stood up, her hind feet on my thigh, and watched out the window along with me. Pickup trucks littered the interstate, sharing the road with more American cars than I saw in California. Of the foreign vehicles, low-end Nissans predominated. My interest in cars was limited, but the vehicular scenery proved to be more compelling than the flat farmland that lay between the two cities.

Inside the trucks and cars, some male drivers wore straw cowboy hats, although oversized baseball caps were more common. Back home, few people wore any sort of hat in their car. Maybe baldness was more prevalent in central Texas. I also saw a cheerleader-like young woman wearing a pink felt cowboy hat. It occurred to me that my mother might like one, which represented a novel notion—thinking about a gift for one of my parents. Meriwether Lewis had been fond of bestowing gifts, so maybe his memories were affecting me.

I suddenly noticed that none of Lewis's memories had bubbled up since we'd departed California. What did *that* mean? And why hadn't I noticed before?

Marc played music from a local country radio station in lieu of conversation. The lyrics were predictable and banal, but the instrumentation intrigued me, especially the use of the violin to produce a scratchy, soulful sound.

The library was only a few miles off the interstate. I'd pictured an older limestone building like some of the ones we'd driven by in West Austin, but it was an ugly, trying-to-be-modern concrete structure just outside the quaint downtown. We drove through two parks, across a river, and past a mermaid statue to get there. A mermaid? In the middle of Texas? What was the story behind that?

When we parked in front of the library, Mildred hesitated and then grudgingly hopped down to the asphalt. Perhaps she thought we were returning her to where she'd suffered on her own before being rescued. I tried to reassure her verbally, but I probably used vocabulary that was above her comprehension level. I'd never felt the urge to dumb down my speech for other humans, but now I wished I'd developed that skill for Mildred's sake.

We still didn't have a leash. Fortunately, Mildred followed us to the back of the building, which we'd determined was the best place to start. Just as we reached the dumpster by the back door, a young woman with a long black braid opened the door with too much force, banging it against the side of the metal bin.

Mildred took off across the threadbare back lawn. Her little legs churned with remarkable speed.

"Let's go!" Marc called as we both began sprinting after her.

She led us across a weedy expanse of brownish grass, past the property line, across a set of railroad tracks, and into a copse of bushy trees that formed the entrance to yet another park. We couldn't keep up, but we could keep her in sight as she continued running, slower now. Marc outdistanced me, but not by all that much. After another thirty seconds, Mildred turned left around the corner of a low, porticoed building—where we had no sightline.

"You go around that side!" Marc called back to me. "I'll go around the other!"

When I arrived on the far side of the building, I discovered Marc panting, standing over an open-ended concrete pipe that was just wide enough to allow a small dog to crawl into it. Most of it was embedded in the hard dirt.

"I saw her here a moment ago," Marc managed to say between deep breaths.

"So she's in the pipe? Do you think she's okay? Do you think the book is hidden in there with her?" I was winded too, but I did a better job of enunciating. We were both sweating like animals who sweated a lot. It wasn't pigs, the idiom notwithstanding, since they hardly sweated at all.

"She's definitely in there, and I'm sure she's fine," he gasped. "This was probably her home before she was rescued. I think our next step is to lure her out and see if there's anything else in there with her." He placed his hands on his knees and bent over. Didn't he ever exercise?

We tried to entice Mildred out of the pipe. Nothing worked, and it was too dark in there to see anything.

Marc spoke up, frustration evident in his tone. "We need to go buy a flashlight, a treat to lure poor Mildred out, and maybe something long enough to fish out whatever else may be in there."

"You go. I'll stay here and keep an eye on her," I said. "Maybe she'll come out for me without a treat once she calms down."

"I'm in a bind here." Marc pursed his lips. "I don't think it's wise to leave you on your own." He glanced around. The park was deserted for some reason. "But we can't risk losing Mildred."

"I absolutely agree. What would it be like for her to be back on the streets if we did? I'm staying here no matter what you do. I can't let that happen."

He sighed. "I guess we have no choice. Call me if anyone approaches you. I don't care if they look like your grandmother."

"Agreed."

When Marc jogged off, I lay down with my face in front of the pipe. A weed prickled my abdomen. "Hi, Mildred. Do you want to come out and sit on my lap?" No response. "What if I told you you're my favorite dog ever?" I waited, and I heard a tiny yip. I tried yipping back. She yipped. Now we were making progress.

Unfortunately, that was as far as I got. After a while, I sat up and just recited the first chapter of the *World Almanac*. I figured that hearing my voice might be reassuring. I hated to think we were the source of her suffering in that dark pipe.

I saw no one, and no one saw me. What public park was so unpopular? Perhaps there was a sign at the front entrance informing people it was closed.

With nothing to do but wait, I switched to researching facets of our situation on my phone, telling Mildred about what I found as I googled various word combinations to discover who else might be interested in the wisdom book—who could've been at the synagogue. When I tried *cult*, *wisdom*, and *book*, I found a distinct possibility. Then *revelation*, *library*, and *wisdom* garnered me information about another organization. Before I researched these groups further, I satisfied myself that they were the only two obvious candidates in the spiritual realm. Did that make them likely suspects? Not really. Not yet.

The first group, a mystical cult originating in Carthage in the fourth century B.C., was apparently still extant, or, more likely, someone had revived it in the early twentieth century. They called themselves the Keepers of Truth, and a former member—a shopkeeper on Cyprus—stated their primary mission was to present the "wisdom of the ages" to the world. He also revealed that in pursuit of this endeavor, members had to pledge they would "sacrifice in whatever manner was necessary, as was required of true spiritual warriors." Unfortunately, the man died shortly after divulging these secrets, so I couldn't contact him to find out more.

I did find numerous conspiracy theories concerning the Keepers, but I doubted that Eleanor Roosevelt, Rock Hudson, and—of all people—Aretha Franklin—were actually undercover operatives.

The second cult, called the Radiant Librarians, maintained a website that declared they were seeking an "earthshaking revelation that will make true wisdom available to every soul on Earth." The bulk of the site was comprised of etchings of holy sites around the world, which they sold in limited editions to raise funds for their "vital, world-saving work." Interestingly, one of these was an ordinary-looking Catholic church in central Connecticut. The Librarians didn't include any contact information or further details about their point of view, which struck me as odd. Why create a website bereft of any beliefs or contact information? What sort of spiritual organization didn't want to share these?

I also discovered a rumor on a wacky spiritual forum that a lineage of "past lifers" had embarked on a "millennial mission to bring wisdom into the modern world." That sounded like my karmic ancestors. How could anyone know about that? I decided it was unlikely it had anything to do with us, especially since the next thread on the forum was devoted to physical descriptions of the aliens who lived under volcanoes.

Marc eventually returned, carrying a bright red packet of beef jerky, a pencil-thin LED flashlight, and a three-foot-long grasping claw. We placed a piece of jerky on the ground about a foot in front of the pipe, and Mildred wasted no time wriggling out and grabbing it between her teeth. I swooped in and scooped her up as she chewed furiously, perhaps fearing I would take it away from her.

"Enjoy," I told her, sounding like a smarmy restaurant server.

I moved to the side, and Marc lay down with the flashlight, peering intently into the drainpipe. "There's something in there. I think I can reach it with the claw."

He went to work while I fed Mildred another piece of jerky. Marc had chosen wisely; she loved it.

"Here we go." His arm emerged with a filthy shred of a baby blue blanket, perhaps a foot square. "Well, that's disappointing. I guess Mildred dragged that in there to help her stay warm at night."

"Let me see." I swapped our dog for the dubious prize. Marc held her distractedly.

Taped to the underside of the crumpled fabric, I discovered a tattered envelope. "Aha!"

I hurriedly tore it open. The only thing in it was a faded black and white photograph of a pair of cowboy boots sporting the embroidered initials B.W. on its tall sides.

I handed it to Marc. "What do you think?"

He took his time answering. "Beats me. Maybe we'll find out what it means in one of your dreams."

My shoulders slumped, and a hollow sensation spread in my midsection. I felt deflated. No book. Just a cryptic photo.

I carried Mildred back to the car, and we drove north. Whatever trauma she'd endured had subsided. She watched out the car window with just as much interest as on the drive down. I studied her more than the central Texas scenery. Periodically she robustly sniffed, implying that her olfactory ability transcended the tempered glass barrier. Her eyes widened, darted to the side, or maintained a steady focus dependent on external stimuli. Several times she prepared to bark, but then didn't.

When we arrived at Chet's, a nasty surprise awaited us. Our space had been ransacked—the time capsule letter was gone—and there was no sign of our host in the jumble of his similarly desecrated home.

Chapter 12

"It's not safe here," Marc proclaimed, his face tight. "Let's grab our stuff and take off."

"Do you think it was the police or the bad guys?"

"I don't know. Get Mildred back in the car."

I'd never seen him so grim. Or bossy. For my part, I was more shaken up by this violation than I had been by the gunplay at the synagogue. My mind raced as we barreled down the driveway and screeched into the sparsely populated neighborhood.

Putting aside the missing letter—my reaction didn't seem to be about that—why would events associated with inanimate things upset me more than possible bodily harm? The phenomenon highlighted the illogical nature of the human psyche.

Marc drove north—at random, he told me—avoiding the interstate, but encountering egregious rush-hour traffic anyway. We didn't talk about the loss of the letter or anything else after he checked in with me to see if I was okay. I said no, and he uncharacteristically didn't reply. Perhaps he'd misunderstood me.

Mildred decided early on to sleep on the back seat, curled into an adorable oblong. I think she sensed our state of mind and wanted no part of it. So far, she'd slept ninety percent of her potential waking hours. Perhaps that was due to her epilepsy. Or maybe dogs were just lazy.

A half hour later, we veered off surface streets onto Highway 183, which headed northwest out of town into hilly topography. While well populated at first, the homes on the limestone outcroppings beside the road eventually gave way to nothing more than scrubby vegetation.

I still felt "wrong" in a basic way I'd never experienced before. I guess it was as much a cognitive as an emotional response. It was as if I'd been flying a plane when an LED on the instrument panel suddenly indicated we had no wheels. I resolved to research psychological insecurity when things settled down a bit.

Marc was still shaken up, too. He didn't even bring up the subject of where we were going or what we might do next. Finding Mildred and a photo of a pair of boots didn't steer us in any particular direction, so apparently Marc just wanted to put some distance between us and Austin.

We passed through Cedar Park and Leander, and then, a half hour after leaving Austin proper, Marc pulled over and parked by a ramshackle convenience store in Liberty Hill. These were all barely settlements, with crumbling, block-long downtowns.

"Let's stretch our legs," Marc said. He disembarked and stood by the hood of the car. He didn't stretch. He stared off into space.

I let Mildred out and joined him. She wandered off to pee under the shade of a twisted live oak. I asked Marc what he thought it meant that someone had my letter now.

He brought his attention back to me with some effort. "I don't know that there's anything new in your letter as far as these people are concerned, but it might confirm things they only suspected."

"You think they already knew about my significant dreams?"

"No, you're right. That would be news."

"What about the lineage of my past lives—the accumulation of wisdom through the ages. That makes the book sound even more valuable, right?"

"Yes, right again. I'm sorry, Tris. I'm not thinking straight."

"Back at Chet's—that got to you, huh?" I checked on Mildred. She'd found a bowl of water by the store's front door and was lapping furiously.

He nodded and sat down abruptly on the warm hood. Now he'd get toasted from the Texas sun and simmered from the bottom up. "I don't know how I'm going to keep you safe," he said. "What if your next dream sends us into a worse hornet's nest? What if these people decide to kidnap you? Who knows what they're capable of."

I took a step closer to him and gestured at our surroundings. "Look around. We're truly in the middle of nowhere, aren't we? We're safe."

"For now, maybe. But even if we pack it in and go home, will you be safe there? I should never have agreed to this crazy trip."

"You can't second-guess a decision that made sense at the time." I made a hand gesture I'd never made before—kind of a cross between a standard wave and finger pointing.

"Try and stop me." He looked off into space again. This wasn't the Marc Dalcour I knew.

"I *am* trying," I told him. "I'm trying to stop you

because whatever's going on with you isn't helping." I was *his* therapist for the moment.

He swiveled his head and stared at me for a moment. Then a couple of guys wearing greasy blue work shirts and matching baseball caps came out of the store, each nestling a six-pack of beer under his arm. They maneuvered around Mildred, who was trying to dislodge a scrap of food from the pavement.

"Howdy," one of them called. "Y'all oughta get outa the sun." He had the broadest Texas accent I'd heard so far.

"Thanks," I called back. "We will."

Suddenly, hunger and thirst asserted themselves. I strode to the Kwikkie Shoppe, and Marc followed. I stooped to scoop up Mildred and carried her in.

"Cute dog," the elderly woman behind the counter said. "Looks like a little racehorse, don't she?"

"Yes, she does."

Shopping for snacks seemed to invigorate Marc, and back in the car with the motor running and the air-conditioning blowing, he crammed miniature powdered doughnuts into his mouth with wild abandon.

"I used to binge on these as a kid," he told me, smiling for the first time in hours.

"They're disgusting. They probably have a shelf life of a hundred years."

"They taste really good." He defiantly stuffed another one into his mouth.

"They're empty calories." Now I was Marc's father.

"Yum." He took a swig of a cancer-inducing diet grape soda.

"All your items are overpriced, too," I pointed out.

"Pretzels are a much better unhealthy snack bargain. And there's nothing wrong with bottled water. It's your best source of hydration."

"I don't like pretzels. And water's boring."

"I give up." I threw my hands in the air—the first time I remember doing that. "If you want to act like a little kid, that's up to you."

"It's fun. You ought to try it sometime, Tris."

I enjoyed my chicken salad sandwich, and I thoroughly hydrated with an unfamiliar but impressive brand of spring water. I could detect nothing but clear, pure water. The flimsy plastic bottle—shaped like a vintage Coke bottle—stated that H2Oh! was pumped from "an ice-age aquifer in beautiful Big Bend country." Mildred ate a small portion of the dry dog food we'd discovered in the surprisingly well-stocked store.

We ran out of gas an hour and a half later—further evidence of Marc's psychological disequilibrium. I walked Mildred by the side of the road, and she pooped, an unpleasant sight for passing motorists, I'm sure. I wasn't too crazy about it either. Cooler now, I still remained uncomfortable in the fading sunlight.

An older white pickup truck with storage compartments on the sides of the bed rolled up behind us on the shoulder. A swarthy man in his thirties emerged and hailed us in heavily accented English. A comical figure, he was about as wide as he was tall. His oversized straw cowboy hat sat on the back of his head, begging the question of how it stayed attached to what appeared to be a bald pate. His dense black beard and hawk-like nose might've lent him a barbarous air but for his giant smile.

"Trouble, my friends? I'm no mechanic, but maybe I can help."

His accent was elusive. Middle Eastern? One of the Balkan states? At any rate, it sounded incongruous in rural Texas.

"We're out of gas," Marc told him.

"Hmm. Maybe this is no problem. I siphoned gas all the time back home. When the power went off, the gas pumps were useless. I just have to find some tubing in the back of my plumbing truck. I'm a plumber."

"Where was that?" I asked.

"I work up the road in Brownwood."

"No, I mean where are you from originally? I'm wondering about your accent."

He'd turned to go get his tubing, but now he looked over his shoulder to answer. "Turkey."

Writing on his truck door proclaimed *Esposito's Plumbing—Personal Service From the Best Damned Plumber In Lampasas County.* Perhaps he'd bought the business from an Italian-American, another scarce ethnicity in central Texas.

He fumbled around for quite some time in the truck's storage compartments before he returned with a long length of clear plastic tubing.

"This'll work!" he crowed triumphantly as he strode back to us. I wondered how different the world would be if everyone felt so satisfied after completing a task as simple as finding an item in his own truck. We'd have a much happier population, I'd guess.

When Bubba—he called himself Bubba, perhaps in an effort to fit in—finished sharing his gas, he stood and chatted. Since we felt we owed him for his kindness, and Marc and I had no particular destination in mind, we listened attentively as he told us how much he liked Texas.

"What brought you over here?" Marc asked.

"Believe it or not, the music. I played Western swing fiddle back home, but no one there liked it. It was hard to get CDs, and there was only one radio show that played it late at night so no one knew how wonderful it is."

"What's Western swing?" Marc asked. "Big band music with cowboy instruments?"

"Oh, it's much more than that. You've never heard of Bob Wills and His Texas Playboys?"

"I'm afraid not."

Bubba grinned, crooked a finger, and pivoted. "Follow me."

The truck cab was surprisingly tidy. A wooden cross hung from the rearview mirror, and a Tupperware container of plain elbow pasta rested on the beige vinyl passenger seat. Our rescuer rooted around in the glove box and then pulled a CD out with a theatrical flourish. "Aha!"

Bob Wills played silly, somewhat frenetic music, which sounded a bit like the soundtrack of silent cartoons. Clearly, this bandleader had appropriated early jazz and blues, and then added a decidedly cowboy flavor. Wills also added an annoying series of noises and comments as his musicians played solos. If I were one of them, I'd consider defecting to another band.

"When I first moved to Texas," Bubba told us. "I lived in Bob Wills's hometown because the name was right and I thought it would be a good place for music. But it's very small, and I could not find work."

"Where was that?" I asked.

"Turkey. Turkey, Texas. And I'm from Turkey. See? There's a Bob Wills museum there, but not much else. Even the museum is a disappointment. They don't even play his music there! It's just photographs, his hat, his boots—things like that."

I pulled the photo from San Marcos out of my back pocket and handed it to Bubba.

"These are his boots! See his initials on them? How did you come to have a picture of his boots when you say you never heard of him? This is very strange."

"It's a long story," Marc said. "And much stranger than you can imagine." He reached out to shake Bubba's hand. "Thanks so much. We'd better get going."

"Where are you heading, anyway?"

"Thanks to you, Turkey, Texas." Marc glanced at me, and I nodded.

On the road again, Mildred on my lap now, I asked Marc what he thought about the plethora of meaningful coincidences. "I'm suspicious about them," I told him before he could answer. "I'm familiar with Jung's theories about synchronicities and the collective consciousness, but I don't think those adequately explain all these uncanny intersections with Chet, Suzanne, and now Bubba. If I wrote this sort of thing in a book, critics would dismiss it as an overly facile plot device. What if it isn't the universe at large that's directing us? Maybe the villains from the adoption festival are arranging all this. Did Bubba seem like a plumber to you?"

"What are plumbers like, Tris? How many have you known? And how many Turks, for that matter?"

"Okay, that's a good point. Putting Bubba aside, though, what do you make of the connections between everyone we meet?"

"It's extreme, I'll admit. I'm accustomed to synchronicities—I get quite a few, but this is ridiculous." He thought it over for a bit, and I let him. His prominent brow drew my attention, the ridge of bone nearly breaking the surface. "When I look for alternative explanations, they're hard to find. How could whoever else is after the book lead us to Chet? You picked his AirBnB yourself. And how could anyone have known what we were up to before they had a chance to steal Suzanne's letter? You didn't tell anyone, I assume, and I didn't, either."

"I did mention it to a kid I know." I told him about Burt, the twelve-year-old who'd been part of the same psychology study as me.

"What are the odds he happens to be associated with a rogue religion, a criminal gang, or whoever these people are?"

"About nil."

"Exactly."

"In her letter to me," I pointed out, "Susan Granger said I should be guided by my dreams, but she didn't say anything about synchronicities. If she wanted us to pay attention to those too, wouldn't she have told me?"

"I don't know. The dreams have been the main thing, haven't they?"

"I guess so."

"How about we agree to keep an open mind about any new coincidences?" Marc suggested, turning his head to look me in the eye. "We'll talk them over before we blindly accept them."

"Sounds good." Mildred shifted positions, so I did as well to accommodate where she wanted to be next, even though it made my knee hurt a little. Then I continued. "Another thing I don't understand is why Meriwether's memories have completely stopped."

"I didn't know they had. When was this?"

"Once we got on the plane to come here."

"Do you miss them?" Marc asked. We were driving through another small town now. This one looked to be even more economically depressed, with decrepit storefronts and even a shack or two by the side of the poorly maintained road.

"No, not at all. It's a relief," I told him. "I just don't know what their cessation means."

"Me neither. Maybe we'll find out as we go along."

"Maybe." I had a feeling we wouldn't, which I recognized as mere intuition.

I petted Mildred for a while and then expressed another concern. "How could my particular lineage have developed precognition—Susan Granger's foreknowledge about me—and who knows what else? It's one thing to remember past lives or dream something meaningful about the present. But she knew my name and address forty years before I was born."

"That was in the dream you and she shared—the first night after you got the letter. Remember? You told her all that yourself on the road in Texas by the menorah trees. I guess Susan got more information from other dreams, too."

"Maybe when people make it their life work to focus on wisdom, they gather a lot of it themselves and special powers come along with that," I suggested.

He sped up for no reason. Was he uncomfortable

talking about this? He'd seemed reluctant to do so, and then hadn't been able to muster any words at first.

I switched gears, seeking a topic that would reflect compassion. "How are you handling all this psychologically, Marc? Any problems?"

"Thanks for asking. Personally, I have a life philosophy, or spiritual point of view, I guess, that helps me accept and make sense out of things like this."

"Well, don't keep me in suspense."

He paused. Mildred woke up in my lap, licked my hand, and fell back asleep. We rolled through farmland now. I couldn't identify the crops. Puffy clouds scudded above the furrowed, brown field beside the road, driven by a strong wind.

When Marc spoke, his voice softened. "Actually, I think it's better if people find their own way around these things. I'm sorry."

"Oh, come on. We're in this together, Marc. At least tell me the general idea."

"All right. I think if something is important to Spirit, it facilitates events. That's what I wrote about in my book—manuscript, I mean."

"Spirit, huh?"

"Substitute whatever word you like—God, Consciousness, Awareness with a capital A. Surely you believe there's something beyond logic and science by now, Tris."

"Well, yes. Based on recent events, I have to. Anyway, I'm sorry. I asked you to tell me about your beliefs, and then I challenged you by questioning your use of the word 'Spirit.' That was rude."

"Wow. First you made a joke this morning, and now you're apologizing."

I shrugged. "So you think God is working everything out for us because he wants the wisdom book published? Is that what you mean?"

"We're always pawns in a bigger game, aren't we?"

Down the road, my phone acquired reception as we passed through a slightly bigger town. Marc pulled over to the shoulder and took Mildred for a walk on her leash. I made a reservation online for the one AirBnB in Turkey. Because of the very short notice, I followed up with a call and spoke to a woman whose voice shook. Perhaps she was old or afflicted by a neurological disorder such as Parkinson's disease. She wasn't the most courteous person I'd ever talked to, either.

While I still had reception, I also researched Bob Wills and his museum, as well as Western swing music. I hated not knowing something that ordinary people knew. According to multiple sources, Wills had served as a seminal figure in several genres of American music, and the Texas Playboys had briefly been the most popular band in the nation in the 1940s. He'd also starred in cowboy movies, despite his banty rooster physique.

Two very boring hours later, after stopping for gas and a late dinner at a restaurant that specialized in frying everything under the sun, we arrived in Turkey. A pale green, spherical water tower, lit by a surprisingly powerful spotlight, announced the town's name and proclaimed it was "The Birthplace of American Music." An occasional elderly tree graced the modest residential neighborhood we drove through, and a plethora of dusty vehicles lined the potholed street. Did everyone in town own three old cars?

We parked on what passed for the main street in front of a locally owned hardware store since our AirBnB was situated above it in an apartment. Sparse exterior lighting didn't afford me the chance to see much of the downtown. Chet called just before we disembarked from our car.

"Hi, guys," he said over the speaker. "I hope you're okay."

"We are," Marc responded. "Are you?"

"I am now. The cops showed up a tad after you left and made a mess of my place. Suzanne bailed me out, which wasn't too expensive because all the witnesses at the synagogue said I'd been defending myself. Of course, cops don't dig somebody fleeing the scene of a shooting, but hey, the guy was chasing me, right? Anyway, my lawyer said I won't do time, even though I have priors."

"Do you think you're safe from the group that wants Mildred?" I asked.

"I was supposed to surrender all my guns, but I hid one on the roof of the cottage. Let 'em try anything, and they'll see what happens."

Marc sighed.

I spoke up again. "Mildred says hi."

"Hi right back at her. She's okay?"

"She likes to sleep, so that's mostly what she's been doing."

"Where are y'all?"

I started to tell him, but Marc broke in. "Another part of the state. I don't think it's a good idea to say more than that on the phone."

"Gotcha. Well, let me know how I can help."

"Sure."

Our BnB hostess—Ophelia—turned out to be an ancient African-American—the only one in town, she immediately told us. "My son and his wife took off for Fort Worth years ago, so that leaves me to carry on out here in the boonies. I retired last year, but I can tell you, that golden years thing is crap. I hurt all the time. My advice is, go ahead and die before you get so old you turn into someone useless like me."

She was about five feet tall, with wrinkles on top of her wrinkles. Her nose and ears had remained intact as her face had shrunk, rendering them outsized. Ophelia wore a beige housecoat, decorated with bouquets of the Texas state flower—the bluebonnet. She dropped onto a plain wooden stool just inside the front door while we stood, luggage and Mildred in hand. Ophelia's large, liquid brown eyes peered at me intently.

"What's that you got there?" she asked. "I don't see so good now."

"It's a little dog. Her name is Mildred."

"What kind of name is that to give a dog? That's an old lady name."

"Is it okay if she stays here, too? She won't be any trouble."

"It's people that are trouble. Give me a dog any day."

She caught me staring at her, trying to figure out how old she was. Ophelia was sharper than she appeared to be.

"I'm ninety-seven years old, young man, if that's what you're wondering. And I was a seamstress, in case you're wondering that, too. Nosy little feller, aren't you?"

"I was wondering both of those things, so thank

you. But I'd like to point out that I didn't actually ask you either one, which would've constituted what you're calling nosiness. A more apt characterization might be curiosity."

"Hmph," and a frown were all I got back.

I'd employed inappropriate vocabulary again and vowed to remain aware of this tendency.

As she showed us our modest, very clean room, Marc asked Ophelia if she hosted many guests.

"More than you'd think. There's only four or five hundred people in town, but we've got that museum, so when the motel's full up or people just want a homier place, here I am."

"What do you think of Bob Wills?" I asked. It was odd she hadn't mentioned his name when she'd referenced the museum. Signs all over town boasted its affiliation with him.

"He stole our music, and he was a big fake. If he were still around, I'd give him a piece of my mind. I surely would." A scathing tone and a bitter scowl accompanied her words.

"Tell us what you mean," Marc requested. He and I stood next to our twin beds, where we'd placed our bags. I continued to hold Mildred. Ophelia stood in the doorway now, whose dimensions rendered her even tinier.

"The man wasn't even from Turkey. He was born outside Kosse, and then when he was eight, his family moved to a farm between here and Lakeview. He just thought it sounded folksy to be from a place with a name like Turkey. And he was a drunk—a mean drunk. When he got rich, he didn't treat people right even when he wasn't drinking, and like I say, he stole our music."

"Black people's music? Like jazz and blues?" I asked.

"No, I mean my family's music." Ophelia looked to the right, as though retrieving memories from atop a diminutive unfinished oak table. "I knew Bob. My mother knew Bob. He stole a song my uncle wrote and one I wrote too."

"You didn't get any royalties?"

"Hell, no. He left me fifty dollars in his will. Can you believe that? Fifty dollars! Anyway, where are my manners? As you can see, there are beds for you and your dad, and the rest room is down the hall to your left. I need my rent upfront and in cash. The hell with the IRS. They're not getting any more of my money—not while they're shooting young Black men on the street and locking up most of the rest."

Marc paid her. It was only twenty-eight dollars.

"I apologize on behalf of White people," I said. I got another "Hmph." "We're a group of entitled, greedy racists," I added.

This garnered a smile. "You got that right, sonny."

Once Ophelia shuffled back down the hallway, Marc and I sat on matching burgundy velour bedspreads facing each other. Our room shared dimensions with the bedroom in Chet's cottage, but Ophelia's out-of-date decor was more pleasing to my eye.

A bedside lamp resembled a dark brown tree trunk until your eye got up to the shade. Then it looked more like a slim African woman with a bundle on her head. A photograph over Marc's bed depicted John F. Kennedy stooping to hand a little boy a toy rocket. The top of the battered oak dresser was adorned with a stuffed baby alligator wearing a straw sombrero.

I liked the wallpaper, even close-up. Blue fleurs-de-lis mingled with black diamond shapes against a cream background. It reminded me of New Orleans, which I'd never visited.

Marc excused himself to go out in the hall to call Ojai to check on his other clients. Ten minutes later, he was back on his bed, where he reclined, as I had.

"I take it that the brevity of your call means all is well back home."

"Yes. No emergencies." He cupped his hands behind his head, and a whiff of body odor assaulted my nostrils. "There are only a couple of people I'm worried about, and they're hanging in there. Sometimes when I'm sick or on vacation, fragile clients fall apart."

"They get scared being on their own?"

"Yes." Marc kicked off his shoes and crossed his legs at the ankles. "Let's go to the museum as soon as it opens tomorrow and nose around."

"Okay. It opens at ten, and since our hostess told me I'm a nosy person, I'll be utilizing my central facial feature when we get there."

Marc smiled. "More humor?"

I nodded. "But less funny this time, I think."

"It's all about stretching—taking risks. It's not about being great at something new right off. Why would you be?"

"I recognize you intended this as a rhetorical question, but I'm going to answer it. I ought to be immediately proficient at humor because I'm capable of doing whatever I set my mind to. If I decide to mimic other people's behavior by introducing anything into my behavioral repertoire, I'd like to think I can be immediately successful."

"That's just it. 'You'd like to think' is the operative phrase here, Tris. You expect what you expect because you want to think of yourself as someone who's capable of being great at everything, including new things. But that's not evidence-based. You couldn't convince a jury of that in a courtroom, could you?"

"I disagree. There's plenty of evidence I learn new things right away. Ask anyone who knows me. Ask the scientists who studied me."

"Within your comfort zone, sure. I'm not talking about intellectual activities or anything else driven by sheer intelligence. Do you think you'd have immediate success asking a girl out on a date or interviewing for a job? When you engage in wishful thinking, you set yourself up to feel like a failure since you can't meet your expectation."

"I have no interest in those activities. And I never feel like a failure."

"Fine. I give up." Marc threw his hands in the air. It almost looked like a martial arts technique—some sort of block when an opponent tried to punch him in the head. "Let's get back to planning. What do you think we need to do?"

"Obviously, going to the museum and looking for the boots in the photo is our best and only option at this point. After that, unless a dream guides us tonight, we'll see how we're directed by the boots and respond accordingly. Maybe there'll be a note hidden in one of them. Then, of course, if we disagree on a course of action at that time, you'll play the 'I'm the adult' card and get your way."

"Be that as it may, why don't we take Mildred for one last walk and then get some rest?"

"That sounds good. I'm exhausted."

The main street of Turkey was deserted, although it was only nine o'clock. Old-fashioned streetlights dimly lit the storefronts, half of them boarded up with weathered plywood. I was sad for this little town that rested its modest laurels on a museum dedicated to someone I'd never even heard of two days ago.

Mildred obliged us by squatting and peeing on the cracked sidewalk by an old-fashioned blue mailbox, and we strolled back to our room. She seemed happy. I realized her happiness was important to me. Here was yet another novel experience.

That night, I dreamt I was in a hot air balloon, suspended high above a coastal town perched on a cliff above pounding waves. I could just see over the high wicker sides of the balloon's basket. The tangy air was redolent with sea smells—brine, seaweed, and wet sand. A wharf stretched into a curving bay, and wooded hills bounded the town on the other side. Mildred yipped. She stood on her hind legs beside me wearing a pirate costume, replete with a black eyepatch. A flash of light caught my eye. Lightning struck a church tower, igniting the building. The balloon began drifting down toward the flames, and alarm swept through me. I scooped up Mildred, frantically trying to think of some way to save us. Just then, a giant pair of black cowboy boots appeared in the sky a few feet away and kicked the balloon's basket, launching us inland. As suddenly as they appeared, the boots disappeared. We whooshed toward a forested area, still losing altitude. As we drew closer to what would be our landing area, a parking lot

beside several rustic buildings, I saw a road sign—
"Welcome to Santa Cruz." Then I woke up before we
hit the ground.

Marc dreamt he fell through a hole in the rocks
beside a beach, entering a vortex of water that sucked
him down until he found a group of Japanese tourists in
scuba gear with stereotypical cameras around their
necks.

Over breakfast in an alarmingly dirty restaurant
down the street from Ophelia's, we examined our
dreams. Mildred waited outside, tied to a yellow fire
hydrant. I worried about her, but Marc said she'd be
okay.

If it were tinier, the restaurant could've served as
an item in Susan Granger's time capsule. Not a visible
thing in it harkened from less than fifty years ago,
including its occupants. The man in the adjacent booth
could've posed for a Dorothea Lange dustbowl
photograph. Stiff red vinyl seats crackled beneath us as
we shifted our weight in a vain attempt to get
comfortable.

"These dreams seem to be less explicit, don't
they?" Marc began. "They might contain clues, but not
ones that compel us into action. In fact, they might just
be ordinary dreams."

"I don't have dreams like this. Well, not until
recently. I'm struck by both of our experiences taking
place by the ocean, and mine being in Santa Cruz. I
know there are several cities and towns by that name,
but it's probably the one in California."

"Why do you say that?"

"The road sign was in English." I looked at the
menu, which featured traditional breakfast items, as

well as something called a "chicken-fried steak."
"Another thing I can do is start googling keywords from aspects of the dreams—stringing them together in meaningful ways."

"I've tried that. I never have much luck."

"It's an art," I told him. "In fact, let me try it now."

A young gal sashayed up to take our orders before I could. Marc and I both asked for the "special," despite the fact that a faded color photo on the menu looked about as ordinary as a breakfast could be. Our server might've been pretty under the mask of makeup she wore. It was hard to tell. After telling us she'd be right back with our drinks—coffee for Marc and orange juice for me—she glided her way to the kitchen as if she were a runway model. I imagined this was her life aspiration and wondered if anyone from a town like Turkey had ever successfully translated such an unlikely desire into a career.

I googled while we waited, trying Santa Cruz, boots, balloons, wisdom, book, and others in various combinations. It took some time to sort through the results to see if anything helpful showed up. Zip. Next, I checked aerial photos and easily identified Santa Cruz, California, as the town in my dream.

I showed Marc the image. "This proves mine wasn't an ordinary dream. I've never seen this in waking life."

"You never know. You might not remember something that's embedded in your subconscious." I shot him a withering look, and he shrugged theatrically. "My dream could still be insignificant, though," he told me. "I dream about drowning regularly."

"Why's that?"

"I mentioned I was in a car accident as a teen?"

I nodded.

"The car went through a guardrail into a lake."

I had an intuitive flash. "Wait a minute. Let me try something. What if we juxtapose words from your dream and mine?" I was aware that my changing the subject without expressing empathy about his accident was insensitive, but I plowed on.

I tried drowning, Japanese, cameras, and everything else I could think of, combining them with terms from my dream. Zip again.

"Try this," Marc suggested. "Santa Cruz and vortex."

"Okay. Why?"

"I think I remember something about that. There are supposed to be energy vortices in certain places like Sedona, Arizona, a town in Oregon, and maybe in Santa Cruz."

"Actually, they say the energy back in Ojai is special too," I mentioned. "Maybe it's even had some effect on us." I googled and checked the results. "Paydirt! There's a place called the Mystery Spot just outside town. Let me find a photo. Yup, that's it. That's where I was about to land the balloon in the dream. It's an old-fashioned tourist attraction."

I read aloud to Marc: "Quite popular in this country in the 1950s—even featured in *Life* magazine—this quaint, bizarre site now draws busloads of Japanese tourists. Japanese-speaking bus drivers double as tour guides as these visitors travel on day trips from San Francisco to Carmel."

"There we go—the next stop on our quest."

"Hopefully, the last." I played with my paper

napkin. "Why do you think we keep getting sent from one place to another? I mean, the book could've been hidden in the pipe in San Marcos, right?"

"I assume there's a reason we'll discover later. For now, we simply need to work with what we find along the way."

"Is there still a reason to go to the museum?"

"We can't know without going," Marc said. "And we're already here, aren't we? Would you prefer to investigate the hardware store or stare at the water tower?"

Our breakfasts arrived, and they were much tastier than the photo suggested. Apparently, our conversation had attracted the attention of the dust bowl man in the booth behind us. Now he stood and moved over beside our table.

"I couldn't help overhearing," he said in a deep, soft voice. "I have dreams such as these. We must honor them when they come."

I studied him. He could've been in his mid-seventies. His wide face and slicked-back jet-black hair were vaguely familiar. I had the feeling I'd seen someone who resembled him in an old Western. Statistically, the odds were that he was Mexican American, but there was a hint of Asia in his eyes, and his slight accent was as hard to place as Bubba's had been. He wore old jeans and a denim work shirt open at the neck. A silver pendant shaped like a lizard snaked down onto his sternum. An out-of-place expensive Swiss watch encircled his hairless wrist.

"If you don't mind my asking," Marc said, peering up at the man, "what tribe are you?"

"Comanche. This was our land. I have something

else to tell you. I used to work at the Bob Wills museum, so I know that when he lived in California in his later years, he occasionally visited friends in the Santa Cruz area. There are details in the museum. Look for the brass fiddle statue—there's a plaque near there."

"Thank you," I said. "I've never met a Native American before." Now that I knew his heritage, I saw that his skin tone and high, chiseled cheekbones certainly fit the bill.

"Now you have," he said. "I've never met a child who speaks as you do. Are you Tris Healy?"

"I am."

"What in the world are you doing here? What is the quest you have spoken of?"

For some reason, I trusted this man, and I guess I'd been yearning to tell someone our story. Marc invited him to sit down, and the man slid into the seat across from me, next to Marc. We introduced ourselves, and then I recounted much of what we'd weathered over the past few days. It took a while.

Theodore—his name was Theodore—listened placidly. None of the fantastic elements of my narrative seemed to elicit any surprise or other emotion. I had no idea if he believed me or thought I was crazy. When I was through, I looked at him expectantly.

"The world can use more wisdom." His dark eyes steadily held mine, and a half smile formed on his weathered lips. "Keep up the good work," he added. Then he stood and departed without another word.

"What do you make of that?" I asked Marc. "Why was that all he said?"

"I suspect he's a man of few words. Maybe a man beyond words."

"What do you mean?"

"There's something about him—something that led you to tell him about us, right? I found I immediately trusted him, too."

"Yes, it seems odd now that I think about it," I mused.

"I think there's a depth to Theodore—maybe some sort of wisdom lineage or maybe just a well-lived life. I don't know. But in my experience, charismatic people like that aren't usually big talkers."

Chapter 13

The outgoing young woman at the front desk of the museum told me I could hold Mildred as we walked through the exhibits. Her red and white cowgirl outfit looked like an inexpensive Halloween costume, but it suited her. I liked her broad smile and her name tag—"My name is Ginnie—what's yours, friend?" When I told her my name, she said Tris was "a beautiful and very unique name." I was tempted to point out that Tris was common appellation in Wales—as a diminutive of Tristan—and that unique was a stand-alone adjective that could not be modified. I resisted.

After walking through several rooms of photos, album covers, movie posters, and other memorabilia, not spying the boots we were hunting, we discovered a panel by the fiddle statue entitled "Bob's Latter Years." Sure enough, it mentioned the Sinclair family of La Selva Beach, California, a small town in south Santa Cruz county. Bob had met Jake Sinclair when he'd acted in Westerns in Hollywood, before he'd moved back to Texas in 1949. Jake had been a stuntman who'd retired to northern California, and the two men had stayed in touch through the years. Wills liked to ride the roller coaster at the Santa Cruz Beach Boardwalk whenever he visited. He'd died in 1975 at the age of seventy, but he rode the coaster until his stroke in 1969.

"Another clue?" Marc cocked his head and smiled.

"Almost certainly."

"I agree. What are the odds of meeting Theodore? He's probably the only person in town—and maybe the entire Texas panhandle—who's on our wavelength. And we were sent to this museum even before we met him, so it's reasonable to expect we'd find something significant."

"What about the boots?" I asked. "We didn't see them anywhere, did we? They've got those fancy ones over in the corner, but that's it."

"Let me ask at the front desk."

He strode away, leaving me alone in the room. We were the sole museum visitors. I stroked Mildred while I waited for him. I never knew how good that could feel, not just somatically, but on many levels. And Mildred would never exploit me, make fun of me, try to boss me around, or...I stopped myself from making a longer list. Why focus on negatives in the midst of a sublimely positive experience?

I peered around the room, which could've used a thorough dusting. Across from me in an ornate gilt frame, a lime green western-style shirt with mother-of-pearl snaps gleamed under a wall sconce. The piping sported sequins, and the black collar was even shinier than the rest. I rated it a nine on the horrid-looking scale, but I supposed it served its purpose back in its day.

On one of the sidewalls, grainy black and white photos documented the various dance halls and ballrooms in which the Texas Playboys had performed, along with two elderly instruments—a mahogany acoustic guitar and a battered violin.

Marc returned. "Ginnie said hey. Not hi—hey. She

told me you were cute, too. I described the boots in the photo. She doesn't remember any like that. Bob was a showman—to a fault, apparently—so all his stage footwear was flashy. I asked her if these could be his everyday pair, and she said maybe a guy in the back would know. He's coming out to talk to us."

Belying our hostess's Ophelia's assertion that she was the only African American in town, Zeke was a Black man in his thirties. Unusually slim, with closely cropped hair and stubble on his cheeks, he wore a faded western-style black shirt with white piping, and designer jeans. The pointy toes of green cowboy boots peeked out under these.

He fussed over Mildred, clearly more interested in her than us, which made sense to me. As the Bob Wills expert at the museum, he was probably asked dumb questions all day long, but how many visitors carried in adorable little dogs? She enjoyed the attention, licking his hand after a few moments.

"Hi, I'm Zeke, the museum director. I understand you have a question about Bob's boots?"

"Do you know Ophelia?" I blurted out.

"Of course. Everybody knows everybody here. Let me guess. She said she was the only African American in town, right?"

"Yes."

"She says I don't count because I have a grandparent who was Jewish. I think she might've overlooked that, but I'm also from New Jersey originally. Apparently, we don't have 'real' Black people there. I love Ophelia—I bring her groceries and deal with her problem guests—but you can't take her too seriously."

"Did Bob Wills steal her song?"

"She told you that, too? She must like you. Yes, he probably did. At the least, he altered it enough to claim it as his own. Even his big hit 'San Antonio Rose' was lifted from a Carter family tune. On the other hand, back then most musicians did that, including the Carters. A.P. Carter scoured rural Tennessee for original songs, bought them for chicken feed, and then called them his."

"You're a music historian?"

"I am. I never thought it would bring me to Turkey, Texas, but they lured me with a great compensation package and all the barbecue I can eat." He grinned. This museum seemed to foster smiling. "It's not so bad here once you get used to it. And most of the time, I'm back in my office researching a book I'm writing."

"I'll bet people here had a harder time getting used to you than you did to them," Marc speculated. I guess he thought Zeke had opened the door to personal commentary by revealing his heritage. "It's hard to be the new kid in a small town, isn't it?" Marc added.

Zeke looked him in the eye, and his smile faded. "Yes, that was the hard part. By far."

I liked this guy. In fact, I'd liked most people we'd met on our trip.

Marc shook his head. "Among other things, when people are embedded in their subculture, they have no idea how racist they are."

"Are you a Black man who got a skin transplant?" Zeke asked, smiling again. "I couldn't agree more."

"I'm a psychologist," Marc told him.

"Pretty much everyone in this town could use one, including me. The nearest one is forty miles away." He paused and looked away, perhaps in the direction of this practitioner. "So what can I do for you?" he asked when he'd returned his gaze to us.

I showed him the photograph of the monogrammed boots. Mildred scrambled to reposition herself while I employed the arm that cradled her.

"Yup. Those are his. His grandson has them now. He's up in Amarillo, but he comes every year for Bob Wills Day, and he brings things like the boots to put on temporary display."

Marc spoke. "Is there anything special about them?"

"I wouldn't say so. Why do you ask? For that matter, how did you come by that photo?"

"It's a long story, and we need to be elsewhere. Thanks so much for your help."

Marc's abruptness once again demonstrated the contrast between his professional and his less sensitive in-the-world personas.

Zeke reached out and touched his upper arm. "I think you owe me an explanation. I've helped you. Now help me satisfy my curiosity."

"We found the photo on the ground in San Marcos," Marc told him. "We're from California, and we thought it would be a fun tourist thing to come up here and see what the story was."

"Fine. Don't tell me. Tris Healy isn't some clueless tourist, is he?"

"You know who I am?"

"Of course. You're on one of the three channels here."

"No cable?" I asked.

He shook his head. "And wi-fi is iffy."

"How can you stand it? I really don't see why you live here."

"Actually, my wife has family down the road in Quitaque. We came to take care of her mother. I'm lucky I'm not still the world's most overqualified grocery bagger. When the former director of the museum retired, here I was. What are the odds?"

"We've been asking ourselves that a lot lately," I told him.

Marc reported we were on a scavenger hunt of sorts to find a spiritual text. Zeke could tell that was true, albeit well short of the whole story.

"Okay, good enough," he said. "Have a safe journey."

"Thanks."

I checked into our travel itinerary to Santa Cruz as we stood under an ancient locust tree next to the museum parking lot. Mildred nosed around. I think she was hunting for a gopher or maybe a mouse. Usually, Marc checked his work email or called his therapist colleague when I researched something on my phone, but on this occasion he just gazed into space.

I was struck by how holistic Marc looked. That is, a unity of his body parts implied an integration of other aspects of him. His long legs flowed into his torso, which sat squarely above the rest of him. His neck didn't so much as connect his head to his body as provide a continuous, penultimate sweep from his feet upward.

Something about the way he stood in that moment made me think he'd been constructed from the ground up with no interruption in the work—rooted in something much bigger than himself. If you asked me why I gathered this impression, I couldn't be sure. Maybe it was the absolute stillness Marc managed to achieve so effortlessly.

****

The airport in Lubbock was an hour-and-a-half drive away. Flights originating from there connected in Dallas/Fort Worth to San Jose, California, which was forty-five minutes inland from Santa Cruz. I used my parents' credit card number to book us a flight from Lubbock to Dallas to San Jose.

"What about Mildred?" I asked as we walked back to Ophelia's in the searing, late morning sun. "Do you think she'll like being on the plane?"

"Actually, I thought about that while you were on your phone. I think it will be better to leave her here and come back for her later."

"Oh, no. We couldn't do that. She'd be too sad."

"Are you sure *she's* the one who would be sad?"

"We all would, I assume."

Marc placed his hand on my upper arm and stopped us both. Fortunately, we now stood in the shade of a store awning. "Try saying 'I will be sad.' " His eye bored into me, seeking a more essential Tris.

"Leave me alone. We need to focus on what's best for Mildred."

"Yes, I agree. I know it's hard to put aside your feelings since Mildred has more or less awakened your heart. But here's my thinking. If I'm Mildred, I'd definitely find the plane ride stressful, so I'd have seizures—maybe lots of them. What counterbalances going through that?"

"She'd get to be with us. She loves us."

"Try saying 'she loves me' or 'I love her.' "

My irritation rose to the surface. "Can you stop being a therapist for just a minute, Marc?"

"Okay, you're right. I'm sorry. The other thing is that taking Mildred might hinder us in Santa Cruz. We'd need to walk her and feed her and either keep her on a leash or hold her, and we'll probably need our hands free."

"Why do you say that?"

He looked me in the eye again. "I didn't want to tell you, but I had a second dream about Santa Cruz last night—a violent one, actually. It worked out in the end, but it wouldn't have if Mildred was with us. The dream confirmed we're dealing with a rogue religious group of some kind—that's who was behind our troubles in Austin. That's all I'm going to say about it."

My face heated up. "You think I can't handle hearing about violence? And when were you even going to tell me about the rest? I have a right to know who we're dealing with, don't I? This is unacceptable, Marc."

"Maybe you're right. It just seemed unnecessary to put you through what I went through dreaming it, and I was planning on telling you the rest when the time felt right."

"Felt right, huh? After you consulted a Ouija board or shuffled some tarot cards? Geez, Marc. Give me a break."

Marc watched me wave my hands around, and I actually worked up a sweat in mere moments, even in the Texas shade. Then I turned my back on him.

I jumped out of my outrage into my head—a familiar refuge from the world of messy feelings. Then I took off on my own, and Marc didn't work to keep up with me.

I considered all that Marc had said as cars and trucks drove by on a busier street nearer Ophelia's. I didn't want to admit it to myself, but he was right about leaving Mildred. On top of all the other reasons I wished I could ignore, disregarding a significant dream would be idiotic.

I pivoted and nodded. Marc was ambling too far behind me to see this, so I found more shade and waited for him to catch up. "Where would she stay?" I asked. "I'm not putting Mildred in a cage in some third-rate kennel."

He joined me as I began walking again. "We could ask Ophelia or Theodore to take care of her. What do you think?"

Now I paused to consider that. We needed to carefully decide what was in Mildred's best interests. She was dependent on us as though we were her parents. I cared about whoever would be her temporary caretaker, too.

"Of the two, I think Ophelia would benefit more from spending time with Mildred," I told Marc. "And Mildred already knows her." I thought about the remarkable native American from the restaurant. "Even though he's old, Theodore might still have a job, but Ophelia's probably always home. Do you think she can make it up and down the stairs to her apartment?"

"I imagine, but I doubt she could take Mildred for long walks," Marc replied.

"Maybe Zeke from the museum could help her with that."

"He has a job, too."

Was he playing devil's advocate to make a point?

The whole thing was *his* idea, wasn't it?

"He could walk Mildred before and after work," I said, more irritation leaking out of me. "And Ophelia and Mildred could commune during the day. He's a good guy. And she's clearly a dog lover."

"All right. Let's see what Ophelia says. I'm glad you're onboard with this, Tris. Inevitably, there will be times when you need to put your dog's welfare ahead of your own. And congratulations for considering the potential benefit for Ophelia."

"She's really my dog? I can keep her?"

"Of course."

"What about my parents? They won't let me have any pets."

"I'll tell them she's a support animal—that you need her to function."

"That would be wonderful." I pictured Mildred sleeping with me and going to quiz shows with me. A warm feeling billowed in my gut and spread throughout my body.

Ophelia was just finishing chopping misshapen carrots when we arrived back at her place. Her tiny, spotless kitchen barely held all three of us. I leaned against the edge of her green Formica-topped table. My legs felt rubbery.

"Hold your horses," she told Marc when he tried to talk to her. A few moments later, she took off her frilly, stained apron and told us she was ready.

We all traipsed to her dimly lit living room. Marc and I perched on overstuffed gray armchairs while our hostess parked herself on a matching loveseat that had clearly seen a great deal of active duty. A professional-looking painting on the wall above her head portrayed a bloody bullfighter being skewered on the horns of an oversized, very angry-looking bull.

"You looking at my picture, Tris? I don't wanna hear anything about it. My granddaughter painted that when she was an exchange student in Spain. I don't care if you think it's wrong to have that on my wall. It's *my* damned wall, isn't it?"

"Yes, ma'am."

I'd let Mildred roam around, but now she pawed my shin to prompt me to pick her up again. She fell asleep on my lap in about two seconds.

Marc outlined our request, phrasing it in terms of what was best for Mildred.

"Hell, no!" Ophelia replied. "I ain't taking on no more work."

"Why don't you hold her for a minute," I said, standing and handing Mildred to her before she could object.

"Oh my, she's a little nothin', ain't she?"

Mildred wriggled, not trying to get down, just seeking a safer perch. Ophelia clutched her tightly. Mildred reached her head up and licked her on the cheek.

"She does kinda grow on you," Ophelia said. "What about food? I ain't paying for no food."

"I'll take care of all the expenses," Marc said.

"Well, I might consider it, but I need to get paid for my labor, too."

"How about two hundred dollars a week on top of expenses?"

"Hmph. When are you coming back for—what's her name again?"

"Mildred," Marc told her. "That's up in the air, but

it shouldn't more than a couple of weeks. What do you say?"

"I'll think on it," she said, holding onto Mildred for dear life. I don't think we could've pried her out of Ophelia's arms if we tried.

Ten minutes later, the matter was settled. Mildred obviously liked Ophelia and vice versa. A phone call to Zeke confirmed his willingness to help.

Ophelia objected to this. "I've got lots of other friends too, you know. I don't need that Jersey boy," Ophelia told us. "I'm popular."

"Do whatever you want," Marc told her. "You're in charge."

"Damned straight!"

Saying goodbye to Mildred brought painful tears, which surprised me. How long had I even known her? The grief intensified. A black hole expanded in my chest, filling the space where my heart was supposed to be. I hunched over on Ophelia's worn chair, holding the first being I'd ever loved. With all my love centered on this one small package, all my heart was breaking. My thoughts made it worse. *Will I ever see Mildred again? Will she be safe? Will my heart ever heal?*

After a time, Marc came over and placed his hand on my shoulder. Then Ophelia sat down on the other side of me and placed her ancient hand over mine. His hand squeezed; hers shook. It helped a little.

It wasn't clear if Mildred fully understood the situation. She seemed confused by my behavior, although she licked my tears and watched me closely. Of course I'd cried before, but never because my heart hurt. Never like this.

When I'd calmed down, we all hugged, and

165

Ophelia told me she loved me. She didn't even know me, and she loved me. Now I cried more, moved by her words. What a compassionate thing to say.

In the car, as we pulled out of town, Marc turned to me. "Perhaps Mildred has so little continuity in her life from her absence seizures that it won't be that hard on her to be separated."

I jumped into my head again, happy for the excuse to do so. "There *is* a certain tyranny in continuity. Our memories, positive or negative, are inescapable, especially mine, since I rarely forget anything."

To distract myself further, I asked Marc what our cover story was—what he'd told my parents about our trip—so I could call my dad while I still had phone reception. Armed with this barely plausible story, I gave him a try.

"Tris! Son! I've missed you so much!"

"Thanks."

"Is that doctor taking care of you?

"Absolutely. And the program here is great. I'm learning so much about how to behave better. I think it's really going to make a difference. Who knew that Romanian scientists were so smart about psychology?"

"Listen, we tried looking up this place and there's no trace of it on the internet."

"Let me pass the phone to Dr. Dalcour."

"Yes, Mr. Healy. How can I help you?"

I only heard Marc's side of the conversation, which was fine with me. The lower the dosage of my adoptive father, the better.

"I see," Marc said. "Well, there's a good reason for that. This program is so popular that they've had to limit attendees to children who've been recommended and accompanied by a psychotherapist such as myself. Only professionals have access to the center's information now. It's for the best. Before they started doing this, there was a line out the door that stretched all the way down the block." He winked at me while he listened to my father's reply. "That's right. Yes, it's just as I described it to you in person. You have nothing to worry about. Would you like to talk to Tris again?"

I shook my head vigorously, but Marc handed my phone back to me.

"Hi, again," I said.

"Are you eating right, Trissie?"

"Don't call me that. Yes, I am."

"Saying your prayers?"

"Just the way I do at home." Which is to say, never. It occurred to me that I ought to revisit that decision. What if there were a way to connect directly to whatever force was behind the wisdom book quest? Wasn't that the function of prayer?

"Hold on for your mom."

I held on.

"Hi, Tris! Are you having any fun? All work and no play makes Jack a dull boy."

"It has been anything but dull. Believe me."

"That's good. I heard it's hot and sunny in Texas. Are you using sunscreen? You know what happened to your great-aunt Irene."

"You've never mentioned it, but let me guess. She died of melanoma?"

"What kind of thing is that to say? Sometimes I don't know about you, Tris. No, she bought shares in a sunscreen company and then she got a wonderful new car—one of those big Chryslers—you know, the one with the grill that looks like it wants to eat you?"

"Okay, Mom. Listen, I've got to go, but don't worry about me. Dr. Dalcour is fixing me."

"Oh, that's great."

We said our goodbyes, and I rolled my eyes as I put my phone back in my pocket. Marc saw me out of the corner of his eye.

"They mean well."

"I suppose."

"Try to look at it from their vantage point." He braked to let a giant orange tractor slide over from the shoulder onto the highway.

"Why? That's a singularly ignorant perspective."

"That's my point. They're ignorant. Would you hold a four-year-old responsible for his behavior based on how a thirty-year-old is supposed to act?"

"Of course not. So?"

"Four-year-olds are supposed to do what four-year-olds do. By adult standards, they're self-centered and obnoxious. Your parents are only capable of their state-of-the-art ability to parent and do life, much as a child can only behave childishly. Can you ask them to be someone else? Your problem is you think they *should* do better than they *can* do. From their point of view, your parents are raising an extremely challenging child, and they have very little idea of how to go about it."

"It's true they got more than they bargained for when they adopted me, and obviously you're right that they're unqualified to parent me." The tractor we'd been following mercifully turned off onto a dirt track beside a partially harvested wheat field. I watched it bounce up and down as I thought. "Look," I said, pivoting on the fabric passenger seat to face Marc, "*you* make a lot of unsolicited suggestions about how people *should* be—how *I* should be. I shouldn't judge my parents, in this case. That's a 'should' like all the others. And a lot of these ideas of yours are virtually impossible to put into practice. Who doesn't want his parents to change? You probably still do."

"I see your point. I guess I state things too absolutely. And I certainly don't mean you 'should' try any of the things I suggest. I just ask that you think about what I say and see what resonates with you."

"Just dial it back, Marc. I don't need therapy 24/7."

"Sure." He cocked his head and smiled. "Look at you. That was two idioms in one sentence. Your rules are loosening up."

"Actually, those were two separate sentences."

"Hi, old Tris! You're still in there too, aren't you?"

I closed my eyes and pretended to nap.

The trip to San Jose was unremarkable—not worth reporting—but the drive from the airport to our AirBnB in Santa Cruz was strikingly beautiful. Most of the narrow highway wound through redwood-covered mountains. I'd never seen these majestic trees before. While obviously not first-growth, their girth surpassed anything I'd seen in the Ojai area, and they soared to amazing heights. They were grouped in well-spaced rings; the center of the rings sometimes displayed evidence of fallen or hewn mother trees.

I opened my car window; their scent was strong enough to penetrate the bubble of our interior air. Similar to pine or fir, with the addition of mustiness, the trees enticed me to sniff them for a long moment. I also smelled a great deal of car exhaust, so I rolled the window up.

No one on the crowded road obeyed the fifty-mile-an-hour speed limit—drivers seemed to be racing each other. Marc kept his attention on the series of sharp curves, steep hills, and irresponsibly driven vehicles.

"Look at the makes of the cars," Marc said after a while. "It's all BMWs, Mercedes, and Lexuses—Lexi? I'll bet these maniac drivers are rich techies commuting from Silicon Valley to Santa Cruz. It's no wonder nobody likes them."

I frowned. What kind of talk was that from a therapist—or even just a nice person? Surely some people enjoyed the company of software engineers, however they drove.

Once we reached the summit and began descending, we occasionally caught glimpses of Monterey Bay. Santa Cruz sat on the most northern point of it, while the Monterey Peninsula constituted the southern arc. San Francisco was seventy-five miles north. The dark blue water looked subtly different than the Pacific I knew from the beaches in Ventura County, but I couldn't tell you why. When I left Ojai someday, this was an area I'd want to explore.

For our stay, I'd chosen a stand-alone granny unit in what I hoped was a quiet neighborhood called Seabright, just south of downtown. It was quite a bit pricier than either of our Texas digs, but that was to be expected.

Our host left the key under an obviously fake rock beside a brick walkway, and he'd also tucked a laminated sheet of paper into the doorframe. It provided a number where we could reach him if need be. Otherwise, he pledged to leave us alone to enjoy our stay. After a list of rules, including no pets, he added that we should read his book about the upcoming apocalypse.

My mother would've loved our converted garage. The exterior photos online had done no justice to the efforts of the owner to tart it up. The predominant exterior paint color was salmon, with two shades of trim—yellow and light brown. Several trellises hung down from its eaves, and purple flowering vines cascaded from these. I felt a pang when I couldn't name the plant, but it passed quickly.

The interior attempted to maintain the mood but didn't quite manage it. While the walls were light turquoise and the kitchenette's cabinets were painted pale green, the overall effect hinted at mild desperation. All the furniture was mismatched and seemingly chosen based solely on its whimsy quotient. A purple vinyl couch sat across from a blue beanbag chair that had seen better days. A slim, cream-colored Corinthian column formed the stand of a torchiere in a corner of the high-ceilinged room, clashing with a nearby Scandinavian-design beech armchair.

In my opinion, once we all accept that furniture, fixtures, and walls are simply utilitarian elements of our existence, the better off we are. Architectural and interior design magazines nauseate me.

After unpacking and abortive naps—my mind raced, as usual—Marc went online and discovered a seafood restaurant a few blocks away. We strolled to it once we cleaned up and changed clothes. Ensconced in an unassuming storefront, Fish Festival was reputed to serve the best sea bass in town, which was Marc's favorite entree.

When we stepped inside, I was pleasantly surprised

by the ambiance, a combination of casual, oceanic decor—fishing nets and small blue and white buoys on the wall—and classical guitar music played at a reasonable volume. At first, I assumed the restaurant was employing a high-end sound system, but then I caught a glimpse of a waif-like girl with long blond hair performing on a stool in a corner of the small room. She wore black slacks and a white, button-down shirt as though she were in an orchestra.

I strode to a table for two that afforded a good view of the guitar player. While puberty had not yet infused me with its chemical stew, I appreciated the opportunity to watch the hands of an accomplished player, male or female. Our server, a stout young woman with rosy skin and hair buzzed as low as Marc's, told us to try the halibut, which I did, but it didn't prove to be memorable. Marc seemed to enjoy his sea bass.

A fellow diner recognized me and asked for my autograph, which catalyzed a parade of other fans, including one of the cooks. Several asked me to say something smart, which has always struck me as an asinine request. This time, I described the atomic structure of several obscure elements on the periodical table. On other occasions I quoted Greek philosophers in their native tongue or elucidated the gross domestic product of West African countries. People generally became bored by my recitations and wandered away, which was my goal in these encounters.

Marc grinned as he watched me in action. "I see what you're doing," he told me once the circus had concluded. "But one of these days you'll meet someone who's fascinated by lawrencium."

"I doubt it."

The guitarist sidled up to our table just as we were rising to leave. Close up, I could see that she was only a few years older than me.

I decided to practice my social skills. "I very much enjoyed your playing," I told her before she could speak. "Unless I'm mistaken, those were Sor and Corelli compositions."

"Yes, they were. Do you play?"

"A bit, but I much prefer hearing you to listening to myself. You have such a light touch, yet there's real authority to your playing."

"Thank you so much. Can I ask you a question?"

Here we go, I thought. What was it going to be this time? Equations? Astronomy?

"Sure."

"Why did those people fuss over you? Are you in movies?"

"No, the only time I act is when I pretend to be an ordinary child." I held out my hand. "Tris Healy. I'm on a TV quiz show. That's all. I'm smart."

I glimpsed Marc's face while I told her this. A mix of bemusement and satisfaction was in his eyes. Perhaps I was projecting these responses onto him.

"Jane Potter-Sussman," she told me as she slid her slender hand into mine. "Pleased to meet you."

"Likewise."

We looked into each other's eyes for a brief moment, which was scary. I wondered what she saw. In a mirror, a Norman Rockwellish young man glared back at me, bearing a misshapen nose, only a hint of eyebrows, and ears that stuck out way too far.

The moment passed. "Well," she said, "off I go. Have a great evening."

Marc slapped me on the back out on the sidewalk. "Way to go, Tris! Gutsy stuff! At this rate, you'll have the pick of the litter in a few years."

My face flushed. I didn't know what I was starting to feel, but I knew I didn't want to feel it. "That's an abhorrent phrase, Marc. Pick of the litter? Really? You don't seem to be yourself today."

His eyes were lasers. "I'm sorry if I upset your precious sensibilities," he snapped. "It's been a long day. I don't need lessons from you about how to behave." The intensity of his gaze was palpable.

I shut down. I didn't think. I didn't feel anything. I just wasn't there anymore. Marc wasn't going to get an opportunity to hurt me again that evening. I read until bedtime, facing away from him.

I slept like whatever proverbial simile you prefer. (Why logs? Why are any inanimate objects presumed to be sound sleepers? And don't get me started on sleeping like a baby).

Marc approached me while I finished dressing the next morning. "I'm sorry about last night, Tris."

"You ought to be. You're supposed to be a role model." I sat down on the edge of the bed and pulled a sock on.

"Who says? I never told you that." He plunked down on the bed across from me and leaned forward. "I'm just a human being doing the best I can like everyone else. If you put me up on a pedestal, then I'm glad I jumped off."

"Oh, so now you're *glad* you were mean to me. What happened to your apology?"

"Look, let's start over. Why don't we each look at our role in the conflict?"

"There's a good idea. Let's regress into therapy-speak." I moved on to my shoes. Marc didn't deserve my full attention.

"Believe it or not, I actually talk like this in real life, too. Maybe you've noticed."

I just stared at him, pretending we were convicts in a prison yard. If I could've mustered the verbal equivalent of a shiv, I'd have said it.

Marc's voice softened. "I know it's hard to acknowledge and take responsibility for one's actions, but let me point out some things to you. We need to get this squared away before we get going on some really important things today. Are you willing listen with an open mind?"

I considered his request. "I'll try." I watched him warily as he gathered himself, straightening his torso and holding his head steady. I was reminded of how he'd stood outside the museum in Turkey, which helped me calm down.

"First of all, I've done an awful lot for you, Tris—off the clock, out of the goodness of my heart and, admittedly, in service of my own psychological needs as well. This trip *has* been healing for me, although I'm not sure why." He glanced down and then up at me again, his eyes slightly squinting. "Have you ever thanked me? Even once? Have you thought about what it's like for me to drop everything in my life and follow the life script of a ten-year-old?" His voice rose. "You never miss an opportunity to show me you think you're smarter than me. You don't care how I feel. And you watch me like a hawk to catch me out saying or doing something wrong. I've witnessed a shooting, driven all day several times, forked over tons of my own money, and I don't even remember what else. Throughout it all, I've held it together. I've helped you in every way I know how." His face relaxed a bit, and he lowered his voice. "Then you told me I said something abhorrent. Did I start the conflict last night? No, you did with that remark. If you didn't like my saying 'the pick of the litter,' so what? Does everything I say have to please you?"

"Uh…"

"I'll own my part in this," Marc continued with even less heat. "I went along with it all past the point I should've. I let resentment build up, and it's coming out now. That's on me. But I don't think it leaked out last night when *I was complimenting you* on your social skills. That's right. I was *appreciating you*—being positive. If I told you you'd won the lottery in a whiny voice, would the tone of my voice be what you'd pay attention to? It was a long, challenging trip here yesterday. I drove that awful road when I was really tired. And did you know you snore? Did you know how much havoc that's played with my sleep? So let's say I spoke carelessly, or even hurtfully. Once again, so what? You can't stand that? You need to give me grief on a zero tolerance basis?"

"Uh…"

"That's it? Uh?"

"Give me a minute. Nobody's ever talked to me like this before."

I felt numb, my brain stuck in neutral. The sensation passed after a few moments, and I realized what he'd said had penetrated my defenses. It was all so obviously true, I couldn't pretend to myself it wasn't.

"Yes," I said.

"Yes?"

"Yes. You're right. I'm sorry." I looked him in the eye and nodded.

"Really? That's it. You don't want to argue?"

"No, I don't think so."

Marc looked so unsatisfied with this that I offered more. "What you said is good feedback. I'm going to work on those things. And thank you for all you've done. You're a great person, Marc. You don't have to be perfect. Just keep being yourself."

He leaned back, whole body relaxed. How had he released the rest of his tension so suddenly?

I stood. "I'm hungry," I said. As far as I was concerned, the conversation had run its course.

We maintained silence on the drive to breakfast in a dark, funky restaurant full of college students. After ordering from a personable young man sporting numerous piercings, and then waiting patiently for our food, Marc revealed he'd dreamt a recurrent narrative in which he was supposed to meet the vice president but couldn't find his pants. "A classic expression of anxiety," he told me.

"Are you nervous about what might happen today? Is that why you're dreaming that? I'm rather excited. Between the Mystery Spot and the Sinclair family near here, we might actually find the book today."

"My dream tends to show up when I travel or when my wife is mad at me. I don't think it's related to nervousness."

"You're married?" I knew nothing about Marc's personal life. There was another deficit I needed to correct. I should've been interested in him all along, including his life when he wasn't with me. "Any kids?"

I asked.

"I misspoke. I'm recently divorced. No children."

"Was it hard to get divorced?" I concentrated on my potatoes while he answered. Crispy and the perfect temperature, I really liked them.

"Surprisingly so. She's also a therapist. Different initials after her name, but doing the same work. We shared an office, in fact. I think that was part of the problem. When she worked, I was off, and vice versa. Our time together was compromised just to save a few bucks. And thanks for asking. I was wondering if you were going to get around to that."

"I really did assimilate what you said back in our room." I took another bite of toast.

"That's hard to believe. I've never had a client who benefited from a diatribe like that, not that I lose control very often."

"I'm not a client." I looked Marc as squarely in the eye as I could. "Not anymore. I'm your friend."

His eyes moistened. "Thank you," he said softly. "I don't deserve that right now."

"Everyone deserves to be treated well. I don't actually pay any attention to that truism myself, of course, but I read it in a book once, so it must be true."

He laughed. "Good one."

By now, we'd finished eating. We stood and solemnly hugged. I could feel his heart beat against my cheek.

"So what's the plan?" Marc asked as we walked to our car, dodging a woman pushing twins in an oversized stroller.

"What do you think? The Mystery Spot first?"

"Sounds good. When does it open?"

"Ten," I told him.

"So we've got some time. How would you like to spend it?"

"Let me get on my phone in the car and research the Sinclairs."

"Sounds good."

Two branches of the family still lived in northern California. One lived in Oakland, an hour and a half north. The other resided in the same house that Bob Wills had visited in La Selva Beach. Rob Sinclair—the elderly son of Bob's friend Jake—was a retired civil rights attorney who apparently lived there with his son's family. The son, Judd, sold real estate, and his wife, Sara, grew wholesale orchids. Their two children had launched and lived out of state. For some reason, this information had been difficult to ferret out.

We continued to sit in our car. Marc used the time to text the therapist who was covering for him. I further researched the rival wisdom book cults I'd discovered earlier. Now that Marc had dreamt about a cult, it seemed likely to me that one of these was behind our trouble.

On an obscure site I hadn't found before, I discovered a great deal of new information about the Keepers of Wisdom, and several credible sources reported their headquarters was right in Santa Cruz. If this was a synchronicity and not an ordinary coincidence, then maybe we were being aimed by Spirit at that group.

The cult worked out of a modest house on the other side of downtown from our AirBnB. Satellite imagery hinted of a minor league operation—perhaps only a few individuals operating out of someone's home. Of course, if anyone had the means, they could've hired people to do their bidding in Texas.

I ran out of time before I could find out much about the Radiant Librarians, the more secretive cult. Their leaders were called guides, and several members had tried to rob an armored car once. That was the only new information.

I asked Marc if he remembered my earlier research on the two rogue spiritual groups.

"I don't."

"I need to fill you in then because one of them may be headquartered here in town."

"Tell me about both. It could be a cult you *haven't* found that's behind all this, but we might as well narrow things down between the two you've identified." Marc leaned his arms on the steering wheel, stretching his back muscles. Through the windshield, a black Labrador retriever simultaneously stretched its back legs on the sidewalk. Its owner, a tiny old man wearing a gray fedora, held its leash with both hands and a surprisingly athletic stance.

I tore my eyes back to Marc. "I'll start with the one that isn't here in town. The Radiant Librarians sell artwork of sacred sites online to fund themselves, and they say they're planning to share 'earthshaking revelations that will make true wisdom available to every soul on Earth.' Some members have broken the law. That's about all I've found out so far.

"The Keepers of Truth work hard at operating covertly, but they're bigger and more global, which has resulted in more leaks. Supposedly they go all the way back to Carthage, but I found out they've only been around since the 1930s. A defector reported that members have to make a scary-sounding pledge to 'sacrifice in whatever manner is necessary, as is required of true spiritual warriors.' There's evidence that they attract people by offering a spiritual pyramid scheme. The more people you recruit, the more tithing comes your way, and the more privileges you accrue. They have a sacred text that you don't get to read until you get to a certain level. People online like to spin conspiracy theories about the group, but sorting through all these would take hours and hours. I don't think it's too likely that Eleanor Roosevelt was a senior member. The Keepers' supposed mission is to present the 'wisdom of the ages' to the world—the same basic deal as the Librarians."

"And us. That's our deal, isn't it?" Marc said. "Let's look at that for a moment. Does it matter who gets the book published? The important thing is that the wisdom gets out there."

"Can we trust people who show up at a dog adoption event with a gun?"

"Like Chet did?" Marc leaned back in the driver's seat and paused before he spoke again. "Tris, we truly don't know these Santa Cruz people were responsible— if the Keepers even *are* Santa Cruz people. Your only real evidence is the fact they might to be headquartered here. We're in town for the Mystery Spot and the Sinclairs, aren't we? Why get sidetracked by speculation like this?"

"They're probably be the ones," I insisted. "It's too much of a coincidence, isn't it? And I definitely don't think we should let the book fall into their hands."

"Okay, I retract my statement. We should be the ones to publish it—as Susan's letter tells us to. Any of these groups—or someone else—might want to keep the wisdom to themselves or profit off it in some way."

"Or shoot us!" I smacked my palm against my thigh.

"Sure. Or shoot us."

"The way I see it," I continued, raising my voice, "we're on a mission—we have a *mandate*—and we have to trust *ourselves* to get the job done. If these people aren't violent, they're still likely to be weirdos."

"I've already agreed. Calm down. But I'm curious why you think they're weird. Did you get that from their website?"

"Do *you* belong to any secret cults?" I stared at him, defying him to dispute my point of view.

"Uh, no, unless you count psychologists."

****

The Mystery Spot sat in the middle of a ring of second-growth redwoods, about five miles inland. The country road we traversed en route wound through groves of mature eucalyptus and live oak trees, peppered with a few well-kept homes. We passed a coed softball team practicing in a park tucked into a meadow across a dry creek. And we almost struck a bicyclist wearing a bright purple jersey as we negotiated a sharp curve. Marc received a single finger salute from the aggrieved party.

We were the first to arrive that morning, so we had to wait for other visitors to gather before they'd send us out with a guide.

The entire operation was rustic—yet another time capsule of sorts. This was how someone would build a mysterious tourist attraction in 1940—and they had. Faded yellow signs with antiquated black fonts were scattered around the steep, wooded property. The faux log cabin gift shop sold a variety of inexpensive Chinese-made souvenirs—any tasteless item that afforded enough surface area on which to print the Mystery Spot's name. From their quantity in a knotty pine bin, I surmised that bright yellow bumper stickers were the most popular item.

The quorum for a tour was eight, but once seven of us gathered, Marc talked the gregarious ticket seller into letting us get started. We wanted to beat a thirty-eight strong Japanese group that was due at ten thirty.

We set out on uphill wooden decking, following our guide, Arthur, a retired geologist wearing a polished stone bolo tie. Why did so many geologists wear those? Maybe they wanted to be able to recognize each other in public. Maybe they just really liked rocks. Arthur's was a dark red oblong with diagonal white streaks. Actually, I liked it and wished I had one just like it.

Skinny and pale, Arthur looked unhealthy, and his careful steps hinted at a mobility issue. How much longer could he do his job, and what it would be like for him when he couldn't?

Our group paused after a few dozen steps. The perfumed woman behind me almost ran me over. She smelled like a combination of roses and chai. Her accented apology told me she was French-Canadian.

Arthur's canned introductory spiel would've struck me as pure hokum a week ago, but now I listened carefully, dismissing none of the gangly man's claims about the "mysterious forces at work that are far beyond human comprehension."

Marc reported that as soon as he stepped over the red line across the path where the "strange exertion of esoteric energy" was purported to take effect, he felt a tingling in his chest and became slightly dizzy. I didn't.

One of the premises of the attraction was that gravity operated differently at the Mystery Spot because of something at the center of the phenomenon—an underground meteor, UFO, or something along those lines. To "prove" that, the founder had built a series of optical illusions on the steep hillside, mostly driven by a radically tilted cabin that served as a cockeyed reference point to trick the eye. Water appeared to flow uphill, pendulums swung asymmetrically, and the like.

Nonetheless, something odd *was* happening. I didn't experience physical symptoms like Marc, yet I was sure of this. I was intrigued by this perception.

Unfortunately, nothing seemed to be conspicuously related to our quest. Perhaps when Marc and I had a chance to debrief one another, we'd discover something.

We didn't. Disappointment and frustration flooded in as we sat once more in our rental car. I didn't tune into the bodily sensations catalyzed by these emotions until Marc encouraged me to talk about my feelings. When I did, my tight face and my drooping shoulders became obvious. By the time I'd finished explaining my emotional response to our fruitless tour, fatigue set in, as though it were ten at night.

Marc shared his disappointment and frustration, too. I didn't press him for details, but I listened attentively. I certainly owed him that.

"So shall we visit the descendants of Bob Wills's friend or check out the cult in town?" I asked when he seemed done.

"As I said before, I think the Sinclairs are more on our radar at this point."

"Okay."

La Selva Beach is a small, unspoiled beach town about twelve miles south of Santa Cruz just off Highway One—a relic of middle-class summer homes from before the extensive development of other geographically fortunate towns. I read this was due to several factors. The 2,800 residents had banded together some years ago and convinced the state to omit the beach part of their name on the highway sign indicating their exit. Also, access to Monterey Bay was limited to residents who purchased a key to an imposing metal gate, a practice that I believe is illegal, but laxly enforced. Finally, the particular location formed a pocket of foggy weather all summer long, inhibiting sun-seekers.

My research determined that the local Sinclairs lived a few blocks inland from a cliff overlooking the water in a New England-looking, dark-green, two-story home. In person, the house was much more substantial than I had expected, dwarfing the cottages surrounding it. A compact silver SUV sat in the asphalt driveway, and a perfectly trimmed hedge hugged the perimeter of the large lot.

We'd neglected to concoct a cover story for why we were knocking on the Sinclairs' front door, so Marc parked our rental car down the street and we discussed it.

"We could say we're doing a survey," I suggested.

"Do you invite survey people into your home?"

"No. What do you think?"

"Let's stick to the truth as much as we can," Marc

suggested.

"Such as…?"

He shrugged. "We could say we're looking into Bob Wills's friendship with Jake. Once that gets us in the door, I guess we'll wing it."

"I studied improvisational theater," I told him.

"Really? That seems out of character."

"Well, it was only for an hour and a half so I could get to Austin on my own. But it might help."

"Let's try it."

A few minutes later, Marc rang the bell and I stood beside him, trying to look like a normal ten-year-old. I unfocused my eyes a little and slumped. I thought of Jane the guitar player in the fish restaurant—what I'd said to her about pretending to be ordinary sometimes.

A woman in her late forties opened the door. "Yes?"

She was short and very freckled. Some of the freckles had joined together to make swatches of reddish-brown skin on her cheeks. She wore black jeans, a sweatshirt that proclaimed her loyalty to a local high school football team, and bright blue running shoes. All in all, she was attractive in a matronly sort of way.

"Hi," Marc said. "I'm sorry to—"

"Tris Healy!" A smile lit her face.

I nodded. "It's me."

"I thought you were sick."

"I'm just taking a break from the show."

"I don't know why you're here, but come in, come in."

Marc introduced himself, and the woman told us she was Sarah Sinclair, which would make her the wife of Judd and the daughter-in-law of Rob, who, in turn, was the son of Bob Wills's friend.

We followed her through a vast, well-lit living room into the kitchen, where she insisted on serving us iced tea before she even asked why we were there.

The kitchen was more modest in terms of dimensions, but no expense had been spared on its decor or appliances. A substantial teak island sported two sinks and a built-in maple chopping board. Matching, expensive-looking light fixtures dangled over all this. Their elongated bulbs resembled oversized yams.

We seated ourselves at a round glass table beside a floor-to-ceiling picture window displaying a landscaped side yard. Tea in hand, Marc told Sarah we had compelling reasons to find out about Jake Sinclair and his connection to Bob Wills.

"You'll want to talk to Rob about his dad. My father-in-law knew Bob when he was a kid, and he's the family historian. Rob's out back gardening. When I'm done quizzing Tris, I'll show you the way."

She glanced at me and raised her eyebrows. Would I cooperate? A swath of wavy brown hair slipped onto her face and obscured one of her eyes.

I nodded my agreement, happy to appease her. She couldn't have been more cooperative.

"Name the smallest bone in the hand," Sarah requested.

I did.

"What is the fourth smallest moon of Jupiter?"

I told her.

"Now I'm going to ask a couple of chicken questions. Why did the chicken cross the road?" She tossed her head to rearrange her hair. It immediately fell back where it had been a moment earlier.

"I don't have enough data to ascertain that. I don't even know which chicken you mean. I'm sure they have varying motivations for their movements."

"That's great. You're just like on TV. I love it when you trash that smarmy emcee. Here's my last question: which came first—the chicken or the egg?"

"There's no answer to that one, either. Whichever I pick contains its paradoxical counterpart, rendering any answer meaningless."

She clapped her hands. "I love it! And you're only eight, right?"

"Ten."

She turned to Marc. "So you're his dad? No, wait a minute. I saw a picture of Tris's parents on his shirt on TV. Who are you?"

"I'm his therapist. I hope you don't mind, but we're pressed for time, and we really need to talk to your father-in-law."

"No worries. Follow me."

The Sinclairs' backyard was a proper English garden. Someone had worked hard to create and maintain it since none of the plants were native to California, and most preferred far different climes. Wide gravel paths snaked through beds of flowers, shrubs, and dense ground cover. A weathered ceramic gnome missing his nose peeked at me from behind a patch of lavender.

At the far end of the winding gravel path we'd taken to our right, a man in his seventies sat on a wooden bench overlooking a bed of multicolored tulips, seemingly mesmerized by them.

"Has he had a stroke?" Marc whispered to Sarah.

"No, he's prone to spacing out, but I suspect he's meditating right now."

"My dog does that, too," I told her. We were close enough now that Rob heard me.

"Well, that's something new—a dog who meditates. What else can he do? Levitate? Attract a group of followers and fleece them for all they're worth?"

Marc laughed. I stared. I didn't appreciate someone ridiculing me. My reference to spacing out—Mildred's absent seizures—should have been obvious. "I mean she has canine epilepsy," I told him with attitude.

"Rob Sinclair, I presume?" Marc interrupted.

"In the flesh. And you are…?"

Marc introduced us. My name meant nothing to him, which was fine by me.

"What can I do for you?" he asked.

I liked his voice. It projected warmth and integrity. He could've successfully hawked most any product on television. Physically, he brought to mind a slew of grizzled actors in old Westerns. Perhaps he'd play the part of an outraged rancher when sheepherders wanted to fence off his range. Or maybe he'd be a saloon owner trying to stop a gunfight in his establishment. Eventually, I was going to be able to cast an entire film from the people we met.

Rob Sinclair wore a worn blue dress shirt with the button-down collar unbuttoned, tucked into baggy gray sweatpants. What was left of his white hair trailed over the tops of his ears, and one of his blue eyes was cloudy.

"We're on a quest," I told him. "And we need to

know about your father's friendship with Bob Wills because it might help us complete it."

"Interesting. Tell me more."

Sarah strolled back to the house. We sat down on another wrought iron bench not quite facing Rob's. The decorative back hurt quite a bit, so I leaned forward. The air was redolent with floral scents—especially the nearby lavender.

Before Marc could pipe up, I continued speaking. "We're seeking a wisdom book that an ancestor of mine left a letter about. It's been hard to find, but we keep discovering clues."

"Like what?"

"At the Bob Wills museum in Turkey, Texas, we were directed here, for example."

"Directed, huh? Was there a new sign next to the one about my dad that said 'Go see some other old guy in California'?" He smiled, but that didn't soften his words.

Marc spoke up. "I take it you've been there?"

"Sure. Waste of time." He paused and sniffed loudly. "So let me get this straight. You somehow interpreted something you encountered at the museum to mean you should come here, right?"

"Well, yes. But we both came to the same conclusion, and we're not crazy or anything," I said.

"Who says? There's such a thing as a shared delusional disorder, you know."

"*I* say," Marc asserted. "I'm a psychotherapist."

"That doesn't mean anything. I was an attorney, and I was still delusional when I was in a cult in my youth."

"It wasn't the Keepers of Truth, was it?" I asked. I

didn't know if fishing for synchronicities voided their significance, but I felt compelled to ask.

Rob stared at us. "It was. How could you possibly know that? I can't think of a more secretive bunch of crackpots—at least back then. Now I hear it's almost like a business."

Marc answered. "It's a long story, but I'm struck by the fact that you were involved in trying to bring wisdom into the world, too. Perhaps that's why we're here."

Rob pulled on his left earlobe. It was longer than the one on the other side of his head. It probably started out that way. "If I'm going to help, I need to know more. I was a lawyer, and I know when witnesses are holding back. There's a lot more you can tell me."

Marc looked at me, and I looked back and shrugged. "What the hell," he said, and launched into an edited version of our story.

Jake listened attentively, occasionally asking a clarifying question. He didn't laugh, shake his head, or even frown, which was a good sign. Perhaps his background in metaphysical matters helped him accommodate the challenging parts of our narrative.

When Marc was through, the first thing Rob did was turn to me. "So you're adopted?"

"Yes. *That's* your response? I don't even know why Marc told you that."

"You look exactly like my son at your age. And his ex-girlfriend gave up his child without his knowledge. You might be my grandson."

Chapter 14

"Where was this?" I asked, skeptical of such a long odds possibility.

"Ventura. All Judd knew was that the foster parents' name started with an H. I don't remember how he found that out."

"I think we need to test our DNA," I said, tingling all over. "I was raised fifteen minutes from Ventura by a family named Healy. This is amazing!"

"Yes, let's run the test, assuming Judd wants to." He gazed at me evenly. "You're not here to get a share of the Sinclair money, are you?"

"No. I've won hundreds of thousands of dollars on *Who's the Genius*? In the media, they call me the smartest boy in the world."

"Really? That's too bad." He shook his head ruefully.

"Too bad?"

"It's a shame you're a public figure at your age. It's not healthy psychologically. It's also a shame you're not like other kids. You've probably been robbed of a normal childhood. It's more evidence you may be my grandson, though. I was a child prodigy myself. Bridge at four. Chess at five. I finished high school when I was fourteen." He nodded toward Marc. "Then four years of therapy. I was a mess."

"Scrabble at three, chess at four, and I aced the

SATs last year." I paused after listening to myself top him. "Sorry," I added. "It's an old habit. Well, not that old, really. Last week, I was still a showoff who tried to make everyone else feel stupid."

"Instead of regurgitating trivia," Rob asked me, "what would you rather be doing with that brain of yours?"

"You know, I'm not sure."

He nodded, and we were all silent for a few moments. Marc finally turned to me, his eyebrows raised. "Do you remember our chat about how we were going to deal with any new, amazing things that might come our way?"

"I remember everything, but I need a better cue to know what you're talking about."

Marc addressed Rob Sinclair. "Do you mind if we take a moment to confer?"

He waved a hand in the air. "Not at all."

Marc walked me down a path lined with yellow ranunculus and orange Icelandic poppies. Once again I caught whiffs of a stew of various flowers.

"Tris, I'm talking about not blindly accepting synchronicities," Marc explained.

"Oh, I see. Yes, you're right. I became excited by the possibility of meeting my birth father. I lost my focus."

"Why would the Sinclairs be your family? This is an old man's wish to solve a mystery and maybe gain a high-achieving grandson."

"How do we know that? It might be exactly what he says," I protested. "And if Rob is simply mistaken or fabricating this for unknown reasons, how could he know where I'm from? Why would he pick Ventura?"

"You're famous, right? Maybe he recognized you and knows your back story even though he's acting like he didn't. There are any number of possibilities that are more likely than this so-called synchronicity."

"You've hit your limit with absorbing strange events, haven't you?"

"I guess I have," Marc conceded.

"Can we just play this out and see how it goes?"

"Sure."

We walked back to our bench near Rob, Marc leading the way again. When we settled back down, he leaned forward and addressed our host. "Do you mind if I ask a few questions?"

"Go right ahead," Rob replied. "This is much more interesting than watching flowers grow." He sat back and crossed both his arms and his legs, which maintained the original distance between the two men.

"Have you ever heard of Susan Granger?"

"No."

"Any connection to Meriwether Lewis?"

"No."

"What about the Mystery Spot?" Marc tried.

"What about it?"

"Is it significant to you?"

"It was. Not now."

"Can you explain?" Marc asked.

"The Keepers of Truth believe it's holy ground—that something mystical is going on there. That's why they got started in Santa Cruz. So I used to think that, too—way back when. I don't know if that's still on their radar."

"What do you mean by 'something mystical?' " I asked.

"I don't know. That was an inner circle secret, but it must've had something to do with their idea about finding hidden texts. They used to believe that if they read pure wisdom, they'd be transformed into some sort of superbeings. Once again, I don't know what they're up to these days. I do know they're still around, though. I ran into Don Stuttgart up at the Whole Foods last year. We started in the cult together. I gather he's in charge now."

"Maybe we should pay him a visit," Marc suggested. "Is he a dangerous character?"

"Back then, you could knock him over with a hard look. At the store last year, it seemed like he'd grown into himself some." He uncrossed his legs with some effort. Perhaps he was arthritic.

I decided to challenge Rob to see how'd react. "How can everything be connected like this?" I asked. "We've got the Bob Wills thing, the mystery spot, my birth parents, and the Keepers all intersecting in this conversation."

"That's the way it works," he said, recrossing his legs. I think he forgot how hard it was going to be to undo the position. "I learned that much back in my seeker days. Everything really is interconnected. It's just usually better disguised."

"So getting back to our situation, we could head over to the Keepers to find out more?" Marc asked. "You think it's safe?"

"I know Don used to be a pussycat, like I said. Beyond that…" He waved his hand airily.

"When can I meet my dad?" I blurted out.

"Whoa," Rob said. "Let's hold off on declaring that's the case. I know you want to settle this in your mind, but he'll be the one to know if it's really a possibility. Maybe Judd will see something of his former girlfriend in your face. And then there's the DNA test. Why don't you both come back tonight for dinner after my son gets home from work—say, around six? That way you can meet him and we can all get to know each other."

"Okay."

Chapter 15

Marc decided we should scout the Keepers' headquarters next, not committing to any particular action beyond that. While we drove back up to Santa Cruz, I was torn between excitement and skepticism about our conversation with Rob. This manifested as physical tension, especially in my gut. This, in turn, created GI-tract discomfort. A minor headache completed the uncomfortable trifecta.

I'd argued with Marc about the synchronicity issue, but in truth neither of us knew enough to draw a reliable conclusion. If Judd looked like me, that would certainly support Rob's hypothesis. On the other hand, perhaps Judd would quash the notion with new input concerning his past. Unbeknownst to his father, he could already be in touch with his son, for example.

The Keepers' headquarters was as unimpressive from our vantage point across the street as it was online. A one-story fake adobe—coated with stained ochre stucco—it tilted a bit to one side, and the forest green shutters adorning most of its narrow vertical windows hung precariously from rusty hinges. Incongruously, the tidy front yard was perfectly mowed and trimmed.

"So shall we approach these people?" I asked Marc. "Rob said they're harmless, didn't he?"

"Not exactly. I've been thinking about this on the

way here. I know I dismissed your point of view before, but now I believe you're right about the Keepers being the cult who attacked us at the synagogue. The synchronicity with Rob's former membership isn't something we should ignore. And remember my dream—the violent one I didn't go into detail about? It didn't take place here, but it still partially corroborates things." He paused at this point, lost in thought. "If I'm the Keepers, even if I hadn't been involved in any of this, I'd still want any wisdom book I didn't already have. So if the group didn't know about us, we'd be revealing ourselves if we go in there, and then what would they do?"

"I understand. That all makes sense. And if Rob Sinclair's synchronicities aren't real—about my birth father and the Keepers—and we haven't settled that—this could be a hoax to lure us to whoever's in that house. I say we stop talking and get out of here."

"Right."

I had another thought as Marc started the car and peeled out on the street. "We might dream something tonight that tells us what to do."

"True. Let's hope."

In all the excitement, we'd skipped lunch, so we each had a taco at a nearby taqueria to tide us over until dinner at the Sinclairs, and then we strolled along a cliff on the west side of Santa Cruz that Marc had read about. I realized it was Saturday when we had to maneuver around throngs of tourists, some speaking unknown languages. This upset me for two reasons.

One, I'd lost track of what day it was, which piggybacked on top of other recent mental lapses. Was I devolving intellectually? As I developed other parts of myself, would those augmentations come at the expense of cognition?

Secondly, along the same lines, why couldn't I at least identify the languages I was overhearing? That was pathetic; it was something I'd studied extensively when I was eight. The most appealing theory I could muster was that the languages happened to be exotic ones I hadn't studied. Basque? Macedonian? Romani?

Marc began to point out scenery he especially fancied, and I followed his lead and managed to wrest my attention back to the moment. The excursion into my head had been a bit unpleasant, actually.

The wide asphalt path wound its way along the top of limestone cliffs above the bay. In one direction, the Santa Cruz wharf sat in the foreground and the taller rides at the Boardwalk amusement park gleamed beyond that. In the other direction, we eventually reached a dead end at the misnamed Natural Bridges State Park, a picturesque beach with a single rocky arch stretching into the water.

En route, I spied surfers, some of them quite skilled, a plethora of sailboats, and a few fishing boats. Several crowded, shallow beaches hugged the mostly rocky shoreline. By a pint-sized lighthouse, the largest of these must've allowed dogs because dozens of them cavorted with one another, some racing through the surf. I missed Mildred and wondered if she'd like the beach.

The tangy air invigorated me, and the exercise didn't hurt either. Both pulled me more deeply into the moment—a series of moments, really—all of them worthy of my full attention.

****

Back in the AirBnb, I successfully napped before dinner. I don't know what Marc did. I should've asked him when I woke up. I only periodically remembered to express interest in him. I *was* mildly interested; I just needed to demonstrate it more.

Judd Sinclair answered the door at his home in La Selva Beach at six fifteen. Rush-hour traffic heading south on Highway One had been horrid.

He looked at me for a long moment and then said, "You're definitely my son." Then he hugged me much harder than necessary.

I didn't mean to, but I squirmed, so he let me go before he otherwise would've. Being held limited my options. Plus I needed to absorb what he'd said, and the sensations associated with the hug drowned that out.

I studied him. He was quite dissimilar physically from his father—much shorter, among other things—and I saw no resemblance to myself, either. If I hadn't been prompted about Judd's relationship to Rob, I would have never suspected it. Based on visual cues alone, *our* relationship seemed even less likely. But why would anyone pretend to be my father?

Judd wore an extremely unattractive navy-blue suit that fit too tightly across the chest and too loosely in the trousers. A white shirt, a blood red tie, and polished black loafers completed what looked to me to be too formal an outfit for a Realtor. If Rob would've been an Old West rancher, and Theodore—the indigenous man in the diner in Turkey—a tribal chief, Judd would've been a storekeeper. Now I needed a school marm, a town drunk, a marshal, and maybe a few villains. My inner film was unlikely to be fully cast. I was thinking about all this to avoid facing the man in front of me, so

I refocused myself.

Judd Sinclair's square face was short on three-dimensionality. A flat nose, thin lips, and no discernible cheekbones created minimal topography. Bushy black eyebrows were his most prominent feature, sprouting forward and then sweeping up onto the lower part of his forehead. He wore his hair straight back—much as Theodore had—but in Judd's case, it was clear he employed some sort of goop to hold it in place.

At first glance, he seemed to be a nice, ordinary person—light years beyond both my parents in every respect—but not the stuff of an adopted boy's dreams. Perhaps no one could've matched my childish expectations of...I don't even know what. Maybe just gravitas of some sort. My birth father ought to be *significant*.

His wife Sarah hadn't cared when we'd been to their home before, but Judd asked us to remove our shoes. "It's new carpeting," he told us. "My dad has suddenly gotten fussy about it."

"Sure."

Since we were late, Judd herded us into a formal dining room I hadn't noticed on our earlier visit. We traversed a not-new-looking taupe Berber carpet in our stocking feet. The light yellow walls of the dining room were covered in amateurish tapestries depicting Hawaiian scenes—surfers, volcanoes, and a majestic waterfall.

Sarah was nowhere to be seen. Rob sat at the head of the oval walnut table, a mostly full glass of white wine in his hand. He wore the same blue dress shirt he'd had on that afternoon. He'd combed his wispy white hair, and it looked like he'd shaved, too.

"Let me guess," Marc said, turning to Judd and gesturing at the nearest wall. "Your daughter is a fabric artist. These are her weavings."

"That's right!" he said. "Aren't they wonderful?"

I stepped closer to see how the tapestries had been made. Apparently, the artist wove in colored threads in some clever way so the desired images created a smooth surface. A tiny signature in a corner of one of the weavings caught my eye, and I leaned in to look just as Sarah emerged from the kitchen holding a platter of food. *Elliot Sinclair*. Not for the first time, I wondered why people gave their daughters male names.

As Sarah emerged from the kitchen, she called a cheery greeting and told us to sit. She'd dressed up for the occasion with a red pant suit and a pearl necklace with matching stud earrings. I hadn't seen pearls in years. They weren't an Ojai sort of accessory. Her cheeks were rouged to an unnatural degree—perhaps to cover the plethora of freckles that nonetheless peeked out from around her makeup. Her shiny lipstick matched her dress, and burgundy high heels completed her outfit. All in all, she had taken the modicum of good looks she'd displayed at our first meeting and obscured them. I've never been a fan of makeup or jewelry.

Our meal was awkward at times. Sarah turned out to be a rather poor cook who insisted on regular feedback about each stage of her meal. I resorted to murmuring incomprehensibly. Marc lied.

All three Sinclairs regaled us with stories about their family that sometimes lacked consistency from one speaker to the next. I guess that was normal—not that I had much personal experience with normal family mores.

Unfortunately, none of the information they shared proved to be useful to us in terms of our quest. Rob was relatively quiet, allowing room for his son and daughter-in-law to connect with me. As Judd provided me with more details that supported my being his long-lost son, my disappointment mounted. My first impression had been quite accurate; he was alarmingly ordinary. Nonetheless, I toyed with the idea of moving to La Selva Beach when I was old enough to emancipate myself. I could adopt Rob as my surrogate father. *He'd* been confident, bright, and articulate earlier that day—he could better appreciate me.

No one brought up the DNA test, so I didn't either. I wasn't in a rush to settle the matter now that I'd met Judd. All in all, I walked away from the evening with anticlimax ruling my mood.

Marc felt the same. "Lots of talk," he commented, "and very little substance. Disappointing, wasn't it?"

"Yes. Now that I think of it, it was almost as if they'd decided ahead of time to block in-depth contact. You tried several times—that question about Judd's childhood ambitions, for example. All you got back was an anecdote about being forced to eat Brussels sprouts. Rob could've exhibited the kind of philosophical depth he'd displayed this afternoon, but he didn't. Why do you think none of that happened?"

"I have no idea."

Chapter 16

That night, I dreamt I was sitting on a beach watching diminutive birds with long stick-legs skitter along the waterline. A line of pelicans soared overhead, and one veered away from its brethren toward me. A diaper or something along those lines was suspended from its mouth—like a proverbial stork delivering a baby. As the bird neared me, it dipped its head and released a wrapped package which tumbled down onto the sand next to me. It should've buried itself, but instead it sat flat, unscathed. The wrapping paper was bright orange with purple script declaring "Happy Christening." I reached out and opened the package, discovering a framed diploma from the "University of Wisdom Book Location." The conferred degree was "Master of Mystery Spots," earned at the "Under the Log-Shaped-Like-a-Flashlight" campus. Where my name would've been written was a row of emoji-stick figures holding shovels. The diploma was signed by "The Entire Millennial Faculty." At the bottom left corner of the document was an X in a circle.

There was absolutely no question about the meaning of this one. After a quick breakfast at the same place as the day before, we headed to a cavernous Home Depot, where we eventually found a long-handled spade. On the way to the registers, I spied a small white dog in the arms of a man standing beside a boy about my age. Despite my sense of urgency, I detoured to the threesome. Marc continued to the front of the store.

"What a cute pup," I said as I drew close, employing my ordinary-boy voice. Close up, I could see that Mildred was much cuter than this one. But they smelled the same.

"His name is Barkie," the boy told me with no evidence of the embarrassment such a name ought to engender.

Barkie's blunt snout resulted in a permanent false smile at the corners of his generous mouth. He turned his head toward me; his eyes were unfocused and unmoving.

"He's blind," the man told me matter-of-factly.

"Oh." I didn't know what to say to that. "I'm sorry," I tried.

"It's okay," the boy said. "We make him happy, anyway."

This kid embodied a markedly positive attitude. I surveyed him as if visual cues might help me understand how he managed that. His skinny frame and narrow face struck me as unusual but provided no clue to his personality. By the time I'd taken in his ordinary clothing—jeans and a logoed T-shirt—and his regular features, only marred by an inch-long scar on his brow, I realized the folly of my effort and returned my attention to his dog.

They let me pet Barkie, who was startled at first by my touch, but then relaxed and enjoyed himself. He felt a lot like Mildred before we'd buzzed her fur off. She'd been softer, though.

I strode away from Barkie and his people to rejoin

Marc, and by the time I found him at the head of a line, I'd wiped my tears away.

We arrived at the Mystery Spot an hour ahead of when it opened. Marc parked up a dirt side road beside a partially oxidized metal gate that led to the charred remains of someone's home.

Light rain fell on us as we walked to our destination. Neither of us had packed any rain gear with us, and a chill seized me after only a few steps. My cotton sweater wasn't up to the challenge of the temperature, let alone the moisture. Even in June, early mornings in Santa Cruz are quite cool.

The fence that looked to be an effective barrier near the front gate of the Spot proved easy to breach once we'd walked around the property's perimeter to a neglected area of the redwood forest behind the vortex.

A strong evergreen scent greeted us as we trod on slippery fallen redwood needles and avoided tripping on the massive roots of the soaring trees. A thrill ran up my spine. The explicit nature of my dream hinted at the end of our quest.

Finding the right downed tree proved to be a simple matter. Lying in the middle of the main ring of redwoods next to the path we'd negotiated the day before, it did, in fact, resemble a giant, old-fashioned flashlight. A ball of withered roots formed the lens housing, and the portion of the trunk that remained constituted the body.

Then we hit a major glitch. The log must've weighed hundreds of pounds, which rendered it secure cover for the buried book. When we tried to roll it to the side, our shoes kept slipping out from under us, and we couldn't even rock it. I should've anticipated this.

Once again, my mental failing spawned keen disappointment.

"What should we do?" I asked Marc, rubbing my hands together. By now, I was a lot colder and wetter.

"Maybe the shovel would give us more leverage," he suggested. "And take a look for a sturdy branch. With both of us on the uphill side using those, maybe we can lever it loose."

Someone had worked at keeping the visible parts of the site tidy. I had to backtrack to where we'd entered the property to find a downed, splintery fence post. It was only a bit shorter than I was.

"Let me take that," Marc suggested when I'd wrestled the post back to where we hoped to find the book.

He handed me the spade, and I dug its point under the log. With a bit of wriggling, I was able to insert most of the metal head under the trunk. Marc had to hunt for an irregularity that created enough space to shove the fence post under, but eventually he found one at the far end from where I stood.

"You ready?" he called. I nodded. "One, two, three…"

I jumped up onto the end of the shovel's handle, and I could hear Marc grunting. A moment later, the log began to shift. A moment after that, it suddenly broke loose from the ground and rolled down the hill.

"Uh-oh."

The weight and friction of the tangled root ball steered the log on a diagonal, and I feared it might crash into the gift shop below. Before it could gather too much momentum, though, the trunk caught on a massive exposed root, rocked back and forth, and then settled.

"That was close," Marc said, gasping from his exertion.

I was already on my knees, scrabbling in the rotted, insect-ridden ground that had lain under the log. My revulsion was suppressed by the urgency that directed my hands. Marc squatted next to me and shoved debris to the side.

A few minutes later, about four feet to the side of where I'd started searching, I uncovered a flat gray rock with a red X painted on it.

"We're almost there!" Marc cried. He scrambled to retrieve the spade while I horsed the rock to the side. Then he began digging furiously. I watched and tried to tame the butterflies in my stomach that were threatening to engulf my body.

When the spade clanged against something solid, a rush of energy surged from my gut up to my head. My hands shook. We were so close now.

It was only another rock. I managed to lift it out of the shallow hole Marc had created.

We hit pay dirt two feet deeper, signaled by a dull clunk. I reached down, extending my arm as far as I could. "I can't quite get to it. Use your longer arms!"

I rolled to the side, and Marc crouched down. A moment later, he retrieved a package wrapped in filthy white plastic.

"It's about the right size," he reported as he tucked it under his arm and stood.

He handed the bundle to me. It was heavier than I expected. Then Marc picked up the shovel again.

"We ought to fill the hole back in before we go. With any luck, they'll just think the tree rolled down on its own."

"The heck with that! Let's open the package!" I trumpeted.

Before we could do either one, we heard a car door slam. A moment later, the first Mystery Spot employee heralded her arrival at the front gate below us by singing an inane pop tune out of key.

We scampered back the way we came, heedless of the steep uneven ground now. I carried the box, and Marc held the shovel for most of the way, jettisoning it into a thicket just before we arrived back at the road.

We piled into the car. With no rhyme or reason, I tore futilely at the plastic encasing the book on my lap. Seeing I was getting nowhere, Marc reached over and took the package from me. "Let's look it over and see if there's an easier way."

Sure enough, the book—I hoped—was inside two sturdy plastic bags, sealed at the top with worn duct tape, which Marc peeled off.

"Open it! Open it!" I felt like the kid I never was on Christmas morning.

He pulled out a sea green and copper swirl of color and handed it to me. "You have the honors, Tris."

I'd never seen anything quite like it. The tarnished copper box appeared to be formed from one continuous sheet of aged, soft metal. The body of the box was rounded on the corners and sides. It was about four inches high and a foot long. A striking parade of bas-relief faces snaked around the sides. The cover depicted a young man's face.

"I think that's you," Marc said softly.

I was beyond words. It did look like me, big ears and all. I found an elaborate catch on the side of the cover and lifted it. Inside lay a shallower eight-and-a-half by eleven-inch paper box. I tore off the yellowed cover.

Underneath shredded newspaper lay no more than fifty or sixty similarly yellowed pages. The title page of the manuscript had been typed on an old-fashioned typewriter.

How Things Are
by It Doesn't Matter Who

Underneath that, someone had handwritten in red ink: *Remember, Tris, DO NOT read the book yet! When it's time, you'll know.*

I'd forgotten about that instruction, and seeing the note made my gut tighten. My excitement morphed into an even stronger feeling I recognized as anger.

After all we'd been through, I was to be denied the satisfaction of reading what was in the book? What was so problematic about wisdom? I was confident I could handle any written words. My recent ability to assimilate all the drama that had come our way proved that. Why didn't Susan Granger trust me?

"You could read it and synopsize it for me," I said to Marc as we sat and stared at one another.

"I'm not going to read it, either."

"Aw, come on." I was a typical kid for a moment, pleading with his mom for candy or a new toy.

"Nope."

I continued to cajole, but I couldn't budge him. "So what do we do now?" I asked.

"I guess we head back to Texas and give the book to Suzanne Granger—unless you have another idea about how to publish it?"

"We can get Mildred back while we're there?"

"Of course."

"All right."

A man suddenly appeared at the driver's side window. He held a pistol. "Out of the car!" he barked.

My heart pounded, and my ragged breath burned. I started shaking all over. The man's face became so detailed, it was as though it had been etched into the air. Yet I could hardly remember later what he looked like in that moment. My mind just wasn't registering the hyper-focused experience.

Another man, this one unarmed, yanked my car door open, which terrified me further. He was extremely ugly, with piggy eyes and a cruel, downturned mouth. He wore coveralls with the name of a moving company on them. Also, he was fat and smelled of alcohol. This was not a spiritual seeker.

"Out!" he called gruffly. "And bring that box."

I clambered out and proffered my prize to the man. He grabbed it, tucked into under his meaty arm, and gestured for me to walk around the car to where Marc now stood in front the gun-wielding thug. This man was extremely skinny and unhealthy-looking, with pale skin and a shaved head. He wore black from head to toe and dark glasses, despite the overcast sky.

"Put your hands on your heads," he instructed in an eerie-sounding falsetto. As I followed orders, I moved closer to Marc. My knees shook, and I held back the urge to vomit. Marc moved away from me. *Thanks. Thanks a lot.*

"If you try to follow us or get the book back," the gunman squeaked, "I'll find Tris and shoot him in the head."

I moaned. I was out of control with terror now. My mind—my trusty protector—failed to step in to ameliorate the horrendous experience. I peed my pants. The urine warmed my thighs.

"Can we at least take a peek before you take off?" Marc asked. "I can use a little more wisdom." He lowered his hands to gesture at the book.

"Hell, no. Only the Senior Guides are evolved enough to understand it."

"Wait a minute," I said, regaining my poise for a moment. "Guides, huh? You're not from the Keepers Of Truth?"

He snorted. "Those idiots? Of course not."

"But we *do* have a spy in the Keepers," the other thug blurted out.

"Shut up!" the one with the gun said, using his natural voice, which was low and guttural.

"Then you're working for the Radiant Librarians, aren't you?" I said. I remembered that their leaders were called guides.

His eyes widened. "How do you know that? Who told you that?"

He was fully distracted now. Marc snapped a kick into his wrist, and the gun flew into a nearby bush. He followed up with another kick to the man's midsection. When our assailant bent over in pain, Marc punched him in the temple. He collapsed and stayed down.

Marc and I both turned and looked at the second, unarmed man. He placed the book on the ground in front of him, held up his chubby hands, and backed away. "I don't want any trouble. I was just doing what I was told."

Marc stared at him for a moment and then took an aggressive step in his direction. The man turned and barreled away.

"Let's get out of here," Marc said, and we did.

Chapter 17

Marc was nice about my peeing my pants. He pretended he didn't notice, even though when we climbed back in the car after hurriedly packing up to return to Texas, I discovered he'd toweled off the passenger seat. I'd jammed my wet pants behind the toilet in our AirBnB after I'd showered and changed clothes, hoping to avoid the shame of being exposed as a coward.

I was still shaking, the copper box jostling on my lap, as we drove over the mountains to the San Jose airport. I didn't know I could feel as scared as I had back at the Mystery Spot. Would other feelings blast me like that some day? Had I only experienced attenuated emotions thus far? If I was ever as angry as I'd been scared, what might happen?

"Adrenaline takes a long time to leave your system," Marc told me.

"I know."

"You did fine back there." I didn't say anything. "Do you want to talk about it?"

"What is there to say?" I asked.

"Let's find out."

I considered his invitation. I had nothing I was ready to share yet, but I also needed to change gears mentally. Ruminating was only going to make things worse. I came up with a strategy I was proud of. "Tell me what it was like for you."

He shot me a sideways glance as he pulled into the fast lane on Highway 17 to pass a tanker truck. The road was less busy than when we'd arrived, but now there was more commercial traffic.

"Okay. I was terrified. That was probably the scariest thing I've ever experienced. And I didn't know if I should just let them take the book or try to stop them. I was concerned you might get hurt if I tried to take that guy out and failed, so I just decided to play it by ear and see if an opening showed up. What you said about the Librarians was brilliant. That's what gave me my chance. I'm proud of you."

His compliment bounced off me. "Where's *your* adrenaline response?" I asked. "You haven't been shaking or anything."

"That's the advantage of life experience. My adrenals don't fire up the same way they used to. But believe me, I was a mess inside. Those men were like movie bad guys—they looked the part, and they acted the part. I'm sure the meth addict with the gun would've used it if he felt he had to."

"How are you feeling now?" I asked.

He half smiled before he answered, eyes locked on the road. "Okay. Not great. I'm more worried now that I know truly dangerous people want the book. What kind of spiritual organization acts like that?"

"Clearly, they're not spiritual. Maybe they started that way and they changed."

"Those two might be independent contractors," Marc said. "Guys the Librarians hired."

"Contractors? You make it sound like they're home remodelers."

"Sorry. I mean they might not be representative of Librarian membership."

"I sure hope not." I turned to face him all the way. There was something I'd been waiting to ask. "Why didn't you call the police, Marc? You said back in Texas you're worried about my safety. Wouldn't that have been the best way to ensure it?"

Marc braked hard as we came around a curve and discovered a dump truck laboring up a hill. "We trespassed today and stole something valuable from whoever owns the Mystery Spot," he said, watching the rearview mirror for his opportunity to pass. "The box alone must be worth a great deal. I think it was made a few centuries ago. And calling the cops would mean we'd lose the book, Tris. Perhaps I shouldn't have decided what to do on my own, but you weren't in good shape at that point."

"But isn't contacting the authorities the right thing to do?" I could hear my voice rising in pitch. "These men might come after us again, and even if they don't, they could hurt other people if they aren't locked up. Besides, we don't have to acknowledge there's a book or that we were trespassing to report what happened, do we?"

"They'd find out we were on the property easily enough if they place us on the road nearby. We left a hole in the ground and moved a log, didn't we? And if they catch the men who attacked us, what's to stop them from telling the police about the box?" Marc slowed down again to keep from ramming into a van that cut us off. Then he continued. "It's true the world would be a better place without these thugs in it, and they may try something else before we can hand off the book. We've got that on the one hand for sure. The main reason I didn't call 911, though, is the responsibility I have to your parents—and to you. I'm not going to precipitate you being locked up."

"They don't lock up ten-year-olds."

"Well, whatever they do, it could ruin your future, and it would certainly kill our chances of getting the book out into the world. Anyway, I think it's too late to call anyone now. Those creeps are long gone."

"How about we talk it over if something like that ever happens again, even if I'm a wreck."

"It's a deal."

I watched cars go by for a while. "There's something else I don't understand," I said as we started our descent into the Santa Clara Valley.

"I wasn't sure I'd ever hear you say you don't understand something."

"Be that as it may, here's my question. You subdued that man with the gun. How could you do that if you were as scared as you say?"

"A healthy dose of adrenaline actually helps in a situation like that. Fight or flight—it's an immediate aid to either one. And I've been so well-trained that my body knows what to do once I set it loose."

"But even so, why didn't your fear hold you back?" I asked. "That's what I want to know."

"In a nutshell, bravery is doing hard things when you're scared. If you don't mind my patting myself on the back, I was brave."

"The way you fight, patting yourself on the back might fracture a few vertebrae."

He turned and grinned. "Good one, Tris."

Later, while we waited for our flight at the San

Jose airport, sitting among a boy scout troop and several unsavory-looking scoutmasters, I reported the sequence of emotions I'd endured back by the Mystery Spot. I still shook slightly, and just talking about what had happened was harrowing. I wondered if I'd develop post-traumatic stress disorder. "Were these feelings appropriate?" I finally finished.

"Absolutely. Like I said, I shared them. And I want to say this again. I'm proud of you, Tris. You were terrified, and you still found a way to speak up and distract that gunman. That's beyond what most people could've managed, and I mean adults, too. That's bravery."

"Thank you."

Marc had proposed that we travel to Turkey, Texas, first, where we could be reunited with Mildred, if only for a visit. He thought whoever was still after the book might have the Austin airport staked out for a while. I couldn't find a way to convince him to commit to bringing Mildred to Austin with us in yet another rental car, but I was still hoping we would.

The flights to Dallas and Lubbock were bad enough, but the drive to Turkey was much more boring than our recent trip in the other direction. The radio was virtually inaudible in the car we received, and something smelled like old socks. The scenery was only novel in the sense that I viewed the same things as last time from the other side of the road. I spent the hours reviewing recent events, sorting out their meaning as best I could. I carried the book wrapped in a couple of shirts in my bag, which I never let out of my sight.

When we acquired phone reception as we passed through a small town, I called Ophelia to let her know we were coming. She was as irascible as ever.

"Who is this?"

"Tris Healy. You have my Mildred."

"Of course I do. I'm not senile, Sonny Boy, am I? I know whose dog I have."

"No, ma'am."

"No, I don't know whose dog it is? Is that what you're saying?"

"No, I meant I know you're far from senile."

"Hmph." Something distracted her, and I could hear her put down the phone and wander off. In about a minute, she returned. "So why are you bothering me with this call? We're doing just fine here."

"Oh, I'm sure. I'm not checking up on you. I just wanted to let you know we'll be there in an hour or so."

"Is that right? What makes you think you can waltz in here without going on the interweb and signing up for my room like everybody else? How do you even know it's empty right now?"

"Is it?"

"Maybe."

"Why are you so mean to me? What did I ever do to you?" I was surprised by what came out of my mouth. I'd never said anything like this before.

Ophelia paused, and I could hear her breathing. "Lordy, Tris, I don't know. I just hurt a lot. I try to live like the church says. I try hard."

"It's okay. I understand. So is it okay if we come? We just flew 1,438 miles to see Mildred—and you too, of course."

"You head on over, honey. I should be pure sugar to you for bringing that sweet little dog into my life."

"Okay. See you soon."

Marc called Suzanne to work out a safe hand-off protocol once we arrived in Austin. She was known to our original assailants, which created risk. For that matter, someone seemed to have kept track of *us* in disconcerting fashion, too. They'd even known about our surreptitious visit to the Mystery Spot. Would physical danger rear its head again in Austin?

Marc and Suzanne worked out a scheme in which she would meet us at a downtown bank, where she'd read the book in plain sight of the security guard. Then we'd place it in a safety deposit box. After that, it was up to her to get it published.

In Turkey, we once again parked in front of the hardware store below Ophelia's apartment. It was about eight in the evening now. A streetlight illuminated a sad-looking old man emerging from the store's doorway, next to a display window of dusty garden tools. He clutched a battered clipboard as though it were a first edition of James Joyce.

Ophelia came to the door with Mildred in her wrinkled arms and let us in. We stood in Ophelia's living room, our luggage at our feet. Marc was to my right. Ophelia stood across from me, barely taller than I was. The weak streetlight trickled through partially closed wonky Venetian blinds, striping her long red skirt on long angles. And a commercial on the radio in the kitchen told us that we could expect to find the best hog feed in the area at Ben's Farm Supply.

I'll never forget that moment. I wish I could. The constellation of upcoming emotions anchored it somewhere in my hippocampus.

I reached for Mildred, and she hesitated to leave Ophelia's arms and venture into mine. When she finally did, her tail failed to wag, and she cried. *She cried.*

Marc spoke up. "Severe seizures erase memory," he told me.

A rational explanation for the phenomenon did little to alleviate my emotions, which in fact escalated. I hurt—a palpable pain in my chest. And then sadness reigned—a heavy weight on my shoulders and a sinking sensation in my midsection.

I handed Mildred back to Ophelia, who gingerly placed her on the threadbare beige carpet. My first love promptly collapsed and fell asleep. I stumbled to the overstuffed brown couch and fell onto it.

Marc spoke up. "I think Tris and I need to talk, Ophelia. Would you mind?"

"What do you mean 'would I mind?' You ain't gonna throw me out of my own home, dammit!"

"No, no. We can be in our room or our car if you prefer. We're your guests here, aren't we?"

"Hmph." She shuffled into the kitchen. Mildred woke up and followed her.

Marc sat down on the couch with me. I couldn't look at him. I buried my face in my hands and began to cry. He pulled me to him, his arm around my shoulder, and I sobbed into his chest.

For how long, I have no idea. The anguish swept me into a novel realm, one with no timekeeper, no witness to my experience, no mind. I guess the roots of my pain were more deep-seated than Mildred's indifference. I'd weathered a series of intense events with little time to process all the feelings these spawned—other than the imperative fear that had seized me earlier that day. When I'd had opportunities to address the emotional backlog, I'd squandered them on mental activities. Even having my own personal therapist by my side hadn't motivated me to fully face my feelings. It took the heartbreak of my so-called reunion with my so-called dog to burst the dam and let the intense emotions loose.

When I recovered and entered the kitchen, I approached Mildred to retest the waters of our attachment. She cried for Ophelia again when I tried to hold her. Our hostess bustled over from the counter and picked her up again.

"Don't pay her no mind, Tris. She goes away sometimes and when she comes back, she don't know who I am either. If I didn't know better, I'd think she was a blackout drunk like my cousin Exodus. Lordy, that man could miss three days in a row and then wonder why he was sittin' in the pokey again."

I gazed at her, no words available, and more tears trickled out. These were for poor cousin Exodus. Very strange.

We decided not to spend the night. It was too painful. Every time I looked at Mildred, I started to cry again. No one spoke about a permanent disposition of her ownership, least of all me. I tried not to think about her as we ate Ophelia's berry pie before we left. My bruised heart simply wasn't up to speaking its truth yet.

As Marc and I reached our car outside Ophelia's to begin our long drive to Austin, Theodore approached us. The older indigenous man wore a perfectly tailored charcoal suit and a straw cowboy hat.

"I sensed you were back in town," he said. "We need to talk."

Marc looked at me and raised an eyebrow. It was up to me.

"Sure," I said. "I could use a distraction."

We leaned against the hood of our rental, and Theodore did the same against the tailgate of a shiny black pickup truck parked just ahead of us. I worried that he'd dirty the backside of his suit pants. His broad, lined face was placid, and his body posture was totally relaxed. His eyes were absolutely present. It was uncanny. I upgraded him from an Indian chief in my imaginary film to a medicine man. The notion afforded me my own distraction.

"You need to leave the dog here," he told me. "It's best for everyone."

"So much for a distraction," I muttered before shifting into a scathing tone. "Did you *sense* that, too?"

"No, it's obvious from simple observation. Your role in Mildred's life was to deliver her to Ophelia. They're a perfect match. Now your role is to let go. I'll tell Ophelia she can keep her."

"Oh, I suppose you know everyone's role," I mocked. "And you think you can just step in and tell her that? Who do you think you are? What right do you have to say that?" It felt good to jump into anger, however displaced it might be. I couldn't very well yell at Mildred, could I?

"You know what I'm saying is true. Anyway, I have something more important to tell you."

"What's that?" Marc asked.

"You think your mission is almost over. It isn't. Things are not the way they seem to be."

"Why do you say that?" I asked.

"I can't say more."

"Can't or won't?" I said. "How does a cryptic pronouncement like that help us?"

He crossed his arms and leaned back farther. "We don't interfere any more than we need to."

"*We?*" Marc and I said in unison.

"We're an assemblage of shamans. We track spirit-related activity and help the universe fulfill its purposes." Theodore stated this as if it were a grocery list.

"Which are?" I asked.

He shook his head slowly.

"So meeting you at breakfast wasn't an accident?" Marc asked.

"There are no accidents. You of all people should know that."

"How do we know you're a real shaman?" I asked.

He smiled. His teeth were a bit yellow, but straight. "Here's some turnabout, Tris. Test me."

"All right. Fine." I paused and puzzled out an appropriate question—something no ordinary man could know. "What happened to me when I was lost in Manhattan when I was four?"

He closed his dark eyes and tilted his head up to the darkening sky. "A woman asked if you if you needed help," he intoned. "You said no even though you were scared because you were also stubborn. You backtracked until you found your father. The woman followed you and told off your father. You liked that. Later, your dad punished you in some way you didn't mind." He smiled again, more broadly this time as he lowered his head, opening his eyes to watch me.

I was speechless. For some reason, Theodore's feat struck me as the most fantastic element out of everything I'd endured. A bunch of mind-reading shamans working behind the scenes to help the universe? Really? And apparently these weren't crackpots or villains. Theodore stood right there in front of us. The experience was personal—immediate—undeniable.

"You asked for it," he said. "Perhaps next time, you'll be more willing to accept not knowing something."

"That's not his strength," Marc said. "Do you know my teacher—Peter Elkin?"

"Yes, he is one of us. He has spoken to me about you." He reached into the back pocket of his ironed jeans and handed Marc a card. "Call me when you need to. That won't be soon, but don't hesitate when it's time. Now I must go. As I said, Tris, I will talk to Ophelia."

"Are you saving the universe on the other side of town tonight?" I asked, still irritated despite my growing awe. I had a million questions, and he was rushing off—more grounds for displaced feelings.

"No, I'm babysitting my granddaughter. Have a good trip."

Chapter 18

We checked into a Holiday Inn late that night on the outskirts of Austin. I slipped from a dazed state—it was way past my bedtime and I was emotionally exhausted—into merciful sleep. I awakened somewhat refreshed. As I pondered recent events, I remembered what Marc had said about awareness being like a benign Pandora's box. Would I always be cognizant of feelings now as I moved through the world? The notion scared me. I wouldn't have even noticed *that* twenty-four hours earlier.

At a too brightly lit coffee shop, facing a plate of canary-yellow scrambled eggs and mushy hash browns, I remained silent while I sorted out my thoughts on this subject. Marc sensed my need for space and emailed on his phone.

"Let's take a walk," he suggested as we emerged onto the sidewalk outside the restaurant. The sun glared at us, reflecting off a nearby car windshield, and when we strode toward a residential street to our right, a FedEx truck nearly hit us as it turned into the restaurant's parking lot.

"So what's on your mind?" Marc asked after a few blocks of nearly identical one-story homes. Their only distinguishing features were the paint colors and the style of the front doors.

I told him I was scared of future feelings. I was aware I was avoiding my grief and happy I could at this point. Since I'd never specifically forbidden Theodore to tell Ophelia I wasn't coming back for Mildred, I had no doubt he had. My dog was gone.

We passed a man with a chubby Airedale, whose snout was buried in a gopher hole beside the sidewalk. "It takes patience to walk the king of terriers," the man told us with a broad accent. His haircut resembled his dog's bushy brown fur. The poor thing had apparently never been shorn or perhaps even brushed. The morning heat wasn't uncomfortable yet, but who wouldn't provide a dog relief from the Texas climate?

"I don't doubt it," I responded. "Royals usually have entitlement issues." I stopped for a moment and added, "You're lucky you get to have a dog. Why not take care of her properly and trim her fur?"

"He's a he, and mind your own damned business, kid."

Marc grabbed my shoulder and pulled me away. We silently strolled a bit farther beside a series of strip malls. After a half mile or so, passing through another neighborhood, this one comprised of upscale two-story brick houses, we circled back, showered, and changed clothes. Then we drove to downtown Austin. I held the box on my lap.

I was struck by the pattern of the patina that covered about a third of the antique copper. On the top of the box, it obscured parts of the bas-relief of my face—my chin and one of my ears. Beside the portrait, the sea green patina formed an array of continents, with the underlying copper color serving as oceans. On the sides, patina dripped onto the carved faces, superimposing various weird hairstyles onto them. I gathered these people were past lives of mine, and I took a few minutes to study them.

They were evenly distributed by gender and age. I'd never seen a photograph of Susan Granger, but I guessed which one was her from the location of the bas-relief and how it matched the expression I would've expected to find on her face. The artist had captured a nobility—something beyond ordinary integrity and kindness. I wished I'd been *her* son.

I glanced up as we approached downtown, an array of new towers and old stone and brick buildings housing stores and offices. The city looked to be thriving.

Parking in a new concrete parking structure proved to be no problem, and neither was finding the prearranged rendezvous—the First National Bank of Austin—which stood beside an old, rather majestic hotel built of decorative limestone. The bank itself was a sturdy brick building that must've harkened from a similar era.

When we met Suzanne in the capacious lobby, she hugged me almost as fiercely as Judd Sinclair had back in California. I didn't feel this was appropriate, based on our brief, fractious acquaintanceship. She merely nodded to Marc.

I stepped back and studied her for a moment. Would I see her differently now—after all I'd been through? She wore a white tunic over black slacks. Her hair was redder—less orange—than I remembered, and shorter as well. I could see she was nervous. She squinted more than she needed to, given the intensity of the ambient light. And her shoulders hunched. When she told us she'd been thinking about the best way to proceed since she'd spoken to Marc on the phone, the words tumbled speedily out of her.

"I'll use my phone to photograph each page and then send them to multiple email addresses," she told us. "Then I'll erase the photos from my phone. It's better to be safe than sorry. We'll put the book itself in a safety deposit box like we planned."

"Good idea," Marc said. "Can you do all that in the bank? Do you think they'll let us use some desk space here to take photos since we're renting a box?"

"Let's find out."

We had to wait a few minutes to ask someone in a position of authority, so I glanced around the bank lobby, picturing a robbery movie to take my mind off my inability to read the book I held. The extremely high, decorative ceiling would either amplify or muffle gunshots. I decided on amplify because the stamped tin panels were reflective. If anyone were conked on the head, the white marble flooring would make falling quite painful. Likewise, if customers and employees were forced to sit on the hard surface, their behinds would start to hurt in short order.

A young security guard with a patchy, fledgling blond beard stood by the front door. He was armed, but he didn't look like the kind of person who'd risk his life. I pictured him placing his pistol on the ground in front of him, kicking it to the robbers, and then slowly lying down. Maybe he'd tell them he had a wife and two small children, although he looked too young for that. I could see him lying to try to save himself.

Eventually, a black-suited assistant manager obliged our request. I think he may have recognized me, although he didn't say anything. People treated me differently—breaking their own rules, for example—simply because I was unusually intelligent. Were Peace

Corps volunteers, hospice workers, and other humanitarians granted similar favors? I always thought I deserved preferential treatment more than they did. Now I didn't.

The assistant manager, a slim Mexican American man in his late fifties, walked us all through a door beside the row of teller's stations and set up Suzanne at a vacant desk in what was the loan department. Just before he departed, he introduced us to Lisa, a nearby officer who was inexplicably wearing a tiara.

"I'm the employee of the month, so I have to wear this stupid thing all day," she told us.

"Do the men have to wear one too?" I asked.

"I'd like to see that! No, they get a gift certificate. That's banking for you. It's still a boys' club."

Marc and I returned to the lobby, where Suzanne would join us when she was finished. He said we'd distract bank employees if we hovered near Suzanne, but I believed it was actually so I couldn't peek at the book while she was reading and photographing it.

"Don't you trust me?" I complained to Marc when we sat down on a quite uncomfortable white marble bench near the front door.

"Trust the lord, and tie up your camel."

"What?"

"Why take a chance? A page of the book might waft over to you on a wayward breeze and position itself in front of your face. You never know."

"I'm serious."

"I'm not."

After a while, I spoke up again. "Can we go for another walk? I'm tired of sitting here, and Suzanne is bound to be a while. Let's go see Austin."

"Sure. The state capitol is right up the street. Did you know they built their dome four feet higher than the national one? It's all pink granite. Have you ever seen pink granite? I haven't."

I sighed. "I'll go, but only if you stop playing tour guide. I *did* know all that, as a matter of fact."

Congress Avenue was even more of a mix of old and new than downtown in general. I definitely preferred the old. We saw a hat and boot store, three jewelry stores, and an upscale chain department store on the way to the seat of the state government. None of them were open yet. We didn't talk.

Neither of us felt an urge to go into any of the state buildings, as impressive as they were from the outside, so we skirted them and strode farther up the hill to the University of Texas campus. There must've been a break between classes because the sidewalks between buildings teemed with hurried students.

As we pivoted to start back, Marc told me he needed to check in on his practice back in Ojai, so he asked me to trail him while he spoke on the phone. "I'll probably need to discuss specific clients this time—you understand."

"I do."

He took a left and then another left, heading south alongside the school on Guadalupe Street, where most stores sold university branded apparel and the restaurants were geared for the campus demographic. Based on the frequency of establishments, University of Texas students favored pizza, Mexican, and Thai food in that order.

After several blocks, Marc turned around and joined me. "Sorry. That took longer than I expected.

My colleague is having trouble talking one of my clients out of punching his boss. Let's hustle. Suzanne will be waiting for us when we get back."

"Sure."

We retraced our steps and resumed our seats on the bench by the front doors. There was no sign of Suzanne. Perhaps she was a slow reader—a major drawback for a literary agent. The security guard eyeballed us from about twenty feet away.

"We're still waiting for someone in the loan department," Marc called to him.

The guard nodded.

I watched the bank's customers. No one wore cowboy boots or hats. Maybe people with money eschewed Texas traditions. Eventually, I browsed the news on my phone. Marc engrossed himself in some sort of phone activity as well.

Suzanne never returned.

The woman with the tiara told us she'd hurriedly departed with the box under her arm after she'd received a phone call.

Chapter 19

Whoever the woman was, she wasn't Suzanne Granger.

We discovered this when we tried to contact her. Her phone number was no longer in service. When we drove to the address in a neighboring town she had told us was her cousin's house, it turned out to be an abandoned pottery factory.

I frantically researched her name, eventually finding the real Suzanne Granger living down in San Marcos, not far from the library. Marc called her from our hotel room and put her on speaker.

"Yes, this is Suzanne Granger."

Marc took the lead. "Susan Granger's granddaughter?"

"That's right. May I ask what this is concerning?"

"Are you a literary agent?"

"I wish. Who is this, anyway?"

Marc introduced himself and explained that someone had impersonated her in order to trick us after we received a time capsule letter from her grandmother.

"I got one from Nana, too, but it was stolen because I left it in my purse on the front seat of my car. What did yours say? Mine was rather cryptic."

"Maybe we can help you decode it."

"She told me if I was contacted by a ten-year-old boy I didn't know, I should tell him to find a dog resembling a horse. How weird is that? Maybe her mind was slipping."

"That's me," I told her. "Tris Healy."

"Well, there you go. Consider yourself told." She paused a beat. "Wait a minute. Are you the quiz show kid?"

"Yes."

"Hmm. Do you think this is all a stunt the TV people came up with? Why would my grandma do any of this?"

"We'll fill you in later," Marc said. "We've got to go."

"Please do."

I felt a kinship with her, strengthened by subsequent phone calls. It was as though Suzanne was family.

Chet wasn't Chet, either. At the AirBnB in west Austin, real Chet—a mortgage broker in his late thirties—told us he'd been lured away with a last-minute free ticket to a music festival. He had no idea what was going on, wasn't related to Meriwether Lewis, and had never sung a folksong in his life.

"We stayed in your cottage while you were gone," Marc explained.

"Then you owe me $190. I can run your card."

"Fair enough. Can we take a look inside in case we forgot anything?"

"Wait a minute. How did you even get in? If there's any damage to my lock, that's going to cost you extra."

"Sure."

Real Chet followed us in. "I see you did leave things. I don't appreciate the hole in my wall you made to hang that picture. That's going to cost you ten extra dollars. And why would anyone travel with a framed portrait?" His eyes lowered to the small table under Meriwether's painting. "That book must be yours, too. You two are careless trespassers. Is this any way to role model appropriate behavior for your son? I want you both out of here as soon as you pay me."

Marc managed to appease the B&B host by complimenting him on his decorating skills, opening the door to a few questions.

Real Chet told us that when he arrived home and found his place an unholy mess, he'd called the police, but they'd been no help. "They told me that luring away homeowners and then robbing them was a common MO. But nothing was missing! The officer had the nerve to look around and say that he didn't see anything worth stealing. Ridiculous!"

"I agree," Marc said.

"Me, too," I added.

Chet looked at me closely for the first time and frowned. I could see that my face was familiar, but he couldn't figure out why.

After a few moments, he shook his head and continued. "I don't guess you're the robbers—I mean the vandals—or you wouldn't have come back. But you were here. What do you know about all this?'

Marc told him a man had impersonated him to collect the rental cash, and that we'd been away when his home was ransacked, which seemed to satisfy Chet. At that point, he remembered he was angry at us and nastily demanded payment from Marc, who obliged.

"Now get out of here with your things and leave me in peace."

Since answers were in short supply in Austin, we returned home to Ojai, where Marc hired a local investigator—John Ruggles—with some of my winnings. Ruggles met with us three days later to fill us in on what he'd discovered so far.

He was a markedly good-looking man in his mid-forties. If John hadn't been a detective, I could see him teaching drama to similarly attractive college students. His bright blue eyes didn't miss anything as Marc and I sat across from him in his spartan office downtown. Did he know more about me than I wanted him to just from reading my face?

"The so-called Sinclairs were bogus, too," he told us in a gravelly voice. "The real family 'won' a last-minute trip to Cancun. These Sinclairs are litigious-minded, by the way, and actual Rob Sinclair's a retired lawyer. The guy's scrambling to find someone to sue, but the imposters vanished. Be aware he might come after the two of you."

Marc nodded. "What about the Keepers' headquarters in Santa Cruz?"

"A couple of innocent lesbian professors share the place. They were both working when you scouted their home. Based on what you told me—and I'm not sure I believe all of it—someone was probably waiting to ambush you inside that house."

"I find your use of the term 'lesbian' to be gratuitous and inappropriate," I told him. "How is that relevant?"

"You're right. It isn't. Sorry about that."

"What else?" I asked.

"I'm running into lots of dead ends in Texas. These people were clever. And of course I'm here, not there.

If you want, I know a guy in Houston, and he can head to Austin. It'll cost you, and I'm not sure feet on the ground will make any difference. I've been able to reach everybody you told me about besides your ersatz Chet and Suzanne on the phone, and I have access to all sorts of databases not available to the general public. I don't know what else he could do."

"What about the other cult—the Radiant Librarians?" I asked.

"I've got zilch on them. I'm not sure they even exist."

"They do. Trust me," Marc told him.

"Here's what I think we ought to do next. I should've thought of this before. I want to send over a tech guy I use to see if they bugged your office. Someone's stayed a step ahead of you all the way through your crazy story. Maybe they're staying a step ahead of me as well now, and that's why I haven't found out more. We sweep my office regularly, so we're safe here, but I'll wager you've been talking about all this in Marc's office. Am I right?"

"Yes."

"There you go."

"Okay," Marc said. "But if they did bug me, that's a terrible breach of confidentiality, and all my clients would be affected."

"I wouldn't tell them about it if I were you."

Ruggles' technical-minded colleague—a chatty Filipino in his early twenties—found a tiny listening device affixed to the underside of a chair. Someone had listened in on our sessions? Outrageous!

When Marc and I calmed down, here's what we pieced together from that scrap of information.

Whoever these people were—and I was leaning toward the Keepers—what I'd said about the book while passing out on TV had galvanized them into swift action. While my words sounded inconsequential to my parents and the ER doctor, who heard the expanded version, they must've served as a clarion call to any cult we'd tangled with. The Keepers and the Librarians surely kept their antennae up for public mentions of wisdom books.

At any rate, I suspect they'd followed me to my first session at Marc's office. "Chet" had probably been the disguised driver following us in a pickup truck. The supposedly anxious woman in Marc's waiting room would've been the one who planted the bug when she briefly preempted my initial session, and chances are she'd been the figure who'd ducked down in the disguised man's truck. It was no wonder she'd seemed so over the top and melodramatic in the waiting room. She'd been acting, and she wasn't nearly as good at it as Fake Chet and Fake Suzanne.

In hindsight, the Texans hadn't always expressed appropriate reactions to the ridiculous synchronicities they'd manufactured. Over the next two weeks, I came to accept they'd certainly manufactured them.

Fake Chet had been too casual—too blithe. Fake Suzanne had been inconsistent, and often her face and her words hadn't matched up. In fake Chet's case, I'd figured he was a little crazy, and gave him the benefit of the doubt. In fake Suzanne's case, my dislike for her overrode other concerns. Perhaps they were cunning enough to know these personas would have these effects on us.

After the bug was planted, they knew everything,

including the AirBnB address in Austin, which I'd mentioned to Marc in his office. After we'd discussed the letter, the book, my dreams, and all our plans, we didn't stand a chance. It was a simple matter to stay one step ahead of us.

The technician wanted to search our clothes and belongings, which I thought was overkill—an opportunity to pad his bill. Marc thought it was a good idea, so I consented.

He found a diminutive tracking disc affixed to the tongue of my shoe, under the laces. It must've been planted at the "Sinclairs" when the pretext of a new carpet prompted me to take my shoes off. How had I fallen for that? They hadn't even *had* a new carpet. With the tracker, our nemeses could follow us at a distance. Perhaps they'd used other devices we weren't aware of.

Two days later, Ruggles provided another report. We once again sat in his office, a modern, well-appointed space.

"I've tentatively identified your assailants at the Mystery Spot. Take a look at these photos." He handed Marc two grainy headshots and kept talking while I leaned over and perused the photos with him. "It took a while because I had to track down lots of gun permit applications. A dealer in San Diego made copies of their driver's licenses."

"That's them!" I told Ruggles.

"Yes, definitely," Marc added.

"These two thugs are employees of a private security company based in Chula Vista. Unfortunately, I can't find either of them. They have relatives in Alaska and Utah, so they probably headed there. I don't think it's worth trying to track them down. They're not going to know anything."

"They might," I protested.

"What would you tell a methhead and a guy with about an eighty IQ if you sent them out to steal something?"

"I see your point."

"The other thing I found out is that the guy calling himself Bubba—the fake plumber who siphoned his gas for you—is a member of the Keepers."

"How in the world did you find that out?"

"It was the writing on the plumbing truck, Tris. Once you told me the name, I hired a guy down in Lampasas to approach the real owner. For a hundred bucks, this Italian-American guy told us he'd rented it to a friend of a friend of his brother who paid with a corporate credit card. The name on Bubba's card was that of a six-foot eight-inch Texas A&M basketball player. So I traced the name of the corporation on the card back through several shell companies on Barbados, and it turned out they're all owned by—get this—KOT Corporation."

"KOT. Keepers of Truth."

"How dumb is that?" Ruggles shook his head and then smiled.

"Very," I agreed. "But let me ask you this. How can you trace a card like that in one of those tax haven countries?"

"Well, just between you and me, we had to hire a local P.I. to bribe somebody down there."

"Ah, I see. It was illegal."

John held a finger up to his lips.

He couldn't find a connection between Bubba,

Fake Chet, and Fake Suzanne—without real names, how could he? Nonetheless, we concluded that if Bubba was a Keeper, so were Chet and Suzanne. All three must've been leading us around by the nose, presenting false synchronicities to explain away their involvement. Now they'd undoubtedly returned to being whoever they really were.

Somehow the cult knew about the photo of Bob Wills's boots we'd found in San Marcos—probably our car had been bugged when we'd talked about it on the ride back to Austin. They'd recognized the boots might be Wills's since he was still an iconic figure in that region. Then Bubba had steered us to where the Keepers believed we needed to be next since we hadn't figured it out ourselves.

The conspiracy theories about the Keepers sounded much more credible now. The cult's elaborate plot to monitor us, create so-called synchronicities, and then trick us into handing over the book had been quickly assembled. And the participants were either professional actors or very talented amateurs. The resources and know-how to orchestrate all this spoke to a sophisticated, well-funded organization. I almost wished the Librarians' attempt to hijack the book at the Mystery Spot had been successful. At least then the creepy, lying Keepers wouldn't have it.

Zeke, the African American man at the Bob Wills museum, was real, and of course Ophelia and Mildred were too. For a while, our shaman friend Theodore's status was up in the air. He kept a very low profile. Eventually John discovered he was, in fact, a full-blooded Comanche living outside Turkey. Nominally, he was a rancher raising cattle, but he still worked part-time as a petroleum engineer in Lubbock.

At first, I found some of John Ruggles's revised narrative hard to believe, but the facts supported it. For example, at La Frontera I'd remembered details of my life as Susan, which had included Suzanne's childhood, and the impersonator had agreed these were accurate. On reflection, she hadn't offered any memories of her own. And the little girl in my memory wasn't all that similar-looking to the woman passing as her adult self. That hadn't seemed important at the time—people change, after all. Now it represented corroboration of the hoax.

Chet had played his part magnificently. Fooling both Marc and me couldn't have been an easy task. By choosing an eccentric persona, he'd pre-excused himself for any untoward acts or speech. For that matter, his nonsense about changing his face with plastic surgery to escape crazed fans covered another base too. If we saw a photo of the real Chet, or someone in town recognized him, he could refer back to that fiction.

Perhaps assigning excellence to the conspirators allowed me to avoid facing my foibles—my willingness to trust strangers and accept unlikely circumstances at face value. The Keepers manipulated us. And I'd let them do it.

During most of the quest, the organization aspired to the same goal we did—finding the book. Without their help, we might not have. From their standpoint, they had no chance of success without my dreams providing essential guidance throughout the quest. So they needed us at least as much as we needed them. The relationship had been creepily symbiotic.

Three weeks after the loss of the book, I rejoined the quiz show, desultorily answering questions correctly and joylessly winning more money. I continued to work with Marc in therapy sessions. I don't think we got anywhere, but at least it was an outlet for expressing thoughts and feelings that had no other venue.

My father was pleased I'd "calmed down and was toeing the line like a respectable young citizen." My mother seemed worried about me. She told me not to hide my light under a bushel basket, and to buck up and face life squarely in the eye.

I couldn't picture either parent as a Nazi now. My mother's broad face and far from alert eyes made me think of a Wisconsin dairy farmer's wife—someone of Scandinavian heritage. She looked reliable and competent, albeit within the parameters of household management.

My father's severe facial expressions finally made sense to me. He wasn't a simple bully or a fool. He was pushing back against a world that stayed a step ahead of him. How would I respond if I was almost always the least educated person in the room? I could bow down to my betters and become meek, or I could seize power in whatever I way I could manage. In my father's case, force of will replaced knowledge. And in many instances, it worked for him.

I no longer saw my dad's burly body as an evolutionary throwback, either. He'd just had a burly dad himself. What could he do about that? And plenty of admirable historical figures had sported barrel chests. It didn't mean anything.

What else had I been so certain about that was

simply inaccurate? That was a question I couldn't answer.

The worst part of those few weeks was the cessation of meaningful dreams. Adrift—without purpose—I felt confused about almost everything. Could I ever trust anyone again? Would I ever get to read the wisdom book? What percentage of our quest had been real? Were all my supposed psychological and personality gains suspect now? I thought about contacting Theodore for help. He'd given his number to Marc and told us to call "when it was time," whatever that meant. I decided to wait. Just knowing I could reach out to him helped a bit. It was like keeping a pain relief pill in your pocket in case your back acted up.

One cool morning, I spied our elderly neighbor walking a short-legged black and white puppy past our house. Without thinking, I ran outside.

"Mr. Santos! Who's this?"

Our long-time neighbor swiveled his round head, bringing his dark, alert eyes to bear on me. The dog did too, with a similar level of attention. When the puppy pulled on his braided leather leash to come see me, Mr. Santos let go of his end as I crouched down, and a moment later, a small wet nose bumped into mine.

"Hey, what's your name?" The puppy licked my cheek and scrabbled to climb up my leg.

"We just got him," Mr. Santos said. "We haven't gotten around to naming him yet. Any ideas?"

"Hmm. Let me see." I pulled my face away to get a better look. The puppy lunged forward.

Mr. Santos started for me, but I waved him off. "I don't mind a little youthful enthusiasm."

"This one might be too much of a handful for the

244

missus and me," he said dolefully. "He was supposed to have been trained at his foster home, but it sure doesn't look like it."

"How about Peanut?"

"I think that's a bit demeaning, don't you? Dogs deserve our respect."

"I like peanuts."

"So do I."

"What about Holsy? His black and white markings are reminiscent of a Holstein cow."

"I think you should stick to quiz shows, Tris."

He stated this gently, but my face flushed and my hands curled into a tight ball. Mr. Santos noticed.

"Of course, I'll mention your suggestion to my wife, and we'll see what she thinks. She named our last dog Anchovy."

"That's a terrible name."

"It sure is."

Holsy let me pick him up, and I stroked his head. His smooth fur contrasted with Mildred's. It felt like warm velvet. I expected the black and the white parts of him to feel different. They didn't. "I've got an idea. Maybe I could help you out by walking him. I could take him to the park and play with him, too."

"Well, I don't know. Have you ever had a dog, Tris?"

"Briefly." I suddenly began sobbing. Holsy licked my tears. I collapsed onto the curb, my shaky legs twisting me away from my neighbor, lost in the feeling.

"I'm so sorry," Mr. Santos said. "I didn't mean to bring up something painful. Has your dog passed?"

In my grief, I didn't know what he meant. "She lives in Texas with Ophelia," I gasped.

"Oh. I see. Well, let's start with a little walk together, and we'll see how it goes. How's that sound?"

His kindness triggered more tears, but I gathered myself, released Holsy, and stood. "Thank you. I loved Mildred, and we never even got a chance to get to know each other."

"Why don't you tell me about her while we walk? Here, take the pup's leash."

Holsy immediately started pulling, and for a little dog with, let's say, a tibia-challenged stature, he was strong. "Whoa, boy. Whoa."

"Try jerking the leash when he does that."

"Oh, I couldn't do that. It might hurt his neck. Maybe if I gave him a treat when he *didn't* pull?"

Mr. Santos gestured at Holsy. "What are the odds that's going to happen? Anyway, a dog isn't likely to connect the dots between a baseline behavior and a reward."

"You know a lot about dogs, don't you?"

"I ought to. I was a veterinarian for forty-one years, Tris. Didn't you know that?"

"My dad said you'd been a farmworker."

He laughed. "There's your dad in a nutshell. I'm not even Latino—my parents were Portuguese. If I didn't see the good in the man, I'd be offended by your father's profound ignorance."

"What do you mean by that?"

We strolled toward to the corner of my street, stopping twice for Holsy to sniff the ground. He was so low to the ground that he barely had to lower his little head.

Mr. Santos turned to face me while Holsy pulled the leash again. "I think racism and sexism stem from not understanding people—or how life works, in general. Sometimes our early conditioning blocks learning about these things. Other times it's simply self-interest. We're all in this deal together, aren't we? That's what a lot of people haven't grasped."

Holsy stopped, raised a leg, and peed on the metal strut of a front lawn political sign—*MacGregor For City Council: His Finger Is On Ojai's Pulse*.

"What about character traits like arrogance or greed?" I asked. "Don't they get in the way too?"

"Sure. How can you be compassionate and empathetic if you're full of yourself or ambitious at the expense of others? You should consider joining our church if you're interested in all this, Tris. Pastor Dave talks about these things a lot."

"Uh, thanks."

Holsy resumed walking, and we turned another corner, steering around a distracted, scantily dressed woman on her phone. Mr. Santos did not eyeball her like most men would've.

"So tell me about Mildred," he said.

I tried, but the grief kept intruding. I skirted the main details so I could continue. Mr. Santos noticed my tears and heard the periodic breaks in my voice, of course, but he didn't comment on them.

When we arrived back at his house, he finally spoke. "My wife and I would be honored if you agreed to share custody of our puppy. You can walk him and keep him overnight sometimes if your parents allow it. But first I'll need to educate you about how to train and care for a dog."

I let go of Holsy's leash and hugged Mr. Santos fiercely.

"Hold it, Tris. That's what I mean about needing to learn more." He broke away and grabbed Holsy's leash. "If you let a dog off his leash willy-nilly, he might chase a cat into the street or be attacked by a bigger dog."

"I'm sorry. I'm just so happy you'll let me help with Holsy."

"Holsy, eh? We'll see about that."

Chapter 20

I woke up from another significant dream the next morning. I related it to Marc the following morning in his office after I told him about Mr. Santos and Holsy. "I was sitting in a rundown public library, listening to a Haydn violin concerto on headphones—no. 5 in A Major, I believe—when Susan Granger's voice replaced the music. I recognized it from speaking exactly the same way in the first dream—the one in which I'd been her on the road in Texas. 'Don't give up,' the voice said. 'The job isn't finished, and your curriculum hasn't run its course. This isn't just about the book. It's also about you.' "

I looked at Marc and raised an eyebrow.

"That's it?"

"Yes. What do you think?"

Diffused sunlight basked the office that morning. Marc had forgotten to fully close the vertical blinds behind him.

"It may be a legitimate lineage dream like the others. You'd know better than I would about that. If it isn't, it probably reflects your understandable urge to complete the task you were set to, Tris. But in either case, what can we do? We're just two people with no way to make a stand against a resourceful international organization. We can't even find them."

"I can tell the difference between dreams. This one

is meant to guide us. And what's the harm in exploring what we've being directed to do? If we're not successful at finding the Keepers, so be it."

"These are dangerous people, Tris." His voice was slow and measured. "There's plenty of potential harm."

I shook my head. "No, it was the Librarians who resorted to violence. The Keepers were simply deceptive—cunningly deceptive."

"All right. Let's suppose we allowed your dream to guide us. What then?"

"I'm being told to resume our attempts to find the book and get it published. We may not know how to do that right now, but so what? That was our original mission, and it seemed equally impossible when we started, didn't it? Yet we did have the book in our hand for a while."

"That's true," he conceded. He leaned back and joined his hands together on his lap.

"The part about my curriculum is more confusing to me," I said. "What do you think she meant by that? Are there specific things I'm supposed to be learning about all this?"

"I don't know, Tris. Perhaps you have another role to play down the line."

Marc's buzzed hair had grown out enough that some of the bristles in the front were flopping sideways. Apparently, standing up alongside their brethren was too challenging for them now. He'd shaved his cheeks recently, but stubble blackened the upper portion of his neck.

"So what shall we do?" I asked, gesturing with one hand for emphasis.

"What do *you* think?" Marc asked in annoying

therapist fashion.

I frowned and spoke sardonically. "That's a rather transparent therapeutic intervention, isn't it?"

"I suppose so," Marc admitted. "But what do you think you should do, anyway? I'm asking as a person this time."

"I used *we* in reference to continuing the quest, and you've switched to *you,* " I pointed out.

"I guess I have." He paused. "Tris, I can't keep gallivanting around the country. I have my work here. I have my life. Let's stay focused on you."

"Fine!" It wasn't, of course. I was still only ten years old. I needed an adult sidekick to be able to travel and do lots of other things.

"We can talk about it later," Marc said. "Let's stay with the dream. How would you proceed if you signed back up for your quest?"

"I don't know. I could hire a team of crack investigators with my quiz show winnings."

"John Ruggles and his associates are very good at their jobs, and he hit a dead end, didn't he? I don't think there's more to find out."

I caught him looking at the clock. That was a first.

"There's always more to find out." My voice was louder than it needed to be. "And if my significant dreams continue, they'll be a source of information unavailable to anyone else. I could steer investigators with what I find out when I'm asleep."

Marc leaned back so far in his chair I thought he might tip over. *Is he unconsciously creating physical distance when he really sought it on another level?* "Let's assume you locate the book. Say it's in a vault somewhere, guarded by the Keepers. Then what?

Where does that get you? Are you going to hire paramilitary troops to storm the place?"

I glared at him. "If I need to. Look, Marc, for thousands of years—literally, *thousands* of years—my karmic ancestors have been working on gathering wisdom. Can I turn my back on my responsibility to fulfill this mission and still feel good about myself?"

"I suppose not. But there's no way for you to do this on your own."

I looked him in the eyes and waited. I had never done this before for more than a moment or two. I was reminded of Theodore's steady gaze. Marc's brown eyes were also very present, as though he lived just behind them—right where he saw the world.

Then he sighed. "Okay. I'm in. Why don't you get on your laptop today and find out everything John may have missed?"

"How do I know what he missed?"

"Tris, he knows what he's doing, but he doesn't have your memory—your brain. Here are some key questions: why would a spiritual group want to suppress a book of wisdom? Was anything fake Rob Sinclair told us about the cult true? Most skilled liars stick to the truth as much as possible. Are there any undiscovered ex-members we could talk to? What's the cult's full history? Who are its leaders?"

"I see you've thought about this."

"Of course." He nodded furiously. He was energized now.

"I tried a lot of that, but I'm sure I can think of additional lines of inquiry," I assured him. Energy flowed through me too, tingling my hands. "You're right. This is a good idea. I'm afraid I wasn't as diligent as I could've been when I originally researched the Keepers. At that time, they were only hypothetically relevant. Then I let Ruggles take the helm after the debacle at the bank."

"Sounds good."

Chapter 21

I didn't set out to scrutinize the Radiant Librarians, but their name popped up on one of the first sites I visited, and I was curious when I happened upon it. Three hours later, I found the origin of their website—an IP address in Kauai. I won't report on any hacking I may have done. Two hours after that, I discovered someone named Kepler had written a book about them which he couldn't get published. Instead, he'd shrunk it down to an article which he published in a University of Colorado scholarly journal. The article focused on the evolution of the organization's philosophy, comparing its original message to secular Buddhism and its current stance to historical messianic Judaism—a God-like figure prophesying an apocalypse. Only one of the references Kepler listed was available online or referenced anywhere else. I suspect he'd fabricated the others, which threw the veracity of the article into doubt.

The legitimate article Kepler had listed in his references provided the first credible, useful information about the Librarians. Of all places, it appeared in a magazine in New Zealand. The cult originally posited that mankind needed a boost of wisdom for it to reach its full potential and enter a new age of peaceful coexistence. For several years, they operated transparently, focused on political action, education, and grassroots fundraising. At that time they called themselves the Wisdom Volunteers. Around 2008, a new leader steered the group toward gathering wisdom in preparation for the apocalypse he or she predicted. The renamed Radiant Librarians ruthlessly appropriated texts from wherever they could find them, using whatever means necessary. Several members were incarcerated in a failed attempt to rob a monastery in Sri Lanka in 2011.

As far as the public was concerned, the cult disbanded at that point, leaving behind only the legacy of their uninformative website. But they simply went underground. A blog originating in Puerto Rico asserted that the Librarians were awaiting "a hitherto unknown book passed on from generation to generation."

A woman on a fringe forum speculated that a defector from the Keepers may have shared information with the Librarians. She didn't provide any evidence backing this notion. How could anyone know something like that? These groups were so secretive that even *I* had trouble uncovering anything about them. But if she were right, that would explain how the Librarians were able to track us. I remembered that one of our assailants at the Mystery Spot had blurted out that they had a spy in the Keepers. However unreliable a source he might've been, combined with what I read, I was inclined to believe it. At any rate, since we didn't have the book, we didn't need to worry about the Librarians for now. The Keepers did.

In reading conspiracy theories about the Keepers of Truth, many of which jibed with my experiences, it was clear the organization was truly international in scale, had resorted to subterfuge before, and acted almost as hypocritically as its more violent counterpart. Ego ruled these people—ugly aspects of ego such as greed, ambition, and a thirst for power. I suspected that the Keepers' leader—whoever he was—wanted to proclaim himself the author of the wisdom book.

I found corroborating evidence that the cult was organized as though it were a pyramid scheme, which explained its proliferation around the world. These people had an even stronger motivation than Christian missionaries intent on saving souls from an eternity in hell. Everyone members signed up meant more money in their pockets. And when these new members signed up more people, and when those members signed up more people...Eventually, Keepers got rich. Very rich. And their leader was the wealthiest of all.

I found one anonymous Keeper ex-member, who posted that the cult had infiltrated the national government. Several other members on the same forum purported to possess first-hand knowledge of this. Someone else claimed to be the leader's cousin, although he didn't name him. It was difficult to know how seriously to take any of the posters' points of view, but the initial post about the government and the purported cousin's information were at least well written.

I decided to research and then contact both the ex-member and the cousin. I had to start somewhere. Perhaps they had just been English majors, but what did I have to lose?

Anonymity was harder to come by other than just omitting one's name from an online post. The ex-member's name was Jan Wing, which took forty minutes to find out. She was a woman in her mid-thirties who lived in Maryland. The cousin was Thomas Sojurner, a high school teacher in Austin. The Austin connection could mean something. Perhaps the Keepers were based there. I certainly didn't believe in coincidences quite the way I once had.

I reached Jan on the phone after paying a site to uncover virtually all her personal information. I was alarmed at how easy it was to trace someone. Perhaps the cults had originally hunted me down by visiting a site such as this one.

"Hello. I'm sorry to bother you," I said. "Can we talk for a few minutes about the Keepers of Truth?"

"Who is this? How did you get my number? This sounds like Bud's son. I don't care what you say, I'm not coming back."

"No, no. I'm sorry. My name is Tris Healy. I've tangled with the organization. I know they're real. I know what they're capable of. I need to find them."

"Tris Healy, the boy genius?"

"Yes."

"Prove it."

"Test me."

"Okay, let me think a minute." She did so. "Name all the states that have land farther south than the northernmost part of Mexico."

"Wow. I don't actually know that, but I'll figure it out." I pictured a map of the US and swept my internal eye across the bottom of it. "There are eleven." I named them.

"One more question," Jan said in a louder voice. The classical music playing in the background had reached a penultimate crescendo—a wind quintet by Reicha, who ought to be better known. "Let me think of a good one. How about this? How many bacterial cells are in our bodies compared to human cells?"

"Ten times more."

"Okay. You're him. What did you say you want? And why are you so depressed now on the show? You haven't given Marv any crap for weeks now. Was it that fit you had on the air?"

"Never mind about my health. I want to know what you know about the Keepers."

"You know they're dangerous?"

"I do, although it's the Librarians who have the guns."

"Uh-oh. You ran into them too, huh? They shot my brother, although he's okay now. Yeah, it's true the Keepers don't resort to violence, but they're up for just about everything else. It's Walter Bradford's fault. An organization's culture drips down from the top. He's a piece of work, I'll tell you."

"How did you get involved?" I asked, just to keep her talking. If I asked tangential questions at first, perhaps she'd be more willing to divulge sensitive information later.

"My brother brought me in. He was a high mucky-muck until he got demoted for sticking up for me when I left. You don't talk back to Bradford."

"What are they planning to do with the wisdom they collect?"

"They're waiting for some last bit of it—something passed on from somebody's relatives or something. Then they're going to put it out as a book written by Bradford, reveal themselves to the world, and get some sort of leadership position in the spiritual community. The whole idea is stupid. I only went to meetings for four months or so before I quit. But I spotted a congressman and an assistant to one of the cabinet members there." Her voice rose in volume as she finished. Clearly, the governmental element was what disturbed her the most.

"Do you work for the government?" I asked.

"Yes, that's why I need to stay anonymous. Please don't tell anyone you know who I am. I wouldn't even have posted anonymously, but I'd had a bit to drink, and I figured that weird little site isn't someplace anyone important visits. At the time, I felt someone had to get the real story out there since the other stuff I found online was way off—probably put out as disinformation by the Keepers themselves. The reality is that they prey on screwed-up people's ambitions—to become enlightened, to get richer, to boss around new members—whatever."

"Are *any* of the other posts real? What about the guy who said he's Walter Bradford's cousin—Thomas Sojurner?"

"I didn't see that one." Jan paused and then she spoke with less intensity. "It must've been after I posted mine. I haven't gone back to the site since then."

"Does Bradford have a cousin?"

"I don't know."

"Where is their headquarters?" This was an important question. I found myself leaning forward to hear her answer, as though that helped on the phone.

"Florence, Italy, actually. But Bradford flies back and forth to Texas, where he's from. He's got some rich old Italian lady who supports the cause over there, so he lives in her palace and keeps her happy in bed." She paused. "Oops. I forgot you're a kid."

"That's okay. I know about sex."

"I can tell you he's been in Texas lately because my brother's there with him at the US headquarters. Instead of a policy aide, now he's just a bodyguard."

"This is in Austin?"

"Yes, how did you know?" She seemed quite surprised.

"It explains some things. How can I find them there?"

"Hmm. I don't know if that's a good idea." Now she sounded like my mother.

"I have a martial artist who travels with me." While technically true, this was certainly a misleading assertion.

"Oh, okay. But be careful. My brother has a black belt in something or other, too. I don't know where their building is or where they stay, but I know that Bradford is a workout nut and goes to a Bodyboy gym wherever he travels. I think he's one of the owners of the chain. I went to one once. They're awful—full of muscleheads dripping smelly sweat. I guess it's the steroids that do that. Eww."

"What does he look like? Are there any photos of him online?"

"Not that I know of, but you can try. He's about sixty, and he looks like he's fifty. He's totally bald, buff, with these dark, beady eyes. Oh, and Bret—that's my brother—says he went to some college in Nacogdoches, Texas. Maybe there's a yearbook picture or something."

"Is there anything else you can tell me?"

"Watch your ass," Jan said. "I'm sorry. I mean your tushy. Watch your tushy."

"Uh, thanks."

"And good luck on the show. Those other contestants are sooo boring."

"You've been a great help. Take care."

I was pleased with my "take care." It was the first time I'd tried it out.

I called Sojurner next, getting his voicemail. It was still school hours in Austin, so he was probably busy teaching. I left a somewhat cryptic, hopefully intriguing message: "Hi, this is Tris Healy, the smartest boy in the world. I need your help. Can you please call me as soon as you can?"

An hour later, he called back. The burr in his voice indicted he was a smoker. "I recognized your voice. How in the world can I help you? You should be helping me."

"With what?"

"I'm teaching an advanced placement physics class, and it's hard to stay a step or two ahead of my best students. Some of these high school kids could give you a run for your money." He laughed at his own comment, something I've always found inappropriate.

"I doubt it. Here's how you can help. I need to know what you know about the Keepers of Truth."

"Really? Why? They're a bunch of scary crackpots. You oughta stay away from them."

"Oh, I don't want to join. They stole something from me."

"No kidding?"

"No kidding," I assured him.

"Did you write a book or something?"

"Sort of," I prevaricated.

"Okay. Well, the thing is that my cousin Walter

Bradford is a major asshole. He beat his wife, who left him a few years back. He raised his son to be an asshole. He conned my aunt out of a lot of money. And his so-called religion is just a way for him to make money and boost his ego."

"Which of these terms describe him best: sociopath, narcissist, antisocial, or criminal?"

"I'm going to go with asshole again." He paused. "I don't really know the difference between all those others. He's totally focused on himself, and he's ruthless in his relationships. I don't know if he's as bad as some of these dictators around the world. I don't think so. I know he's bad enough that I haven't talked to him in years."

"How would you go about getting something back if his organization stole it from you?" I asked.

"I'd let it go. It's not worth it."

"Suppose it was. Suppose it was something of immense value to you."

"Uh, let me think." He paused this time for an inordinate length of time. "I know a guy who's still active in the Keepers," he finally said. "He's an actor. We used to be in a band together back years ago. I can't imagine he'd want to help you, but it's worth a shot."

An idea flashed into my brain. Maybe we'd lucked out. "Is he a tall guy in his sixties with a gray ponytail? And he has circular scars on his torso?"

"That's a good trick. Are all you geniuses psychics, too?"

"No. What's his name?"

"Frank Sitkova. His wife is in the Keepers too, actually. She might be more cooperative. I don't know."

I described the woman impersonating Suzanne Granger.

"Yeah, that's Arlene. We dated briefly twenty years ago before I made the mistake of introducing her to my cousin. If you see her, say hi for me."

"Sure. How can I find them?"

"I don't know what Frank is up to, but last I heard, Arlene Sitkova was teaching drama at Austin Community College."

I asked him quite a few more questions. None of his remaining answers were helpful.

Chapter 22

I walked Holsy three times—once by myself. His official name was Groucho now, which I refused to employ even though Mr. Santos said it was better for him if we all called him the same name. After each opportunity to spend time with Holsy, I cried myself to sleep. I was learning to love my new dog, but it wasn't the same as Mildred. I guess it was like a teenager's first love.

I finally told my mother about Mildred. I could hardly get the words out. She held me and stroked my hair.

"Maybe you could ask this Ophelia person to send a photo of Mildred," she suggested. "Or she could put her on the phone. Your aunt talked to her dog all the time while she was away in the navy."

I couldn't bear to do it.

****

I really wished I'd researched everything more thoroughly weeks ago when it might've saved us from losing the book.

Marc told me that wasn't a helpful thought when I mentioned this at our next session after filling him in on what I'd discovered. "Let's focus on what you found out," he continued. "And what to do, if anything."

"We could turn the Sitkovas over to the police."

"For what? Impersonating people?"

"Arlene stole our book."

"We gave it to her, Tris."

"Well, technically. But what she did might constitute fraud." I paused and considered the matter. "Fake Chet—Frank—shot that guy at the synagogue, right? He probably wasn't arrested like he said, so maybe he's still wanted for that."

"John Ruggles told me he checked the police blotter during the stretch we were in Austin. There wasn't a shooting. That was staged, too. I'm sorry. I forgot to tell you."

"Why would they do that?"

"I don't know," Marc replied. "To keep us from contacting the authorities? To create a psychological bond with Chet—I mean, Frank? Going through trauma together will do that. Maybe it's something else. Anyway, how would arresting Frank and Arlene get the book back?"

"It's leverage for getting their cooperation. On TV, criminals usually make deals for reduced sentences." The room was warmer than usual even though the blinds were closed this time. I shifted in my chair as if a new position might afford me a breeze.

"Hmm. That's true—on TV, anyway. But they won't have the book themselves, will they? What do they have to offer as far as a deal goes?"

A car alarm shrieked nearby, and I had to wait quite a while before I could reply. "I don't know. More information about the Keepers? Something incriminating?" I thought a moment. "What if we told the world about the book, so when it comes out, Bradford can't pretend he wrote it."

"Well, since we haven't read it, we can't refer to

specific content to identify it, and we have no way of announcing anything on a grand scale. For that matter, who would believe our story?" He thrust both his bent arms out sideways, which startled me. I guess he was symbolically encompassing a disbelieving world.

"Maybe we could trick them somehow," I suggested. "That would be satisfying after what they did to us, wouldn't it?"

"We're not actors like they are, are we? But there's nothing wrong with scheming along those lines. Can you think of anything?"

"Let me think a minute." I probably took two. "We have a way of contacting the Keepers now—through the Sitkovas," I pointed out. "Suppose we tell them we only gave part of the book to Arlene? There weren't all that many pages in the copper box. Or there could be a second volume, or we could've discovered more of the book since we last saw her. If I were Walter Bradford and we made a convincing case about one of these through someone he trusts, I'd at least want to investigate further."

"How could we convince them we were being straight with them?" Mark asked, clearly skeptical. "Why would they believe us?"

"We could supply sample pages of the additional material," I suggested.

"Could we?"

"Sure. You wrote a book—remember? It sounds like it's full of wisdom. Or we could plagiarize something obscure."

"My book is overly psychological, I think. And how could we come up with something in the same style as what they have? We don't even know what that is."

"It's worth a try. Unless you have a better idea."

"I still don't see how it helps us get the book back."

"We can use the supposed extra pages as leverage—to make demands. We'll give the material to them if…"

"If what?"

"I don't know. Maybe we could say we want to read what they have, and then pull a switcheroo somehow when it's in our hands—like con men do."

"How does that work?"

"Distraction. Hiding an identical item nearby. Giving them a motive like greed to do something to our advantage. I don't know. I've only seen this in movies, but I can research it."

"Okay. Why don't you? If you come up with something that isn't dangerous, we'll talk about it again."

"Agreed." This was about as much of a sign-up to proceed as I was likely to get from Marc.

Arlene Sitkova was reachable at Austin Community College. Frank was off the radar; it was as though he'd ceased to exist four years ago. Walter Bradford was a member of the Austin Bodyboy gym—it was an easy hack into their database.

Next I researched the relevant laws that applied to the Sitkovas's actions. I found enough to support a credible threat, if not a conviction.

I decided to act unilaterally once I'd refined my plan. Marc had agreed to the general idea, and impatience ruled me. I just couldn't stand to wait until I met him again to implement it.

I left a message on Arlene's work voicemail, reading from a script I'd painstakingly composed.

"Hi, Arlene. This Tris Healy, and obviously I know who you and Frank are. Congratulations on fooling us for so long, but you need to know that by the end, we knew what you were up to, which is why we only gave you a small fraction of the wisdom book—just enough to make you leave us alone. Of course, we kept copies of what we gave you. Listen carefully to me, or you may end up imprisoned for your role in all this. You and your husband have violated numerous statutes. At the least, you'll lose your job and serve a few years.

"We can publish the full book, but we'd like your pages back before we do. It's better if the provenance of a book like this is free and clear. You can tell Walter Bradford about this call—yes, we know about him, too—but I wouldn't recommend it. You are pawns in his game, and you know as well as I do that he'll sacrifice you to get what he wants, which is the entire book. If he comes after us, the story goes public. We have an extensive file in the care of several lawyers who will see to that. Your roles are the centerpiece of the file.

"If you don't have a way to wrest the pages from your leader, you can help us trick him into supplying it. Either way, we'll sweeten the pot with twenty thousand dollars if you're successful. I'm rich from my quiz-show earnings, so that's no problem.

"I'll expect your answer by this time tomorrow. Call this number or face the consequences." I recited the number of an anonymous forty-dollar phone I'd bought at the grocery store.

Three hours later, Frank called. "You'll be talking

to me about this. Don't call Arlene again. Is that clear?"

"I'm setting the terms here. I'll do as I please. As it happens, I'm happy to talk to you. Now what's your answer?"

"You have us over a barrel, Tris. What choice do we have? Our lawyer says we're screwed if you finger us. But Bradford keeps the book in a safe in his mansion, and so far he hasn't let it out of his sight. So that's a no go. What else will satisfy you?" His authentic voice was smoother and less accented—like a radio announcer.

"Nothing. Where there's a will, there's a way. We need to use the leverage the rest of the book represents to manipulate Bradford. You two are obviously creative people—I don't know how you came up with half the things you said and did with us—so figure it out."

"Let me think. Walter is smarter than hell. He's got his faults, and I'm sure you have a low opinion of him from what you went through, but don't underestimate him. He's been a godsend for the Keepers, and if it wasn't for you and your damned brain, we would've been able to launch our plan weeks ago."

"And that plan is…?"

"Never mind."

"What are Bradford's weaknesses—his vices?" I asked. I needed to know more about him from an insider. What could we prey on if we tried to con him?

Without hesitation, Frank replied, "Vanity. Ambition. Sex."

"Sex?"

"Yeah, he's a sucker for redheads. Go figure. They're all nuts, if you ask me."

"Isn't your wife Arlene a redhead?"

"I rest my case. She's the one who pulled me into the Keepers. She was already on his radar when I met her. If I hadn't come along, I think they would've gotten together. The thing is, she thinks he's infallible. Well, almost."

"But she's onboard with helping us, anyway?"

"Begrudgingly."

"If she told Bradford I'd contacted her to make a legitimate deal, would he believe her?"

"Sure."

"You don't sound much like a true believer," I pointed out. "Why don't you idolize your leader?"

"I'm a realist, and so is Bradford. The Keepers aren't successful because he's charismatic or a great orator or something. He's just a man who came up with a novel way of building a spiritual organization. I'd still be begging for crappy dinner theater parts if it weren't for him."

"You're talking about a Madoff-style pyramid scheme."

"Call it that if you like. It's much more." He paused, and I didn't fill the silence. "Look, I know you're smart," Frank continued, "but I also know from hanging out with you that you're inexperienced and immature in a lot of ways, including being so full of yourself that you're probably rehearsing persuasive arguments against what I'm saying right now instead of listening. I don't think it's a good idea for us to take orders from a kid like you, Tris. Have you ever met anyone like Bradford—someone with that kind of power? Can you predict how he'll react? I can."

"I've hired a team of experts."

"Oh, you have, huh? Let me guess. Dalcour? And

some hired muscle, maybe?"

"That's none of your business." I made a mental note to look into finding someone proficient with firearms. Perhaps Ruggles would be willing to accompany us to Texas.

"I'll talk it over with Arlene and call you back tonight," Frank told me. "If we're going to do this, it needs to be soon. Bradford's planning to hold a press conference in a few days to reveal the book."

"Have you read it?"

"No. I think my wife peeked at it despite our orders not to, but she won't admit it."

"All right. I'll wait to hear from you," I agreed, "but if I don't like what I hear, my next stop is the police station."

"Got it."

"Wait a minute. There's something I want to know. How did the Keepers learn about me—about the book—in the first place. Was it from the TV show?"

"We don't watch TV. It's not allowed. Your ER doc happened to be a member. It was just random."

Chapter 23

I spent the rest of the day devising an updated, detailed plan. Was I less experienced than a typical adult? Sure. Unfamiliar with characters like Bradford? Thank God, yes. Too immature to manage the situation? Hardly. Like many lesser intellects, Frank underestimated the ability of a world-class mind to compensate for deficits in other arenas.

I also let Mrs. Santos know I'd be away for a few days. Her husband was at a meeting to raise money for some civic project. She was a sturdy Australian woman who always wore bright colors. Old people's ages were difficult for me to ascertain, but I suspected she was at least ten years younger than Mr. Santos, who was clearly in his seventies.

"I hope *Groucho* won't miss me too much," I added.

"He'll be fine. Puppies are resilient creatures. And he'll be so happy to see you when you get back. You can look forward to that, Tris."

I devoted the bulk of my session with Marc the next morning to a detailed explanation of my plan. He wasn't pleased I'd initiated contact with the Keepers without him and told me so in no uncertain terms.

"Well, that's in the past," I replied. "Do you think it's helpful to dwell on it?"

"I suppose not." He grinned. "That sounds like

something I'd say, doesn't it?" Then he gazed distractedly at the oak bookcase across the room. "I think it'll work," he finally said. "We'll be using Bradford's untrustworthiness against him, won't we? And it's less dangerous than anything I was able to come up with. Well done, Tris."

An unfamiliar warmth radiated throughout my chest. The energy expanded, heating up. Here was the individual who knew me best telling me I'd done a good job with something quite important to both of us. I attempted to identify the specific emotion that might be generating the energy. Pride? Joy? Satisfaction? None of those felt right. I gave up and just felt the bodily sensations for a while. Marc let me. Our time ran out before either of us spoke again.

Frank called shortly after I'd finished dinner— roast beef, green beans, apple cobbler, and a long story from Dad about his army post in Alaska. Gee, Dad, I didn't know it was cold up there. Thanks for the news.

"Okay. What do you want us to do?" Frank asked. "We didn't come up with any brilliant plan on our end, but we'll go along with whatever you've dreamt up."

"Have Arlene call Walter and tell him exactly this: you and Frank fooled us for quite a while, but by the end we knew what you were up to, which is why we only gave you a small fraction of the wisdom book— just enough to make you leave us alone. Of course, we kept copies of what we gave you. We could publish the full book, but because it doesn't matter to us who takes credit, we'll sell you the rest of the manuscript for two hundred thousand dollars. You have twelve hours to gather the money and text us at the following number, or we'll go ahead and tell our literary agent to email the book to a list of interested editors, *and* we'll contact the police."

"Wait a minute. I can't remember all that. If you want it exact, I'll need to write it down."

I repeated it slowly a few moments later, including the number of the other burner phone I'd bought for Bradford to call. I didn't want to leave a written trail of texts or emails.

"How does this get you the pages back?" Frank asked.

"Leave that to me. You are the most deceptive person I've ever met. Why in the world would I tell you? I'll dictate more terms later." The truth was, I hadn't figured out a logical reason for the Keepers to bring the book to a handoff with us. It was the weak component of my plan.

"Point taken. You know, on the one hand, it was fun fooling you and Dalcour—a real challenge given who I was dealing with. I did feel bad about it sometimes, though. I want you to know that."

"Screw you, Sitkova." I hung up, and another surge of energy rocked me, this time in my gut. Anger. Definitely anger. I liked it. So far, it was my second most favorite—right behind love, which had proved to be a double-edged sword. I thought about Mildred, and the anger morphed into tears.

She was a regular source of anguish now. Ever since we'd left Turkey, bouts of sadness periodically interrupted whatever else was happening.

Two days later, after some preparation and a long talk with the *Who's The Genius?* showrunner about taking a break from taping, we flew back to Austin, as did John Ruggles, who sat several rows behind us on the familiar flight. Marc convinced my parents I needed a refresher course at the fictitious institute run by Romanian scientists to maintain my progress as an upstanding young man. My father bought this. My mother wanted me to stay home.

"He's good enough now, and I don't want to have to miss him more. He's my baby boy, and I'm his mother. We belong together."

I was moved by her words. My mother loved me in her own way. My father overruled her as usual, coercing my mom to sign the new paperwork for the airlines. She did so with tears in her eyes, and I felt sorry for her. Nothing ever happened based on her say so. What would that be like?

At the Austin airport, we rented our car at one company and Ruggles at another. I could write a book about vehicle rental contracts at that point. While we drove to our hotel—the historic one downtown, next to the bank—John called to tell us we hadn't been followed.

"Great," I told him. "On to the next phase of the plan."

"Right."

I called Frank from our cramped, dark room in the old hotel. Apparently people were smaller and needed less light in olden times. Furniture back then seemed to have been built purely for its aesthetic qualities, too. The hand-carved antique armchair I sank into immediately hurt my lower back, and it wasn't as though I'd spent years digging ditches or something.

"Walter Bradford agreed to a deal," Frank told me. "In theory, anyway. He wants to set the details, though."

This didn't surprise me. "No way," I answered. "Here's how it's going to go down." I'd carefully scripted these phrases based on how people talked on TV crime shows.

I dictated our terms and gave Frank his orders. Then I reported to Marc once I'd hung up. He stood next to me, but I hadn't wanted the hollow sound of my voice on a speaker making Frank wonder who else was listening.

"We're okay so far, but let's hope John is successful," Marc said, looking a bit grim. Had he lost faith in our plan? I hadn't. "It's hard to leave such a crucial part of our strategy to someone we've only known a few weeks," he added.

"Like you said the other day, John's good at his job. I trust him to play his role, but I have to admit I'm not sure how Bradford will react when push comes to shove."

We spent several hours playing chess on Marc's phone in our room while we waited for Ruggles to report back. Remarkably, Marc defeated me handily. Was he a highly skilled player or was my churning stomach distracting me?

"You're anxious," Marc told me, noticing my discomfort.

"I don't feel anxious. It'll turn out however it turns out."

"Anxiety expresses itself in various ways, including physical symptoms. It doesn't care that your mind tells you to be calm. It's energy looking for a home."

I tried Ophelia's response. "Hmph."

This started me thinking about Mildred again, and I

almost cried. It was no wonder I lost at chess with all these feelings roiling around. On a level playing field, I'm sure I could've thrashed Marc in short order.

John Ruggles finally called. "It worked."

Marc put the phone on speaker. "Tell us about it."

"I got to the Bodyboy gym a little bit before Bradford. From the way they treated him at the front desk, it was obvious who he was. Plus, he was definitely an older version of the college yearbook picture you showed me. When he made a beeline for the elliptical, I got to an adjoining machine first and made a big show about being unfamiliar with how it worked—like a grown man can't push a start button. That got his attention. When I asked him for help and tried to chat him up, his suspicions intensified, and he switched to a weight machine on the other side of the room. I kept watching him in an obvious way and faked a phone call. Then I waited until he'd entered the locker room, gave him a few minutes, and followed him in. He had a towel around his waist in front of his locker when I approached him again.

" 'I hope you don't mind if I presume on our earlier conversation. You seem to know your way around this place,' I said. 'Maybe you could recommend a good Thai restaurant in town.'

"Bradford grabbed me the lapels, spun me around, and slammed me into the wall of lockers. The guy is way strong.

" 'Who the hell are you?' he yelled. 'Are you working for that California scum?'

"I feigned fear. 'I don't know what you're talking about,' I told him.

"He patted me down and extracted my wallet from

my back pocket. Flipping it open, he scanned my California driver's license and my PI license.

" 'John Ruggles. And you're a private investigator. I thought it was something like that. Let's just see what else is in here…'

"I watched his face as he found the forged receipt. He freaked."

I'd fabricated the paperwork myself—a forty-five hundred euro retainer from Walter Bradford's patroness in Florence. Under "services rendered," I'd typed in: "Conducting a thorough investigation of Walter Bradford's finances and the Keepers of Truth's financial transactions." At the bottom, I'd done a passable job of forging the woman's shaky signature, which I'd dug up in an archive on a Sienese courthouse website. Bradford was sure to recognize her handwriting from checks she'd written to him. Apparently, she'd been bankrolling the cult for many years.

"He immediately returned my wallet and backed off," Ruggles reported. "His tone was pretty reasonable now. 'What do you want? Why'd she sic you on me?'

" 'It's about the latest book you found. She got word that something's not right there, so here I am, investigating on her behalf.'

" 'Nonsense. It's the final piece of the puzzle. I told her that.'

" 'I've done some checking, Bradford. You better make sure things are in order in your house, because I verified this from an inside source. You only have part of the book, and you're planning to buy the rest with the contessa's cash. That's not why the contessa backs the Keepers. She's not happy about you spending her money that way.'

" 'Look, let me get dressed, and we'll talk about this over a couple of drinks.'

" 'Sure,' I said.

"So we adjourned to a nearby bar, and he tried to bribe me—with an insultingly low amount—to tell this Italian woman he wasn't doing anything against her wishes. He said he knew she'd earmarked her 'contributions' for charity, but she didn't understand the cult's current priorities. When that didn't work, Bradford finally leveled with me. He *really* doesn't want to piss off his sugar mama.

"As we suspected, he's only pretending to go along with your deal, Tris. He's going to have his bodyguards hidden at the exchange site. They'll take what we bring to the meet. I pressed him for details, saying I needed to be sure his plan was sound. It's a dumbass scenario we can circumvent easily enough. These are amateurs.

"I promised to tell Bradford's sugar mama he was cleverly acquiring valuable new wisdom—the final piece of the puzzle—without spending a penny. That seemed to reassure Bradford. Then I took whatever he had in his wallet as a bribe after all. Five hundred and eighty dollars. Why not? I'll take it off your final invoice."

Marc laughed. "Great work! Why don't we split Bradford's money?"

"Sure."

"So go ahead to the next stage of the plan, okay?"

"I'll get on it," Ruggles said. "Based on what that asshole told me, two more men ought to get the job done. I'll call the guys I talked to before we left. You've got room in your budget for all this, right?"

"I'm rich," I told him, which was sort of true. I didn't hold the purse strings to my winnings, but I knew I could find a way to cover all the expenses.

Chapter 24

I found a self-published book from fourteen years earlier which had sold two copies. Didn't the author have any friends or relatives? Titled *The World According To Sid Bromberg,* it impressed me as surprisingly wise. I printed it out on old paper I found in the bottom of my dad's desk drawer; it would survive a cursory examination if need be. At least, I hoped it would.

Frank called later that afternoon. "Okay, it's all set the way you want. I had to get creative to get Walter to go along with bringing the box and the first part of the book. That was the hard part. Saying both parties need to have something to lose to make it fair was not gonna fly with him. I didn't even try that. He couldn't give a crap about fairness. Anyway, I told him that after all you went through, you were anxious to make sure the book got published, so you wanted us to prove we still had our portion of it. If we'd already sold it or something, you wouldn't go through with the deal because we wouldn't have the whole thing to publish."

"And he accepted that?"

"Not at first. I got Arlene on the phone with him because he trusts her judgment, and she said he oughta bring the box, but then make sure he hangs onto it no matter what. Bringing it gets a meeting, she told him. It doesn't mean he actually has to hand it over when all was said and done. She argued with him for a while, trying to convince him it was our best bet."

"And it worked?" I asked.

"Yes, eventually. I hope you're appreciating what we're doing here. Convincing an inherently suspicious man like Bradford of something that doesn't make much sense isn't easy."

"Sure. I'd thank you if you deserved to be treated civilly."

"If you're trying to hurt my feelings, it's not working. Anyway, he wants me at the meet too, so we'll see you at six fifty-five tomorrow morning. What's with the wacky time, anyway?"

I was ready for this question and hoped my answer would satisfy him. "We have a plane to catch."

"Oh, okay. Remember, these aren't people you want to double-cross, Tris."

"I know. Why does Bradford want you there?"

"I don't think he trusts me. He knows I'm along for the ride with Arlene as far as being a member goes, and there's a rumor we've got a snitch in our midst."

"Let him know we're not people to double-cross, either. I'm smart enough to exact all kinds of creative revenge if he messes with us. He won't know what hit him." Once again, I'd borrowed this crude phrase from TV.

"I'll convey that. You have nice day, little buddy." He hung up.

I didn't like his cocky tone. He should've been scared, or at least nervous. What was he up to? After some thought, I decided he was in on Bradford's plan to hijack the hand-off. That was probably why Bradford had agreed to bring the book, too. He didn't have to worry about losing it with his minions lurking near our meeting. The more I thought about it, the more that made sense. Frank's story aside, our request was unreasonable. A good-faith negotiator wouldn't have kowtowed to it. Frank couldn't tell us the real reason Bradford agreed to bring the book without revealing the Keepers' treachery.

Marc agreed. "A lot of liars include too much detail. As good an actor as Frank is, an actor's only as good as his lines. I can't imagine Frank and Arlene could've convinced Bradford with those lame arguments. The important thing is that the glitch in your plan has been resolved."

Between Frank's call and getting ready for the next morning, I engrossed myself in studying Mandarin online. I needed something to keep me from either perseverating on negative outcomes or indulging my feelings about giving up dear Mildred. And despite earlier efforts, I had yet to master spoken Mandarin's intonations—four possible versions for each word, all with varying meanings. Memorizing thousands of Chinese characters had been much easier.

When it was time, Marc and I drove north, heading to a previously scouted parking spot a few blocks from a huge Amazon warehouse. We didn't speak on the way. There was little traffic due to the early hour. I kept my eye on the time. Timing was the key.

The car ahead of us at a long stoplight proclaimed on a well-worn bumper sticker that I shouldn't believe everything I think. Another one I spied down the road suggested that we eat the rich. Rather than dwell on either of these intriguing notions, I watched a series of sidewalk scenarios. A stooped old man in blue

Bermuda shorts, black knee socks, a white dress shirt, and a tweed English driving cap strode purposefully beside a young girl—maybe six—who struggled to keep up as she stared down at her phone. A green iguana lay languorously across the shoulder of a very tall, longhaired man climbing out of a parked red SUV. And a deliveryman labored under a stack of pizza boxes in the doorway of an old-fashioned barber shop. Who ate pizza at six thirty in the morning? For that matter, who cut hair at that hour?

I'd designated the grassy median at the front of the crowded Amazon employee parking lot as our meeting location for two reasons. One, it gave Bradford's men facile places to lurk—behind nearby cars. We wouldn't have to wonder where they were. Also, John Ruggles's crew could easily hide behind them in a farther row of cars, making it a simple matter to take them out of the picture. These local hires were armed, as was Ruggles at this point.

Once we arrived and began talking to Bradford, the second, and most important, component of the location would come into play.

We arrived exactly on time in the warehouse parking lot, double-parked to the side of the front door, and disembarked. Walter Bradford and Frank stood waiting on the median, the latter clutching the metal box containing the book. His boss held a green fabric grocery sack, which presumably held cut newspaper or some other facsimile of the cash he'd promised to hand off.

Marc carried an attaché case with the loose pages of Bromberg's substitute book in it. My knees began to shake again. I was sick and tired of all the shaking, but what could I do? Our acting skills were about to be tested in person—mine for the first time. And the stakes were high.

"So here's the infamous smart boy," Bradford growled as we approached. "Smart and greedy, it turns out."

He was as advertised—a muscle-bound, bald, middle-aged man. He wore a tight brown T-shirt and pressed khaki pants. Frank stood beside him, looking much the same as he had as Chet. His combination of African American features transposed onto a Caucasian face was especially striking in that moment. Perhaps anticipatory adrenaline had heightened my senses again.

"It's not greed," Marc said. "We simply need to get paid for our troubles. We've been through hell and back."

"Well, let's get this over with. Show me the rest of the book." A sneer seemed to be Bradford's baseline facial expression. His fierce dark eyes glared at us as well.

He'd have been a classic Western villain—maybe too typecast to be believable to a modern audience. For that matter, who had gleaming white teeth or such smooth skin back in the 1880s?

Marc held the case up waist-high and clicked it open, revealing the pages I'd copied. Bradford took a step forward.

At that moment, a loud whistle blew, and employees began noisily streaming out the front doors of the warehouse. The night shift was over. As waves of workers hurried past us on both sides, Ruggles stepped out from the crowd, a compact pistol held low against his leg.

"We meet again, Walter. I guess you can't trust everyone you rough up in a gym locker room."

"Now!" Bradford called to his men.

"They're not coming," I told him.

Ruggles raised the gun, aiming it at Sitkova, shielding it with his other hand from passersby. "Let's have the box, Frank."

As the former Chet stepped forward, two men burst through the crowd on our right, holding pistols of their own. Big guys with fierce expressions, they seemed capable of anything. Bradford's frown and compressed brow made it clear that these were not his men. One of them wore a white tank top and army fatigue pants. The other one was clad in a black button-down shirt with the sleeves raggedly ripped off. Baggy yellow basketball shorts completed his I'm-a-loose-cannon-who-means-business look. Their faces reiterated the intensity of the threat they represented. Both men scowled through dark stubble and glared for all they were worth.

"Put your gun down," the smaller of the two—the tank top—said. Ruggles lowered his weapon but hung on to it. Then the man turned to the rest of us while his partner kept Ruggles covered. "We'll take the money and both books. Move it!"

He winked at me, thank God. His performance was excellent; I'd begun to wonder if he was really Ruggles' man.

"Who are you?" Marc asked in a scared voice.

"We're Radiant Librarians," the ripped-sleeves man said. He turned to Sitkova. "Thanks for your help, Frank."

"What do you mean? You're not the Librarians!"

"Shut up!" the man commanded. His lean face was venomous. His eyes gleamed.

Suddenly, Ruggles raised his gun, but before he could use it, tank top shot him in the chest. Or seemed to, I should say. Realistic blood leaked through his shirt, and he crumpled onto the grass.

The sea of employees had begun to diminish. Now the loud gunfire created panic, and they scattered.

The shooter grabbed the box from Frank's arms and the grocery bag from Bradford. The other man snatched Marc's attaché case, and they both started to run, planning to disappear into the fleeing crowd.

Two more men blocked their exit. They held bigger guns—sawed-off shotguns. They were the thugs from the Mystery Spot attack.

"Not so fast," the skinny one said.

Oh God. Would I pee my pants again?

Our fake Librarians yielded to the genuine ones. I didn't blame them. They'd signed up for pretend gunplay, not the real thing. Both men laid down their guns and stood with their hands locked behind their heads.

"It's about time!" Frank barked. "Where the hell were you?"

"Traitor!" Bradford snarled.

"We got held up by all these asshole Amazon people," the fat gunman said. He was the one who'd run away after Marc had disarmed his partner.

"Shut up!" the skinny, bald one bellowed. He wore black from head to toe again.

"Let's get out of here," Frank barked. "Grab the bag and the book—move it!"

"Right."

When the threesome seized the books and the bag full of cut newspaper, they turned their backs to run off. Ruggles rose up just enough to train his pistol on them. "Whoa, pardners," he said. "Not dead, just resting."

They halted in their tracks. I couldn't tell if they were planning to comply or resist.

Just then, an enterprising citizen opened fire from somewhere behind me. Another shot came from my left. These weren't geeky Amazon engineers. They were gun-toting working-class Texans taking the law into their own hands.

I flattened myself on the grass, face down, as did Ruggles and Marc. Bullets flew for a while. When the cacophony finally stopped, I looked up. Everyone besides us was gone. There was a splash of blood on the ground under where Bradford had stood.

We ran to our cars and piled in as sirens screamed in the distance. Fortunately, we were able to blend in with the departing workers.

What a mess. No book. And I *did* pee my pants again.

Chapter 25

Later in our hotel room, as adrenaline drained out of me—once again, a very uncomfortable process—I took stock. Our classic con had been successfully hijacked. My plan would've worked, too. If Ruggles's men had taken off with the book following a fake murder, what recourse would've Bradford had? Surely, he would've fled and been happy to see our backs. Even if he continued his pursuit of the book, he'd clash with the Librarians, not us.

John Ruggles joined us in our room after once again making sure we weren't followed. I was struck anew by his matinee-idol looks. Why would a guy like that become an investigator? He told us both of the men he'd hired were unharmed, very angry, and heading for the hills—literally. One of them owned a cabin west of Austin. Ruggles reported that the man recommended we leave town as soon as possible, too.

We did, catching a flight to Albuquerque, and then to Los Angeles, where the three of us rode a shuttle to Ojai. The last thing Ruggles said before we parted company was that our rental car in Austin may have been identified, so we might find police knocking on our door soon.

For the next few days, every time I heard a noise, my startle reflex kicked in. I looked up this phenomenon. I was exhibiting hyper-vigilance. Marc told me that even if we weren't "on the lam," this was a typical post-traumatic symptom, along with insomnia, and several other now familiar phenomena.

My fears even kept me from enjoying my walks and playtime with Holsy, although our reunion was epic—basically, the opposite of what happened with Mildred. His skinny black and white puppy's tail threatened to wag right off his sausagey body. And he rained kisses onto my face, necessitating the use of a towel prior to our initial stroll.

No one came knocking, and no one approached me while I was out in public with dear Holsy. I guess we were lucky. But what crimes had we committed, anyway? The shooting was staged, and witnesses must've noticed Ruggles miraculously arising from the dead. It was legal to carry guns in public in Texas, except for the sawed-off shotguns, which weren't ours. All we did was stand, talk, fake a shooting, and drive off. The Librarians were the ones who needed locking up, and if I were a cop, I'd want to get the Amazon shooters off the street, too.

In hindsight, it was a miracle none of the warehouse workers had recognized me, a variable I hadn't considered at all. Perhaps Austinites were less interested in quiz shows, or maybe I was such a fish out of water in that parking lot that onlookers presumed I was merely a kid saddled with an irresponsible father.

If I were a witness or a police officer, I'd assume our fiasco had been a drug deal "gone bad," as they say on TV. No investigation would get far operating from that premise, and we were three states away, so I eventually felt safe. I told Marc so in our next session.

"Yes, I agree. I think we're okay. How are you

feeling?"

"I'm still shook up—much the same as after we were attacked at the Mystery Spot, with the additional element of keen disappointment since we lost the book."

"I think it's time to call Theodore," he said.

"*I* think it might be time to give up," I said. "The Librarians are really dangerous. I don't think I can go through another scary mess like that. It's just too much."

"Why don't we talk to Theodore before we decide?"

I nodded begrudgingly.

Marc dialed the number and put the call on speaker.

"Hello, Marc," Theodore answered.

"Is that a shaman thing?" I asked. "Knowing who's calling?"

"It's a caller ID thing, Tris."

"Oh, yeah. Sorry."

"What can I do for you?" he asked.

I spoke up. "Bad people have the wisdom book."

"How bad?"

"What do you mean?"

"It's a subjective term. One man's bad is another man's lovely and delightful."

Marc spoke. "I don't think anyone would be delighted by the Radiant Librarians' behavior."

"Ah, those people. I understand." He paused and considered our situation. "After all you've been through, you still don't have your book, Tris. Are you feeling discouraged?"

"Very much so," I told him.

"It's going to work out in the end. It always does," Theodore told me.

"Always? What about when people die young? What if a Librarian kills me?"

"You need to expand enough inside to gracefully hold that sort of thing as a version of working out. There's a bigger picture that transcends your individual life."

"I don't think metaphysical reassurance is going to help Tris very much right now," Marc said.

"Perhaps not. My job in a conversation is to say things. Yours is to make of them what you will. Be reassured. Don't be reassured. That's up to you."

"Once again, I don't think that's an appropriate thing to say right now," Marc asserted. "So can you help us decide what to do?"

"You still want to get the book?"

"Yes," Marc replied.

"No," I said simultaneously.

"Like I said when I met you," Theodore replied, "the world can use more wisdom."

"So you're saying yes, too? You think we should keep going?" I asked.

"Yes, at least as far as I'm concerned. Let me discuss this with my associates and call you back later."

"Okay."

Later that day, I received word that *Who's The Genius?* had changed its rules to end my reign. Now there was a limit on how many times a contestant could win. Ratings were down because the public had grown weary of watching me every time they tuned in. That was fine. The show wanted me back for one more competition, and I was in no rush to even do that.

My father was livid. He talked to a lawyer about suing, but then he got a call from the production company that was developing a new show with me as the emcee. The working title was *Beat Tris!* They were ready to negotiate a contract, and even if the show never aired, we'd still get paid quite a bit.

That's all it took to transform my parents from outraged to happy. Sometimes I wished a simple shift of external circumstances could prompt *me* to adopt such a positive mood.

I lay awake that night projecting negativity into my adolescence, and beyond. Was this to be my future—schlocky TV shows? What about discovering new scientific truths, writing a groundbreaking novel, or any number of other meaningful, non-venal pursuits? Would I have to emancipate myself before I could direct my genius toward these?

Theodore called back while I was in my next session with Marc—no accident, I'm sure.

"We've decided to help," he told us. "Only one shaman kept it from being unanimous. That's as good as it gets with us."

"That's great!" I said. Hope swelled in my chest, the section of my body that seemed to be most affected by emotions.

"Tell us more about your group," Marc requested.

"We're a loose association of shamans and others who know how to leave our bodies while we sleep. We meet in Antarctica on alternate Thursday nights. I usually bring the snacks."

"Antarctica? Snacks?"

"Just kidding about the snacks. We like it in Antarctica, though. It's quiet. With no bodies, we can't get cold, and since there's no time or space in the subtle realm, there aren't any problems with any of that."

"That doesn't make sense," I chimed in. "If there's no space, how can you be in a specific location? And what do you do? Fly there? Teleport?"

"It doesn't need to make sense to you."

"What happens at these meetings?" Marc asked.

"We complain about politics, gossip about celebrities—all the usual stuff."

"Really?" I asked.

"No, just kidding again. You two need to lighten up." He paused. "It's hard to characterize what we do. It varies. And there's only so much that would be helpful for you to know."

Marc spoke up, irritation in his voice, which surprised me. "So yesterday you wanted to talk about metaphysics instead of helping Tris with his feelings, but now you want to 'help' by *withholding* metaphysical information?"

"You said it was better not to know some things back in Turkey, too," I said before the shaman could reply—if he was even going to. "Why's that?"

Theodore's voice softened. He was in teacher mode now. "Suppose I told you we talked in our meetings about how cockroaches were going to rule the Earth in twenty years. Wouldn't that knowledge interfere with your well-being?"

"Is that true?" I immediately felt like an idiot for asking.

"Hell, no. They won't be in charge for at least a hundred years. And they're coming from outer space, so they're different than our cockroaches."

"You're kidding again, aren't you?" Marc asked.

"Yes. You see what I mean? We're only configured to hold so much weird stuff before it messes with us. Antarctica is enough for today."

"I've done some reading about shamanism since we met that second time," I told Theodore. "Are you affiliated with a particular tradition or lineage?"

"Yes, but that doesn't matter. Here's what we're thinking…"

He launched into a long, detailed plan that certainly bested any of the ones I'd concocted. I was able to add input that refined it—several details they'd overlooked. I don't know how they knew enough about the Librarians and the current situation with the book to make any sort of plan. I also wondered about their motives. I liked Theodore, but what did we really know about who he was affiliated with? Could every member of his organization be trusted?

"And that will work?" Marc asked when Theodore and I finally finished hashing out the minutiae.

"We had some disagreement about the possibility of success—as you would define success, I mean. This was before Tris's contributions. The consensus was that we had a fifty-eight percent chance of pulling it off."

"What does the other forty-two percent look like?" Marc asked.

"That wouldn't be helpful to know."

Marc looked at me and rolled his eyes. "You can be really irritating," he told Theodore.

"Sure, a lot of people tell me that. Shall we get on with this? Let me fill you in about some things."

Theodore's shaman network—he alternately called them Shamans R Us or Amalgamated United—knew quite a bit about the Radiant Librarians already. He told us they'd had eyes on the cult for several decades.

The organization was based on the north shore of Kauai, near Princeville, where they operated out of a timeshare resale office—sort of a low-rent real estate business. Their goals were different than the Keepers' ever since their current leader—Sue Popp—took over. As I'd read online, she directed her small, loyal cult to gather whatever materials might support her apocalyptic prophesies—using any means necessary. Popp had personally recruited the gunmen we'd run into twice—her brother owned the private security company they worked for. Once again, I couldn't imagine how the shamans could know all this, but I believed him.

Ironically, according to Theodore, the wisdom book didn't have any material in it that had anything to do with Popp's agenda, but she couldn't have known that until she finally got hold of it. "So the Librarians have no reason to publish or even hang on to the book," Theodore told us. "If I were her, I'd sell it back to the Keepers."

"You know what's in the book?" I asked.

"Yes."

"Don't tell me," Marc said. "It wouldn't be helpful for *us* to know, right?"

"Bingo."

All that effort, expense, and violence for nothing. The book was useless to the Librarians? Was Popp so sure of herself that she assumed any wise words would corroborate her point of view? Perhaps she'd been steered wrong by whoever was spying for her within the Keepers. None of those possibilities made much sense to me, but I guess religious maniacs weren't the most logical demographic in the world.

More than ever, I wished I'd read the book. What *was* in it? I was only finding out what wasn't. The Keepers knew, the Librarians knew, and now it turned out the shamans did too. Everyone but me. It wasn't fair.

"What about giving the book to us?" I asked, my tone hopeful. "Would she do that since it's no use to her?"

"No," Theodore said. "That's not the way these people's minds work. And whoever she sells it to, it's going to be for more than we can afford."

Marc spoke up. "Frank Sitkova is a convert to Librarianism, right?"

"Based on his pattern of behavior, I think he's just a greedy turncoat. Don't worry about him. The universe is self-regulating."

"What do you mean?" I asked.

"Sooner or later, there's payback for everything dishonorable we do to one another."

"I like the idea of sooner better than later," I told him. "Can't you do something about that? Shamans have all sorts of powers, right?" I hated to think Frank might remain unscathed until some future incarnation.

"You don't work the system," Theodore said. "It's what you surrender to. If you surrender enough, these so-called powers show up. We call them tricks. They don't matter much."

"Those tricks might be what save our planet," Marc said. "Wisdom book aside, it doesn't look like ordinary people are going to be able to stop the powers that be from ruining the world."

"Oh, don't worry. There are plenty of other planets

to reincarnate on."

Chapter 26

I talked my parents into taking a family vacation in Hawaii, somewhere my mother had always wanted to visit. This was the first step in our plan. I'd miss Holsy while I was gone, but I knew he'd be fine since all was well with him once I'd returned from Austin.

"I'm going to sip margaritas on Waikiki beach!" my mother shouted, throwing her hands in the air. "Yippee!"

"They don't have Mexican drinks there, Betty," my dad told her. "You get those girly drinks with fruit and little umbrellas. You'll like those too, though. And Tris could use a break before he goes back on the show for the last time."

He could be a decent father and husband sometimes. I tended to focus exclusively on his faults since he didn't have enough self-awareness to hide them.

Marc sent my folks an email with an attachment detailing Freud's practice of taking his patients with him on vacation so their work could remain continuous. Then he volunteered to go to Hawaii too, as long as it was Kauai, which neither of my parents had ever heard of. I filled them in about the island and said I thought it was a good idea if Marc came with us. Without any background in psychology, they had no idea we were proposing something wildly unorthodox.

"Tris needs to keep working on himself," Marc told my father in a follow-up call. "I fear he'll backslide and become the old Tris again if we don't do this."

I'd been much less hostile since we'd returned from Austin—verging on civil—so this was a powerful argument.

"Well, it's no skin off our teeth if that's what you want to do," my dad replied. "But we're not paying any extra."

"I'll square it with your health insurance company."

That'll be the day—an insurance company paying for junkets to Hawaii. Sometimes my parents' ignorance was opportune.

I created a slideshow of photos and descriptions of Kauai, and we looked at them together, which pleased my mother immensely.

"Oh, Trissie, this is what I always wanted—to be a real family and do things together. This place is gorgeous!" Her face lit up as though the sun was shining through the walls of our condo.

"We gave him every chance, Betty," my father said, frowning his aggressive frown. "He wouldn't go bowling with us, he said car shows were for greasy morons, and he even told us he'd rather be burnt alive than go to the county fair. Lord knows we tried."

"Let's focus on now," I said. "Right now, we have something positive happening, right?"

"Good point," my dad said. "We live in the now, don't we?" He smiled as he said this. He knew he was speaking my recently acquired language.

"What? That doesn't sound like you, Dad. Where'd that come from?"

"I picked up that book you left on the table the other day—the one Dalcour told you to read. *My Fullness*, or something or other, by some foreign guy. He says on the back of the book he's a Buddhist, but a lot of people say that and then it turns out they're something else. You can tell the real story from this guy's last name. Anyway, he sounded pretty smart."

I got up and put my arm around his shoulder. "That's great. I'm proud of you, Dad."

My mother's jaw dropped, and my father looked down quickly so I wouldn't see tears leaking out. That was a first.

"That therapist of yours is worth every penny!" Mom proclaimed.

Ever since I'd watched a movie filmed in Kauai as a young child, I'd looked forward to visiting someday. Marc had honeymooned there, which I imagined would introduce a bittersweet element to his return. I asked him about that at our next session.

"It might be hard. But it's where we need to go, regardless."

"Let me know if I can help with that when we're on Kauai. You know, if you need to talk about it or something."

"Thanks, Tris."

I reported my father's remark about the present moment, which tickled Marc.

"We'll shape that guy up yet."

"I doubt it," I said. "I think my best strategy is to shift my attitude—stop trying to change him."

"Absolutely. I was joking."

"I realize that," I said, although I hadn't. I suddenly remembered something I wanted to discuss. It kept

301

getting pushed onto a back burner as more urgent material drew our attention. "Let's talk about how I don't have past-life memories anymore," I said.

"Sure."

"It's not just that I'm not having them. It's that I hardly notice their absence. What a profound phenomenon to lose awareness of. If I can't trust my mind to stay tethered to experiences this intense…"

"It could be a positive step." Marc paused to take a sip of water from a glass on the table beside him.

"I hardly think so. I find it deeply disturbing." Just talking about my diminished cognitive abilities scared me. I remembered how Marc had stated in our initial session that I was basically fear-based.

"You're moving away from an internal focus toward a fuller participation in outward situations." He crossed his long legs, revealing purple socks. "It's coming at the expense of tracking things, and that's hard for you to accommodate."

After further discussion, Marc suggested that the absence of memories was probably a response to trauma. "You may have circled the wagons psychologically to protect yourself, blocking difficult material. How many ten-year-olds endure shootings, let alone all the rest? Anyway, let's just keep an eye on it."

"Okay." I felt about two-thirds reassured.

Several days passed in an ordinary fashion—I studied metaphysics and social skills, for the most part—and then we all headed to the San Francisco airport. My mom and dad sat together on our flight, and Marc and I parked ourselves across the plane's aisle. We'd found a relatively inexpensive nonstop to Lihue, one of only two towns on Kauai with a population exceeding five thousand, and just barely that. For the most part, I watched movies to pass the time. I gave out a few autographs and posed for selfies, too. My fans' excitement about meeting me meant something to me now. My presence brightened their day.

My mother had bought all of us matching Hawaiian shirts, Marc included. Talk about bringing coals to Newcastle. On sale at Target, our orange polyester monstrosities sported a smorgasbord of not-to-scale pineapples, coconuts, and macadamia nuts. It was a good thing we weren't planning to visit an impoverished country populated by hungry people.

When we arrived at the modest, open-air Lihue airport, my mother asked where we could change our money. My father remarked that no one looked Hawaiian until he saw one extremely large brown man at the baggage carousel. "Finally," he said to him, "a real native. Talk some Hawaiian, would you?"

"I'm from Samoa, asshole. Go screw yourself."

My dad stood paralyzed, his face redder than I'd seen in a long time. His hands balled into fists. He finally realized the Samoan could knock him over with a casual forearm. "Sorry," he muttered as he turned away.

I could see that Marc was about to step in, but I preempted him. "Dad, most people here are a mix of nationalities. There aren't many pure Hawaiians like in the movies."

"Well, I hope they're not all as touchy as that man. What did I say that was so bad?"

I patted him on the back. "Don't worry about it. He was just a big jerk, and he isn't even from around here. If you do your best to be nice to the people who live here, they'll be nice back. They've got this thing called aloha spirit where they try to be really friendly."

"Ooh," my mother said, "that sounds wonderful. There's never any reason to be mean. Mean people should be kept locked up someplace out in the desert. Where's Samoa, anyway? It sounds like some kind of food."

"It's another tropical archipelago 2,618 miles southwest of here."

"It's a South Pacific island, you mean? Goodness, he's come a long way. No wonder he's so cranky."

"Actually," I told my mother, "we just flew…let's see…nine more miles than he did, assuming he wasn't on our plane."

"Oh, Trissie. You know everything. You're so helpful." She gave me a big hug, burying me in her ample bosom.

When she finally released me, I glanced at Marc, who winked and gave me a thumbs-up.

Marc hadn't checked any luggage, so he headed over to a car rental van. He'd rendezvous with me later that day after checking into his lodging—a studio AirBnB in the heart of Princeville.

My dad had uncharacteristically splurged on our accommodations. As we waited for the Westin Princeville's shuttle, he paraphrased what he read from a brochure he'd found in a rack on the wall in the baggage claim area.

"Our hotel has a crapload of swimming pools and amenities, including beach access at an even fancier hotel down the street. The rooms aren't rooms. They're suites, so Tris can have his own room, and there's a little kitchen and a living room, too. They've got brand new barbecue grills on this cliff overlooking the water and anyone can use them—well, anyone staying there. There's ping-pong and a pool table, too. Once we go shopping for groceries, and there's a shuttle for that, we won't have to go anywhere. We can just relax."

"I might want to look around the island, Dad—see the sights, as it were. Maybe Marc could take me if you'd prefer to relax."

"Sure, sure. Whatever."

Perfect.

We climbed into the gleaming white resort shuttle with several older, wealthy-looking couples. It was a forty-minute ride to the other side of the island. I hoped my parents didn't embarrass themselves too badly in the van or while we stayed at the high-end resort.

A friendly woman from Iowa sat behind my mom and struck up a conversation. After exchanging basic facts about themselves, the woman—Helen—cajoled my mother into sharing her best recipes. Clearly, my mom was making up the specific quantities of the ingredients, and she probably didn't remember the actual cooking times either. Just as clearly, Helen wasn't retaining any of the details. They didn't care. It was about making a connection. I hoped they'd reconnect at the resort. I pictured the two women dangling their feet in the shallow end of a vast swimming pool, moving on to sharing sewing tips and their hopes for future grandchildren.

Personally, I thought they were foolish to focus on one another instead of the spectacular landscape we drove through. Jagged green peaks jutted up from the lush tropical landscape. We passed farms, open spaces, orchards, and groupings of modest homes in the mostly rural north end of the island. The main highway was just a two-lane country road, often bordered by uncrowded beaches as it periodically hugged the shoreline. Occasionally, hotels and restaurants competed with the natural beauty, and we passed through several towns that were littered with shops dedicated to exploiting tourists. Did anyone really need a miniature Hawaii license plate with his name on it? Personally, I only bought necessities at sensibly priced stores. Anything else felt irresponsible, given the state of our planet. I'm sure if I ever mentioned this to Marc, he'd want me to "step outside my comfort zone" and purchase ten tiny license plates. Loosen up about *everything?* No, thank you. I'll hang onto my core values.

Situated near the south border of Princeville, the Westin sprawled behind a neighborhood of two-story condominiums. The town didn't seem to be a town, per se. A planned development of homes and golf courses, carved out of something that probably didn't need carving forty years earlier, Princeville nonetheless embodied a certain charm. Every property owner, especially our resort, had spent a great deal of money on landscaping—an array of tropical plants and trees I'd never seen before.

Under the capacious portico in front of the resort's lobby, several men in matching, *tasteful* Hawaiian shirts stood poised to welcome new guests. You didn't buy *those* shirts at Target, and they probably didn't itch.

I became aware of the catch-22 of the island as I stood and watched two men efficiently unload luggage from the back of the van. It was *humid*, at least by my standards, borne of inland California. And the tropical sun was fiercer at a lower temperature than back in Ojai. I weighed Hawaii against June in central Texas, and at least Hawaii won that contest. I hadn't noticed the humidity or the intensity of the lower latitude sun in the shade outside the airport, where a strong breeze had moderated the heat. I imagined that thirty feet away from the shelter of the resort's canopy, I'd be sunburned in a quarter hour.

The aloha spirit was quite evident and seemed to be a sincere expression of goodwill. If I had to work at a tourist-centered business, I'd be unhappy and probably surly. Perhaps the job market on Kauai was so limited that unloading vehicles and checking people into their rooms represented career success.

Online photos hadn't done justice to the Westin. Comprised of seven or eight three-story buildings sprawled across eighteen acres, its low-slung design implied non-greedy developers. I later discovered the island's building code precluded any structures higher than a coconut palm tree. What a wonderful idea.

Despite the accurate images of the suite on the Westin website, our living quarters were more modest than I expected. I'd believed the dimensions and furnishings would catalyze some sort of feeling I wasn't having. I wasn't even sure what that would be.

A Polynesian theme was evident in the brown and beige decor. Complex straw matting adorned several walls, and mid-twentieth-century Hawaiian landscape paintings were clearly unique works of art. A substantial dining room table was artfully shaped from an unfamiliar dark hardwood. The small kitchen included every modern appliance we might need. And the beds were firm and comfortable, with marvelously smooth sheets. What more did the expectation-generating part of my brain require to feel satisfied?

By now it was late afternoon. Once we unpacked and I slathered on sunscreen, I was ready to shed my parents.

"I'm going out to explore the grounds," I announced.

My mom frowned, her bow of a mouth turning down sharply at the corners. "Ooh, do you think it's safe? Jim, should we let him wander around by himself?"

"*You* try to stop him from doing whatever he wants. He'll just tell us some obscure fact about hotels that shoots down whatever we're saying."

Mom nodded, and I took off. It occurred to me for the first time that my father might be intimidated by me.

My first stop was back at the main building to ask one of the concierges where I could buy a sturdy sunhat. This older Eurasian woman steered me to the compact gift shop across from the upscale restaurant at the rear of the lobby. Armed with my purchase of an outrageously expensive toquilla straw model—the only hat in my size that didn't reek of poor taste—I found an unoccupied lounge chair under an enormous umbrella by the main pool, where I watched young children splash and play. The children's energy, as always, amazed me. I suspect that kids under a certain age instinctively know how to appropriate energy from nearby adults for their own purposes.

A twentysomething female server sidled up in the ubiquitous Hawaiian shirt that all the employees wore—a swirly white pattern against a light green background. "Can I get you anything, hon? A coke? Some fruit juice? We have guava if you've never tried that."

This perky blonde gal looked as though she'd been a cheerleader at a school like UCLA. Her smile was wide and inviting, so I decided to test my social skills.

"I haven't. Is that your favorite?"

"No, I actually like the orange/passionfruit combo the best."

"Tell me about passionfruit." Of course I already knew all about it, but if I limited myself to novel topics, I'd hardly ever speak.

"You know, that's a good question. I know they have them at the grocery stores here, but I can't even remember what they look like."

"That's okay. How long have you been on the island?" I asked.

She frowned. "Oh, you can tell? Bummer. I'm trying so hard to fit in. It's been three months."

"Where are you from?" I patted the seat next to me. "Sit if you like. I'm enjoying talking to you." This was a major stretch for me. What if she said no? How would I feel?

"I'm not supposed to, but sure. My feet are killing me." She plopped down unceremoniously with a sigh. "I'm from Oregon."

"Where in Oregon?" It was time to show off. I couldn't resist.

"Beaverton."

I closed my eyes for a moment to retrieve the information. "That's the sixth largest city in the state, population 99,000 as of 2018, in Washington county, comprising 18.73 square miles."

"Whoa." She stared at me. "I don't know all those details, but you got the county and the population right. Have you been there? Are you from Oregon?"

"No, that's just the way my brain works. I pretty much remember everything, and I read a geographic almanac once."

"Wow." She stared more. "Wait a minute. You're that kid from the quiz show, aren't you?"

"That's me."

"What's it like?"

"You mean being on TV?"

"Yeah. Is it fun?"

"No, it's nerve-wracking. Imagine millions of people are watching everything you do."

"God, that would be horrible. I get self-conscious when a table full of drunk men look at me."

"Well, that's different, isn't it? I'd hate to be a woman and have men stare at my body."

"Yes! It's the hardest parts of this job. Some of the other servers—even the men—flirt with guests all the time to boost their tips. Not me."

Neither of us said anything for a few moments.

"I'm Tris."

"I know. I'm Natalie."

"It's on your name tag," I pointed out, instantly realizing that this comment may have made her feel stupid. "I'm sorry," I added.

"What for?"

"I didn't need to mention your name tag."

"No biggie. Listen, I better get back to work and bring you that juice."

"Sure. It was nice talking to you." I'd never specified which variety of juice I preferred. It would be interesting to see what she would bring.

She stood and smiled again. "You're cool, Tris—nothing like that jerk you play on TV."

"Thanks."

She strode off into the intense sunlight.

I'd connected with someone completely ordinary and enjoyed it too. Natalie was a nice person doing the best she could to make her life work. What was wrong with that?

Marc called and told me he'd drive over in a few minutes. I called my mother and told her I'd be seeing some local sights with him and we'd probably have dinner while we were out.

"Are you sure, Trissie? We're going to go to that fancy place back where we checked in. The stewardess on our plane said it won stars, and there's a menu in the room..."

I heard my dad shout, "The suite, Betty. The suite!"

"Oh, sorry. I found a menu in the *suite* here, and they have something called Huli Huli chicken. Can you imagine. What a silly name. We could try it together. What do you say?"

"That sounds like fun, Mom. We'll see how it goes. Why don't you make a reservation for three, and I'll join you if I can."

"You think we need a reservation?" Her voice sounded worried.

"It's a way to get an especially good table, even if the restaurant isn't crowded."

"Thank you, Tris. We'll do that. Have a good time with your therapist. He's a nice man, isn't he?"

"He certainly is."

Natalie returned with a tall glass of orange-passionfruit juice and several beers on a round metal tray. She seemed to be in a hurry, so I told her my room number for billing purposes, and she scurried away with the other drinks.

The juice was, in fact, delicious. Obviously fresh-squeezed, I'd never tasted anything like it. Unfortunately, I couldn't savor it since I needed to meet Marc out front.

"Hop in," he said when I found his mid-sized Japanese sedan idling under the portico. "There's been news."

Chapter 27

Once I settled into the passenger seat and Marc maneuvered out of the parking lot, he briefly turned to me. "We need to move up the timeline. Theodore called and told me the Librarians arranged to sell the book the day after tomorrow."

"To whom?"

"To Shamans R Us, actually, as planned—or so they think—but the Librarians insist on that particular day to complete the deal, which certainly wasn't in *our* plan. So we've got to move quickly. Instead of getting the lay of the land tonight, we need to go on to the next step."

"Okay, but remind me why we don't just go ahead and actually buy the book."

"That's right. You don't know how much they're asking." He turned to face me for a moment again. "Half a million."

"That's ridiculous!"

"It certainly is," Marc agreed, returning his eyes to the road. "I guess Theodore had no reason to negotiate them down. I don't know the details. You know how he can be when you ask him a question."

On the ten-minute drive to Hanalei, Marc outlined what Theodore had set forth in their phone conversation while I took in the sweeping views of the most breathtaking bay I'd ever seen. A sandy beach stretched uninterrupted from one end to the other of the almost perfect parabola. Graceful, bowed trees provided shade along the grassy area on the back edge of the beige sand. Dozens of surfers plied tall, forceful waves while others swam. And all of this was the mere foreground of a panorama that encompassed lush farmland, steep, bright green mountains, and distant inlets.

At the bottom of a long hill lined with jungly tropical vegetation, we queued up to cross a one-lane bridge that marked the beginning of a coastal plain planted in taro, which Marc recommended I not try, no matter what any Hawaiian told me.

The town itself was about five blocks long— typifying the scale of Kauai. At first glance, it looked funky, as though fringe people eked out meager existences tucked away in this remote corner of the island. Upon closer examination, it was clear that the modest, weathered buildings housed expensive businesses and that the local residents were by no means poor. Living beside Hanalei Bay came with a steep price tag.

Tourists in rental cars patrolled the two parking lots and side streets searching for spots. We lucked out after cruising by a kayak rental shop, a Polynesian-style restaurant, and several art galleries. A red jeep backed out of a prime location.

A high percentage of tourists wore Hawaiian shirts or T-shirts with writing on them, new-looking shorts, and either thong sandals or hiking boots. The locals wore upscale versions of 1960s fashions, including tie-dyed tank tops, homemade-looking jewelry, and surfer shorts. If you swapped each group's clothes, it would still be easy to tell the two groups apart, given the purposeful air of the locals. They were downtown to either grocery shop or sell things to the tourists. The Hanaleians also seemed a bit full of themselves—the kind of people who thought they were better than you because they could hold a downward dog yoga pose without grimacing.

Now they were here, some of the tourists didn't seem to know what to do. Families wandered from store to store, read menus in front of restaurants, and sat on benches to watch cars go by. Perhaps they'd already been to the nearby beach and were now content to pursue this passive array of activities.

The timeshare resale business that served as a front for the Radiant Librarians operated out of a stand-alone storefront at the far end of the downtown. As we strode there, I could feel the strong ultraviolet rays on my bare arms, SPF eighty notwithstanding.

Butterflies fluttered in my gut again when I glanced at the manila envelope under Marc's arm. Life was bringing me a lot of bodily sensations lately. In fact, it was as if someone had turned the volume knob of life in general from four to nine.

We entered the building, and an especially aggressive aloha greeted us. The young African-American woman behind the modest desk—the only furniture besides two kitchen chairs set before it— smiled and told us they were fresh out of listings. "The real estate market's a funny thing," she added, shrugging as though we should share her perspective about the vagaries of her profession.

Clearly, the entire operation was geared toward discouraging potential clients. The threadbare furnishings hinted at failure, and the woman's words—

which couldn't possibly be true—scarcely encouraged anyone to even remain in the room. My online investigation of timeshares on Kauai indicated a thriving marketplace.

"Real estate certainly is a whimsical realm," Marc agreed, smiling back at the woman.

"You seem like nice people," she said. "Why don't you try Island Sales? You might have better luck there."

Above her continuous smile, her alert brown eyes demonstrated depth. In that moment, as those eyes widened, I realized she had recognized me, which was a good thing.

Instead of asking for an autograph, she rose and sidled to a door behind her. "You know," she said smoothly, "let me get my boss. She might be able to help you more."

Marc laid the manila envelope on the desk as we waited for about two minutes. I began sweating despite the office's perfectly adequate air-conditioning. Our mission might very well rest on the next few minutes, and whoever was back behind the door had time to call in thugs.

The fiftyish woman who emerged from the inner office bore an air of authority, which I initially attributed to her upright posture and a hint of indefinable charisma. Tall and slim, she wore a sky-blue polo shirt and white shorts. She'd tied her long, dark hair in a ponytail. Overall, she was attractive in a slinky sort of way—as if Modigliani had painted his usual model in the twenty-first century.

Her eyes drew my attention, as they exerted a magnetic effect. *They* were the seat of her authority. As dark as her hair and oversized to a fault, something else was odd about them. She never blinked. How could that be? Maybe she timed her blinks to mine, so I couldn't see them. More likely, her ducts weren't functional and she employed artificial tears. Either way, it was disconcerting.

We remained seated as she stood behind the desk, arms crossed.

"Hello, Sue," I said, fairly certain this was Sue Popp—the cult's leader.

"Tris. I wondered if we'd ever meet." Crisply delivered, each word was distinct from its brethren. The pitch of her voice was lower than I expected.

"You'll want to read the materials on the desk," Marc told her.

"Mr. Dalcour, you have no idea what I want."

"Nonetheless…"

After a long staring match between Marc and Popp, she finally picked up the packet, opened it, and began reading.

We had assembled all the damning evidence the shamans could muster, along with an account of our own experiences at the hands of the Librarians.

"What do you want?" she asked without looking up. Her tone was steely now; she wasn't shaken. Based on my first impressions, I didn't think she would be.

"Money," Marc told her. "And the book you stole."

Popp sat, a graceful, flowing movement as though she'd been a dancer, and perhaps she had. No one seemed to know her history prior to nine years ago.

"I'm not falling for that. Who do you think we are? We're not the Keepers. I know you two don't care about money. What do you really want?"

"I'm curious," I told her. "What do you think sets

you apart from the Keepers? From my vantage point, you're just a more ruthless version of the same organization."

"I'm disappointed in you, Tris. Hasn't that brain of yours been able to discern something as simple as that? Unlike Walter Bradford, I am sincerely dedicated to our cause. I have a vision for a better future for all of humanity—a world without war, without hate, without old white men in charge of everything. The world as we know it—this morass of corruption and filth—will end soon, and my people are preparing to give birth to a new era in human history. You've met Bradford, haven't you? And for that matter, you know Sitkova—a Keeper willing to betray him. There are others like them. These people are scum. A spiritual organization's culture develops from the top down. Ours embodies loyalty, conviction, and obedience. These don't happen by accident. I've *made* them happen."

"*You're* sincere?" Marc said, which surprised me. It was evident to me she was.

"I am," Popp stated with intense, eerie conviction.

"Are you talking about the Revelations version of an apocalypse—the end of days?" I asked.

"No, we're not Christians. And that's not for the likes of you to know—unless you decide to join us. We could use someone like you." She paused. "I'll tell you this much. Perhaps it will entice you into attending one of our services. The end of life as we know it will start with a pandemic, originating in China."

"Be that as it may," Marc said, "there's nothing new about your message. Countless gurus and charlatans have espoused the same thing for millennia, and yet here we are. And hasn't modern medicine pretty much eliminated the possibility of a worldwide epidemic?"

"Human illnesses, yes. This will be a crossover from the animal kingdom—karmic retribution for all our cruelty to those souls born into the bodies of other species. I assure you, every one of us has been a cow, a pig, and even a mosquito."

"I appreciate the glimpse into your worldview," Marc said. "But let me tell you more about the material in that envelope. Whether you believe we want money is irrelevant. Perhaps we don't. What matters is there's no way you want the information in that folder leaked to the press, and we'll do exactly that if you don't do what we say."

"If you do, I'll have you both killed. In fact, I might, anyway." Her tone was flat—expressionless.

I was struck dumb. *Did she really mean that? Or was it a strong bluff?*

"Try me," she said, reading our expressions. Her gaze remained penetrating, and quite convincing.

Marc spoke. "You're telling me you're a sincere prophet leading an organization to help the world, but you'd commit murder?"

"Oh, not me. It would be those gentlemen you met in Santa Cruz and Texas. Do you think they're incapable of that?"

Our plan had not included responding to direct threats on our lives. I let Marc continue to take the lead. I was out of my depth, and the strong adrenaline response my fear catalyzed froze my mind, among other familiar sensations.

"Jason, Carl! Could you come in here?" Popp called.

Two young men emerged from the door behind Popp. Neither was particularly imposing physically, but each had a fervent gleam in his eyes. These were obedient drones.

They stood beside her, each at parade rest with their hands behind them. Were they ex-military?

Marc fidgeted and then blurted out, "The information is on Tris's laptop, and a back-up thumb drive is locked in the hotel safe where he's staying. So think twice about your threats. Harming us won't get you the damning evidence."

"Hey, don't tell her that!" I said, alarm in my tone.

"Why don't we just take a break and think things over?" Popp suggested. "Have a nice meal on me, and then come back and we'll see if we can work this out."

She opened a desk drawer, and I held my breath for an instant. When she reached in and pulled out a gift certificate to a nearby restaurant, my breath whooshed out. She handed it to Marc. "We give these to people who won't go away after our receptionist talks to them."

So we adjourned to a seafood restaurant down the street, just past the third shaved-ice stand I counted. From the outside, the Opakapapah House looked like something you'd find in a film set in the bayous of southern Louisiana—a rambling shed constructed of weathered, vertical wooden slats. Inside was another story. We could've been in a French restaurant in San Francisco. Despite the Hawaiian name, the dining environment was decidedly anti-Hawaiian.

We waited by the vacant hostess's podium—an incongruous black-lacquered Chinese piece.

"My wife and I ate here on our honeymoon," Marc

told me matter-of-factly. "Well, not exactly here. It was an Asian fusion restaurant back then."

"What's it like?"

"It was excellent, but we drank too much."

"No, I mean what's it like for you now—being here?"

"Oh, sorry." He closed his eyes for a moment as a diminutive Asian hostess glided through the dining area toward us. "It's bittersweet. More sweet than bitter, I guess."

We both tried mahi-mahi in a rich, cream-based sauce while we discussed our meeting. The fish was outstanding.

Marc pointed out that parts of the scary encounter with Sue Popp had followed our plan and parts hadn't. After we looked at that, we shared our thoughts on Popp herself, and Marc agreed she was sincere in her misguided beliefs.

"I was just challenging her to see how she'd react," he told me.

"Does she have some sort of mental health diagnosis?" I asked. "Did you see her eyes while she was answering you—saying she really *was* sincere? Nobody should be that sure of *anything*. She looked crazed."

"I've seen high-functioning delusional disorders like hers before, although it's rare. She believes and will continue to believe whatever she thinks about all this, no matter what real-world evidence comes her way to dispute it. This isn't a biochemical thought disorder like schizophrenia or bipolar disorder, so there's no medication that can help."

"Do people with this disorder usually focus on

spirituality?"

"There are several common themes: grandiosity—which might entail a spiritual element—persecution, jealousy, erotomania—believing someone is love with them who isn't—and somatic—fictitious medical problems. I might be leaving something out. In my experience, the grandiose version totally lacks insight about who they truly are."

"So she's a combination of the spiritual and the grandiose versions?"

Marc nodded.

"When they get support from followers like Popp does, does that make it worse?"

"Definitely. Look at famous cult figures from the past. Typically, they started off with modest claims. By the time they gained enough followers for the world to notice them, they'd declared themselves God or something. You can be both spiritual and crazy; how much one or the other flourishes depends on circumstances."

"That's really interesting. I need to read more abnormal psychology, and I'll definitely research delusional disorders in the morning."

We agreed we'd have to wait to see how it all played out before we'd know how much any of that mattered.

The dessert menu seemed impressed with itself for offering Lappert's ice cream, so I tried macadamia coconut fudge. It was exquisite. I had no idea anything could taste so good.

When I'd finished, Marc asked me if I thought we'd given the Librarians enough time.

"Yes, I think so."

"Let's head back."

When we walked in, a laptop and a thumb drive sat on the metal desk. Popp sat behind it, and a much more imposing minion stood behind her. As we took our seats in front of the desk, he stomped around us to the front door, which he locked. I turned to watch him. He glared back as he assumed a parade rest stance.

If you could cross a wild boar with a larger, more erect species, you'd have the animal kingdom version of this guy. He wasn't just tall or broad. He was startlingly fierce, like photos I'd seen of Afghan warriors. In his case, if he'd started life with a hawk-like nose typical of that region, someone had squashed it since, spreading it to the sides. His forehead was pitted with small dents, and his patchy stubble was jet black. He radiated violence by the way he stood on the balls of his feet, leaning forward just a bit as though he were a pit bull on a leash, waiting to be released.

"So all we need," Popp declared in a self-satisfied tone, "are the passwords for these."

I turned around and crossed my arms. "No way," I asserted. I attempted to project a scared variety of bravado—not too much fear and not too much stubborn resolve.

"Maybe we have other copies," Marc said with a distinct lack of conviction.

"I told you I'm not a fool, Dalcour. I read people. You just told me you don't. So I think it's time for me to resort to a cliche. We can do this the hard way or the easy way. It's your choice. Bart has an unfortunate mean streak that I haven't been able to tame. It comes in handy in situations like this."

"I take it that Bart is standing behind us," Marc

said.

"I am," Bart rumbled. "I don't think the term 'mean' really does me justice, though. I'm the guy in your middle school class who tortured cats. You know what I mean?" His voice had been damaged in some way, so the sounds were about two-thirds low frequency noise and one-third words.

Acting scared now came easily. Just being in the same room with this guy was terrifying. My hands trembled, which could only help our cause.

"I'm not giving you any passwords," I squeaked.

"Sure you are," Popp said calmly. "Can't you see that?"

"Screw you!" I tried.

"Dalcour," she said. "How do you feel about watching Bart torture your young friend?"

"Tell them, Tris!" Marc called, frantically waving his arms.

"No!" I crossed my arms and glared at him.

Sue leaned back in her chair. "Let's try this another way. Tris, how do *you* feel about watching Bart burn holes in Marc's genitals?"

I ducked my head and pretended to sob. Then I mumbled the passwords. She used them to open the laptop, insert the thumb drive, and reveal the contents of both.

"If you try anything else," Popp told us, "we won't be so nice to you."

"Yes, ma'am," I said.

"And Tris, despite the fact that you've hardly lived up to your reputation as a genius, remember you're welcome to come to one of our services." She handed me a card on which only a phone number was printed.

"Perhaps when the pandemic starts, you'll rethink things."

"We'll see."

She ordered us out of the office, and I tried to slink away in shame.

Marc called Theodore from a wooden bench down the street. "It worked like a charm."

Chapter 28

The shamans knew one of the assistant managers at the Westin was a Librarian, so they'd incorporated that into the plan. The laptop and the thumb drive in the resort safe—not mine—were loaded with false information. After mining the computer and the thumb drive, Popp would think she'd neutralized our efforts, and she'd believe she knew a great deal about who she was selling the manuscript to. My bogus file of intercepted shaman-to-shaman messages suggested a foolproof way for the Librarians to cheat them on the upcoming transaction—getting their supposed cash without yielding the book. We all agreed Popp would act on the information.

So far, so good, as harrowing as it had been.

By the time Marc dropped me off at the resort, my parents were long gone from the restaurant. As I walked from the main building to our suite, I devised a tale of impersonal misfortune to spare their feelings—a flat tire and no spare.

My mother was mollified by my tale of woe. My father was livid that I'd made my mother suffer. She hadn't even enjoyed her meal, he told me.

"Oh, Jim. That's not true. It was delicious, and you know it. You had three bites, didn't you?"

He grunted and turned back to the TV, which was showing a University of Hawaii men's volleyball match. "You'd think a place like this could get better sports," he complained. "Look at these guys. They're a bunch of basketball rejects."

"And so skinny," my mom said. "They don't look right. That reminds me, Tris. Did you have a good dinner? As your mother, I'm in charge of keeping you filled out, aren't I?"

"Absolutely. It was a very good dinner. If you get a chance to try mahi-mahi, I think you'll like it."

"More weird chicken?" my father asked.

"No, Dad. It's a type of fish."

"Do you understand why they have all these crazy names here?" he asked me. "Can you tell me that?" This was new. He'd never asked me for information before.

"I think I do. They only have sixteen letters in the Hawaiian alphabet, which limits their word construction, and they have more words with multiple meanings than any other language."

"You mean like how they say aloha for hello *and* goodbye?"

"Exactly."

"Hmph. Strange people."

"But friendly," my mother added. "Very friendly."

"Most of them," I said, thinking of Popp and her crew.

All four of us played tourist the next day after an uneventful night—no significant dreams. In the face of pressure from everyone else, my father let go of his plan to remain at the resort for the duration of the vacation.

Since Marc had rented a car, he drove. My dad sat up front with him, and my mom and I roosted in back.

Every few minutes, my dad commented on Marc's driving. He couldn't help himself. If he was forced to be a passenger with a non-professional driver, he became nervous and regressed into verbal incontinence.

Marc was endlessly patient as we retraced our route on the two-lane highway we'd traversed the day before on the way to a waterfall beside the Wailua River. Every few minutes my mom commented on something she spied. Surprisingly, when I followed her lead, I was afforded glimpses of engaging sights I would've otherwise missed. A smiling family in matching red T-shirts rode an assemblage of three tandem bicycles on the narrow sidewalk in Kapaa.

"Ooh, look how fat that dad is. He should not be riding a bike in his condition," she proclaimed. "What if he has a heart attack? That little boy on the bike with him could get hurt."

In a parking lot down the road, several boys in multi-colored board shorts clutched shiny surfboards. As we watched, they began jousting with them, racing at one another and then veering away at the last minute, their surfboards banging into one another. Apparently, fat people's activities were more worrisome to my mom since she said, "That looks like fun!" this time.

My favorite sight was the facade of a ramshackle restaurant that displayed huge, grainy, black and white photographs of three of its menu items, with captions under each: "Pork Supertacos—like being in Mexico, but better," "Assorted Lunch Plates—everything you need," and "Ono Poki Bowls—our speciality."

My mom's comment, which drew my eye to the scenario: "Look at the black and white food! That's soo cute! It's like they don't know what kind of film to put in their camera."

Shortly after that, I spotted someone following us in a black minivan. If this was a Librarian, so much the better. Our innocent activities would satisfy Popp that we weren't scheming against her. By the time we pulled into the parking area by the falls, the van had disappeared.

Since he'd been to Kauai before, Marc appointed himself our guide. He marched us to where the view was the best, answered inane questions as best he could—where's all that water come from?—and told an anecdote or two about his previous visit. My parents were charmed and delighted by both the scenery and my therapist.

We toured another waterfall, several beaches, and even hiked briefly through a bamboo forest. My mother was not a hiker, so this latter activity challenged her. As she mentioned several times, she preferred to walk on level ground since she'd tripped over a root once as a child and then her knee had hurt for a week.

I had a fun day, despite two brief rain showers later in the afternoon and lingering anxiety about the following day—when we would enact the next phase of our plan.

My parents genuinely loved the island. Other than Marc's driving, our hike, the service where we stopped for lunch, the humidity, and a homeless man who "looked at my mother funny," they didn't dwell on the negative at all.

"I really do like your therapist," Mother told me that evening after Marc had returned to his digs. "The more time I spend time with him, the more I can see how he's good for you, Trissie." We were watching TV as a family—a show about an interracial family who lied to each other about trivial things, got caught, and then lied anew. A laugh track followed each iteration of immoral behavior.

"Yes, Marc has been a tremendous help," I said. "Look at us. A month ago, I'd have been isolating in the other room with my headphones on."

One inane show followed another. My mother pronounced each her favorite until my father told her she could only pick one since that was how favorites worked. She picked a reality show in which contestants attempted semi-impossible physical feats, failed to complete them, and then fell into vats of various unpleasant substances.

I didn't mind. The entire experience was edifying from a sociological perspective. It strengthened my opinion that the term "mainstream" scarcely deserved any sort of association with the term "culture." Juxtaposed, the words formed a classic oxymoron.

The next morning, Marc and I took off to eat breakfast together in Kilauea, a smaller town six miles to the south. I called Theodore en route to make sure the shamans had been able to complete their preparations the previous day. They had.

"Don't worry, be happy," he told me.

"Hey, did you steal that from a song?"

"Sure. I get my best material from songs. Anyway, the songwriter stole it from Meher Baba, who was an Indian shaman."

"That sounds like a guru's name."

"That's right. He was the other kind of Indian. And it doesn't matter what word you assign to someone. Guru, shaman, teacher, sorcerer, medicine man, sage—

who cares? The map is not the territory, Tris."

I had to think about that one once I got over being impressed by his thesaurus-like list. "I understand. Did you steal that axiom, too?"

"Absolutely. I don't even remember from who. There's no original metaphysical material left, just new ways to package it. You'll probably be disappointed when you read your book of wisdom. What could it say that hasn't already been said? Hell, Marc's probably mentioned a lot of it to you by now. He's wiser than you think."

"Really? I think he's quite wise."

"You'll see."

Something puzzled me. "Why would you help us if that's what you think about the book?"

"Several reasons. First, why not? Do I want to spend all my time in my barn having visions and whatnot? That gets boring, and I like variety. Secondly, having age-old wisdom assembled in one modern book might move some people to shift to a more compassionate stance toward their fellow man. And lastly, our shaman meetings have been kind of dull lately. Your problems have spiced them up."

"So two of your reasons are self-centered—a benefit to you personally? I thought holy men were supposed to be altruistic."

"Who said I was holy? Shamans are just people."

"People who read minds! And God knows what else."

"Exactly."

At a bustling breakfast place filled with working class locals, I tried taro pancakes on the recommendation of our enthused server. Big mistake.

"I told you so," Marc said.

"That's definitely not a therapeutic approach to suffering."

"So sue me." He was in high spirits. "I guess I'm feeling close to the finish line."

"You're confident about this morning?"

"I am."

When we'd finished, we drove to the Makai golf course back in Princeville, where Theodore had made a tee time for us at nine.

Neither of us had ever played golf, and we weren't about to start now. Could there be a stupider sport? We needed a golf cart, though. That was a key part of the plan.

Fortunately, Theodore had clued us in about proper golf attire before we left the mainland. I'd packed a white golf shirt, navy blue shorts, and a brand-new golf cap that prominently advertised a brand of golf equipment. I didn't want to leave my straw sunhat back in my room, but sacrifices had to be made to save the world, after all. All the other golfers, who looked to be wealthy retirees, wore similar caps with similar embroidered logos. When did corporations sign us up to be unpaid walking billboards?

Based on quite a few films, I expected a sprawling, pretentious-looking country club, with a huge banquet hall, and perhaps a tasteful bar with a soaring, beamed ceiling. Instead, a living-room-sized pro shop, a walk-up snack bar, and a long row of golf carts awaited us. Expanses of emerald green stretched in all directions. I would've thought we'd arrived at a prime time for golf—midmorning—but the shop was empty except for a chubby young man behind a tall counter. He failed to deliver an aloha.

Marc asked him why the course wasn't busier.

"People go out early here to beat the heat and the wind," he told us from behind the counter. "Especially this time of year." Worried that we might decide not to play based on this information, he added, "Oh, you'll be fine. It's not supposed get above eighty-four today."

He was dressed exactly as I was, except the logo on his golf shirt was bigger than the one on my cap. I could see him eying me, trying to ascertain if I could hold my own on the course. Poorly-skilled players delayed everyone's round.

"Tris is an eighteen," Marc said.

"Wow, that's great at his age."

I had no idea what an eighteen was. Fortunately, I didn't care. Whatever it meant, it got the job done.

We rented clubs—they had a "junior" set for me—bought enough balls to be able to theoretically lose a few and still play, and paid exorbitant fees for the cart and the round.

"I think you should change the name from 'junior' clubs to something less demeaning," I told the man.

"It's the industry standard." He didn't even look up.

I pictured him saying this about everything. "How about 'height challenged set,'" I suggested, "or 'younger player' set?"

Now he looked up. "Not going to happen."

"Where's your aloha spirit?" I asked.

"Tris, let's get moving." Marc steered me by the shoulder out into the brilliant sunlight.

Ten minutes later, Marc guided our cart toward the first tee. The path wound around a practice putting green and several maintenance sheds. It was fun riding around with no doors or windshield. For some reason, I wasn't nervous. Yet.

We passed the first tee out of sight of the clubhouse and zoomed up the asphalt path beside the first fairway. Well, as much as a golf cart could zoom.

Beside the vacant first green, we switched places, and I practiced driving alongside the second fairway. I'd need to be behind the wheel when we rendezvoused with the shamans in another fifteen minutes. As usual, I learned quickly, although I braked much too sharply several times.

The course wasn't crowded, but the golfers we passed all glared at us for interrupting their sacred activity. Why a nearly silent electric vehicle fifty yards away represented a serious distraction was a mystery to me. Other athletes performed perfectly well surrounded by thousands of jeering spectators.

On another occasion, I'd have stopped to soak up the scenery. The park-like grounds afforded periodic vistas of nearby Hanalei Bay, and the closely mown grass was impossibly green and smooth. The surface of the greens resembled the felt of a billiard table, in fact—albeit an enormous, undulating one. The spacious fairways stretched out in curving fashion, sporting sand bunkers, berms, and drastic changes in elevation.

We passed through all that, staying on the path, until we found our designated tree beside the twelfth tee box, which I parked behind, nearly ramming into a four-foot-tall fern. The hole was devoid of golfers since players hadn't gotten that far on the course yet. Both Marc and I could just barely see around our respective sides of the tree's trunk as we sat in our cart. We waited.

Mild anxiety arose, and I permitted myself to feel it. My tolerance of alarm and fear had suffered recent inflation, and it wasn't as if the tree was holding a gun on us.

Finally, fifty yards ahead, by the side of the cart path, two dyads converged after emerging from separate side streets. I recognized Theodore and his description of an Amazonian blonde woman colleague, as well as Sue Popp and Bart the psychopath.

The laptop the Librarians had stolen from the Westin safe "revealed" that the golf course meeting was a red herring, designed by the gun-shy shamans to send the Librarians on a wild goose chase that would culminate in a safe handoff a half hour north at Tunnels Beach. There would be no cash on hand until then. Knowing this ruse meant Popp could use it to her advantage by planting her men at the beach where the shamans wouldn't expect to find them. Once again, based on our consensus of Popp's psychology, we were fairly sure she would.

We certainly stood a better chance of enacting our plan on the golf course if her main force waited where they thought the real exchange would take place. Also, if she didn't expect our gym bag to be filled with money, she probably wouldn't be as nasty when it turned out it wasn't.

While we watched, Theodore and Popp talked. The shaman held a lime green gym bag, and Bart held what looked like the book box. We'd reasoned Popp would want to let Theodore examine it to prove she had it—as he'd requested—in an effort to play along with the shaman's plan. Then when no money was actually forthcoming at the golf course, she'd have Bart retrieve the box from Theodore. After pretending to be unsettled by Theodore, Popp wouldn't need to bring the book later to Tunnels Beach in order to hijack the shaman's money. She'd probably already picked out the next group to sell the book to.

If we were wrong about any of this, Marc and I would stay hidden and we'd move on to plan B. I didn't like that one nearly as much.

As Popp and Theodore began to step toward one another, the shaman's female colleague ostentatiously scratched her head.

I gunned the cart forward, narrowly missing the tree. We'd pulled our caps down over our faces, and now we tried our best to look like golfers heading up the course, our bags lashed behind us.

I'm sure if the Librarians scrutinized us, our identities would've been obvious, but Popp was engrossed in looking in the gym bag Theodore had just handed her, and Bart watched Theodore as he passed him the copper box, which gleamed in the sunlight. We could only hope the book was actually in it.

As we approached them, I slowed just a bit just before I ducked down. Theodore tossed the book over me to Marc, whose hand-eye coordination was far superior to mine. He caught it handily, and I gunned the cart again.

I kept my eyes on the path; Marc narrated what was happening behind us.

"The shamans are sprinting back to their car. Now Popp is running, too. For some reason Bart is running the other way—onto the course. Uh-oh. There's a cart coming up from the other side of the fairway. It was hiding in a hollow behind the fairway bunker. Crap! Bart's climbing in, and they're heading our way."

We had half a hole's head start, which wasn't much. My heart raced and my hands tingled. "They had a backup plan."

"They certainly did."

"Do you think we can make the same getaway now?" I asked.

"No."

"Is their cart faster than ours? Are they catching up?"

"Golf carts have a governor, so the top speed on all of them is virtually the same. That means we're being followed more than we're being chased—they can't catch up. In fact, we're gaining ever so slightly. You weigh less than they do."

"Do you think they have guns?"

"It wouldn't surprise me, but they're too far away to use them, thank God."

"Here's my thinking." I said. "The longer we drive around, the bigger our lead will become. I don't know the battery life on these carts, but maybe in a while, we'll be able far enough ahead to proceed with the original plan."

"There's plenty of juice for that, but it's a risk, Tris."

I continued to follow the path past the next tee box, down a steep hill to a dogleg fairway. Marc gripped the package with both hands, leaning into the curves to stay erect.

He spoke up again. "They're still on our tail." After a pause, he said, "Here's the thing. Popp's men at Tunnel Beach can get here in a half hour. If we're still on the course trying to lose these guys behind us, what's to stop them from driving a car onto the course to catch us? And we're only increasing our lead on an incremental basis. I don't know how much difference even a half hour would make."

"Why don't we see if ten or fifteen minutes matter. I'll drive a circuit of nearby holes."

We must've been quite a sight—a fifteen-mile-an-hour chase. They couldn't catch up. We couldn't pull away. In an action movie, our scenario would constitute the most boring fifteen-minute stretch of film ever produced.

While I drove, Marc called Theodore, who consulted Melanie—his local colleague who'd signaled us. She suggested a new plan. The thirteenth hole ran parallel to the Westin resort. When we next approached it on our fourth lap around the nearby holes, we were about a hole and a half ahead of our pursuer. We were still in their sightline, so they could follow us into the Westin parking lot, but hopefully that wouldn't matter.

Cutting between resort buildings, and unfortunately damaging some perfectly-trimmed shrubbery, we careened into the top end of the parking lot. Theodore jumped out from between two parked cars and tossed Marc a card key. "The last building! On the far side! Number 116! Leave the cart in the portico!"

"Right!"

Melanie backed her Honda into the opening from which we'd just emerged. Through the car's window, her fierce countenance exuded personal power. She was a different variety of shaman.

"That should slow them down," Marc told me.

"Great!"

I accelerated toward the parking valets who stood under the capacious portico in front of the Westin's main entrance. As we screeched to a halt, Marc threw money at the men. "You didn't see us!" he called. "You don't know where we went!"

We took off running toward the far side of the building, and he shouted over his shoulder, "In fact, call the police on the men chasing us. They're dangerous!"

We arrived breathless at the room Melanie had procured in her name, locked the door, drew the curtains, and called Theodore. Marc put it on the speaker.

"How are things going out there?" Marc asked.

"All they know is that you left the cart out front. The attendants came through for you. Good thinking. And listen…" Straining, I heard sirens in the distance. They'd be much louder outdoors. "The sirens are spooking the Librarians. They're are taking off in their cart—back to the course."

"You two are safe?" Marc asked.

"Yes. You have the book?"

"Well, we have the copper box. We haven't opened it."

"Why don't you?"

I retrieved it from the bed where Marc had tossed it. I fumbled with the latch and pulled back the lid of the ornate copper box.

There was the same title page—*How Things Are*, by It Doesn't Matter Who—replete with Susan Granger's admonition not to read it yet. I decided that only applied the first time around—a convenient rationalization—so I lifted up the pages and placed them on the beige bedspread beside me. Then I nodded to Marc and began reading.

"It's here," Marc reported.

"Excellent."

Chapter 29

Later that day, after both of us had finished reading the manuscript, we handed it off to yet another shaman. Apparently, Kauai was a hotbed of them. This imposing figure, a full-blooded Hawaiian man if I'm not mistaken, would scan it, email it, make copies, and send the original manuscript to Marc's sister in Tucson.

The complete wisdom book follows this narrative as an appendix. More on that later.

I didn't return to my parents' suite since I was unlikely to be safe there, and Marc had already packed up his things in the trunk of his Toyota, so he didn't need to return to his AirBnB. We felt as safe as could be under the altered circumstances.

I wished I knew just how vengeful the Librarians truly were. When it served her to threaten us, of course Sue Popp presented things as though that were so. And Bart was either yet another great actor or an actual psychopath. I thought the latter more likely.

One thing in our favor was that surely Popp now realized we'd wanted her to steal the laptop and the thumb drive. Therefore, she also knew we still possessed information that would be extremely damaging to the Librarians.

At first I had no success at all convincing my parents on the phone that Marc and I needed to go home sooner than planned. We'd decided this was the wisest course of action. We'd travel circuitously with Theodore, which promised to be interesting.

Marc finally waved me aside and spoke to my folks on the speaker. "Those Texas people just let me know that they're going to do an all-day therapy event in Los Angeles tomorrow. I think Tris needs to attend, and he's willing. It's vital to his mental health."

"He seems fine now," my mother argued. "And we're all having so much fun. Don't they have something for him here?"

"Mom, it really would be best if Marc took me back to California. We can come back sometime as a family, and you can take me around and show me everything I missed. That would be fun, wouldn't it?"

"This is ridiculous," my father said. "Tris just got here. What kind of idiot thinks this is the right way to do things?"

After quite a bit of back and forth, my dad agreed and my mom followed suit, although I could tell she didn't want to. We still had to concoct a story that explained why I wasn't going to collect my things at the suite.

"There's no time," Marc told them when they brought it up. "Our plane leaves right away. We're already at the airport."

That garnered him an earful for a while, but when Marc put his hands over his mouth and called out a garbled fake flight announcement, my parents let me go. Marc had the foresight to bring the last letter giving him permission to accompany me, so we didn't expect any trouble at the airport.

We actually stayed in our room for three days—talking to each other and on the phone to Theodore, reading, watching movies, and eating room service—until Melanie ascertained the Librarians had abandoned their search. Then she arranged a boat ride to Oahu for Marc, me, and Theodore for the next day, followed by a flight to Los Angeles.

"It's easy to monitor the little airport here. Better safe than sorry," Theodore told me during one of our long chats. He was holed up in the Hawaiian shaman's home in Lihue.

"Really? 'Better safe than sorry?' " I'd taken to teasing him when he resorted to platitudes.

"I made that one up myself," he asserted.

"No, you didn't."

"How do you know? Maybe it was in a previous life."

"Maybe you just say those things to get a rise out of me," I said.

"Maybe."

For the next several days, I peppered Theodore with questions during our calls. He answered some, obfuscated others, and completely stonewalled at times. I began to see a pattern—a lesson—in his responses. My shaman friend was teaching me how to manage my curiosity and determine what I truly needed to know versus what I simply wanted to know.

"You need to let the mystery be," he finally told me. "You know enough to be a good person and live a good life. If you need more, it will come."

"But there are still aspects of what I've been through that I don't understand," I protested.

"So?" This was probably Theodore's most common response, and as it turned out, his most effective one. Gradually, I came to understand there was never a meaningful rejoinder to his "so?" When he chose to say it, that single word highlighted the hollow quality of what concerned me. His "so?" was like a proactive barometer giving me real-time readings on what mattered.

By the time we disembarked from our boat on a pier outside Honolulu—somewhat the worse for wear, in my case—he'd convinced me to stop trying to find out more. My new motto—my main takeaway from my time in Hawaii: "Knowledge isn't understanding, and understanding isn't awareness." Theodore added, "So screw knowledge," when I told him this.

There's a lot to both of those statements. Think it over.

Epilogue

That's the end of my story. The wisdom book follows as an appendix.

As a compendium of information, it's rich and thought-provoking, but cramming dense ideas into philosophically packed paragraphs scarcely makes it reader-friendly. It was as if the authors wished to create as compact a book as possible, no matter how inaccessible this might render it. Perhaps they wanted to filter out all but the most resolute seekers. I don't know.

I haven't allowed anyone to change one word of the book. That may have been a mistake, but I owe an allegiance to my karmic ancestors. Who among us has the discernment to second-guess them?

Despite an enthusiastic literary agent's sustained best effort, no publisher could be persuaded to print the wisdom book as a stand-alone work. Among other things, it was just too short.

I don't blame them. Perhaps if I'd been willing to attach my name to the manuscript, we might've enjoyed earlier success. I didn't feel comfortable pretending I wrote it, and I'm not sure anyone would've believed I had, anyway.

When our agent finally hit on the idea of offering to combine the smartest boy in the world's memoir with the wisdom book, a bidding war ensued. I'd been out of the limelight for a year or so at that point, but people still remembered me. We applied the resultant large advance toward promoting the book—making sure as many people as possible know about it. Since you're reading these words, we appear to have been successful in your case.

I had no plan to start writing a book at such an early age, let alone labor at the task for so long, much to the chagrin of my editor. I was loath to turn in a subpar effort and hesitant to share the crazy-sounding material before publication. I know this memoir could've been more skillfully penned with the help of a writing coach from the start, but I've done my best.

Ironically, I don't know if any of that matters. One thing I learned the hard way was that words alone—mental activities in general, in fact—are insufficient to bring awareness into one's in-the-moment experience. And without functional awareness, how can we make new choices? An unrecognized crossroad ensures we never vary our path. The wisdom book discusses this, and also addresses a remarkable amount of other themes that emerged during our quest.

So read away, but keep your expectations low. What use is mere understanding if a supporting set of life events aren't concurrently levering you into *doing something different?* Verbiage merely primes the proverbial pump for personal transformation. Or it doesn't.

So the text might serve as a call to action for readers who have had their proverbial jar lids loosened sufficiently by their life experiences, as someone described it during my quest. One more firm twist by the universe—reading the book—might pop their lids off. Or perhaps some readers were recently cracked open by personal crises—as I was. This, combined with the book, might make a difference. Otherwise, who knows?

I've come to the conclusion that the world at large will not be converted to a compassionate, loving place by the publication of yet another book, even if it truly contains all knowable wisdom—and who knows if this one actually does. Change on a species level happens slowly. Revolutions devolve into evolution. That's just the way it works.

I suspect most readers will abandon their effort to plow through the information that follows, and that's fine. I thought about not including the wisdom book at all—an idea my editor heartily endorsed—but I know I'd feel short-changed if I read about a harrowing scavenger hunt and the author failed to reveal the payoff.

I recommend savoring a paragraph at a time, taking in the (sometimes) counter-intuitive notions slowly. When I tried to zoom through the book, even *I* felt overwhelmed. Alternatively, you might want to skip to the end, where there's an easy-to-digest list of original aphorisms. I keep these on the refrigerator at home, and every now and then even my parents refer to them. Sometimes I wish I could share them with Holsy, who seems to be destined to be one of those dogs who remains an eternal puppy.

I do believe every word in the book is true, however helpful or unhelpful. Take it from me. After all, I used to be the smartest boy in the world before I wised up.

Appendix

How Things Are
by It Doesn't Matter Who

We are like intricate origami.
Our multi-lifetime mission is to unfold ourselves
And return to the simple sheets of paper
We once were before we were us.

Introduction

Wisdom is useless unless it is applied toward how we live. So what does living informed by the ideas in this book look like on an ordinary day? It looks exactly like kind, loving common sense. Ideally, what is known these days as "ego" is in check, to be drawn on as needed. We have transcended a self-centered approach to our lives. We neither avoid nor seek out conflict and suffering. We don't devalue the present moment by craving for it to be different, although we take action as called for. We sign up to experience what comes our way. And then we *pay attention*, squeezing the learning out of all we go through. No one can actually manage all this on a consistent basis, of course.

You may know someone who tries to live this way. Be like them as best as you can, and then apply these principles of understanding and kindness to yourself when you inevitably fail. Accept it all, including the long-term, frustrating nature of making changes in the way you think and live. Give yourself permission to be where you are. Love yourself.

Basically, life asks us to learn how to thrive in free fall. Everything's always changing. There's no place to stand that's exempt from this. We can't freeze life in a futile effort to establish psychological security. We need to learn how to accommodate this truth gracefully. In practice, this might look like adaptability, acceptance, non-reactivity, resourcefulness, patience, and such.

It is not necessary to do any of this perfectly or even enthusiastically to derive benefit. All movement in the direction of surrendering our arrogance and misdirected willpower will help restore balance. Eventually, we may learn that if we don't just do what we like to do, but instead learn how to enjoy what we *must* do, the adversarial relationship between ourselves and the world melts.

Accepting Reality

Everything is how it needs to be at any given moment—even the aspects of life that our hearts and minds believe to be nothing more than gratuitous horror. As we work to eliminate war, starvation, and epidemics, we need to understand that a transcendent element has played a role in their formation. There are unknowable "reasons" why the world is the way it is. In other words, what looks like "wrongness" can be a subset of a greater "rightness," and we need to honor both.

In hindsight, don't we sometimes see how an

undesirable situation in our life served a purpose we weren't able to understand at the time? There's something beyond us that's partnering with our efforts. This synergy will nearly always produce more valuable, relevant life circumstances than what we try to create from a purely individual perspective. We may not *like* how things turn out when we cease our futile efforts to control life, but nonetheless, it's best to let go of short-term desirability as a primary criterion.

Who are we to say how life *ought* to be? If we think we know, aren't we declaring ourselves omniscient? Our job is to respond to *how things are,* not squander energy on wishful thinking. When we compare reality to our idealized version of how *it could be*, we foster unrealistic expectations, resentment, frustration, and a sense of failure when we can't convince the world to be the way we want it to be.

As humans, we are only capable of observing the world through subjective eyes, colored by our preferences, experiences, and emotions. And naturally we prefer to promote circumstances and outcomes that we believe will reduce our suffering and align with our values. Our vantage point, then, rests on these limited aspects of the human condition, rendering us ill-equipped to evaluate something as vast and complex as the universe.

Don't try to arm wrestle life into submission. Why would we want to establish an adversarial relationship with the world at large? If we fight reality, it wins. It's much bigger than we are.

Instead, let's struggle as called for *within* the world we've accepted as best we can. This is a key element. Passivity doesn't help us create social justice, or reject abusive relationships, or speak out about other universally objectionable aspects of life. Acceptance of reality as a whole doesn't entail turning the other cheek to everything others do, or saying it's all okay with you, or letting anyone evade responsibility for their actions. On the contrary, when one pays attention, accepts reality as it is, and acts in cooperation with what is needed, proactive and sometimes even aggressive behavior may be called for.

Generally, specific exceptions aside, when we attempt to assert our will in realms in which we are *not* empowered—and these are far more prevalent than most of us suspect—we bang our heads against an impassable wall. It will hurt, get us nowhere, and cause collateral harm.

We are all accustomed to thinking of the weather as beyond our sphere of influence, for example. We need to face the unpalatable fact that most people—and many situations—are like the weather. Let other people be who they are and let them do what they do, then make choices in regards to them based on the clear sight that this approach brings. One possible choice is to ask someone to change a behavior. Perhaps they will. But asking them to turn into someone else to suit you is fighting reality. It doesn't work that way. When we struggle to make fixed things different, our relationships suffer, along with everything else.

We will be less effective with all life tasks if we don't come to terms with the fact that things are never going to be exactly the way we want them to be. It also helps to know this isn't necessarily something going wrong. Sometimes "right" is well disguised to the likes of us. Our inability to gracefully accommodate reality is simply a limitation of ours—not a valid negative judgment about what we've encountered. So let's all make ourselves and the world a better place without condemning it for being what it is. Here's an aphorism to ponder: everything is perfect the way it is, *and* there is tremendous room for improvement.

When we engage in a wisdom-based sincere effort, we can better accommodate undesirable outcomes. What more than that can we do, after all? Since even a masterful process doesn't guarantee a particular outcome, we need to do what we can and then let go.

The universe operates opaquely, impersonally, on an infinite scale, and with access to ultimate truths that will always escape us. So in trying to understand its true nature, we will either remain largely ignorant or, if we think we know, delusional. We recommend ignorance. False knowing is more problematic than *not* knowing. Like fish, we may not be equipped to understand the water we swim in, but as higher order beings, *we* have the ability to recognize we can't understand *our* "water." This awareness shifts things.

Of course, our book would be pointless if there weren't *something* to know, so the next chapter will address this.

What's a sensible response to all this? How do we change the way we live to reflect a humbler, more cooperative attitude? Try aligning yourself with your best sense of how things need to be in any given moment in order for things to work out the best for everyone and everything who is a part of that moment—including yourself. Pay attention to make this possible.

Pay attention. This is the key to everything. How

can we choose a different way of living without noticing what's happening around and inside us? When we're not in the moment, we meet our mind instead of the world. We tell ourselves about life, and we assign meaning to it. We don't let it tell us about itself.

Reality

There are some things we *can* know. For example, everything is an expression of an animating energy that underlies all we experience. We are complexly organized versions of this energy. There is no matter. What we perceive to be matter is what this array of energy looks and acts like to us. Other animals are composed of the same energy, which is simply organized in a less complex manner. Trees, rocks, and air are imbued with primitive, simple consciousness. Many strange aspects of physics are being discovered, and this will continue, eventually confirming what you are reading here. In the meantime, like Plato's allegory, we will only see the shadows of what exists beyond us while we sit in our caves.

We call this essential energy Love. Why Love? For one, because there is no proper word in English. Also, when we encounter this energy directly, we feel a depth and intensity of love flooding us unlike any other. Historically, prophets have been guided by these experiences. In its pure form, the energy is much more than what we're capable of experiencing. The love we feel is simply the aspect of the energy we can assimilate without becoming overwhelmed or damaged.

With electromagnetic energy, humans only experience a portion of the full spectrum. Other creatures see colors beyond the ones available to us. Still others employ radar or sonar—wavelengths unavailable to most species. Our access to animating energy is similarly limited because of our configuration and evolutionary needs.

Perhaps "energy" strikes the reader as an odd term for what we are describing. Scientific energy implies force that a physical or chemical circumstance can produce—the potential to cause change in some way. Even this common usage of "energy" is an elusive concept. Can you see gravity? Or sound, or heat, or electricity, or atomic energy? We can experience the effects of these forms of energy, but they would seem magical to a less-educated population. Is it so unlikely that an additional form of energy exists that seems magical to us now?

If reduced to another one-word description, Consciousness can substitute for Love or energy. Like Love and energy, it represents something intangible, yet powerful. Are we our brain cells? Our minds? Our hearts? Does consciousness manifest as an individual package of energy roaming around, bumping into other people at random?

Hardly. Consciousness is beyond the physical, beyond the illusion of separateness, beyond *beyond*, if you can imagine that. It seems to interconnect everything, none of which needs to be connected to anything else since it is already One in the first place.

When we look at the world through the eyes of a chemist or a physicist, we see that we make artificial distinctions between this and that. The molecules in the air which interact with the molecules of so-called solid matter are composed of the same tiny sub-parts, which in turn are illusions created by energy fields. So the space between things isn't space at all. It's a continuous web of varied molecules—a glue that connects things, which happens to be invisible to the likes of us.

Why is it important to know these things? Without a general understanding of what we typically dismiss as esoteric, we are likely to operate on false premises, as if we are dealing with a completely different animal than the one in front of us. If you think you're feeding a kitten, but it's actually a lion, how's that going to work out? We can't respond appropriately to life without knowing more about it.

Also, out of ignorance, we take many things very seriously that either don't matter or are simply not helpful to focus on. What's the value of looking down on someone else, fantasizing about living forever, fearing what might happen next week, or rolling into a ball and trying to block out the outside world? These sorts of activities drop away when our ignorance is vanquished. They are supported by mistaken ideas about life.

Our Hearts

Being in a body is like wearing an outlandish disguise. Who's in there? If we metaphorically describe the root essence of the universe as an ocean of Love, then perhaps we are tiny droplets of the same Love, encased in flesh. When we are in our hearts, approaching the world with Compassion, we are closest to our ocean home. Compassion with a capital C is universal Love as a stance—a baseline—not merely an emotion (lower case c.) A Compassion-based individual recognizes we're all in this together. If you fail, I do too. If you feel joy, I'm happy for you. If you need a helping hand, helping you helps me. And so forth. When you understand we're not really separate, a great deal changes. And when you directly experience this Oneness, you may transform in profound ways. You may live primarily in your heart, with all the benefits this brings to yourself and others.

In contrast, while compassion with a lower case c might encourage us to act in a loving fashion, it might also impel us to say yes when a firm no would be more helpful in the long run. Such a choice might stem from sympathy or empathy, only manifesting when these emotions motivate us. Perhaps we feed a stray cat and ignore a stray dog based on our fondness for cats. In other words, lower-case compassion is more capricious—more determined by happenstance, judgment, and our idiosyncratic personalities.

The human heart is an interesting phenomenon. It's a process like everything else—not a fixed object. But unlike other spiritually affiliated processes, it straddles the two worlds—the mundane and the metaphysical. In other words, it serves an in-the-world function, and also something far greater than that.

From some vantage points, these two aspects of heart—which could also be described as the personal and the universal—seem as though they are opposites, pitted against each other. Actually, both elements simply coexist and have their place in the scheme of things.

Here's a germane saying: truth embodies paradox. In many circumstances, we need to find a way to accommodate so-called opposites. Fortunately, there is always a vantage point that transcends our initial misunderstanding—one in which both elements operate concurrently with no adversarial relationship. This is so with our hearts.

On the one hand, the universal heart serves as a gateway to universal Love, Compassion, and a deeper non-mind understanding of life. As we already discussed these earlier, let's examine its more personal counterpart.

Our human hearts hurt when we're grieving, when we feel rejected, when things don't go our way, when medical problems plague us, when we encounter painful scenarios, and such. Since we are configured by evolution to avoid pain, we often attempt to escape experiencing these heartaches, which lead to actions that don't serve us. When our spouse leaves us, do we start drinking? Do we isolate ourself when we receive a cancer diagnosis? Do we settle for a pallid version of love from an inappropriate partner in order to soothe or distract ourselves? Our *response* to what's happening in our human heart can be antithetical to what our heart itself knows is in our best interests. In other words, feelings themselves aren't a problem. It's what we *do* with them that determines whether we are helping or hindering ourselves.

Of course, there's nothing *wrong* with hindering ourselves. We all do this regularly. Who can do life perfectly? In fact, our struggles to managing emotions and life difficulties are a major part of our life curriculum—our reason to be in a body. So emotions such as heartache are natural and useful, and in no way incongruent with the big picture.

It's possible to soften when our hearts are bruised

and focus compassionately on whoever "hurt us." We can stay in our hearts when our reactions to painful experiences tell us to go into a hardened stance. We have choices, and these can be decided by a Compassionate heart, not the mind, nor our urge to escape discomfort.

Back to the universal heart. When we are aligned with universal Love, we see that the usual human striving for more and more, both materially, psychologically, and even spiritually, is a dead end. The deeper we explore both our human and universal hearts, the more we find an intersection of values—one that directs us to be in service to others. In other words, our path is likely to eventually lead us to conclude that, above all else, we are here to help others reduce their suffering.

Opening

When you can open your heart to pain
And open it to your enemy
And open it to a rock
And open it to an idea
And open it to the sky
And open it to itself
And open it
And open it
And open it…
Everything shifts.

Thoughts

Thoughts are less real than the rest of life. Why do we trust what we invent in our minds as though it's telling us true things about ourselves and the world around us? The question to ask ourselves about any thought is "How do I know?" A very common answer to this is "I don't, actually." As stated earlier, our perspective is always subjective to some degree. Because we'd like to be able to fill in life's blanks, we pretend to ourselves that we can. Other thoughts serve our short-term self-interests at the expense of our life goals.

Here's an example of how blindly believing our thoughts can be harmful. Perhaps a given situation or context feels boring, unfair, or even disgusting. These are not actually feelings. They're the judgments—the excuses—that our minds concoct to protect us from the supposed horror of fully experiencing those moments. So we end up assigning meaning onto life instead living it and letting it tell us what it is.

Our thoughts con us, singing siren songs of false knowing, impossible psychological security, and self-interested ego fulfillment. Don't believe your thoughts unless you have a good reason to do so. The mind is a useful tool, essential for many life activities. But we have allowed it to serve as a petty dictator, promoting its own self-centered interests as it attempts to supervise parts of ourselves about which it knows very little.

For example, how could a rational part of us effectively supervise an irrational part? The world of emotions will always remain a mystery to the mind. Its rules and aspects are akin to the difference between dreams and waking life. In the former, forms morph into other forms, time is fluid, and perhaps we can fly. In waking life, all of this would be disturbingly absurd. So should the waking mind use its judgements and interpretations to regulate dreams?

Like any dictator, our thoughts want to hold onto their power and will muster resistance to ideas that challenge their rule, including this book. Notice what you are thinking right now. Are you creating a list of objections to what you're reading, or assembling justifications for why your usual way of approaching things is right for you? How many of your thoughts are designed to maintain the status quo?

Certain categories of thought are particularly suspect:

- Many thoughts are outdated. We made a decision about how to live when we were ten years old and never notice we've failed to update this policy as we age.

- Inherited or legacy thoughts are passed down to us. We often adopt them regardless of if they fit who we've become. Perhaps we've been conditioned by our parents, our church, or our school to think in ways that serve them. It can be difficult to sort out which thoughts are truly ours. Who did you vote for? Which sport do you like the best? What is your religion? Did you arrive at all of these on your own?

- We often overgeneralize or construct stereotypes as a misguided shortcut to understanding the world. One or two experiences aren't enough to draw conclusions from. Everyone from Italy isn't short and swarthy. We aren't bad at math because we flunked one test. It's easy to believe these thoughts since, like most, they serve us in some way. Overgeneralizations keep the world simple, which is comforting. Of course, in the long run, they don't help us gather the skills we need to navigate the complexities of life.

- Some thoughts are simply unwieldy—an array of ever-growing concepts that are virtually impossible to sort through. Depending on your particular mind, you may have the equivalent of the IRS tax code in your head when you try to order from a restaurant menu.

- Rigid or absolute thoughts simply aren't useful. They don't match the ever-changing shades-of-gray world around us. Hardly anyone is *always* anything. Hardly anyone is *never* anything. Since nothing is fixed, rigid thoughts can't describe life accurately.

- Thoughts driven by reactive emotions can't be trusted. They are not in service to us as a whole—just to the feeling that triggered them. Later, we often regret acting on these thoughts since they interfere with our life goals. If I want to live harmoniously with my spouse or keep my job, how does yelling epithets help me achieve that?

- Finally, there's a catch-all category of unrealistic thoughts. Jumping to conclusions, thinking we know what's in someone else's mind, thinking we know the future, magnifying or minimizing something, and unrealistic expectations all steer us wrong in various ways.

If we know all this about problematic thoughts, we can dispute them when they show up. We don't have control over our first thoughts, but if we are aware enough, we can choose a second one that serves us.

Almost all of us also think too much as well, at the expense of what else we could be doing. Here's an exercise. Look at something nearby—a houseplant, for example. Try to just observe it for a minute or two. Nothing more—just pure observation.

If you're like most people, your mind pulls away

after scant seconds and starts processing what you're seeing: "That's a healthy-looking plant. I'll bet it cost a lot. It reminds of the one my aunt has. Look how shiny that one leaf is. Did somebody polish it? Why would anyone polish just one leaf? Oops, I'd better get back to observing."

Noticing this tendency to overprocess our ongoing experience is an important step toward learning to step away from overthinking—to master where we put our attention. How different would life be if we could decide when to think, what to think about, and whether another mode might serve us better in a given circumstance? Emotions, body sensations, intuition, and a host of other information sources are underdeveloped and underutilized in the modern world.

Life Is Change

We have a choice to either hunker down and resist being changed by what comes our way or grow and evolve even as the ground underneath us shifts. Trying to maintain our historical sense of ourselves through thick and thin can be subtle, using psychological defenses, or it can be obvious, arguing away others' point of view or freezing our development by drinking. If the world around us stayed the same, perhaps trying to limit its ability to influence us would work better. As it is, these attempts to make ourselves feel safe and secure are doomed. Impermanence prevails.

When we're willing to experience life as it is and let it shape us, we're trusting the universe to provide us with what we need in order to evolve. And when we're curious about what that curriculum will be, knowing we will not opt out of a working relationship with it, life becomes more interesting.

Everyone, everything—every speck of anything—changes. Always. Sooner or later. In that sense, life is a process and all content and outcomes are merely milestones along the way. But we grab onto these because it's our nature to be fearful of uncertainty. We have been conditioned by evolution to do whatever best helps our species survive. That includes a wired-in imperative to avoid whatever we fear or can't control, and it's still operating today. Now we might be facing an unpredictable co-worker instead of a pack of wolves. We grab onto whatever feels safe and secure in a similar manner in both cases.

We all sometimes try to hold tight to things that are merely processes. Perhaps you created a career based on how you look. What happens as you age? You either fight a losing battle against wrinkles or you find a way to create another rewarding career based on something else. The former is grabbing onto something, the latter is responding to change. Some people stay in unhealthy relationships, dead end jobs, and other painful circumstances—clinging to what they know, however miserable they feel.

Like many aspects of the human condition, we have to work with our nature about these things, never finding a way to fully transcend how we are configured. And why should we?

So if change cannot be controlled, does this make it our adversary? Adopting a friendly attitude toward change creates more congruence with how things are, so our insides and the big picture line up and work together more harmoniously.

At the risk of repeating ourselves…Change brings us lessons to learn—the ones we need to learn, as determined by forces greater than ourselves. Do *we* know what we need at a deep level? No, we know what we want, what suits us, what's easier for us, and the like. How well would your life work if only these were in charge of your fate? Don't worry. They can't be.

Choosing growth in response to impermanence isn't always a simple thing. The first step—again—is *paying attention*. If we don't proactively override evolution when it seeks to dictate our behaviors, we simply repeat our ingrained patterns, whether they help us or not. That which we don't bring into the light of day runs things from behind the scenes. When we don't *pay attention*, we become puppets whose strings are being pulled by the old part of our brains.

At first, the uncertainty associated with change triggers fear. So we avoid things that might lead to it. For example, if we are truly seen and understood by others, whatever happens with them has greater weight—greater power to *change* us. So we hide who we are, blocking deeper human connection out of fear. But at what cost? If we could learn to accommodate the uncertainty associated with personal transparency, wouldn't our lives be richer? Couldn't we offer more to others?

When lessons come our way—and they will—some of us muster direct resistance to them, even doing the opposite of what we are being directed to do just to spite the unseen forces that seem to be pushing us around. Perhaps we were planning to play tennis, but we sprain our ankle walking to the courts. Some people find something else to do. Some stand on the sidewalk and shake their fist at the tree whose root buckled the concrete. Others go play anyway, worsening their injury.

A subtler way to stifle change entails constructing life circumstances in which it simply doesn't make sense to change. We might choose a spouse we can't get along with unless we keep treading our old, familiar path. We might join the military, where regimentation is rewarded. We might sign up for inappropriate or dangerous change so we can "learn" that change is bad. When we do things like this, we no longer have to keep making up reasons or concocting stories to justify our resistance to personal development. Real reasons surround us on a daily basis.

We enter a more glorious realm when we are willing to face our fears and allow ourselves to be shaped by what we encounter in life. A great deal of difficult or unpleasant experiences are a side effect of trying to be a rock in a river instead of an alert boatman, rowing gently downstream with the force of the river. Even a rock will eventually be worn down by water, whether a torrent or a trickle. In the meantime, who enjoys life more?

Pain and Suffering

The universe employs many methods to help us. Some of the most valuable ones don't feel much like help.

Without suffering to pry our eyes open, engage our hearts, and provide challenges we must respond to, what would life be like? Comfortable circumstances don't usually motivate us to improve ourselves. When we're suffering and we want to suffer less, we extend ourselves, take risks, and do what's called for.

There's no dodging pain and suffering. It's built into being alive. At some point, we will all fall down and hurt ourselves, disappoint someone, grieve, go hungry, become ill, and be mistreated. These are painful. There's no getting around it. Of course, we need to try to minimize all of these for ourselves and others, but no matter what we do, they will show up sometimes.

Nothing is going wrong when we "fail" to protect ourselves from suffering. Like so much else, it's what we do when it shows up that determines our fate. Minimizing suffering in the first place makes sense. Avoiding experiencing it when it surfaces is problematic.

Avoidance provides short-term relief since it allows us to sidestep potential or actual suffering and provides a more pleasant experience. So we do it again next time. It becomes a favored tool in our life tool kit.

But long-term, our range of approved experiences shrink down. We might minimize challenging, novel, difficult, and emotionally risky experiences—anything unwelcome—based on our preconceptions of what might bring us suffering. We try to line edit life—keep the parts we like and eliminate the others. Some of us devote our lives to establishing personal safety—both physically and emotionally.

When we do things like this, we preempt the universe's ability to provide us with what we need. Our pain isn't random; valuable lessons are embedded in it that could be crucial to our lives. Suppose as a small child, we ignored how it much it hurt when we fell out of a tree. We'd be likely to repeat a similarly dangerous feat, wouldn't we? If our spouse left us because we drank too much, why would we stop drinking if we didn't feel the emotional consequences of her departure?

Some avoidance is helpful, of course. Extreme circumstances void many of the recommendations in this book. We might need to soothe or distract ourselves from the consequences of overwhelming events, such as intense physical pain or the loss of a loved one. Perhaps we'll distract ourself with a crossword puzzle or plan what we'll have for dinner. We might soothe ourselves by stroking our cat's fur or taking a warm bath.

It's important to moderate the dosage of intense suffering by taking care of ourselves when we truly need to—when the consequences of not doing so would be destructive. The problem is, we do such things when they are *not* necessary because many of us believe we are more fragile than we actually are.

So it's our resistance to experiencing pain, employing avoidance in many cases, that layers secondary suffering atop mandatory, initial suffering. If we can find a way to tolerate and accept pain as an unavoidable condition of being alive, we won't make things worse for ourselves. And when we allow pain and suffering to be part of our experience—on *their* terms—the information they provide help us devise effective responses. We learn. We grow. We change.

In general, the more we act incongruently with the big picture, the more we resist experiences of any kind, the more we do the opposite of the principles in this book, the more we suffer in the long run. If we're willing to learn a given life lesson—about how to manage suffering or anything else—we no longer need painful circumstances to motivate us. Since we have been co-creating these circumstances with the universe for our benefit, they drop away, and new agendas take their place.

The Path

There are many paths to the top of the mountain, although we believe that the metaphor of digging and exploring a deep hole would be a more apt description of personal development. Aspiring to an outward, upward goal is a type of ambition, a desire to achieve. Ironically, the more one outwardly strives, the less distance one traverses on one's true path. Focusing inward, digging ever deeper into our personal foibles and issues, brings us somewhere quite different.

It's easy to think that the goal of working on ourselves is the abdication of personhood—stepping away from the difficulties of being human—standing on the mountaintop. But we have to start where we are—rooted in our own imperfect way of doing life—and move through the idiosyncratic problems associated with this. There are no shortcuts or bypasses to circumvent this work. You can't even take a piggyback ride through it, no matter how broad the shoulders are beneath you.

What do we mean by "our imperfect way of doing life"? Nothing more than how we typically cope with what comes our way. We planned an outdoor wedding, but now it's raining, so perhaps we feel sad or angry. What do we do when the rain comes down and the feelings come up? We could call off the wedding and go to a bar and drink all day. That's one person's coping strategy. We could frantically try to buy raincoats for all two-hundred-and-fifty wedding guests. There's another path. Some of us might yell at our affianced for picking the wrong day. Some wouldn't be able enjoy the altered ceremony even after they located an indoor venue. Our "stuff"—our patterns of responses to life—are all different. But it's all just stuff. No one's is any better than anyone else's.

Maybe our problem is a phobia, or a tendency to overeat, or poor impulse control. There's no long-term escape from the indignities these spin out. We may think we can ignore problems such as these, but sooner or later, there's a day of reckoning for whatever we shrink from or deny or rationalize or act out without awareness. Our willingness to do our inner work is an essential element in staying "unstuck." Even if we only develop willingness after we've been pummeled by life, willingness still opens the door to something new.

The suffering we endure from moving forward through the sometimes unpalatable muck inside us is hardly gratuitous. There is bang for our buck in this effort, in contrast to the energy we throw away when we fight reality (as per an earlier chapter.) We are human; we need to be human; being human is a messy, bumbling deal. So let's all get used to it.

Maybe we'd prefer to be taller. Or to never feel disappointed. We're not saying the universe at large has no interest or mercy around these types of concerns, but if a particular form of suffering needs to be a part of your life to move you through your issues, you will not be magically relieved of it. Nor would you want to be if you could fully understand your long-term life path.

(Which you can't).

Let's forget the mountain with various paths, the hole in the ground metaphor, and our personal problems, and picture a wagon wheel for a moment. Imagine we're tiny, and we all start off living on the outer edge of the rim. Perhaps we wander around the circumference for a while before we wish to know more than what that realm offers us. Eventually we discover we can explore ourselves and the wheel world by journeying down one of the spokes toward the hub.

As we slowly make our way down, we learn more and more. Sometimes the journey is rewarding, sometimes it's harrowing. Some of us rest on our way or settle for only going so far. Others persist. As we go farther, the different spokes, taken by different tiny people with different outlooks, grow closer and closer together, as they literally do on a wagon wheel.

Finally, we reach the hub, where all the knowledge and wisdom along our route has been fully developed. It's the same realm with the same truth that all the other spokes have led to. We find brethren there, even though, back on the rim, other people seemed wildly dissimilar to us. In fact, we may realize we may have been One all along.

Now let's translate that into the non-tiny world we live in. The outer edge of the wheel represents a superficial, unexplored existence. Many of us live our whole lives there, and that's what these folks are on this earth to learn about. It's not wrong or bad.

The spokes represent religions, philosophies, traditions, and such. A Buddhist chooses to go down one "spoke," a Christian another, and a Muslim yet another.

Each religion/philosophy/"spoke" looks separate—differentiated—at the start, but the differences shrink as an adherent perseveres and approaches wisdom. Eventually, perhaps many lifetimes later, all seekers arrive at the same destination—the "hub" where universal wisdom dwells. So any and all paths can bring one to truth. There is no right way to do anything, let alone this.

When we sincerely tread our path—whatever it might be—the universe will meet us more than halfway, creating a conspiracy of events to lever us where we need to go. This won't be a straight route like a wheel spoke. If we need a teacher, one appears. If we need to move to another continent, the universe will orchestrate this. If we need to experience a loss, it happens. If we need to make many false steps driven by our untamed ego, we will.

Various clues help us know if we're truly on a path and not trudging down a dead-end pseudo-spoke. Have we become more kind and loving? That's the primary one. Are we less selfish, impatient, judgmental, dishonest, competitive, aggressive, and greedy? In other words, have we softened, become less directed by our egos, and become more interested in the welfare of others? Even attaching moral values to our preferences, especially in reference to other people, is a tip off we may have strayed.

Unexplained phenomena are another clue about the legitimacy of our path, although they mean nothing if they are unaccompanied by the favorable elements above. Perhaps we notice a series of amazing coincidences that defy all odds. Perhaps we know something we have no business knowing. We may directly experience Oneness or another sublime mystical state. We will probably see the world sometimes as the exquisitely beautiful place it is, however we formerly perceived it.

These are not achievements, or milestones, or badges of status. We can't use them to bypass the hazards of our lives or accelerate our progress. They are simply side effects of various phases of our particular path. Some paths produce many. Some don't. It doesn't matter. Don't get entranced by any of this.

In a way, the entire concept of a spiritual path is silly. We don't go anywhere. We just learn to shed all that obscures who we are and what's available to us to know. We don't need to augment ourselves or add anything. We just need to strip away what stands between us and our true nature.

This might happen suddenly, when we least expect it. It may develop incrementally over decades. Or it may not happen at all. We just need to live our lives with full attention and sincerity. Then what happens, happens.

All our life curriculums are exactly the way they need to be. Do you yearn to be at the "end" of your path? Let's look at that. By the time it happens, if it does, no one you'd recognize would be left standing to find it thrilling. The glorious state you imagine you'd experience would actually be incomprehensibly matter-of-fact to your future "self."

The Clearing

There is a clearing at the center of the woods
And each path—

The one along the creek,
The one up the hill,
The well-marked one,
The new one,
The raggedy one,
The familiar one,
And the dangerous one
All meet there
Where it's still and luminous.
And in the clearing,
How hard or easy,
Slow or fast,
Long or short,
Odd or usual
The path taken
Is a matter of some amusement.

Reincarnation, Afterlife, Enlightenment, and Other Mysteries

Forget about these, unless they serve you as metaphors. It's not helpful to know about them in detail. We can't become caught up in the drama that constitutes our life curriculum if we know *too* much about what lies beyond it. As we said earlier, it is by facing life challenges, becoming engrossed in them, and working through them—or whatever else our lesson might be—that we change and grow. And we're prepared by the journey to meet the challenges that await us at the "destination." Shortcuts don't work.

This book itself walks a fine line between edifying its readers and making sure the cat is not too thoroughly out of the bag. We all need to buy into our misconceptions about ordinary reality some of the time. Why even be in a body, dancing this amazing dance, if we've completely transcended our gritty life curriculum? Also, at any given point in our spiritual development, some of us need what helps us maintain ourselves and some of us need what helps us dissolve ourselves. Information that too thoroughly loosens what binds together a vulnerable reader endangers his mental health.

Let's look at the concept of heaven and hell. Suppose we could settle the question of whether these exist once and for all, delineating all the details? Who could invest in life on Earth in the same way after that? Everything would change. One example: how many individuals would break society's rules—"sin"—if they knew for sure there were horrible eternal consequences in Hell? (Don't worry about that, by the way). We need to fill all the human roles to make the world work, including the villainous ones. Even a seemingly benign change such as the omission of gross misbehavior would be severely destabilizing.

Knowing the details of one's death is another example of unhelpful information. Would we attend to our personal business the same way after that was revealed to us?

By the way, helpful and unhelpful serves as an effective filter for evaluating almost anything. Right and wrong, comfortable and uncomfortable, good and bad, and even true or false lead us astray. Is it more important to live a life that works or to be "right?" Discriminating helpful from unhelpful promotes happiness. The others generally don't, especially in relationships with other people.

Experiments

Life is an experiment. Every developmental step in our lives involves trying things—testing ourselves and those around us—including learning to walk, learning language, and learning to relate to others.

As we wrote earlier, talking and reading are like priming a pump. They might help you gather motivation and get ready to work on yourself— assuming you even want to—but sooner or later, you have to begin *doing*.

We suggest that a sensible first step is to tinker on a small scale—run a minor experiment of your own. Find your "edge" about something, beyond which you've been too uncomfortable to venture. Then intentionally step one baby step past it and see what happens.

The simplest, most literal form of this process might be someone who's afraid to leave their house standing a foot beyond their front door for ten seconds. In other words, choose something small enough that you can virtually guarantee your ability to follow through and do it.

What might happen next to the shut-in? Some people will discover the brief sojourn outdoors was more tolerable than they would've guessed. Others may find it worse.

What feelings arose? What was the aftermath of the experience? What else did they find out about either this one foot of world or the depths of themself? Now they have a working relationship with their problem— data to sort out—and clues about what might be a useful experiment to try next.

What if we try this approach with something more complex? Suppose we've recognized that when we feel criticized, we lash out and counterattack. We tell ourself this isn't who we want to be, yet we keep doing it.

Next time the opportunity arises, perhaps a behavior just past our edge would be to say, "Tell me more about that." Or perhaps that would be too ambitious and a more appropriate experiment would be to take a break and go for a walk. Trial and error—that's the best way to gather practical information when we wish to institute the principles in this book.

Without a doubt, any behaviors along these lines will provide novel experiences—new perspectives on the situation. How does our problem "criticizer" respond when we don't counterattack? How do we feel? How could we fine-tune our new comment? How did the conversation turn out?

Once again, the goal isn't to force a particular outcome. Perhaps the new behavior makes things worse. Even this constitutes a successful experiment. Now we know more about the scenario—what not to do—which may imply what would work better. And now we're moving—we've left resting inertia in our wake.

There's a story about an inventor who announced a success to the press following five thousand tries to find the right substance to make his invention work. A reporter asked him what it felt like to fail so many times. He responded that he'd never thought about it that way. He considered it to be a successful experiment with five thousand steps.

It may not seem so, but small experiments that

walk us into our problem arenas also bring us a bit closer to becoming more kind and loving. Often, these qualities lie on the other side of the personal muck, which is finite, so we can eventually traverse it. En route, it may feel as though we're making things worse. The muck might be thicker or deeper than we thought. We might be alarmed by the slow pace of our progress. We might lose faith in what we're doing.

The trick is to stay at it. Keep your momentum. Work on things every day. Establish a spiritual practice if that helps. Meet with others on a similar path. And no experiment will amount to much if you fail to *pay attention.*

Aphorisms to Ponder

Many of the following phrases have appeared in our wisdom book. Others are presented here for the first time. We could easily write a chapter about each one, but some people learn more from deciphering the meaning in encapsulated wisdom. We imagine that of these forty-six sayings, some will prove helpful for a given reader, some will merely be thought-provoking, and some will make no sense at all. We hope all of them stimulate readers to think for themselves about what our ideas might mean to them.

Yield gracefully to what is.
When you're not in the moment, you meet your mind instead of the world.
Find a way to cooperate with how things need to be.
All craving is a devaluation of the present moment.
We're prepared by the journey to meet the challenges

that await us at the destination.

Love animates and illuminates us.

Paying attention isn't about inventing what you want to pay attention to. It's about being with whatever's there.

The benign gears of karmic machinery turn slowly.

When you open your heart to the pain in the world, everything shifts.

If you attach moral value to your preferences, your suffering will increase.

Dissolve yourself to become who you are.

Life asks us to learn how to thrive while in free fall.

One person's dead parrot is another person's dead mother.

We're all in this together.

You can count on impermanence.

It doesn't tend to work out if you try to waltz with a badger.

Everything's impersonal.

Love kills fear.

The universe is self-regulating.

Consciousness dreams us.

The best response to the challenge of grace in action is ruthless compassion.

Our default setting is kindness.

The universe will meet you halfway if you do your work.

The way to find out everything that's knowable is by simply paying attention.

Comfort and discomfort are very poor criteria for making choices.

Don't be fooled by the illusion of control.

Most problems are a side effect of not having a straightforward relationship to reality.

Every life path is unique, so all comparisons are invalid—between apples and oranges.
Time is an illusion, solid matter is an illusion, separateness is an illusion, and so is pretty much everything else you can think of.
What's "real" is beyond thought.
Life is not a serious business.
Literally, the root energy of the world is love.
The opposite of compassion is not hate. It's ignorance.
There are no thought police.
Beauty, truth, and love are all aspects of the same phenomenon—that which underlies our world.
Don't make things happen; let things happen.
Death is profoundly mundane.
Everything is perfect exactly the way it is, and there's tremendous room for improvement.
At any given point in our psycho-spiritual evolution, some of us need glue and some of us need solvent.
Truth embodies (apparent) paradox.
We are like complex, completed origami. Our task is to unfold ourselves and return to the simple, blank sheets of paper that we once were before we were us.
Being in a body is like wearing an outlandish disguise.
Give yourself permission to be wherever you are.
Our thoughts are like stories written by drunk burros.
Internal attitude affects external events.
Learn to enjoy what you must do.

Summation: The Meaning Of Life

In a nutshell, the meaning of life is loving connectedness. Of course, the concept of meaning is a human construct, prone to interpretation. One person's meaning might be meaningless to another. Yet if we adopt this simple sentence in lieu of continually seeking something more, we can live a better way.

Harmony between ourselves and the big picture which surrounds us—a cooperative stance—is promoted by establishing congruence between our insides and the way the world works around us. If in the long run, we can orient ourselves to the possibly true, possibly metaphorical concept that the universe serves as a benign teacher, we can agree to learn our lessons.

After all, the dualities of inside vs outside, us vs them, and all the other ways we divide the world are illusory. Oneness rules—loving connectedness. Live as though we are One, whether you currently experience life that way or not. It works.

****

Last Words from Tris

There you have it—the slim, somewhat redundant text for which we risked our lives. As Theodore predicted, there's nothing novel in it, and both Marc and Theodore have said similar things.

I still found the wisdom book to be helpful, and I hope other readers do. If you bought this book for the memoir alone, congratulations on slogging through the wisdom section to the part you're reading now. I know this wasn't easy material to absorb. In fact, you probably disagreed with a great deal of it. It's counterintuitive to how we've been raised in this country.

Personally, I now believe every word in the book is true. Take it from me. I may only be an intelligent adolescent these days, but after all, as I said before, I used to be the smartest boy in the world.

A word about the author...

Verlin Darrow is currently a psychotherapist who lives with his psychotherapist wife in the woods near the Monterey Bay in northern California. They diagnose each other as necessary. Verlin is a former professional volleyball player, country-western singer/songwriter, import store owner, and assistant guru in a small, benign cult, from which he graduated everyone when he left. Before bowing to the need for higher education, a much younger Verlin ran a punch press in a sheetmetal factory, drove a taxi, worked as a night janitor, shoveled asphalt on a road crew, and installed wood floors. He barely missed being blown up by Mt. St. Helens, survived the 1985 Mexico City earthquake, and (so far) he's successfully weathered his own internal disasters. He maintains a website: marcd@cruzio.com

Thank you for purchasing
this publication of The Wild Rose Press, Inc.

For questions or more information
contact us at
info@thewildrosepress.com.

The Wild Rose Press, Inc.
www.thewildrosepress.com

CPSIA information can be obtained
at www.ICGtesting.com
Printed in the USA
BVHW040211230721
612410BV00040B/704

9 781509 236909